By EM LYNLEY

PRECIOUS GEMS SERIES
Rarer Than Rubies
Italian Ice
Jaded

THE DELECTABLE SERIES
Brand New Flavor
Gingerbread Palace
An Intoxicating Crush
Lighting the Way Home (with Shira Anthony)

NOVELS
Hostile Takeover
Out of the Gate

NOVELLAS
Disguises

Published by DREAMSPINNER PRESS
http://www.dreamspinnerpress.com

OUT
OF THE
GATE

EM LYNLEY

Dreamspinner Press

Published by
Dreamspinner Press
5032 Capital Circle SW
Suite 2, PMB# 279
Tallahassee, FL 32305-7886
USA
http://www.dreamspinnerpress.com/

This is a work of fiction. Names, characters, places, and incidents either are the product of author imagination or are used fictitiously, and any resemblance to actual persons, living or dead, business establishments, events, or locales is entirely coincidental.

Out of the Gate
© 2014 EM Lynley.

Cover Art
© 2014 Reese Dante.
http://www.reesedante.com
Cover content is for illustrative purposes only and any person depicted on the cover is a model.

ISBN: 978-1-62798-682-3
Digital ISBN: 978-1-62798-683-0

Printed in the United States of America
First Edition
April 2014

For my parents, who indulged my horse-craziness far longer than I expected. Who knew it would last this long?

CHAPTER 1

"I SEE exactly what you're doing."

Wesley Tremayne put down his binoculars and turned around to see Vanessa Vandermere wagging a long pink-and-black fingernail at him. Best not to reply. He willed his heart—beating like a jackhammer—to slow as he pasted the perfect, innocent grin on his face. Years of acting—onstage and off—had taught him to dissemble.

"Think you can spot the winners before they even get to the ring?" Vanessa continued, her tone teasing, cheerful, not accusatory. "Or were you checking out the shapely blonde leading the third horse?"

He inhaled slowly when he really wanted to gulp in much-needed oxygen. He'd overreacted. No, he'd responded just in time to what could have been a disaster. As much as he was enjoying the day out at the racetrack with his friends, he was restless. He'd been the center of too much attention, and he was fraying at the edges.

"You caught me," Wes replied, playing up his right dimple.

"Oh, Jules, good thing you're here." Vanessa grabbed onto Julia Compton's arm. "You need to keep Wes on a shorter leash. He's got a wandering eye."

Julia gave Wes an appraising look, then turned back to Vanessa. "Vee, I'm not worried Wes will run off with another woman. I trust him completely." She slid an arm around Wes's waist and he gave her a suitably adoring look. "Only we're not a couple. How many times—"

"You can fool some people, but not me. You two are the worst-kept secret in Hollywood, honeybuns." Vanessa gestured as she spoke, and Wes wondered how she didn't poke her own eye out with her outrageously long fingernails.

"Think what you like." Julia let go of Wes and took the binoculars from him. She held them to her face and trained them on the track.

"I'm heading down to watch them saddle the horses so I can decide which one to bet on." Vanessa gave them a dangerous wave of her talons and left them alone in the private grandstand box.

Julia gave the glasses back to Wes. "He's gorgeous." She winked.

"Which one do you like?" Wes asked, again looking through the binoculars.

"I thought we were talking about which one you like?"

"Number four." Wes glanced down at Julia's head. She was a good six inches shorter, and it was the view he often had to settle for.

"Oh really? I thought you'd go for one. Or at least his trainer." She gave a silvery laugh and put her arm around his waist again.

Wes kept the glasses focused on runner number one's trainer as he reached up to adjust the horse's bridle. His navy sportcoat rode up, giving Wes—and anyone else looking—a nice view of his arse in well-fitting dark blue jeans. Wes held in the smile the sight induced and resigned himself to admiring the good-looking man from a distance. His light brown hair fell in wavy curves and the full-lipped smile made Wes want to lick his own lips. Something about the chiseled chin and the shape of the man's nose twigged a hazy memory Wes couldn't quite bring to the surface.

A quick glance at the program told Wes the attractive trainer was named Evan Taylor, but that didn't explain where he might have seen the man before.

"Let's go down to the saddling ring so you can get a closer look, Wes." Julia tugged his hand, then gave an encouraging squeeze.

He didn't know what he'd do without Julia Compton. She'd gone from costar to friend to lifesaver in the space of a year. He followed her down the steps and into the sunshine as the runners for the third race at Santa Alamita were saddled up. Wes pulled the baseball cap out of his back pocket and settled it onto his head, a moment too late.

"Look, is that Wes Tremayne?"

"Wes! Hi, Wes!"

"Go ask him for his autograph."

"He's with Julia Compton. I *told* you they're dating!"

Wes smiled and waved but didn't stop for autographs. By the time they reached the paddock, the hot horse trainer was gone. Probably just as well; someone might have noticed if Wes paid him too much attention. There was a limit to his acting abilities, but so far he'd fooled everyone. Some days he fooled himself, but during lonely nights he wished away the talent and fame he'd achieved.

If he hadn't upped sticks and made his way from the London stage to Broadway and then to Hollywood, he might be living a boring, settled life with a man he adored. He'd chosen a career he loved over a private life.

But Julia was tiring of her role as Wes's love interest. When she quit the production, he'd have some tough decisions to make. For now, he replaced his mask and took Julia's hand and kissed it.

The audience should love that performance.

"COME ON! Gray horse, come on!"

Wes chuckled to himself as Vanessa Vandermere shouted to the horse she'd put twenty-five dollars on to win. "That's not how it's done. Come on, seven! Come on, seven! That's it." He didn't wave at the horse the way she had.

"Oh, so you're the expert?" Lance Robbins said.

"I don't care what he says, as long as it's in that gorgeous accent of his," Vanessa said. She'd stopped shouting at her horse as the pack rounded the turn into the homestretch.

"Come on, four. Come on, four!" Julia Compton said, standing up and pounding a fist into the air. Her usual ladylike demeanor was discarded as she got more excited: shades of Eliza Doolittle at Ascot.

Wes hadn't bet on this race, but he enjoyed watching the antics of his friends. They'd come here on a last-minute whim, in celebration of wrapping the first season of *Zero Gravity*—currently top of the ratings in the key demographics—which he and the fifth member of their party, Brent Bell, starred in together. Wes was content to observe the others. He was exhausted by the filming schedule. He hadn't realized how much hard work a television show really entailed, but he was finally in a hit, and he wouldn't trade it for the keys to Buckingham Palace.

Now they had about eight weeks off, assuming the network renewed the show for another season. If not, he'd be hitting the pavement again, looking for a new role. His agent had an array of meetings and events for him to attend in the meantime. It simply never ended.

"Fuck, fuck, fuck!" Julia said, still punching toward the finish line. "Lost by a hair, damn horse!"

"Ha, ha, beat you!" Vanessa gloated and waved her winning ticket under Julia's well-powdered nose. Julia grabbed the ticket away and pushed it into her bra.

"Go on, Vee, get it now." Julia winked at her friend.

"Oh yes, please, Vanessa, go after that ticket." Lance's attention was fully on Julia's cleavage now.

Wes wasn't particularly interested in it, or in watching Vanessa tease Lance by pretending to go for the ticket.

"You can keep it, Julia," Vanessa said. "Just put the winnings on a horse in the next race and split whatever that wins. Fair?"

"More than fair," Julia said. "Who's coming down to the paddock with us?"

"I will." Lance didn't pass up a chance to spend time with Vanessa. He didn't seem to realize she'd never see him as more than a platonic sidekick, certainly not a bed partner. Wes found the sexual dynamics between his friends fascinating—and was glad to be on the sidelines.

"Wes, come on. You have only bet one race. I know you're sitting there watching us throw our money away. It's your turn to lose." Julia tugged at his hand and raised an eyebrow flirtatiously.

"I can't say no to you, Jules." He glanced back toward the bar inside. "But we shouldn't all go. Brent's not back yet with the next round of drinks. I'll catch up to you." He gave her a pat on the behind as she stood and followed Vanessa and Lance from the box.

Lance tried the same move on Vanessa, and she smacked him hard enough for Wes to hear, but it didn't faze Lance.

They'd been gone less than five minutes when Brent Bell arrived with their drinks. "Where'd everyone go?" he asked as he looked around. "Cashier?"

"Vanessa won and Julia's choosing bets for the next race. They went down to the paddock to watch them saddle the runners."

"Fine. I could use a break after the line at the bar."

"We could have sat in the clubhouse," Wes suggested.

"You can't come to the track and sit inside. Got to be outside where you can see them, and if you're close enough, feel the hooves pounding down the stretch."

"I agree." Wes noticed how Brent's face lit up and he became more animated as he talked about the excitement of watching the horses run.

"First time I've been to the races yet out here. I'm actually glad Vanessa suggested it. Always a fun day with the gee gees."

"Gee gees." Brent chuckled. "One of her few good suggestions." He sipped at one of the drinks. "But it's only coming up on the third race. I bet you twenty bucks she's bored before the fifth and wants to leave to go shopping or for cocktails. Or both."

"No bet. I expected she wouldn't make it to the third race." Wes chuckled and finished his drink, a tonic water with lime. It looked like a gin and tonic, but only Brent knew it wasn't. Wes couldn't keep up with Lance and Vanessa's alcohol intake, and he didn't particularly want to. He couldn't afford to make any stupid mistakes because of alcohol, or he'd be heading back home with nothing to show for his eighteen months in Hollywood. He hadn't spent years acting in small plays to ruin his big chance at being a star. A stint on Broadway as Marius in *Les Miserables* had resulted in his being cast in his first series: a critical success that no one actually watched. Now he starred on a hit series, but his goal—like many other young actors—was a film career.

"Can you take a couple of these drinks? Then we can go down to the paddock and meet up with them."

"No problem," Wes said and took two. Brent carried the others, and they made their way down the steps from the reserved box and followed the throng toward the paddock to watch the horses for the next race get saddled and parade around the enclosure.

"There they are!" Brent spotted the other three. He couldn't wave because he had his hands full of their cocktails. Neither could Wes, so they moved through the crowd.

"Hey, look, it's Wesley Tremayne." A young woman dragged a friend up to him. "Wesley Tremayne? Oh my God, it's really you!"

"Yes, it's me." He gave them a smile. He still couldn't get used to being recognized. He liked it, so it was easy to act pleased to meet fans.

"Can we get your autograph?" the other girl asked. She shoved her racing program toward him and he shrugged, hands full of drinks. "Oh, I'll take those." The girls each grabbed a drink, and he pulled a pen out of his jacket pocket.

"Who should I make this out to?" he asked, beaming at them. He signed something for both girls and had a photo taken with them. Now, three other fans were waiting. They recognized Brent when Wes introduced him and asked for his autograph as well. "Thanks, everyone. Our friends are probably anxious for their drinks…."

"Oh, sorry!" The fans shook their heads and apologized. "Thank you!"

"You did that very well," Brent said. He turned down one corner of his mouth. "But then again, you could say 'creamed corn' and the girls would be chasing after you. Damn you. Just keep hanging around with me, though. I need the exposure."

"Shut up, Brent. You're doing well. Don't you have a film lined up after this season's over?"

"Yes, but...."

"But nothing." Wes grinned. "I can teach you to say 'creamed corn' with a British accent if you like?"

"Please. I could certainly use your overflow of female admirers."

"Gladly." He could have them all if it were up to Wes. He didn't want any of them, but he wouldn't say that to Brent.

"I won't mention anything to Julia." Brent gave a conspiratorial grin.

"What the hell *is* creamed corn, by the way? Anything like mushy peas?" Wes shook his head. He hated mushy peas and didn't think anyone back home would find the phrase sexy, even when uttered by the hottest American film star.

They were still laughing when they finally made it to the spot where the others waited for them.

"Oh, there you are. What took you so long?" Vanessa grabbed for her drink almost immediately, and then Lance took his. Julia waited for Wes to hand hers over.

"Thank you, Brent," Julia said. Neither of the others bothered to thank him. "What do I owe you?"

"Nothing, Jules."

Wes waited to see if the others offered, but they didn't. Wes handed Brent some money, but Brent waved it away. Of all of them, Brent probably earned the least, but he was always the one offering to get the drinks. Like Wes, he wasn't drinking today and usually only had one when he did. He liked to stay in control and didn't like showing up on set the next morning at less than 100 percent.

"I think we should bet on number five this time," Julia said after they watched the horses take a turn around the enclosure.

"Why?" Lance asked. "Number two looks like a winner to me." He tapped his finger in the racing program.

"I like his name. Jelly Jones. It's cute." Julia gave a little shrug.

"I think we should bet on the shimmery red one. He's the prettiest." Vanessa pointed.

"Chestnut," Brent said. "But looks don't often have anything to do with running ability. Lance seems to have the most scientific approach."

"Yeah," Lance agreed.

"But that's how I picked the winner in the last race. The prettiest one. Lancelot, how much have you won today?"

He grinned and edged closer to Vanessa, clearly enjoying the nickname and the attention. "Nothing yet."

"Then don't waste your time reading that little book." Vanessa's laugh sounded like water bubbling up from a mountain stream as she turned back to the horses—and away from Lance.

Julia had her head down, scanning the entries on the form. Brent showed her how to find the horses' previous records, then turned his own attention to the horses in the paddock.

"Wes, honey, what's a claiming race? The program says this is a claiming race."

"We have them in the UK, but Brent should explain. He's the resident expert here today," Wes said. "The rules are likely to be different here."

Brent turned to Julia with a soft snort. "Just because I have a friend who's a trainer doesn't make me an expert on everything at the track. But I happen to know the answer to that one." Julia gave him an I-told-you-so smile. He shrugged and continued. "It means you can claim—or buy—any of the horses in this race. See the description?" He pointed to the page in the program. "It indicates the price. In this race it's $20,000, a pretty good set of horses, but nowhere near top quality."

"And anyone can claim a horse? How do you do it?" Julia asked.

"You have to fill out some forms and deposit the selling price at the racing office. Then at the end of the race, you own it, whether it wins or not."

"Really?" Julia sounded excited. "I just fill in some forms and then I'd own a racehorse? That easy?"

"Well, you need the twenty K," Wes added. "Do you *want* a racehorse?" Julia got excited about a lot of things that didn't manage to keep her interest for long. He didn't relish having to talk her out of buying a racehorse.

"Oh, I want one too!" Vanessa chimed in again. Wes was surprised she didn't already have one. She had one of everything else. It was a tough life being the granddaughter of an oilman who'd made his will before he'd actually had any grandchildren and died before any of them had grown up to disappoint him. Honestly, Wes couldn't fathom what Julia saw in her.

"Yes, I think I want a racehorse, too, Wes." Julia jumped up and down like a little girl. "What do we need to do, Brent?"

"What's this 'we'?" Wes asked.

"Let's buy one." Julia tugged at Wes's arm. "I always wanted a pony!"

"This isn't a pony, Jules," Wes said. Did she think she could ride it around between races?

"It would be a good publicity thing for you, Wes," Julia said, now sounding more like an agent than a six-year-old girl.

"Buying a racehorse seems kind of extreme. Besides, don't they cost an absolute fortune to own? It's not just the up-front price, but the ongoing costs," Wes said. He admitted he rather liked the idea of owning a racehorse, but it simply wasn't practical.

"If it wins it will pay for itself, right?" Julia replied, her voice rising on the final word.

"*If* it wins...."

"Oh, Wes, you're always concerned about money." Vanessa got back into the discussion. "Let's buy one together, as a group... then we'll split everything, and we can have lots of days like this, coming to see our horse run." She turned to Lance and started playing with the collar of his shirt. "Lancelot, don't you want to buy a horse with us?"

"Sure, Vee," Lance replied, true to form. Had Wes expected anything different? Vanessa could have asked him if he'd cut a toe off and he'd have agreed. *Idiot.* "Actually, it would be fun."

"So, Brent, how do we sign up?" Julia asked again.

"Why is he the expert?" Lance asked.

"He's got a friend who's a trainer, Lance. It's why we're here, because Brent's friend has two horses running today," Julia replied.

"Are you guys serious about the horse, or is this just a moment of temporary insanity?" Brent asked, mouth open. "If you are, I'll call Evan and ask, but don't just wind me up—or him. He takes his work very seriously and doesn't care for capriciousness when it comes to horses." He looked at Wes.

Wes shrugged. "Go ahead and ask him. But I don't think we should do anything today on the spur of the moment." He gave Julia a pointed glare, and her excitement deflated a few notches. "Let's think about this...."

FOUR DAYS later, Wes found himself back at Santa Alamita racetrack. After a discussion—and not over cocktails—four of them agreed to buy a horse together. Brent opted out. Vanessa had even come to the discussion with a check for her share of the purchase price. They'd agreed not to pay more than $10,000 for a horse, only $2,500 each. Brent consulted his trainer friend about decent horses scheduled to run during the next week, and they all agreed on a horse to claim.

"Wes, you should make the claim in your name, with the others as fractional owners. It's much easier than the paperwork for a partnership," Brent suggested. "Of course, you'll want to consult your accountant."

"My financial advisor told me this is a good way to cut my taxes, even a little," Vanessa added.

"Cut your taxes?" Lance asked.

"Yes. You can write off the losses against other income." Vanessa shook her head, as if everyone should know this. Wes was surprised she knew anything about taxes. Either she'd learned a lot from her father, or she wasn't as dumb as she pretended to be.

"But he's going to win," Julia replied, ever the optimist.

Wes filed the necessary forms in the racing secretary's office at the track and deposited the funds in an account. The others watched him fill in the claim form.

"Evan said you need to name a trainer on the form or it's not a valid claim." Brent pointed to the line in question, which Wes had left blank. He looked up at the clerk behind the counter, and he nodded his agreement.

"Why not?" Julia asked. She glanced at the clerk but he didn't respond. He was staring at Julia, mouth open, eyes a little glassy. Clearly he recognized her and was struck speechless. Apparently not a lot of film stars showed up here.

"I think it's to ensure the horse will keep racing. You can't just claim a horse and not race him. But I don't know all the rules; just passing the info on." Brent flipped the form over. "You can use Evan's name for the time being and then switch to your choice of trainer—or even stay with the current one if you want."

"Doesn't he want to train Mister Twister after we buy him?" Julia asked. Wes knew she'd voted for this horse because she liked the name.

"He'd have to see him run and then check him over himself, so he won't guarantee anything," Brent replied.

Wes finished the form and had one of the racing secretaries check to make sure it was correct. Then he sealed the envelope and was directed to punch it through the time clock as proof he'd filed the claim before the cutoff.

"Oh, I have butterflies in my stomach," Julia said, hanging on to Wes's arm.

The five of them watched the horses—including Mister Twister—as they were saddled and walked around the paddock before the parade to the post. They moved up to view the race from box seats. Julia was biting her nails, but Vanessa shouted encouragement as the horses took each turn and the pack roared down the homestretch. Mister Twister was still in the middle of the pack, and Wes's heart beat in time with the thundering hooves, and he was on his feet as they flashed across the finish line.

Mister Twister came in third.

"Hey, that's not too bad," Brent said. He accompanied them to the Winner's Circle where they would find out if they had succeeded in their claim. If a competing claim had been made, the racing secretary would rely on the roll of the dice for the outcome.

But no one else had tried to claim Mister Twister, so Wesley Tremayne and his three friends were the newest and proudest owners of their very own racehorse.

CHAPTER 2

EVAN TAYLOR edged the mare into the starting gate and Nicky Holloway, his assistant trainer, closed the grate behind them and stood out of the way. According to the horse's papers, she was called Singing Skirt. To Evan and his staff, she was just Sable.

Sable pricked up her ears and stamped one hoof.

"Easy, girl. Steady," Evan whispered. He nodded at Nicky and tensed, waiting for the gate to open.

When the bell sounded and the grill dropped, Evan didn't even have to urge Sable out. She knew what to do, charging forward and quickly moving through her gears until she hit gallop. Evan held her back for the first furlong, then loosened the reins and let her set her own pace. She was alone on the track, but he suspected in her mind, she was at the head of the pack, running for home with the rest of the field trailing her.

Her mane whipped into his face, the coarse hair stinging his chin as he bent down over her neck. The wind whistled and hummed in his ears, and he felt as exhilarated by her youthful burst of speed as she apparently did.

Sable had retired from the track five years ago and now worked as an exercise pony, accompanying the runners to and from the track, or on practice laps. Once in a while, he treated her to a fast run out of the gate. She would have made a great broodmare, but complications with her first foal left her unable to have another, so Evan found another use for her. Who was he kidding? He loved the runs as much as she did. He was too big and heavy to ride the racehorses, so his only taste of racing glory from the back of a horse came infrequently.

He took her six furlongs, but she could have gone another six and wouldn't respond as he tried to slow her down. It took another two furlongs—a quarter of a mile—before he had her completely under control.

"Hey, Sable, trying to show off for everyone?" he asked as he leaned forward to scratch behind her ears. She swiveled them in his direction and tossed her head—an affirmative. Evan slapped her neck and continued to talk to her as he brought her back to the opening in the rail.

"Good time, Ev. I clocked her at 1:15. Not bad for an old gal," Nicky said as she met him at the gate.

"Who you callin' old?" He patted Sable's neck again. "Bite your tongue."

"Want me to walk her?" Tim Hartsock—Timbo—asked as he hopped off the fence when Evan exited the track.

"No, Timbo, I'll do it myself. But you can clean the tack for me." Evan dismounted and walked Sable to the side of the barn. He unsaddled the horse and let Timbo take the tack while he brushed her down and washed her. This was one of his favorite parts of the day, spending time with the horse.

Once Sable was clean, he walked her around for a cooldown as he went over his plans for the rest of the day.

His cell phone vibrated in his pocket, and he pulled it out. "Evan Taylor."

"Hey, Evan, it's Brent."

"Hey, Brent. It was good seeing you at Santa Alamita the other day. What's up?"

"Remember those friends who were interested in claiming a runner?"

"Yeah." Evan figured they had changed their minds pretty quick once Brent passed on Evan's warnings. "Talked them out of it?"

"No, quite the opposite. They put in a claim and yesterday became the proud owners of Mister Twister."

"You're kidding me?"

"Nope. And they put you down as the trainer."

That stopped Evan in his tracks. It also forced Sable to stop, and she tossed her head when the lead pulled taut. "Sorry, girl." Evan rubbed her nose in apology and started moving again. "Well, I did say they could. But I really don't want another horse right now."

"I've never heard of a trainer turning down another paying customer. You got every stall in the barn occupied?"

"A group of new owners, Brent. They take five times the effort of one new owner and ten times as much work as one experienced owner. Pass."

"So charge them more," Brent said with a chuckle. "But not too much. Wes Tremayne is one of my costars, but he's also a friend."

Shit. Evan hated actors, except for Brent, and he only got a pass because they'd been friends since college. "For actors, I charge double."

"At least meet them. You can always negotiate a rate if you don't like them. Or you can send them packing, but don't turn them down just because one of them is an actor."

Evan made a grumbling noise.

"Look, Evan, you can't be a trainer in SoCal and not deal with the rich and famous. They've got to be a good portion of your business."

"It doesn't mean I have to like them." Evan led Sable back inside the barn and put her in her stall. "Okay, text me a contact e-mail address, and I'll send them an official application and arrange a meeting. You better come along with them."

"Don't worry. I can see both sides may need me as a go-between. Thanks, pal." Brent disconnected.

Evan hoped he wouldn't regret meeting them.

THAT EVENING Evan checked his e-mail, wondering whether Brent's friends had gotten their act together and sent the application. Instead, he found a message from one of his owners.

Dear Mr. Taylor:

A formal greeting was never a good sign. They'd been on a first-name basis. He steadied his nerves and continued.

We regret to inform you we intend to move our horses to another trainer at the end of the month. Thank you for your contribution to their racing careers.—Thomas and Ellen Hall.

Evan glanced at the calendar. Was this Monday? Just what he needed. Luckily, the Halls only owned two horses, but he was just covering expenses with them. Without their daily fee—the amount he charged to train—he'd be cutting the budget mighty close.

Brent's comment about a trainer who turned down a paying client came back to haunt him. Despite his reservations, Evan no longer had a choice about whether he took on Mister Twister, but he decided to boost the fees for him. If the Hollywood group balked, he could always negotiate back to his regular rate.

While he was staring at the Dear John letter from the Halls, an e-mail with the application from Brent's friends arrived. He printed it out and was sitting on the couch skimming the details when Gary came home.

"Hey, hon, good day?" Gary brushed his hand across Evan's shoulder, and Evan took hold of his wrist and pulled him down for a kiss.

"Might have a new horse," Evan said, not wanting to admit he'd also lost two. He watched Gary head down the hall and heard him drop his bag in the office and come back via the kitchen. He heard the sound of a cork popping, and Gary came in with a glass of red wine. He took a swig and sat down with Evan on the couch.

"Who's the owner?" Gary glanced at the papers.

"I wouldn't mind a glass, too."

"Really? Okay." He handed Evan his glass and went into the kitchen to pour himself another. He came back to the couch and reached for the printout.

"It's got personal information on here, Gary."

"So, who am I going to tell?"

"It's not mine to share. Sorry." Evan folded up the papers and put them into the pocket of his jacket. He shouldn't have brought them inside. They belonged locked up the file cabinet in the barn office. He trusted Gary, but it wasn't good business practice.

"So, can you tell me anything about the owners, if you're so intent on protecting their secrets? Warren Buffet? Brad Pitt?"

"No." Evan grinned at Gary's wide-of-the-mark guessing. "But one *is* an actor. Wes Tremayne. He's on Brent's show."

"Wes Tremayne?" Gary nodded. "It's more like Brent is on *his* show. Interesting. Who else?"

"An actress I never heard of and another woman who, based on what Brent inferred, is apparently best known for being rich and partying."

"Oh, a Kardashian?"

"What's a Kardashian?"

"Seriously? Sometimes I wonder if you ever notice anything besides horses."

"Only you." Evan kissed Gary. Sweet, but too short as Gary pulled away to take a sip of wine.

"So why don't you sound very excited about this new horse? Is he a hay-burner?"

"No, he's not half-bad. But you know I hate dealing with actors." He paused and Gary looked at him, as if waiting for something. Evan blinked and continued. "They want everything their way and think they're experts because they played a horse in a film or something."

Gary burst out laughing. "Nothing wrong with their money, though, is there? If you like the horse…."

"I can handle the horses, but not the owners."

"I wouldn't mind having Wes Tremayne as a client," Gary said as he drained the wine in his glass.

"I don't think he does documentaries. Does he?"

"Don't you even know who he is?"

Evan shrugged.

"Let's watch something he's been in. Then you'll see what I'm talking about."

AFTER DINNER Gary found *Zero Gravity* on the network website, and they watched two episodes. The premise was familiar: a group of people lost in outer space, searching for food and answers on various planets.

"Kind of a cross between *Firefly* and *Lost*," Gary said.

"Now I see what you're talking about." Evan was amused how the writers found a way to get Wes Tremayne out of his shirt at least twice per episode. No complaints from Evan on that count, no matter how ridiculous the excuse.

"He's like Henry Cavill's better-looking brother."

"Who?"

"I forgot you don't go to the movies anymore either. He was in the new Superman movie. As Superman…."

"Superman," Evan said absently, eyes still glued to a shirtless Wes. "This is on TV every week?"

"Yeah, but now I'm sorry I mentioned it." Gary turned the television off and put an arm around Evan. "Come to bed, Ev. I'll make you forget about Wes Tremayne's incredible nipples."

He hoped he could figure out how to find the show again and watch without Gary. Evan was technologically challenged in general and Gary usually came to his rescue in that regard. Not that Evan had even remotely considered cheating on Gary, but Wes Tremayne was some serious eye candy.

THE NEXT afternoon, Evan was in the kitchen reviewing some training reports over a very late lunch when Gary came home. "In the kitchen," Evan shouted, and Gary appeared, a huge smile on his face.

"So, Ev, it looks like the itinerary for my Brazil trip is shaping up. I'll be leaving Friday or Saturday." He pulled a bottle of beer out of the refrigerator and sat down across from Evan.

"So soon? I didn't realize you got your funding sorted out." Gary had been trying to fund a documentary about birds in Brazil, and with the economy, money for docs had really dried up.

"Yes. Well, almost. I found another backer to cover the shortfall, and we just have to work out some details and paperwork."

"Who?"

Gary exhaled but didn't reply immediately. "Let me get everything finalized, then I'll let you know. Don't want to jinx anything."

"If you're already making travel arrangements, you must be sure it's going to pan out."

Gary stared at him and got halfway out of the chair. "Evan, stop poking your nose into every single thing I do. I don't do that to you. I'll tell you when I tell you." He slammed the beer bottle onto the table and snatched up his messenger bag, then left, letting the front door crash shut behind him.

Gary's quick temper always surprised Evan. He wondered how he ever stayed quiet and still enough to film his nature docs. But he was a genius with the camera and had won a dozen awards for his filmmaking. That was how he and Evan had met in the first place—at one of the award ceremonies.

But Evan didn't know what he'd said that could have upset Gary so much today. He was merely showing an appropriate level of interest and concern. A damn sight more than Gary had shown for Evan's work lately. He used to come to races, or get up early for workouts, but not lately. He'd only seemed to be interested in the horse Evan was training for him.

Evan heard Gary start his car and race the engine before peeling out of the driveway. He cringed, knowing the noise would travel to the barns and frighten the horses. It seemed no matter how long Gary lived here, he never quite understood how easily horses could be frightened. It was nearly time for evening rounds of the stables, so Evan grabbed a jacket and put a few apples in his pockets from the bowl on the kitchen table. He pulled one more from the bowl and shined it on the front of his shirt before taking a juicy bite. It dripped down his chin, and he wiped it away with the back of his hand, glancing around as if his mother might have seen it.

The thought amused him and brightened his mood as he locked the door and headed down the hill to the stable office. He'd meet up with Nicky for rounds, but first he'd check to see if any of the horses were jittery after Gary's noisy departure. Sure enough, two yearlings at the near end of the barn were restless in their stalls. He heard the chestnut kick at the wall a couple of times, further frightening the bay filly.

"It's okay, fella," Evan said as he glanced into the chestnut colt's stall. The horse stopped moving and swiveled his ears in Evan's direction. "Come over here." Evan pulled a pocketknife from his jeans and cut one of the apples into quarters. He held one out on the palm of his hand, and the colt took a step toward him before throwing his head up and shying away again.

"Okay, I'll just give this to her." Evan nodded in the direction of the filly next door. He waited for a count of five, and just as he stepped away, the colt moved toward the door. "I knew you wouldn't pass this up." He offered the apple again, and this time the colt took it, fluttering his soft lips against Evan's palm. With his other hand, Evan scratched the colt just below one ear and listened to him munch the fruit, grinding his teeth and making a low noise in his throat. Evan wanted to see if the colt had hurt himself during his kicking fit, but he decided to wait a few more minutes for him to settle down.

He moved to the other stall and fed the bay filly some apple. She'd been more frightened by the colt, Evan guessed. He'd speak to Gary again, but so far it had done no good. It made more sense to move the sensitive yearlings to stalls away from the road. Just in case.

But Gary would be leaving in a week. Was it worth upsetting the horses' routine? He'd see what Nicky thought. He headed down the corridor and made a turn at the next aisle and into the barn office.

Nicky Holloway sat behind the desk, typing at the keyboard of a desktop computer.

"Hi, boss," she said without looking up when he entered.

"How'd you know it was me?"

"It's time for rounds. Who else would it be?"

He looked around and realized that a visitor had easy access to the barns and the office. "It could be anyone. Maybe we should start being more security conscious. I think I should look into a security system, video feed, that sort of thing. Just in case."

"Just in case. Good idea." Nicky nodded and got up for the evening rounds.

THE NEXT morning, Evan got up earlier than usual and drove to the track. He had another runner today, and Nicky could handle the morning workouts back at the farm. He found that Mister Twister had been put into one of the vacant stalls in his barn at the track.

He peered into the stall, which was still dark, but the horse came up to the door and nuzzled Evan. He was alert and friendly. A good sign. He'd wait till it was light out to give him a good look over, then have one of the exercise boys—even the female riders were called boys—give him an easy jog for a lap or two to stretch his muscles. He'd raced a couple of days earlier, and even if he was sound, he wouldn't be up to a fast workout for at least a few more days.

He gave the first set of riders instructions for workouts and watched from the side of the track.

"Got yerself a new horse, there, Evan?" Frizzy Johnson asked. He was a regular at the track. He'd been an assistant trainer, and now he was a handicapper for one of the racing papers. He was bald as a cue ball now, but once his moniker had been a genuine description. Now it was merely ironic.

"Maybe, Frizzy. Gotta check him out and decide whether to take him on."

"He looks good. Definitely was the best in Bing Watson's barn. He's probably crying into his cornflakes over it." Frizzy nodded.

"He should try Wheaties. Then maybe he'd do a better job and not be losing claimers."

"Yeah, Wheaties." Frizzy laughed so hard he started coughing. His solution was to grab a cigarette from his pocket. He coughed again and couldn't get it between his lips.

"Frizzy, maybe you should take up drinking instead," Jose Chavez suggested. He was another trainer, and he settled in to watch his horses work.

"I only started smoking so I wouldn't drink," Frizzy replied, rasping. "Haven't touched a drop in twenty years."

"Good for you, Frizzy," Evan said. He took notes on his horses' performances.

It was light by the time the first group finished, and he went to get a good look at Twister. He had recovered from his race and was still sound, so he sent the rider out for a one-mile jog to see how he moved. The horse needed to bulk up a little more, and he would benefit from the quiet, more hygienic barn and workouts on Evan's hills instead of the track.

He already had a deposit on Twister's training fees in the bank, even though he hadn't yet agreed formally to train Twister. He'd get the rest when the group came out to the farm on Friday if everything was mutually acceptable. Brent's friends insisted on seeing the setup there. Evan didn't want a Hollywood horse, but he'd liked Twist's personality and after seeing him work again knew he had a lot of untapped potential. Evan convinced himself the arrangement would be for the horse, not for the money.

By the time the second set of horses were back in their stalls, it was time to meet the owners of that day's runners.

Evan needed to get in the money now more than ever. Only one of the two had a fighting chance. He debated putting some money on it to win, but decided against it. Betting was a slippery slope. Winning felt so damn good some people couldn't stop. Evan was too smart to even risk it. His owners often gave him a ticket for their horse, and that was the only way he'd get involved.

It was a good day. The better horse came in second, and the other managed third place in his race. The trainer's share of the purse, ten percent, felt good. He paid the groom his bonus in cash, then headed back to the farm.

He drove up the hill from the barn, anxious to get home and take his boots off. He noticed a black Cadillac Escalade in the driveway at the house, parked next to Gary's Lexus, but before he reached the house, someone got in and drove it away.

"I WISH you were going to be there when I meet these people today." Evan's chest felt tight as he contemplated the visit from the Hollywood owners. He sat down on the edge of the bed. He'd already supervised morning exercises and come back home before Gary had even gotten out of bed. Normally, their divergent work schedules weren't an issue, but Gary would be leaving that evening. Nicky had graciously said she'd handle some of Evan's duties so he would have part of the day off before Gary left.

"The main thing is meeting the horse, right?" Gary rolled up close, put a warm arm around Evan's waist, and pushed a finger through one of his belt loops.

He smelled woodsy and warm. Evan was going to miss him while he was down in Brazil for a month. He stroked Gary's shoulder.

"Yeah, but… they're Hollywood people and you know how I feel—"

"The guy's harmless. Come on, we watched a few episodes of *Zero Gravity*, and he's just a kid. He doesn't know anyone or have enough pull in town that it should worry you. Besides, you're out of that world now. You're overthinking the Hollywood connections." He reached up to stroke Evan's arm.

"I know you're right…," Evan said, though he didn't believe it.

"Come on back to bed, and I'll make you stop worrying about Wes what's-his-name, okay?" Gary said, unbuttoning Evan's shirt enough to pull it over his head easily. Evan let him undo his pants, too, then slipped them off and climbed back in bed.

"I've got two whole hours before they'll be here…."

"This won't take that long," Gary said. "Promise."

"Pity," Evan said and let Gary pull him down onto the bed.

"Still plenty of time to give you something to remember me by." Gary rolled Evan onto his stomach. "Don't want Wes Tremayne turning your head while I'm gone." He squeezed Evan's ass.

Evan noticed Gary's suitcases sitting in the corner. This would probably be the last time they made love before he flew out that evening. "Slow down, Gary."

Gary didn't reply, unless a slick finger up Evan's ass could be considered a response. "Ev, I want you so bad." Gary's voice was low and raspy, and it got Evan's engines going every time. He spread his legs wider.

"Me too."

Then Gary pushed inside, hard and sudden enough to knock the breath out of Evan. He tensed up at the intrusion and unexpected pain.

"Ooh, so good, Ev." Gary grunted as he started moving.

"That... hurts," Evan said, his voice muffled into the pillow, and he tried to turn his head. Gary had reached up to pin Evan's arms. "More lube?"

"I'll slow down." Gary didn't reduce the intensity of each thrust. "Want you to remember this when you meet that pretty Wes Tremayne."

"Pretty?" The word popped out of Evan's mouth on a gasp as Gary rammed in again.

Gary stopped moving and leaned down, mouth against Evan's ear. "He's pretty now. Once he hits thirty, he'll grow out of it, start being handsome and manly, like you did. You were awfully pretty when I first met you."

That was one word Evan hated, especially when someone used it to describe him. Hearing it again produced an ache in his gut. "Why are you talking about Wes now, while you're in bed with me?"

A cell phone rang. Gary reached toward the nightstand where it vibrated across the surface. He twisted so he could grab it without pulling out. "Yeah?"

"Fuck, Gary, the phone, now?" Evan said. His ass was on fire, and not in a good way. He tried to move out from under Gary but couldn't manage it under his weight.

"Yeah, yeah. Got it. See you then." He flipped the phone shut and tossed it onto the table.

Evan didn't want to ask, but who could be that important that Gary would pick up the phone while they were in bed?

Barely missing a beat, Gary started thrusting again.

"Hon, it still hurts. Please, more lube."

"I'm almost done. Hang in there, 'kay? I'm not gonna see you for a couple of months. Just let me...."

Evan bit his lip and squeezed his eyes shut. This was not how he wanted their last lovemaking to be. This wasn't even making love. It barely even qualified as a decent fuck. At least not for Evan. Gary came a few minutes later, sinking his teeth into Evan's shoulder hard enough for Evan to think he'd drawn blood. Evan cried out and Gary kissed the spot, but it throbbed and ached, bringing tears to Evan's eyes.

"Oh yeah. God, that was good. C'mere, it's your turn." Gary slid an arm around Evan and rolled him over. "Hey, don't cry. I'll only be gone a month or so."

Evan closed his eyes as conflicting emotion swept over him. Would he miss Gary this time? Part of Evan couldn't wait for Gary to leave, but the other part was afraid to be alone.

Gary brushed a finger across Evan's cheek, catching the tears, oblivious to their cause, but the tenderness of the gesture tugged at Evan's heart.

"Kiss me," Evan said, trying not to make it sound like a question. Gary bent down and kissed him, then slid his hand down to Evan's cock "Let's see what I can do for you...." He tugged to get Evan hard again, then jerked Evan off skillfully. Afterward, Gary pulled him in for a cuddle, spooning up behind Evan.

"They're moving up our flight this afternoon, Ev. That was the pilot calling before. He's gonna contact me when he knows for sure." Gary kissed Evan's shoulder and neck.

"I thought we'd have the afternoon...."

"Sorry, but I've got no control over the logistics." He pinched one of Evan's nipples, getting Evan's full attention. "Promise me one thing while I'm gone?"

"Don't sleep with Wes Tremayne?" Evan chuckled, recalling what Gary had said about him earlier.

"No. Just promise me you'll run Jet in a big race at Del Mar next month on my birthday?"

"What?" Evan rolled toward Gary. "Jet? She's not ready for that company yet." Evan had bought the filly, Shapely Shadow, for Gary as a birthday gift the previous spring, but Gary insisted Evan keep a half-ownership stake in her. Evan loved the filly, though she reminded him of better times with Gary.

"Sure she is. You're a good trainer. She'll be ready by then. For me?" Gary kissed a spot under Evan's jaw, turning him to jelly.

"For you."

Gary played his fingers through Evan's hair and held him close.

EVAN WOKE up alone. A glance at the clock told him it was nearly eleven. He had just enough time to shower before Mister Twister and his owners would arrive.

"Gary?"

It was only when Evan got no answer that he realized Gary's suitcases were gone. There was a note pinned to the other pillow.

Flight got pushed up to 1:00. Didn't want to wake you. Talk to you soon.

—XO G

Evan heard a car engine. "Gary?" Maybe he could catch him for a proper good-bye. He grabbed a towel and raced out onto the porch just in time to see Gary climb into a sleek black Escalade.

And then he came face-to-face with Wesley Tremayne.

CHAPTER 3

WES COULDN'T take his eyes off the gorgeous, half-naked man barely holding on to a towel. Not a good idea with Vanessa and Lance there....

Vanessa ruined the mood—and the view—with a snigger that snapped Gorgeous out of his thoughts.

"Excuse me," the guy said, turning away in clear embarrassment. "Uh, this is...." He scratched the back of his neck, which was a peculiar shade of salmon, matched only by his cheeks. "Let me change. Please, wait here?"

"Okay," Wes said. Julia didn't say anything, and even though Wes couldn't see Lance, he knew his mouth was open to comment, but the door slammed shut before he had a chance.

"Evan?" Brent took the steps up the porch and knocked on the door. "It's Brent...."

Wes heard a muffled reply, and Brent opened it and went in.

"Well, he made quite an entrance," Vanessa said. "Too bad I didn't have my camera!"

"Vee, that's not cool," Julia replied, shaking her head.

"Maybe this horse racing thing will be fun after all!" Vanessa rubbed her hands together and sat down gingerly on one of the chairs on the porch after examining it for a moment.

"Yeah, don't get your hopes up, hon." Lance said. "He's not exactly your type."

"Everyone's my type, Lance-a-lot!"

Everyone but Lance. Wes bit his tongue to keep from speaking out loud.

"Not this one. The dude with the suitcases is his, you know, *partner.*"

"So? This is a big place. I'm sure he can't run it on his own."

"Not that kind of partner. Boyfriend kind. You know?" Lance made a limp-wristed gesture. "Even *you* can't ungay a faggot."

"Lance!" Julia snapped. "He can hear you."

Wes saw her glance in his direction without making eye contact, and he knew she hadn't only meant Evan Taylor. He appreciated the gesture, however small and ineffective.

"Okay. Don't be so damn touchy. He knows he's gay. It can't be any surprise at this point."

"I don't think you're supposed to say 'faggot,'" Vanessa added, frowning at Lance. "I hate that word."

"Okay, Vee. I won't say it." Lance said probably just to appease Vanessa. Small victory, but Wes appreciated Vanessa's comments, especially because she was still in the dark about him. He wasn't likely to enlighten her anytime soon, despite her reaction to Lance's homophobia.

"I don't care if he's not into me. I can still enjoy looking at him. I don't even care if he's a good trainer. I like him." Vanessa winked at Julia. "What do you think?"

Wes tuned out their chatter, smiling as he replayed that first encounter in his mind. It had been only a few seconds, but it made quite an impression on Wes. Evan Taylor was damn fine. Lively hazel eyes reminded him of vintage champagne, and the straight nose, and strong, square jaw wouldn't have been out of place on Wes's interpretation of a Greek god. He was several inches shorter than Wes, who had a thing for tall men. But with a face like that, well, he could make an exception.

In fact he already had. This was the good-looking trainer he'd been ogling through binoculars the previous week and occasionally daydreaming about.

But only in his wildest fantasies, because Evan already had a boyfriend, though anyone who wouldn't turn around when he shouted didn't deserve him. Wes thought the dark-haired guy leaving as they arrived had glanced at the porch as if he hoped Evan wouldn't come out. What was going on there?

Wes's daydreams were preempted when Brent came out of the house, followed by Evan, who now wore faded jeans and a pale-blue button-down shirt.

"Evan, these are my friends Julia Compton, Vanessa Vandermere, Lance Robbins, and Wes Tremayne."

Evan shook hands with everyone, though Lance couldn't seem to let go quickly enough. Wes, on the other hand, was in no hurry to let go of Evan's firm, warm grip, but he didn't hold the handshake a fraction of a second more than expected. Wes took a chance meeting Evan's gaze, letting the gold-brown eyes melt his self-control just a little.

"Nice to meet you, officially," Wes said.

One corner of Evan's mouth turned up, a tiny half smile Wes could tell wasn't from amusement. The look in his eyes radiated embarrassment, but his shoulders were straight and square, as if he was fighting the emotion. Wes gave an infinitesimal nod to relax Evan, and it seemed to work. Evan didn't mention Wes's accent, something nearly everyone remarked on at first meeting. It was another point in Evan's favor as far as Wes was concerned.

Up close, Wes reassessed his initial impressions. No, Evan's face wasn't quite perfect after all. Lips a little too full, mouth a little too wide. And there was a tiny scar on the left side of his chin, visible in the bright morning sun.

"So, let's take a look at your horse," Evan said after the introductions. "My assistant Nicky Holloway has him ready."

He led them down the hill from the house to the barn, and Wes tried unsuccessfully to stop staring at his arse. The pale jeans hugged his curves enough to give an idea of what lay beneath the fabric without being uncomfortably tight for riding, Wes guessed. They certainly did justice to Evan's arse, even if it was off-limits.

A bloke could dream, right? And Wes certainly would.

Evan led them through the barn, which was actually a row of stalls under a roof but only partially walled in. The horses could look over the barriers and see what was going on but were still protected from the weather. The floor was clean swept, and each horse had a black rubber water bucket and a mesh bag of hay hanging where they could easily reach it. A few nickered as the group passed. Evan paused to rub a few muzzles.

Vanessa stopped Wes at one stall and rubbed the horse's forehead. "Shapely Shadow," she read the nameplate on the wall. "She's beautiful." Wes patted the dark filly's neck, then realized the group was far ahead and raced to catch up. Vanessa stumbled on high heels and grabbed Wes to keep from falling.

Evan turned at their commotion, and though he didn't say anything, his pursed lips and narrowed eyes telegraphed his thoughts perfectly. When the group reached the end of row, they found Twister with a sturdy, efficient-looking woman who was running her hands along his legs and inspecting his hooves.

She straightened up when they stopped. "Hey, boss. Hiya, Brent."

"Nicky, these are Mister Twister's owners." Evan glanced at them with a glint of fear in his eyes, "Uh, Julia and V-Vivien? No…."

"Vanessa," she prompted with more graciousness than Wes had seen before.

"Vanessa, thank you. Lance and Wes," Evan concluded.

Wes liked the way his name sounded on Evan's lips.

Nicky shook hands and gave Wes a glimmer of recognition. They watched Evan inspect the horse from head to tail to toe, and Wes thought he heard Evan whispering.

Lance tugged at Wes's elbow. "Wonder if the horse will talk back." He sneered and pointed his chin at Evan.

"Sure, he talks to 'em. Spends some time with each horse every day."

Wes turned around to see one of the grooms, a man in his forties with a sunburned face and muddy jeans.

"He talks to them all?" Lance sounded incredulous, just this side of mocking.

"Something like that."

"And do they talk back?" Lance scoffed.

Wes preferred not to say anything, but he listened to the groom. He'd discovered long ago he learned far more by listening, not speaking.

"'Course they talk back, boy! Just they don't use words like you or me. But they communicate all right," the groom said condescendingly. "Secret to being a good horseman is understanding what they mean. Some folks can get it, and other ones, it's like they're deaf and blind."

"Oh," Wes said, embarrassed just from proximity to Lance and his snark, the smarmy git. He hoped the groom didn't consider *him* to be deaf and blind as well. "So how do you learn to understand them?"

"Listen with your hands and your eyes… and your heart. You'll figure it out if they want to talk to you. Horses don't talk to everyone, y'know? Ya gotta *earn* it." The man turned and headed down the barn to take care of a horse that had knocked the hay out of his feedbag. He rubbed the horse's nose and whispered something, followed by a hearty laugh. Wes focused on Evan again.

The grizzled groom finished his tasks and returned, then went up to Evan and spoke softly. Hopefully, it wasn't to say how useless Wes would be around the barn. He'd come today as one of Twister's owners, but he already knew he liked the atmosphere in the barn and wanted to be more involved in Twist's training and racing than just writing checks and watching him race.

It was more than just enjoying the way Evan Taylor looked and moved. Wes found his attention split between Evan and the quiet efficiency of the rest of the staff as they bustled around the barn.

But after hearing the old man's words, Wes would pay more attention to the horses and less to the people around the barns and see if he couldn't learn more that way.

Evan nodded and turned back to Twist's inspection.

"He looks pretty good. Better than most of Bing's horses. He's sound. Looks like he's recovered nicely after the last race. Nicky, let's saddle him up and have Cheryl take him for a few laps."

Once Twister was saddled, they watched the exercise rider put him through his paces, including breaking from the four-stall starting gate. Wes was impressed with Evan's facilities. The barn was clean, the horses lively and attentive to the visitors, and the training track had its own starting gate.

Evan timed the horse on the last lap, when the rider had him warmed up and really moving.

He nodded as he clicked the stopwatch. "Not bad considering he just vanned down here. He's got a good head on him, doesn't let too much upset him. That's a good trait in a racehorse."

"You think he's a winner?" Julia asked.

"He could be. He's not at his peak. Needs a different training regimen, better quality feed, and some TLC, and then we'll see what he's really capable of."

"Sounds like you know what you're doing," Lance said, and Wes could tell the words were difficult for him to say. "When will he run again?"

"Three, four weeks. I wouldn't even think about evaluating for at least ten days. Depends on how quickly he settles in here and how he responds to some high-quality food. There's only another week of racing at Santa Alamita. The next meet's up in the Bay Area. Golden Gate Fields. He might be ready in time to go up there."

"That long, huh?" Lance shook his head.

"He's not a car. He needs more than a new set of tires and a tank of gas. I only run horses when they're ready, not on your schedule, unless we're aiming for a stakes race when I'll tailor the workouts so he'll peak on the right day. But this guy just isn't in that league—yet." Evan's jaw tightened as he spoke, and he slowed his words down. Lance had clearly hit one of his hot buttons. "Any more questions?" Evan glanced at each of them, but his gaze lingered on Wes for a fraction of a second longer than the others.

"Do you think he could be good enough for a big stakes race?" Julia asked, her tone polite, not quite deferential. She gave Evan the smile that had gotten her at least three juicy roles, and it seemed to work.

"I can't say yet, but I won't rule it out. Some horses, you can tell right away they don't have what it takes. Others you can tell they have it. And some, like Twister, keep their cards close, and it's going to take some work to see what he has to show me."

"Now what?" Julia asked.

"I'll take him for a one-month trial period. Time for both sides to see if this relationship is going to work. If it does, then we can draw up a proper contract."

"Just one month?" Wes asked.

Evan glanced over at him. "There are two main kinds of owners I meet. The first kind likes the idea of owning a racehorse. It's exciting, a little sexy." He glanced at Lance. "It's a status symbol."

Lance resumed the skeptical frown he'd worn practically since he'd arrived.

Evan turned his gaze on Julia and Wes. "The other kind own horses that race. They like the track, but the horses come first. The excitement of racing and winning isn't their main motivation. One group asks how the horse is doing, wants to visit him here even when he's not running. The other group calls to see when he's running, then only shows up in the Winner's Circle." Evan glanced around the group again. "What kind of owners do you want to be?"

Julia stepped forward again. "I—"

He cut her off. "Don't answer yet. Think about it. There are four of you. You decide among yourselves. I don't want to be part of your discussions. And I only want to deal with one of you. That's it. *One* liaison or the deal's off. Do you want to discuss this among yourselves?"

The four of them looked at each other and shook their heads. "Works for me," Vanessa said.

Lance had been staring at Evan with particular interest as he explained his general philosophy. Wes hoped he wouldn't open his mouth and fuck this all up. Lance cocked his head, and Wes's stomach churned.

"I know where I've seen you! Weren't you Troy Evans?" Lance blurted, and everyone turned to him, except Evan.

"One month. Who's going to be my liaison?" Evan asked, pointedly ignoring Lance's question.

"I will," Wes said. The sound of his voice startled him. It was the first thing he'd said to Evan since their introductions.

Evan gave him another appraising glance. "The quiet one." His gaze bore into Wes. "Suits me perfectly." This time he smiled.

Wes planned to google Troy Evans as soon as he got home.

"THAT WAS a helluva result, wasn't it?" Julia asked as they drove back to LA. Brent, Vanessa, and Lance had come in a second car, and Wes was grateful. He didn't want to spend an hour listening to any more fag comments from Lance or smell Vanessa's lip gloss and $1000-an-ounce perfume. He felt sorry for Brent, who had refused Julia's offer to drive back with them.

"What do you mean?"

"Let me count the ways," Julia chuckled, venturing a quick glance before turning her attention back to the road.

"He wasn't what I expected," Wes replied. "He was kind of a prick, douchebag, or whatever you Americans say."

"Yes, he was. I didn't expect him to be so serious, and I did expect him to be nicer to us," Julia replied, absent-mindedly twirling the ends of her hair with one hand as she spoke. "It was like he would rather hang out with Mister Twister than with us. Even before Lance put his entire leg in his mouth."

"So, who is—or was—Troy Evans?"

"Evan's stage name. He was in a few films and a series. I can't remember off the top of my head. He kind of faded away, but that happens a lot. I thought he looked familiar, so I asked Brent when Evan was watching Twist run."

"He must be cleaning up training horses for actors, producers...."

Julia shook her head, eyes still on the road. "Brent says he avoids everything to do with actors and Hollywood. He only took Twist at Brent's insistence."

"I reckon owning a racehorse is more serious than we've been taking it so far. I mean, it is his job and his livelihood. And he really cares about the horses. The owners can go fuck themselves."

Julia chuckled. "It's too bad, though."

"What's too bad?" Wes asked, glancing over at Julia.

"His personality. Definitely not what I expected from someone so pretty." She giggled.

"Pretty? You think he's pretty?"

"Don't you?" She took a quick glance at Wes, and he shrugged. "I saw your reaction when he came out of the house in that towel." She laughed.

"He's more pleasant to look at than to speak to. A moot point, since he's not available even if I found him more than remotely attractive. He gets along better with horses than people." He paused. "But he must be decent if Brent likes him, though."

"Brent's known him since junior high or something."

"Remind me what junior high is again."

"Seventh to eighth or ninth grade. About age twelve to fifteen."

Wes nodded, though he knew he'd forget again. Couldn't retain all this American minutiae. "So what else did Brent say?"

"He got fed up with Hollywood bullshit and just quit. That's all Brent would say, but I got the feeling there's more to it."

"Now everything makes sense," Wes replied. "He probably just saw us as more Hollywood bullshit, especially Vanessa and Lance."

"Probably…. Maybe he'll be different with you, one-on-one, so to speak." She turned toward Wes and winked. "You did volunteer to be our liaison."

"I don't know what got into me." Wes had been responding to Evan's appearance and his rapport with the horses, somehow blotting out the facts that Evan acted like an arsehole and wasn't available.

"I do. If he'd looked at me the same way, I'd have volunteered too."

"How did he look at me?" Wes had only seen Evan glaring, which wasn't exactly a turn-on, no matter how good he looked in a towel.

"Like he wanted to eat you up. But only when you weren't looking. His words said he was a jerk, but his eyes…."

"Shut up. You're imagining things."

"We'll see. Once you two start 'liaising.'"

Liaising.

"We should watch something he's been in later, unless you have plans?" Julia asked.

"Not really. Sounds good." Wes's only plan was to learn more about horse racing. He decided he wanted to take owning their horse more seriously. He was curious why Evan Taylor had found the horse racing world preferable to being a Hollywood star. He also wanted to know why Evan's boyfriend had run off and left him, without even a glance back.

What was going on there?

CHAPTER 4

BY THE next day, Mister Twister had settled into the Taylor routine. Nicky assigned him a groom, and within a couple of days, Evan detected a little more spark in him. He kept him on a light workout schedule, alternating jogs with gallops, but no speed work. He needed to put on some more muscle. Then he might really turn some heads on the track.

Gary called from Brazil three days after he left and spent ten minutes answering Evan's questions with vague responses. He didn't say exactly where they were, but he did send Evan some photos of their rustic accommodations in a small rainforest village and some incredible shots of colorful birds. Evan felt embarrassed he'd doubted Gary was really in Brazil when he flipped through the images on his phone. Gary could get as immersed in work as Evan, and sometimes communication came second.

But Evan couldn't deny he still had some unanswered questions about how Gary had suddenly found funding to fill the gap between his main backer and the amount needed to do a first-class job on this documentary. He wouldn't pry, but the lack of information gave him a worrisome ache in his gut.

He walked into Twister's stall to examine the horse's legs for any heat or soreness after the morning's gallop. He heard the phone burr over the intercom. Nicky was in the office, and he knew she would get it.

"Evan? Phone," Nicky shouted from the barn office.

Evan was only two stalls away, so he got to his feet and poked his head into the office. "Who is it?"

"Wes Tremayne," she said with a schoolgirl twinkle in her eye, hand over the mouthpiece.

Evan tried not to react. "I'm not here." It was the only answer, because he wasn't about to talk to the man when just hearing his name sent a little shiver up his spine. Too dangerous.

"I already told him you were...." She furrowed her brow. "Sorry, I didn't know."

"What does he want?"

"To talk to you."

"Shit. Doesn't he realize we're busy around here in the afternoons?" He snatched the phone from Nicky, then felt bad for taking his frustrations out on her. He mouthed, "Sorry," before answering. "Taylor."

"Hello, Evan, this is W—"

"I know. Nicky told me." He used his impatient voice.

"I can see this is a bad time. Let me know what would a better time to ring back for five minutes of your time."

Surprisingly, Wes remained polite, even in the face of Evan's rudeness. Wes's enchanting British accent smoothed his ruffled feathers a bit. "I guess I can give you five minutes right now."

"Thank you."

"What did you want?"

"Actually I was hoping you could recommend some books to me, about racing."

"Racing? You mean betting?"

"No. About American horse racing and things an owner should know."

The answer surprised Evan. "Books about horses? Didn't you just google it?"

"I might be old-fashioned, but I prefer books. I like to know whose information I'm reading, so I don't always trust the Internet. Not a fan of Wikipedia."

Another surprise. Tremayne's interest in horses was a good thing, unless a little knowledge meant he'd start second-guessing Evan's training. "Sure. I can suggest a few." He listed two books he'd found helpful, but they were not for a novice. They would convince Tremayne this was serious and complicated work. But it would get him out of Evan's hair for the time being. He could hear Wes writing on the other end.

"Anything else?"

"A couple of others might interest you…." He mentioned two more.

"Thank you. I appreciate your time. I'll let you go."

"No problem." Suddenly he didn't want the conversation to end. "If you do want to call, evenings are better. Between seven and nine." Why did he say that?

"Thank you. I'll do better next time." Wes hung up.

Next time. Evan stared at the phone for a moment, wondering when that might be before he realized he shouldn't be looking forward to talking to Wes Tremayne again.

WES HUNG up and smiled. He hadn't expected Evan to sound so annoyed when he first answered, but thankfully by the end of the conversation, his attitude seemed less hostile, if not exactly welcoming. Now Wes had some resources to study so he wouldn't waste Evan's time with stupid questions. He quickly found two of the books for sale online and ordered them for next-day delivery. He searched all the online sources for used books, and local libraries, but couldn't find any copies of the others. He had enough to keep him busy while he kept searching.

Julia called the following afternoon, and Wes was already halfway through the first book.

"Got any plans for dinner?" she asked.

"No, but I'm not up for going out. Why? Do you think we need to make an appearance?"

"It's up to you, but it couldn't hurt. Once a week is probably sufficient when you're filming, but on hiatus…."

"Why can't we let people think we've gone on holiday together?"

"That means I can't go out, either."

"Okay, fine. Dinner." He let out a pent-up breath but it didn't dissolve the increasing tension in his shoulders. "Where should we be seen?"

"I'll find someplace new and out of the way so someone thinks they've caught us."

"Whatever."

"Wes, we don't have to keep doing this. You have options."

"Let's talk about it later. I'll pick you up around eight thirty?"

"Sounds good." She hung up.

He picked up his book and lay down on the couch. He turned the digital radio on and chose a jazz station, then cracked the book open and read.

The phone chirping startled him. He glanced at the number before answering. Julia.

"It's nearly nine. You okay?"

"Nine? Really?" He looked at his watch. "Sorry, I got distracted."

"No problem. Do you want to cancel?"

He did, but then he'd just have to do it the following night. "No. Give me forty minutes."

He hopped in the shower and dressed in black jeans, with an Armani shirt and jacket, and put a little gel in his hair to keep it from frizzing in the California heat. It beat the typical British chill, but he'd never quite got used to it almost year round. He went to the underground garage beneath his building and slid into the smooth leather of the Porsche Boxster. It was the first car he'd ever owned—he'd never needed one in London or New York—and he hadn't got used to either the left-hand drive, or the LA traffic yet. It was luxurious enough to match his star image, but not so expensive he'd feel embarrassed driving around in it.

God, how he hated all the identities he felt expected to wear, even when he wasn't in front of a camera. He was seriously considering chucking it all in and going back to the stage. Maybe television just wasn't right for him, and if that was the only way to get into films, then he could just tick that one off the list too.

He thought about Evan Taylor, and his exodus from Hollywood began to make more sense.

He drove to Julia's apartment and rang her from the street. She came down and slid into the passenger seat. He leaned toward her for a brief hug. Only someone standing two feet away would be able to tell it wasn't a kiss. They separated, and then he pulled her close again. That should be good for whoever was watching. He sensed a camera flash and whispered into her ear before they parted and he put the Porsche into gear.

"Wes, I think we really need to talk about this."

"What's to talk about?"

"I don't want to keep doing this either."

"Did you meet someone?" He glanced over quickly and saw her shake her head.

"No. But it's making you miserable. Is it worth it?"

"Saul thinks so."

"You really want to keep playing this game for the media and your manager? This kind of deception only sets back wider acceptance of gay actors. No one's lost their roles over coming out lately. The homophobic actors are the ones losing out. Remember Isaiah Washington? Where's he now? Even Alec Baldwin lost a job for his big, fat mouth."

"I'm not established enough here to take that chance." He turned right at the next light and went two blocks until they arrived at the restaurant. He handed the keys to the parking valet, then went around to open Julia's door. A few cameras snapped, and several women asked for his autograph. None of them asked for Julia's, but two men did, and Julia took photographs with both of them. Then Wes held out his hand.

"Sorry, guys, I'm claiming her back," he said with a grin.

Julia waved to the fans as Wes slid an arm around her waist.

Inside they were immediately shown to a table off in one corner, which provided them some privacy from eavesdroppers. It was perfect.

Once they ordered and the waitress brought their drinks, Julia brought up the topic they hadn't finished discussing in the car.

"Wes?"

"What?" He waited for her answer, but all he got was a raised eyebrow. "Okay. As much as I agree, I'm not ready to risk the alternative." He sipped his drink. Julia had ordered both of them something pale green and tasting of vegetables. Julia seemed to be enjoying hers, so he pushed the nearly fully glass towards her.

She grinned and signaled for the waitress, who came over immediately. Being recognized did have some perks, Wes admitted.

"What beers do you have on tap?"

She rattled off about a dozen.

"I'll have the weissbier." Wes grinned at Julia.

"I'll be right back with that."

And she was.

Wes took a sip and smiled, vowing never to drink anything green again. "Look, Jules, let's go one more month. If there's a good reason then, I'll drop the charade. Unless you want out. You can break up with me. Say I cheated on you or something."

"Did you?" She grinned and finished her cocktail. She started eating the fruit out of the glass.

"Not with another woman...," he whispered and grinned back.

"Is that a good idea? I'm not saying be a monk, but what if he tells someone else?"

"I guess I would be forced to deal with the issue at that point." He took a long pull of his beer. He hadn't been reckless, but he hadn't been as careful about possibly being recognized. Maybe at some level he wanted to get caught.

"If and when we break up, I don't think cheating is going to help your reputation any. Look at Kristen Stewart."

"I'd rather not, thank you."

"You know what I mean. We can just part ways and stay friends without accusing anyone of cheating. What's wrong with that?"

"No one believes that friends crap," Wes replied. He reached out and held her hand across the table, in case anyone was watching them.

A wine steward arrived with the bottle Wes had ordered, stopping their conversation. As soon as he left, the waitress brought their food— appetizers and main dishes served together at Julia's request.

They ate in silence for a few minutes. Wes's braised short ribs were delicious. He gave Julia some, and she offered him a taste of her lobster chowder.

"One month, Wes. Then we reevaluate the situation. The longer you wait, the worse the blowback," Julia said. "One month."

THE NEXT morning, photos of their intimate dinner appeared in the paper on the celebrity-sighting page. Evan spotted the photos as he sipped coffee and ate breakfast in his kitchen after morning workouts. He hadn't even glanced at that section for years and he would rather not think about why he had today. He pushed the paper away, almost gagging at the thought of another bite of scrambled eggs. He'd made too much, still cooking for two.

Why did the sight of Wes and Julia get to him? Sure, Wes was attractive, and he seemed more serious about owning the horse than his friends, but that didn't explain why Evan kept thinking about him after Wes's phone call.

Wes Tremayne was straight, and even if he weren't, Evan had Gary.

Gary. Evan hadn't begun to miss him, and that worried him as much as his perplexing attraction to Wes Tremayne.

Back when Evan was acting, the advice was to craft a persona where men wanted to be you and women wanted to sleep with you. If you could manage that, you'd hit the big time. You couldn't be a guy men thought was any competition. You had to be someone guys wanted to hang out with.

When it came to Wes, Evan wanted to sleep with him, not be him. Maybe that was the secret of success with gay viewers. Agents and managers should remind up-and-coming male stars they should appeal to men and women. Whatever they'd told Wes Tremayne was paying off. Now that Evan had started paying attention, he spotted stories about Wes everywhere. He had some good PR folks on his staff. Word around town seemed to cast him as the new Harrison Ford, and there was even talk of him becoming the next James Bond when Daniel Craig hung up his license to kill.

His cell phone vibrated—a reminder it was time to leave for Santa Alamita. He had two runners today. With the meet ending in a few days, he vanned the runners back each evening so he wouldn't have to make more than one trip next week when he closed down his barn there.

IN THE paddock for his first race, Evan thought he spotted a familiar face in the crowd: Vanessa Vandermere. She was standing at the rail with the boorish Lance. Was Wes with them again today? He hoped they wouldn't flag him down because he didn't want to speak to either man. Vanessa gave him a little wave and a smile, and Lance nodded without any enthusiasm. The feeling was mutual. Then two other people joined them near the rail. Brent and Wes. Julia was nowhere in sight.

Brent shouted a greeting, and Wes waved and flashed Evan a smile he was quickly coming to appreciate. Seeing Wes with the full sunshine on his face, Evan knew what Gary had meant when he said Wes was still "pretty." His hair looked almost golden, but his smile nearly outshone the sun. The horse Evan was saddling skittered away while he had his attention elsewhere, then danced back and stepped on Evan's foot. Half a ton of horse hurt, even through his sturdy boots.

"Need a hand, Evan?" Timbo, his groom, reminded him he hadn't finished tightening the cinch.

"No, I've got it." Evan felt like an idiot in front of the crowd. He finished the task at hand and let the lead pony take his runner Nautical Knot away for a few turns around the paddock so the betting public could get a good look at the runners.

He saw Brent and Wes at the rail again, and he strode toward them.

"Your runner looks good," Brent said. He pulled a ticket out of his pocket. "I put a little bit on him."

"Me too," Wes said and flashed his own ticket, along with that smile that melted Evan's insides far too much.

"You're not supposed to tell me that!" Evan joked. "Now I'll feel guilty if he doesn't win."

"What's the occasion for a suit on race day?" Wes asked. Evan felt Wes's gaze travel along his body as surely as if he'd been caressed.

"It's our 'dress uniform,' so to speak. Like an athlete who wears his uniform only on game day, but not during practice." Not strictly true, since he preferred a nice jacket over jeans. But today he had two reasons for the suit: two big stakes races, and the fact Wes might be here. Evan was hard-pressed to say which had been uppermost in his decision.

"I like it," Wes said. The smile reflected in his eyes gave Evan the impression he wasn't speaking in general terms. Evan grinned but turned away to avoid meeting Wes's—or Brent's—gaze. He was afraid he'd give away how much he'd appreciated the indirect compliment.

The announcement sounded for the horses to move to the track for the post parade. "Gotta go," Evan said, never sorrier to have to attend to his runner—and the horse's nervous owners. It was customary for trainers to sit with the clients during the race.

The thought of sharing the box with Wes when Mister Twister ran brightened Evan's mood, until he remembered the horse's other three owners, including Julia Compton.

EVAN'S RUNNER came home first by four lengths. The jockey got him out of a tough spot when they got boxed in at the first turn and took a chance moving close along the rail, but Nautical Knot had plenty of speed and shot forward as a tiny space opened up. The second-place jockey lodged an objection, claiming Nautical Knot bumped him, and Evan rushed to the track to find out what had happened when the "Inquiry" sign went up and an announcement advised the crowd that the stewards would determine the final order of the runners momentarily.

Jorge Diaz, Evan's jock, had to recount his actions during the race, while up in the booth the stewards watched the video.

"Evan, if we bumped them it wasn't on purpose, but I don't remember feeling anything. He was crowding me against the rail, and it was only because Knotty still had so much in the tank I could get him out of there."

"I believe you. Sometimes things happen. We'll take a look at the video later, no matter the outcome." Evan trusted his riders. But from a few feet away, the owners glared at Jorge. Evan went over to try to calm them down. He wouldn't let them insult or intimidate his jock.

A tense five minutes later, the stewards declared Evan's runner the winner and the second-place horse was disqualified to fourth because the stewards found the objecting jockey had impeded the progress of another runner earlier in the race.

Nautical Knots's owners—an Orange County stockbroker and his overly bleached and Botoxed wife—hugged Evan and Jorge as if nothing had happened.

Evan was used to it, and so was Jorge, but he still tried to shield his jocks from the owners whenever possible. He'd give him an additional bonus from his share of the purse to prevent Jorge from turning down another ride on this horse.

The purse for the race had been $40,000, which paid Knotty's owners 60 percent—$24,000—and Evan's share came to 10 percent of that: $2,400, not a king's ransom but not bad for a day's work.... The second-place trainer took home only $800.

AFTER SADDLING his runner for the sixth, an $80,000 stakes race, Evan spotted Brent and Wes Tremayne again. Evan met them at the fence, secretly glad Vanessa and Lance were nowhere to be found and neither was Julia.

Evan wondered how Wes managed to look like he'd just walked off a fashion show runway. The guy's hair looked perfect, even in the heat, while Evan felt like he'd walked through a swamp. He brushed at his temple, feeling his hair was damp from sweat. Even Brent looked a little soggy around the edges.

"What happened in the last race?" Wes asked.

Evan gave him a summary.

"What did they do before the video replays?" Wes asked.

"They guessed. Maybe they flipped a coin. Who knows? I'm just glad it's more likely they'll see what really happened."

"Now I wish I'd put more on Nautical Knot," Brent said. "I could have bought a new car like Wes."

"I didn't win enough for a new car. Possibly a second-hand car that doesn't have an engine." He laughed.

"It sure beats losing," Evan replied.

"Evan, I meant to thank you for the suggestions on those books. I was able to find all but one. The Landers book. Can't even find a second-hand copy for sale anywhere. Did I get the title wrong?"

"No. That's the book. It's out of print, I guess."

"Oh well. I'll have to ask a book dealer to track one down." Wes looked disappointed. Evan hadn't expected him to read one, much less buy all of them and go to this effort to find the last title.

"I have a copy back at the farm." The words were out before Evan realized it. "I could lend it to you." Jesus, that was a bad idea. Evan pressed his lips together to keep from blurting out anything else.

"I'd love to borrow it. I noticed several other books mention his work, so I would like to read the original."

"Sure. Next time I see you." Damn mouth betrayed him yet again. Next time, like this was going to happen on a regular basis.

The trumpeter called the horses to the post, and Evan waved as he followed his horse out of the paddock.

"WELL, THAT was quite a turnaround," Brent said to Wes as they made their way back inside to place bets for the race.

"What do you mean?"

"The other day at the farm I thought Evan was going to bite everyone's head off, and here he is offering to lend you a book. What happened between then and now?"

Wes shrugged. "I don't know. I called him the other day for some recommendations of books about American racing. He didn't sound too happy to hear from me at first, but once he started talking about horses, he loosened up. He was very helpful."

They stopped at one of the self-service betting machines. Wes used half his winnings from the first bet to place a second bet on Evan's runner, Baited Hook, wondering at the coincidence of two runners with maritime names. If he lost, he'd still come out quids in. He didn't plan to keep any of the winnings. He'd find a worthwhile local charity to donate to. His manager would be all over that. Wes didn't need to cash in on a charitable donation to boost his image, but he knew the publicity would help the charity much more than it helped him. He considered it an acceptable use of his public image.

They got back to their box seats. Vanessa and Lance had left after Evan's first race. Or rather Vanessa had left, and Lance trailed after her. The guy would never learn.

THE HORSES were at the gate, and Brent watched through the binoculars. "Evan's horse broke late. He's going to have to make up a lot of ground to have a shot."

Sure enough, the jockey slowly moved the horse up, fifth place, then fourth, then third, as they roared around the final turn and into the stretch. Just a furlong left and Baited Hook was half a length back.

"Come on, four! Come *on*, four!" Wes shouted as Brent joined in, and they jumped up and down as if that might influence the outcome of the race.

Baited Hook put on a last-ditch burst of speed and the result was a photo finish. The crowd buzzed as they waited for the officials to determine the winner.

Again, Evan's runner beat the odds and won, by less than a nose.

Now Wes really had won enough to buy a new car.

He already had a car he loved. He'd just give more to the charity.

Wes trained the binoculars on the Winner's Circle as Evan and the owners posed with the horse for the photographer. Was it his imagination or was Evan looking in Wes's direction?

Imagination, or wishful thinking. Wes put the glasses down, and he and Brent went inside to cash in their winning tickets.

"Two close finishes," Wes said. "My stomach was in knots. I hope it's not like this when Mister Twister runs."

"I'm sure it will be worse," Brent said.

Wes really wasn't thinking that far ahead. Instead, he was calculating how long he should wait to ring Evan to follow up on borrowing that book.

CHAPTER 5

"YOU DID what? And he said what?" Julia stared at Wes from across the table in the bar at Indigo 7, a new restaurant off Sunset. When she raised her voice, other bar patrons glanced in her direction, and Wes saw some of them recognized her. She was wearing a slinky white dress with bare shoulders, and he shouldn't have been surprised at the admiring stares.

"He told me he'd lend me the book, so I e-mailed, and he invited me out to the farm tomorrow since Twister is doing a fast workout. That's not as fast as a race but—"

"I get it. Now you're an expert on training racehorses." She gave him an impish grin. "Or racehorse trainers? What do you think he means by the invitation?" She sipped her drink, which true to the name of the place was a vibrant indigo. Wes had already added blue to his do-not-drink list, placing it even higher than green.

"Why does he have to mean anything by it?"

"Right, he doesn't know you're gay too, does he?" She lowered her voice as she spoke. Wes credited her with not glancing around to see if anyone overheard—a telltale sign there was something worth overhearing. She was smart *and* a good actress. "I should ask what do you mean by this sudden interest in horse racing?"

Wes had been asking himself the same questions, without much insight into the answers. "Why does it have to mean anything? Why can't I be interested in the horse, and spending time with Evan is just an added bonus? It doesn't mean it's going anywhere it shouldn't."

Her smile dissolved. "Shouldn't?"

"He's involved with someone, remember? Besides, just because two gay men hang out doesn't mean there's anything going on between them. Do you end up fucking every male friend you hang out with?"

"No, but it doesn't mean I wouldn't like to." She reached out and stroked his chin, rubbing her fingertips back and forth along his stubbled jaw as she gave him a look he wouldn't have minded from Evan Taylor. This, however, would keep up the illusion Julia had helped him craft.

They had dinner, and she stayed at his apartment in the guest bedroom. She kept some clothes and makeup there. When she left she would put her things away in his closet and bathroom. The ruse had been her idea, in case their friends snooped when they were in his apartment.

Sometimes they went out together, came back here, and then he left through the garage's rear entrance to go out on his own to a bar or club. He felt restless tonight as he lay in bed staring at the ceiling. He could use something—someone—mindless and anonymous tonight, but he wouldn't go. He needed to get up early to get to Evan's farm for Twister's 7:00 a.m. workout.

The promise of seeing Evan again was incentive to stay in. Wes didn't know what he was doing or thinking. He just knew he wanted to spend time with Evan Taylor. He brushed away Julia's question about where this was leading. Nowhere. It couldn't go anywhere now.

But in a month?

EVAN WAS up at five as usual and down to the barn by five thirty.

"Getting a late start today?" Nicky teased as she poured fresh coffee from the pot in the office.

"No."

"Wet hair?" She didn't say more, but he ran his hand across his scalp in response.

He didn't generally shower this early, waiting until after helping with the stalls so he could wash off the mess.

The grooms started on their charges while he and Nicky went over the horses' exercise schedules. They had a chart tacked up on the wall, showing each of the sixteen horses and whether they would walk, jog, gallop, or do speed work and which horses would work alone and which with company—in a small group intended to simulate racing conditions.

The first group of six horses was ready for their exercise by six. When they started back to the barn, Wes Tremayne was walking out in the direction of the track. He waved. Evan's spirits lifted in the morning gloom.

"Wes Tremayne's here?" Nicky asked, moving her pony even with Evan's. She nodded, and Evan noticed her glance at his still-damp hair again.

"I told him he could watch Twister's workout if he got here early enough. I'm surprised he made it."

"Twister's not going out till eight."

"I know. I told him seven, figuring he wouldn't show."

"Surprise!" she said and gave him a wink that knocked the smile right off his face.

Wes waited at the barn for them to ride up, and he took hold of Evan's horse's bridle while he dismounted. He rubbed her muzzle and held out his hand, open palm up so she could see he wasn't hiding any treats. She explored his palm with her lips, and Evan watched to see Wes's reaction, which was a grin.

"Good morning, Evan. Thanks for letting me come out."

"Hi, Wes. Want some coffee? There might be a fresh pot in the office. Or I could make some tea if you prefer?"

"Coffee's fine. Prefer it first thing. But I do love a good strong cuppa later on."

Evan clipped his mare's bridle to a ring on the outside wall of the barn and scritched her ears before going inside with Wes. As Wes poured himself a cup of coffee, Evan took the opportunity to assess him. Wes wore jeans and a thin navy sweater over a black T-shirt. The navy was a nice complement to his dark hair and brought out the color in his eyes. He wore sturdy leather boots, similar to Evan's, only they were obviously new and only a little dusty from walking through the barn. Evan approved. In truth, he approved of much more than the boots, but he put those thoughts out of his brain. Didn't want to scare off the straight guy.

"There's one more group to work before Twister. You can hang in the barn or come out to the track and watch those horses."

"I'd like to watch, if I won't be in the way."

"Just stay away from the gap—the entrance to the track—and on the outside of the railing."

The grooms had saddled the next set of horses to work, and Evan inspected each one, feeling all four legs. Wes stood a few paces back, watching.

"Checking for heat, right?" Wes said, and Evan stared at him.

"Yeah. That's right," Evan replied. Maybe Wes really had read those books. "This guy, Baited Hook—Ben to us—has a little right here on the inside near foreleg, just below the knee."

"Could I feel it?" Wes asked.

Evan stared until he realized Wes was talking about the horse's leg. "Sure."

Wes bumped knees with Evan as he sank down and gently reached out, sliding his fingers along the horse's leg. The heat was just above the rough oval spot called a chestnut. But the heat from Wes radiated up Evan's thigh, and he fought to concentrate on the horse.

Wes moved his hand to the other leg, comparing.

"I see the difference. What will you do?"

"I'll keep him at a jog—trot—today and ice him after. If he's still warm tomorrow, then maybe just a walk with a pony, no rider. If it's worse, I'll give him a day off."

Wes nodded, taking in the information.

Evan finished checking the horses, and he noticed how Wes stayed out of the way, or kept to the near—left—side of the horses. On the way past the office, he grabbed a pair of binoculars for Wes to use.

"Thanks, Evan."

"You spend much time around horses before this?" Evan asked as he headed outside to mount Sable.

"I rode as a kid. My school, I guess you'd call it high school, had a stable of horses, and I have friends who own hunters."

"You seem really natural around them."

"Thanks," Wes said and smiled, warming Evan despite the chill of the gray morning. "Need a leg up?" Wes added and Evan nodded.

He bent his leg and propelled himself up as Wes gave an added boost so he landed softly astride the mare. He tried to ignore the sensation of Wes's fingers around his calf and composed himself as he gathered the reins.

Evan glanced back, watching Wes make his way behind the horses to the track.

WES WATCHED the first set of horses work out and listened to the riders give Evan reports on how the horses worked. While Evan supervised the horses on the track, Wes noticed Nicky worked with two others at the little starting gate at the far side of the track. He watched through the binoculars as she helped the rider get the horses into the gate. One was skittish and nearly tossed the rider as it moved sideways away from the gate. The other wasn't as nervous but didn't go in smoothly. Nicky moved her own horse into the gate and waited as the riders finally got their horses inside, though one backed out as soon as he could. From this distance Wes couldn't tell if that was on purpose or not.

He watched the horses working around the track, mostly jogging. Another horse on a gallop blew past a chestnut filly, and she broke out of her trot to try and catch up. The rider got her under control, but she fought him the rest of the way around the track. He could see the rider patting her neck and talking to her the whole time.

He got a good feeling about how Evan Taylor ran his stables by watching how his staff worked with the horses. They all talked to them, gently easing them into their workouts and keeping open communication even as they moved around the track. As each horse finished, the rider came up and reported to Evan.

"She really wanted to move."

"He's still pulling hard on the left rein, even with these blinkers."

"She kind of sputtered and got winded after a mile."

Evan made notes in a pad he kept in his shirt pocket, then sent each horse back to the barn. By then Nicky and the two horses she was coaching came back and reported to Evan.

Then, as a group, they returned to the barn, with Wes following behind, forced to move at a jog to keep up.

The first set of horses were being bathed when they got back, and Evan felt each horse for heat or injury and asked the grooms to ice two of them.

Wes went back to Twister's stall to watch his groom tack him up, and he rubbed the horse's muzzle.

"You remember me?" he asked. The horse nickered. Wes decided to believe that was a yes.

When the rider took him out of the stall for Evan's inspection Wes was surprised how much the horse had changed in only a week. He seemed fuller though the chest, more muscular, and his coat even felt softer. Maybe it was his imagination.

"He looks really good, Evan." Wes ran his hand along the horse's chest.

"You see the difference?"

"What do you do differently? Just feed more?"

"No. Better quality, probably. And I give them vitamin supplements and an ulcer treatment."

"He's got ulcers? How do horses get those?"

"Horses are grazers and tend to eat a little bit at a time all the time. Their stomachs produce acid continuously, expecting them to be eating continuously. If they don't eat, they can get ulcers. We also feed three times a day, instead of two, so there is a shorter period between their dinner and breakfast. And they have access to hay all day, which cuts down on the problems. Twister has a mild case."

Now Wes was even more glad they'd claimed the horse and taken him away from the trainer who didn't take proper care of him. It also made him wonder how many other horses out there weren't being looked after.

"Would you think I was crazy if I took some photos?" Wes asked. The last thing he wanted was for Evan to consider him as anything less than a serious owner.

Evan chuckled. "Sure. Take whatever you like. At least you're showing more interest than some of the owners."

"Really?"

Evan shrugged. "I ask people if they want photos or workout reports, and most of them don't. Others come by for workouts or want to be involved. I appreciate the interest."

Wes pulled his phone out of his jacket pocket and snapped some photos. He was worried Twister would shy away from the flash, but he didn't. Instead, he perked up his ears.

"Oh, this one is a ham," Evan said, tugging at the horse's forelock. "I think he likes having his photo taken. Maybe he remembers the Winner's Circle. Is that right, Twist?" He smoothed a hand down the horse's face. "Okay, let's get this group to the track."

Wes gave Evan a leg up again, and he noticed Nicky watching from astride her own horse, but she didn't say anything. He wondered what she was thinking and decided he didn't care.

Out at the track, Nicky worked with two more horses at the starting gate while Evan supervised the track work. He slid down off his mare to stand with Wes at the rail, then handed him a spare stopwatch out of his pocket.

"You time him too, then you can see how he's doing."

"What am I looking for?" Wes squinted as the exercise rider jogged Twist up the track in the wrong direction.

"He'll take him down to the far turn. Then they'll turn around and move in the right direction. He'll start speeding up as they approach that green and white pole there." Evan touched Wes's arm as he pointed across the track. Wes used the binoculars to see the spot. "Then the rider'll bring him up faster as they hit each pole. You count the time between poles, then total up to see how he's doing. They'll work five furlongs, or five-eighths of a mile."

"I'll do my best."

Wes watched as the rider sped Twist up, and when they were even with the pole, he clicked the watch. It was hard to watch the horse and the stopwatch. Before he realized it, the workout was over, and the clock read just a few seconds over a minute.

"One-oh-four and change," Evan said.

"Is that good?"

"It's not race pace, but that's not what we're aiming for here. What matters is how much energy he still had when they finished."

The rider jogged back and reported. "He moved really well and didn't fight me until the last furlong. I know he wanted to go faster. I could have done it in about three seconds less, but I didn't push him at all."

"Good work, Danny," Evan said. He clocked the other horses and made more notes before he pulled his mare's reins off the fence.

Wes noticed he didn't get on again, choosing to walk with Wes rather than ride. The horses jogged another half a lap before coming back to the barn. The second set of horses was cooled and bathed, and Evan examined each of them before the grooms returned them to the stalls. Wes watched as some of the horses had icepacks strapped to their legs.

"Those stay on about an hour," Evan explained. "Now the horses who worked in the first group are iced, and we'll apply a poultice—a clay and liniment mixture—to take away any swelling."

Wes nodded. He was overloaded with information. He should have taken notes.

"Did you have breakfast?" Evan asked.

"No," Wes replied. His stomach had been growling, and he hoped Evan hadn't heard it.

"I usually grab a bite after the last group. You're welcome to join me at the house, unless you have to be somewhere. Then I'll be able to get that book for you."

Wes remembered he'd originally come for the book. "Nowhere. I left the day free since I didn't know how long the workout would take."

"Let's take a break." Evan poked his head into a stall where Nicky was slathering something on a horse's forelegs. "I'm taking a lunch break. Back in an hour."

"Okay, see ya." She waved and nodded at Wes.

Wes followed Evan up the slope to the house. From the outside it looked like a cross between a bungalow and a farmhouse. The front porch wrapped around. The day had started to heat up, and the shade felt good as they went up the front steps. Evan unlocked the door and waved Wes inside.

The décor wasn't what Wes had been expecting. Burnished wood floors were covered with Oriental rugs. The living room was painted a soothing cobalt, with mahogany wainscoting and a few golden stars twinkling on the coved ceiling with its gentle curves instead of right angles where walls met ceiling. The furniture was comfortable and plush looking and appeared to be antique, made in a time when craftsmen built everything to last. There was a television with a home-theater system set up and two sets of speakers.

He followed Evan into the kitchen, painted a buttery yellow, with mustard-colored wooden floors.

"Do you like eggs? Bacon?"

"American streaky bacon?" Wes asked as he sat down at the table. There were two chairs. He noticed one seemed slightly more worn than the other. Who was the one who had so many meals alone?

"What other kind is there? You mean Canadian bacon?"

"No. Back in the UK, we have meaty rashers, and it doesn't get dark and burnt and shrivel up when it's cooked. It's cut into juicy pink strips, but not like Canadian bacon. Something in between."

"Really? I only have the American kind, sorry." Evan sounded apologetic, and Wes wished he hadn't sounded so negative. He felt like he'd insulted Evan, who hadn't needed to invite him for breakfast. How ungrateful he must sound criticizing Evan's generosity.

"That's fine. Sorry. I'll have some after all."

Evan poured two mugs of steaming coffee. "It's fresh. I have it on a timer so it's ready when I get back."

"Thanks. Can I help?"

"Not necessary. It takes the same amount of time to cook for two as for one." Evan pulled food from the refrigerator, set a skillet to warming on the stovetop, and filled another with water.

Wes hadn't cooked for two for a long time. He wasn't very good at it in any event. If Julia stayed over, they ate out. He also hadn't had anyone cook for him for even longer. He never ended up with guys who knew how to cook. He watched Evan move comfortably around the kitchen, setting bacon to sizzle in one skillet before cracking eggs into the other.

The bacon smelled divine, and Wes's stomach rumbled again. Evan drained the poached eggs, added some cheese and salsa, and served them with flour tortillas.

"It's kind of a cross between huevos rancheros and eggs Benedict." Evan sat down and gave Wes a hopeful look.

"If it tastes half as good as it looks and smells...." Wes cut a portion and took a bite. It was delicious, streaky bacon and all. He was nearly finished before Evan was halfway through his own. He smiled as he watched Wes devour his breakfast.

"Glad to see you enjoying it. I wasn't sure you'd eat bacon at all, regardless of its nationality," Evan said, still grinning. "I figured your personal trainer kept you to a strict food and exercise regimen."

Wes glanced up at Evan and cocked his head, wondering where that idea had come from.

Evan glanced away for a moment, then replied, "I watched a few episodes, and uh...."

Wes nodded. "Yeah, the writers seem to figure a way to get my shirt off in nearly every show. So yes, I do have to keep fit. And I don't tell my trainer about the bacon, so I'd appreciate you keeping this our secret."

"Promise." Evan crossed his heart.

If only he could tell Evan his real secret. Their gazes met for a moment, and some ineffable connection formed. Wes wanted to say something, and he could tell Evan did as well, but neither spoke. It was somehow even more powerful in silence.

"Evan, I was wondering about how you ice the horses after the workouts?" Wes chose to keep to a neutral topic. He couldn't trust himself if they talked about anything personal.

"What about it?"

"If the workouts stress them so much, isn't that bad for the horses?"

"Do you run? How do *you* feel after a workout?"

"Sure I run. Do cardio and weights. Afterwards, I feel exhausted, but good."

"And the next day?"

Wes nodded as Evan's point hit home. "Achy, if I've done a useful workout."

"Same with horses. They're athletes too, and when they exercise, they get aches and pains. We try to minimize any pain and make sure a little ache doesn't become something serious. But most of these horses love running and want to run. I try to care for them to minimize any aftereffects. But we don't run them to the point they are in actual pain unless they pull a muscle, the same way a human athlete might."

Wes nodded as he popped the last bite of eggs into his mouth. He closed his eyes for a split second, savoring the tasty meal as much as the company of the man who'd cooked it for him.

"I have some fruit salad if you're still hungry." Evan went to the refrigerator and came back with a plastic container. He put the tub down on the table and handed a serving spoon to Wes, who helped himself.

"This is a lovely house. I like the colors and all the wood."

"Thanks. It's what's called Craftsman style, built in the '30s.

"It's not what I expected this far out of town."

"This place was originally owned by a film star who made a fortune during the silent era, then couldn't get a role once the talkies got popular. He retired out here, far away from the Hollywood people who rejected him."

Wes didn't see a flicker of irony on Evan's face as he recounted what sounded like his own story, save for the rejection part. Wes still wondered why he'd left, but he'd never bring the topic up. "I suppose a lot of stars were in the same boat. I wonder what will make me obsolete."

"CGI?"

They both laughed. "With the amount of animation in some 'live-action' films, it does seem they don't need actors."

"Or stunt men. Those guys are in much less demand too."

"I hadn't thought about it. It's only lately I've even needed to think about stunts. Until I came here, I was mainly on the stage, where you can't fake anything." Back home, Wes had been the stage version of a

Hollywood star, and in many ways he preferred the simplicity and challenge of stage work, not to mention the spontaneity and immediate feedback from the audience.

"Would you like to see the rest of the house?" Evan asked, keeping Wes from expressing any of his doubts.

"I'd love to. Let me help with the dishes"

"I have a dishwasher. Don't worry about it."

Wes pushed the plate away, stomach comfortably full. Evan led him down the narrow hallway, hung with exquisite framed photographs of animals in an array of habitats, from the desert to the rainforest to the African plains.

"These are brilliant. Absolutely gorgeous. I can practically hear and smell them."

"My boyfriend took those."

Had Wes just imagined the pause before the word "boyfriend"? "He's a photographer, then?" What a fucking idiotic question....

"No. Documentary filmmaker, actually. He takes photos, too, but just as a sideline." Evan paused at the doorway to his office, which was a dramatic dark red with white accents and a pale coved ceiling, curving as it met the walls.

"Incredible. Who would think to use this color on a room?"

"It's the original color, or pretty close."

Wes stepped inside to get the full effect of the room, which wasn't as overwhelming as he'd expected. "I thought I'd feel like I was inside the mouth of a whale." He chuckled as he glanced at the desk, carved from dark mahogany, a complement to the gleaming wood accents on the walls. At one end was a pile of papers, a bold red border on the top one with the ominous header "Last Notice" in huge letters he could read from halfway across the room.

As Evan led him to the next room, he turned toward Wes. "He's in Brazil. For a couple of months."

"What?"

"Gary. My, uh, boyfriend."

No doubt about that pause, but why had Evan mentioned him, or the trip?

The next room was the bedroom. Wes almost didn't want to look, but the dark emerald walls drew him in. He didn't want to see the bed where Evan and Gary were together. Evan's bedside table held books, a clock, and a notepad, but the other nightstand had only a lamp. One side of the dresser top held a cluster of toiletries; the other was bare, as if the person who used it had disappeared—or never existed.

Evan brought one hand across his chest to rub absently along his shoulder. Through the shirt Wes could see the outline of a small bandage, presumably covering the memorable bite mark from the day they'd met. Anything deep enough to require a bandage couldn't be a good thing, Wes decided.

In the mirror Wes could see a pained expression on Evan's face as he continued to touch his shoulder and stare at the empty half of the dresser top. He didn't look as if he missed Gary very much.

Evan glanced up and noticed Wes looking at him in the mirror, and they shared a silent moment. Wes expected Evan to look away, but he didn't.

A soft chirping from Evan's pocket shattered the mood. He finally looked away and answered the phone. "Yeah, Nick?"

Wes couldn't hear her words.

"Did you call them? Talk to Sandy? … They still won't deliver?" Evan looked at the ground and turned so Wes couldn't see his face directly or in the mirror. "Did the winnings from the other day show up in our account yet? … Then have him…. Cash? Fine. I'll take care of it today." Evan snapped the phone shut and looked toward Wes.

"I need to get going too. I've taken up too much of your time." Wes walked out of the room and down the hall. He could feel Evan's eyes on him. He stopped in the living room. "Thanks, Evan, for letting me come to see the workout, and for lunch."

"My pleasure." He sounded like he meant it.

If only, Wes thought as he hurried toward the Boxster.

EVAN CURSED the feed man who hadn't yet made his regular weekly delivery. Yes, Evan owed him money. Most likely so did everyone else. Evan hadn't been paid yet by the Rosarios, another set of clients who had taken their two horses to another trainer the previous week. They owed forty-five days of training expenses for two horses, plus vet bills, nearly $8,000 total. He paid salaries first, then feed, and the vet was last on the list. His accountant warned him against using his personal account for farm expenses, but he couldn't wait. Even with the trainer's share of the winnings from this week's two runners, this month would be tight.

But he couldn't help smiling as he cleared up the kitchen. He'd enjoyed cooking for Wes Tremayne far more than he should have, but Wes had been so obviously interested in the horses, asking serious questions and being so damned normal and genuine, nothing like the overblown ego Evan had expected. It didn't hurt that Wes was easy on the eyes, but the little sparks, the underlying current Evan had felt in Wes's proximity had little to do with looks, and everything to do with his eagerness to learn about horses and racing.

Well, maybe that didn't explain everything. Evan was charmed because it couldn't possibly be an act. Wes had no reason at all to feign interest in Evan or the horses. No wonder Wes had already achieved relatively quick success.

It had been a very long time since anyone had paid that much attention to Evan and the effect was exhilarating. With a twinge, Evan recalled it had been when he first met Gary that he'd last felt such a kick.

What did it mean that a couple of hours with Wes boosted Evan's mood more than a weekend with Gary? Not that Evan could remember the last time they'd spent a whole weekend together.

Instead of helping Nicky with the afternoon chores, Evan drove to the bank and got cash from his personal account to take to the feed company. Only then would they promise to deliver the order the following day. Evan had enough feed on hand for a week, but he liked to keep a buffer, just in case. This week had probably been that case, but he'd rather not owe anyone.

As Evan drove back to the farm, throbbing in his shoulder jolted him back to the reality that was his relationship with Gary. He smoothed two fingers over the bandage and felt a chill settle into his bones. Brent had put the bandage on the day he'd brought Wes and Twister. He'd come in and given Evan an earful about Gary, not for the first time, as he patched up Evan's shoulder.

"Evan, you deserve better. While he's gone, please think about whether you two even belong together anymore."

Brent's warnings and worries took on a new veracity for Evan. Though Wes would never be more than a friend, he'd shown Evan that he had options. He didn't have to settle for Gary's see-sawing between apathy and ill treatment.

He pulled into the farm's driveway and as he rounded the bend, Gary's Lexus came into sight and Evan felt his jaw clench, even though he knew Gary wasn't home. He sat in the car for a few moments calming himself before he made his way down to the barn.

He found Nicky in the office, frowning at the telephone. She looked up as he entered the room.

"I tried calling Mr. Rosario again today. Voice mail. What should we do?"

"I'll warn Raymond about them." Evan smiled. The new trainer the Rosarios had chosen was a friend of his. Most of the trainers knew each other, at least by sight, and they exchanged information about horses and owners.

"Knowing him, he'll send you part of whatever they pay him," Nicky grinned. "If they pay him."

Evan nodded. "He's a good guy."

"So, Wes Tremayne?" Nicky asked, eyebrows raised.

"What about him?" Evan didn't particularly want to talk about their lunch up at the house.

"Maybe some of his rich friends will buy horses, and you'll fill the barn up again. I can just see it: 'Horse trainer to the stars....'" Her voice turned wistful.

That would be awful. It was the last thing Evan wanted. He didn't want to see or hear from any of those people. The idea turned his stomach, in fact. He wouldn't even go with Gary to awards dinners anymore, in case he saw someone from his past. Nicky didn't know why he'd left Hollywood, and she never even mentioned his previous life, but she was clearly star struck by their newest clients.

The last thing Evan would do was be the trainer to the stars. Even if he was down to his last dollar.

CHAPTER 6

AS WES drove away from the farm, he realized he'd never gotten the book from Evan. That was a good reason to go back, he decided, then realized how foolish the thought was. He'd spent a couple of hours with the guy, and they'd both obviously enjoyed each other's company, but that was as far as it went. He'd told Julia that two gay men could have a friendship that didn't involve sex, and here he was, dying to prove she was right after all.

But Evan was off-limits. He had a boyfriend, however ambivalent he might be about their relationship. Wes had never cheated and didn't condone the practice. He didn't want to be the "other man," because he never wanted to be the mug were the situation reversed.

He drove out of the green, rolling hills, the dusty cloud over Los Angeles growing more distinct as he reached the edges of the sprawl. It felt like another world at Evan's farm. Quiet, with sunshine and fresh air you couldn't see or feel on your skin at the end of the day. Even London—not a particularly clean city—never felt as dirty as LA, literally or figuratively.

He was too restless to go home, and he didn't want to hang out with any of his friends, so he headed for the gym. He spent an hour doing cardio on a treadmill next to a plastic-perfect blonde who batted her eyelashes at him if he happened to glance in her direction. How he missed running cross-country over grassy hills like he had at home in Wiltshire—like the ones on Evan's farm. The one time he tried running on the beach, he was mobbed by fans.

It would be nice to run at Evan's farm. Maybe he could— He stopped that idea in its tracks.

He moved onto weights and then the sauna before showering. He knew some of the other men recognized him, and a few even gave him appraising glances. This gym wasn't a favorite of gay men, but he got the message anyway, and ignored it.

When he was dressed, he found a voice mail from Lance and rang him back.

"Dude, where've you been? I tried calling this morning."

Wes had deleted the three missed-call notifications from him. "Where's the fire?"

"A guy I know is taking his boat to Catalina for the weekend, and he's got room for us. We leave at three thirty."

"I don't want to go to Catalina."

"Yes, you do. One of the guys coming along works with Spielberg. You want to meet this guy."

Spielberg? Wes would give his left nut to meet someone who worked with Spielberg. But he'd just come from Evan's farm, and his clothes were dusty and dirty. Shit.

"Where should I meet you? I'll just ring Julia and we'll grab a bag."

"No, Julia. It's not a couples thing."

Uh-oh. Alarms sounded in his head. "You know, Lance—"

"Spielberg. Focus."

"Okay. Right."

"Swimsuit and jeans. It's casual. Maybe you won't even need the suit." Lance's leer came through the phone loud and clear.

The trip sounded like a disaster waiting to happen. But Spielberg. He reminded himself this was what he wanted—a chance at something really big. He called Saul, his agent, from the car on the way home to make sure Lance wasn't setting him up.

"Wes, don't miss this opportunity. The guy's legit. I've been dying to get someone in front of him for years. Do whatever you can to get this guy to like you. To remember you." The tone of Saul's voice caught Wes off guard.

"Whatever? What does that mean?"

"Whatever. Suck his dick if he wants. I don't know. You'll figure it out."

Suck his dick? Saul couldn't be serious, even for Spielberg.

What the hell had he gotten himself into?

NINETY MINUTES later he stepped on board a gorgeous tri-deck motor yacht. Lance was lounging in a swimsuit—beer in hand—at the edge of a hot tub situated on the rear deck. Wes had never seen a hot tub on a boat before. This one had two girls in it. Closer to the front, blue-and-white striped umbrellas shielded the three men engaged in animated conversation from the intense afternoon sun. They wore T-shirts and cargo shorts or chinos.

"Hey, glad you made it before we left." Lance thrust a beer at Wes, who still had his overnight bag slung over his shoulder. Wes took the bottle but didn't drink. "Come meet the guys.

"Daniel, Wes Tremayne."

Wes shook hands.

"This is Walt and Sam," Lance continued the introductions.

"Glad to have you aboard. Make yourself at home." Daniel was obviously the host. He and the others were so well-known, last names were unnecessary. Walt worked with Spielberg. Wes had promised himself if the guy didn't show, he would leave before they left port, but Lance hadn't exaggerated or lied. Wes grudgingly admitted—only to himself—that he was impressed with Lance's connections.

Wes shook hands with the other two. "I'm flattered by the invitation to join you."

Another group of buxom, bikini-clad girls came onto the deck, a few slowing to touch Wes's arm or shoulder as they passed. That almost sent Wes back onto the dock, but he figured he could handle this. He needed to learn how to handle this.

"Let me find you a cabin, Wes." Daniel led him down a set of steps into a room that could put an international hotel to shame. Polished wood and gleaming metal reminded Wes of his wealthy school friends' homes and boats. But it was still luxurious, even by Hollywood standards. "Doug Patton and Mick Correll are around somewhere," Daniel said over his shoulder as Wes goggled at the luxury of the yacht's interior on the way to his cabin. Doug was a studio exec and Mick a massively successful Oscar-winning screenwriter who had graduated to producer.

Wes stowed his bag and came back onto the deck. Doug and Mick had materialized, and Daniel made introductions.

He didn't even attempt to keep up with the drinking—led by Lance and Mick—and no one noticed. As long as he had a glass in his hand, even if it was tonic water, he was in good shape. He did notice Walt wasn't drinking much either. It raised Wes's estimation of the guy.

One of the women sat next to Wes. "I'm Amber."

Of course she was. "What's your real name?" he asked.

"Amber."

"Not interested."

Fear flashed across her face. "Susie."

"Hi, Susie. I'm Wes."

"I know." She grinned like the million fans he'd met. "Is Wes your real name?"

"Yeah, it is."

"Do you like to party, Wes?" She scooted closer to him on the seat near the stern.

"Depends on what you mean."

"Goldie's got some weed."

"No thanks." He raised his glass. "I'll stick with this, thanks." He was glad to see that only two of the guys were smoking, and Walt wasn't one of them. Lance was, and he took a hit and coughed, so Wes knew he was just trying to fit in. That was Lance's problem. Always trying to be someone else and never happy being himself. He could be a real wanker sometimes, one of the reasons Wes wasn't thrilled with the idea of this weekend. But one-on-one when he wasn't trying to "charm" some woman, Lance approximated a decent guy. He'd certainly come through with getting Wes invited along this weekend, and he vowed not to judge the guy too harshly, despite the waves of homophobia that practically rolled off Lance now and then.

The girls rotated around the boat, talking to all the men in turn, and two of them took their tops off. Wes found a seat where no one could sit next to him. The last thing he needed was for photos of him with topless women to hit the tabloids. He kept an eye out for cameras or phones. One of the girls might be snapping shots. It would do his image no good to be seen cavorting on a yacht and cheating on Julia. Fans loved her, and this would turn them against Wes. On the other hand, it would cement his image as a red-blooded heterosexual, but it wasn't worth it.

Walt pulled a deck chair over to Wes.

"How are you settling into Hollywood?"

He'd been here over a year, but he supposed that still made him a newcomer, even if he was on his second series. "I'm still getting used to it. This, for example." He waved an arm, taking in the boat and the girls.

"Some people think you need that kind of entertainment in LA. I just ignore the girls."

Wes nodded, wondering if this was Walt's way of saying he wasn't into women. Maybe Saul's dick-sucking comment wasn't just a joke. He kept waiting for Walt to make some kind of move on him.

"You miss the stage?"

"Oh yeah, I do." Wes bit his tongue. Shit, he just told a film director he preferred live theatre. Saul would wring his neck!

"TV's quite a change."

"I like the opportunity to get it perfect," Wes replied.

"Bullshit." Walt chuckled and met Wes's gaze head on. "No one who's had your kind of success on the stage likes doing twenty takes on a set. Look, you don't have to feed me what you think I want to hear. This isn't an interview or audition."

Wes wiped a hand across his brow with an exaggerated stage motion, and Walt laughed again. Wes already liked him. "What is it, then?"

"Just wanted to meet you and see what you might be interested in doing. Steven's noticed you. Loves you in *Zero Gravity*. What do you hear about it getting picked up?"

Wes heartbeat sped up. Spielberg watched his show? He counted to five before trying to breathe. "Million dollar question. We're on pins and needles waiting for the network decision. Worst part of this job." Wes had three missed calls from Saul—could he have news? Maybe he should have rung him back.

"I hear you." Walk sipped his beer. "So, Steven's got a few projects bubbling and asked me to sound you out."

Wes tried not to gulp. "What's he thinking?"

"He's looking to adapt a play, something different for him. Maybe Shakespeare, maybe going back to a Greek or Roman classic drama.... Looking for a new character study of the lead role."

"Interesting." Wes nodded, a little deflated. He'd been thinking Indiana Jones. Seeing those films as a kid had been an inspiration for him to take up acting.

"What plays do you see translating to the screen, Wes?"

Unfortunately, Wes's mind blanked. He might not remember his middle name right now with the prospect of working with Spielberg rendering him incoherent. He shook his head, hoping Walt couldn't smell his brain frying.

"No need to answer right away. We've got a couple of days to continue this conversation."

"You really want my opinion?" Wes was flattered beyond words. He was also scared shitless. What if he made a poor suggestion? He pushed the worry out of his mind and shifted the topic to travel. Walt asked which city Wes preferred, London, New York, or LA.

Then inspiration struck. "I do have an idea...."

Walt raised his eyebrows.

"Did you read *Mary Reilly*? A supporting character's take on *Dr. Jekyll and Mr. Hyde*."

Walt nodded. "Saw the film."

"How about spotlighting a secondary character, and the original lead is no longer the focus." Wes bit his lip before voicing his other idea. "Or... it might be interesting to swap the main character's gender."

"That's brilliant. A female Hamlet, a male Portia?" Walt's smile spread across his face.

Wes's phone buzzed in his pocket.

"Go ahead and get that. I don't mind."

Wes glanced at the caller ID. A text from Evan. He grinned. He'd save it to read in private. Even if it was about horseshoes, he was just thrilled to get any text from Evan.

"Your girlfriend?" Walt asked. "Julia?"

"What?"

"The way you were smiling, I just figured."

"My girlfriend?" His brain finally connected itself to his mouth. "Yeah."

"I wish I had someone who put that look on my face," Walt said.

I wish I *could* have someone like that, Wes thought.

THE REST of the weekend went smoothly. Wes didn't have to pretend to sleep with any of the girls, and he chatted more with Walt and his host Daniel, who was working on a project for Pixar. He wondered whether Wes would consider voicing an animated character for a project on the drawing board. Of course he would. Daniel said he'd give Wes's agent a call in a week or two, when the project firmed up.

And like a giddy schoolgirl, Wes texted with Evan a few times over the weekend. He asked about Twist and Evan reminded him about the book they'd both forgotten on his previous visit. Evan had a horse come in second on the last day of racing at Santa Alamita. Wes planned to go for Twist's next fast workout.

Everything was neutral and aboveboard. They were becoming friends, bonding over the horses, Wes told himself. He had another month before filming started up again, and spending a day now and then at Evan's farm would be just the thing to unwind in the limited free time he would have in the hectic filming schedule. And no one could question it.

But by then Gary would be back from Brazil.

So much for Wes's perfect plans.

TWO DAYS after the Catalina trip, Wes, Julia, Lance, and Vanessa went out for dinner at one of their regular places. Brent was at the bar with a couple of other friends, but he stopped by their table for a drink and to catch up with Wes's apparently successful introduction to the Hollywood heavy hitters.

"Don't forget the little guys when you're the new Brad Pitt, okay?" Brent joked.

"Brad Brit," Vanessa said, and everyone laughed.

"I don't think I'll ever be Brad Pitt. I'm not even trying." Wes wanted a film career, but the prospect scared him. He'd never be able to be himself if he had Brad Pitt's level of scrutiny from fans and tabloids. Julia's deadline loomed, and he still didn't know what he'd do.

"Onto another subject," Brent began. "I hear you're becoming quite an expert on horse racing? Even going to morning workouts?"

"Morning workouts? Aren't they at some ungodly hour before the sun's even thinking of coming up?" Vanessa asked.

Julia chuckled and Wes flashed her the don't-say-anything look just a shade too late.

"About seven, right, Wes?" Julia asked.

"You've been going to see our horse work out at the track?" Lance asked, leaning in closer to Wes. "I didn't realize he was back at Santa Alamita."

"At the farm," Brent added.

"At the *farm*?" Lance raised his eyebrows. "All the way out there? So, how's our horse doing?"

Wes gave an update based on what Evan had told him, including what kind of exercise he'd done over the past week.

"You really are getting into this, aren't you?" Vanessa seemed amused by the concept. She shook her head, her dangly silver earrings sounding like little wind chimes.

"Don't spend too much time with that trainer, Wes. He might have his eye on you." Lance smiled and elbowed Wes, but his comment held more malice than Vanessa's innocent observation.

Wes could have made a disparaging comment about Evan, or he could have said he wouldn't mind if Evan did have his eye on Wes. He chickened out and didn't say anything, and he felt Julia's glare from across the table. What the hell should he have said?

To Wes's surprise, Julia insisted on going home with him after dinner. He thought they'd acted enough like a couple in public that she wouldn't feel the need to extend the ruse, especially because he needed to be up at the arse-crack of dawn to get to Evan's.

They had barely gotten into the apartment when she started. "Wes, how many times have you been to the track or the farm?"

"What's got your knickers in a twist? You knew—"

"I thought once or twice, but it sounds like it's a lot more than that."

"And?"

"Wes, when have you been doing publicity? That's your job during hiatus. Keep your face—and the show—in fans' minds. Saul called me to say you canceled an event to sign DVDs?"

"The show got canceled. Who cares?"

"The fans, Wes. That show got canceled, but your current fans will flock there to see you, and those crowds help the execs make decisions on what to renew. You don't know yet if *Zero Gravity* got picked up for another season, do you?"

"No." He hated that she was talking to his agent and telling him what to do. "It's got fantastic numbers. Not like the last one." He wouldn't even say the name of the previous series. Bad luck. Not that he was superstitious or anything. "Brent doesn't look too worried."

"He's petrified, but he's not going to show that in public or in front of Vanessa and Lance. I hear his agent's got meetings and auditions lined up just in case."

"Really?" Brent hadn't told Wes that. Come to think of it, Wes hadn't returned Brent's calls. He'd been busy reading one of Evan's books last time Brent rang.

"Get your priorities straight, Wes. Focus on your career. You don't get second chances around here. Take a few days off and the next hungry actor will crawl over your dead body to get a part you should have had." She let out a little huff and stalked off in the direction of her bedroom.

Wes watched her, knowing she was right.

Just tomorrow. He'd go out to Evan's as planned, then get back to work. It wasn't like he had a chance with Evan anyhow. Tomorrow would be his last day of fun.

CHAPTER 7

THE NEXT morning Wes drove in the dark to Evan's farm and watched Twist do a fast workout with company—in a group of four horses. Twist was the fastest of the group, but he didn't know if that was because Evan wanted to work the others at a slower pace.

Evan invited him for breakfast after the workout, and he accepted, a mixture of excitement and dread coursing through his body. They had another egg dish and a delicious watermelon salad with lime and chilies.

"You're a fabulous cook, Evan." Wes couldn't help speaking with food in his mouth.

"Thanks. You're the only one who appreciates my attempts." He gave a crooked grin.

"More than attempts. Successes." He grinned. "You do the cooking when Gary's here too?"

Evan just nodded. Wes figured with Evan's long hours, Gary should at least help. He liked the guy less and less.

"So, how's his film going?" Wes dreaded the answer, knowing if it was on schedule then Gary would be coming home soon. But if they were going to be friends—platonic, which was the only real option—then it was a normal topic of conversation.

"I don't know, actually. I haven't heard from him in about a week."

Half of Wes wanted to get up and cheer, and the other half took a more realistic approach.

"Are you worried? Is the area dangerous at all? I've only heard about problems in the urban areas down there."

"Not really. He's been in worse places. Afghanistan, for example, and he spent some time in Bosnia that he won't talk about. I probably don't want to ask, either."

"I thought he does nature films?"

"It's kind of a new thing for him. He's tired of war and death. He did a doc in Central America about the farmers who have to choose between drug crops and legitimate crops, and he got an idea to explore how drug and legitimate agriculture is affecting the environment. I'll show you some of his other photos after lunch if you're interested."

Wes nodded. He was interested, but he didn't want to find anything about Gary to like or admire.

"His work is incredibly important. I just don't have the heart to suggest he choose safer projects and safer locations… or closer to home." Evan's voice sounded small, sad, as if he were talking to himself and not to Wes.

Wes didn't reply. He really didn't know Evan well enough to offer relationship advice, but staying with Gary appeared to be doing Evan more harm than good, and Wes felt a little less like a letch moving in on Evan while Gary was away…. It was disingenuous to bad-mouth Gary, and Wes felt as if he'd stepped into a twisted, real-life *Tootsie*—merely pretending to be just a friend when he really wanted to be so much more—only he wasn't in drag.

They turned their conversation back to horses.

"So, where's the next race meet?"

"In the Bay Area. I'll take the runners up there in about a week and settle in. Then I'll play it by ear on which horses are ready to run. I'm also meeting a couple of prospective owners who might be sending me some horses. Whether that pans out probably depends on how often my horses are in the money up there."

Wes opened his mouth to ask a question, then thought better of it.

"You were wondering about Twist?"

Wes shrugged.

"I'm taking him. He's in good shape and getting better every day. As long as we keep him at this level of fitness, he should be ready to race opening week."

"Really?" Excitement bubbled up in Wes.

"Really." Evan grinned. "Hopefully, I can keep that smile on your face when he runs."

It wouldn't take a win by his horse to keep Wes smiling when he was with Evan.

After they ate, Evan showed him some of Gary's work in the living room and dining room. He'd barely glanced into these rooms on his first visit. The work was incredible.

Over a dozen photographs hung in the living room and as many in the dining room, displayed simply under frameless glass. They had been grouped by topic. One cluster of pictures showed a series of what were probably refugee children in Africa, and another was of people going about daily life in a city that had been bombed and destroyed—probably Bosnia. The photographs all inspired a strong emotional response, and it made Wes wonder what Gary was like. He clearly had a talent for bringing out a subject's thoughts or emotions so powerfully on film. The photographs were painful and raw, and Wes couldn't look at any of them for more than a moment.

Near the back corner of the living room, he found a much more enjoyable display: photographs of Evan. They'd been taken over a period of years—that was clear by the changes in Evan's appearance—and in all but a couple taken at a beach, he was fully clothed. But what struck Wes was the level of intimacy the photographs conveyed. Evan's personality shone clearly even in the candid shots.

The best shot was Wes's least favorite: It was larger than the others and depicted a much-younger Evan close-up in black and white, looking almost shyly at the camera from under thick lashes. His hair was mussed, and from the angle and background, he was lying in bed. His full lips were parted, sensual. The look of complete love in his eyes ripped through Wes's body. No one could doubt how the subject felt about the photographer.

No one had ever looked at Wes like that in his entire life, and if someone had, then he'd never let go of him, ever.

Wes recognized Evan's habits and quirks he'd seen—the way he'd look down and scratch the back of his neck when he was embarrassed or the way he'd bite the tip of his tongue when he was focused on something. One image of Evan with a horse made Wes believe Evan actually *could* communicate with the animal. Though he didn't yet know Evan very well, somehow looking at these photographs made Wes feel as if he'd seen him in a new and intimate way and made him want to get to know Evan even better.

None of the images were recent, Wes noted. Had Gary stopped wanting to photograph Evan, or was he simply not around enough? Wes took another look at the black and white print to remind himself Evan was not available. When Wes glanced back over at Evan, he saw the same shy, uncertain look flash across his face, blended not with love but with pain.

A WEEK later, Evan was scheduled to leave for Berkeley and Golden Gate Fields with nine of his horses. Nicky stayed at the farm with the other seven.

He still hadn't heard from Gary, and now he was getting worried. Gary's assistant director was Michael Barton, and Evan knew him and his wife, Celia. The four of them had socialized on various occasions, though not lately.

He called Celia the night before he left town.

"Hi, Evan. How are you?"

"Good, Celia, thanks."

"How're your horses doing? Any big winners lately?"

"Quite well, actually. But I don't want to jinx it."

"Sure. What's up?" she asked, her voice still friendly and open.

"I haven't heard from Gary lately. I figured there's no Internet or phones wherever they are."

There was a pause so big it could have swallowed Detroit. "Evan, I spoke to Mike last night. They were taking a few days' break in Brasilia."

"Oh." Suddenly his throat closed up, and he couldn't speak or breathe.

"You okay, Evan?" He couldn't stand the concern bordering on pity in her voice.

"Yeah, fine. I'm sure he's just busy or voice mail's not working." He rushed the words, wishing he hadn't said anything.

"I'll pass a message on through Mike. How's that?"

"Thanks, I appreciate it."

"And you have Mike's cell number, right? Give him a call and he'll give you an update."

"Thanks." He disconnected. An update? What kind of update? What did Mike and Celia know that Evan didn't but should?

He'd give it a few days, then consider contacting Mike.

He was leaving early the next morning, and he couldn't afford to stay up half the night worrying what Gary was up to.

CHAPTER 8

THE NEXT morning Evan was up before the alarm went off at 3:00 a.m. He hadn't slept much. He pulled on jeans and a long-sleeved shirt and headed to the barn. Nicky and the grooms would arrive shortly to help him load the horses. They'd packed the horse van and minivan with tack, meds, and other supplies.

Evan flicked on the barn lights, and several horses nickered in response. He'd disturbed their regular routine, and it would take a day for the remaining horses to get back to normal after he left. He was still on autopilot when he went into the office and headed straight for the coffee pot. He put an extra scoop of coffee in, since they could all use plenty of caffeine this early. Evan had to be extra alert, since he was driving.

Nicky arrived before the coffee finished brewing. Evan was sitting at his desk going over checklists, and her arrival surprised him.

"Evan, you didn't have to get up this early. We can load the horses without you, and you can use the extra sleep. It's a long drive up there."

"I'm fine." Evan brushed off her concerns as he poured the first cup of steaming java. He handed it to Nicky. She added milk and four spoonfuls of sugar. He cringed at the thought of how her coffee tasted.

He put a splash of milk and half a packet of raw sugar in his and sipped. It was too hot to gulp or he would have. He and Nicky went over the checklists to be certain they hadn't forgotten any equipment.

The four grooms arrived and were in the stalls checking their charges when Evan and Nicky emerged from the office to greet everyone.

"Any problems?" Evan asked.

Most of the men shook their heads, except Andy. "Jet's acting a little strange this morning. She's really skittish and just not herself."

"Is she injured?" Evan asked.

"Not that I can see. She wouldn't let me close enough to check her legs, but she's moving okay."

"Bring her out of her stall and let's take a look." Evan followed Andy to Jet's stall. He'd given so much attention to this filly, though she hadn't lived up to her potential, only starting once as a two-year-old, where she finished sixth. But she'd improved dramatically lately, and Gary had asked Evan to run her as a birthday wish, so he'd decided to take her to Golden Gate Fields.

"Something's definitely up," Nicky said. Andy had trouble calming the filly enough to lead her out of the stall, and she kicked out and tossed her head. Her eyes were wild, showing the whites.

"Want a hand?" Evan asked. He'd never just take over from one of the grooms; it showed a lack of trust and respect.

"Sure," Andy replied.

Evan entered the stall, and Andy backed out. Evan spoke in low tones to the filly. She stamped one foot and stared at him, clearly still frightened. Evan kept talking, and she calmed enough for him to approach her. He took hold of her halter and stepped close to her side so she couldn't clip him with a kick. He stroked her face and muzzle, feeling tension ease out of her.

Evan had high hopes for her, but sometimes even looking at her brought him to the edge of tears. She represented his entire relationship with Gary, such a waste of potential. Had he transferred his disappointment to Jet and let her down? He promised to give her more attention going forward.

"Let's get out of this stall," he whispered, and she let him lead her into the aisle, where he clipped her lead to a hook in the wall. He continued murmuring as he bent down to inspect her legs. She was still a little jittery and kicked out once more. "She's not injured, but Andy's right. She's upset about something."

"Think we can risk shipping her?" Nicky asked. She and Andy stood a few feet away so as not to upset the filly any further. "Do you want to tranc her for the trip?"

"I'd rather not give her any meds if we can avoid it, Nick. Andy, let's leave her for last. Go ahead and load your other horse, and we'll see if she's calmed down enough. Otherwise, for her safety, I'd rather leave her here for now. If she's this riled up getting into the van, she won't settle easily up there."

"Sure." Nicky nodded. "We can always send her up later."

"Do you want me to go up?" Andy asked. Trips out of town were a treat for the grooms, so Evan wouldn't penalize him.

"Yes, Andy. I can use the extra help. You can rotate through the other horses so everyone gets a day off."

"Sounds good." Andy grinned and went to prep his other charge. He'd probably do anything Evan asked for the chance to go up to the Bay Area.

"I really thought Jet was improving." Evan folded his arms across his chest and stared at the filly. He'd worked extra hard schooling her, and he was eager to run her, so the behavior problems were a disappointment as well as a setback to her racing debut. "Gary wanted me to run her later this month."

"Speaking of Gary," Nicky said. "When's he leaving for South America?"

Evan whipped his head in her direction. "Nick, he left nearly a month ago."

Her eyes widened. "He did?"

"I didn't mention it?"

"No. He never comes to the barn anymore, and you never mention him. Before, I could tell from your moods when he's away. But this time I hadn't noticed the usual signs. You've been so cheerful lately, I honestly would never have guessed he—" She stopped herself, but there wasn't a trace of irony in her voice. "How's his film coming along?"

He ignored her comment about his moods, but he wondered what she meant. This wasn't the time to ask. "Great. The film's going great," he lied. He walked down to the other end of the barn to avoid any follow-up discussion of Gary.

Evan entered the tack room to see if there were any last items to collect for the trip. As his gaze touched on racks of saddles and bridles, he mulled over his feelings about Gary, and his behavior before and during this trip. The truth was something Evan hadn't wanted to admit: that he and Gary no longer worked together as a couple. Their lives were more separate than ever, and it had nothing to do with Gary's trips or their work schedules. The caring and consideration had evaporated. Gary had become moody and demanding—at times bordering on violence—and Evan had lost the will to make the extra effort to close the ever-widening gap between them.

Was anything different about Evan now? It didn't take him long to realize he hadn't missed Gary at all. In fact, Evan felt guilty for being glad he was gone. He wasn't sure how much of his recent good mood had to do with Wes Tremayne.

This trip to Golden Gate would be a good opportunity to assess that particular situation. Evan found himself all too eager to spend time with

Wes. Even with Gary out of the picture—Evan was seriously considering asking him to move out as soon as he returned—Evan's growing attraction to Wes Tremayne could not end well. He didn't need to set himself up for failure by falling for a straight guy. Worse, he was Hollywood. Still new but becoming more entrenched in the mire every day.

Were the reasons to avoid him what made Wes so attractive? He was off-limits, so Evan didn't have to worry about potential rejection; it was built into the situation. For the time being, Wes made Evan feel good about himself, knowing their friendship was real, unconditional, and Wes had no expectations of him.

BY THE time the other horses were loaded, Jet still hadn't calmed down.

"I'll leave her here another few days to settle down," he told Nicky as he climbed into the cab of the horse van. "Keep to her regular training schedule, and let's reevaluate her condition in a few days."

"Think she might run at Del Mar instead?"

Evan considered for a moment. "She's not ready for that quality-wise, but it's a shorter van trip. I'd rather not run her at all than put her in the wrong race. What's your opinion?"

"I agree. She's green, and any bad experience could put her off racing." Nicky nodded. "I'll just walk her today to calm her down, then get back to training tomorrow."

"Good plan. We better hit the road. I'll check in later." Evan swung the door shut and started the engine. Nicky slapped the door then stepped away. She waved as Evan pulled out of the driveway, followed by the van with the grooms.

The drive north was uneventful. They stopped every three or four hours to make sure the horses had water and that none of them had injured themselves. After the first stop, Ricky, the lead groom, slid into the cab with Evan so they could discuss plans for the week.

Ricky had a clipboard and took notes about each horse, even though Evan knew he knew every detail off the top of his head. "The list is in case I'm not around and someone else has a question," Ricky had told him. Whatever the reason, Evan liked Ricky's attention to detail. He'd intended to make him an assistant trainer within a year, assuming Evan still had enough horses in the stable to justify the expense.

At the rate his clients were dwindling after the Halls and Rosarios had taken their runners, he might need to lay off some grooms rather than promote anyone. The thought made Evan's stomach churn.

Why the hell was he losing owners all of a sudden?

Evan's cell phone chirped. It was sitting in one of the coffee-cup holders, and Ricky reached for it.

"It's Mr. Wes," he said, looking at the screen.

Wes. Evan hadn't spoken to him for a couple of days and hearing his name caused an unexpected flutter in his stomach that blew away his earlier concerns about Jet and the fleeing client base. He wanted to hear Wes's voice, but with Ricky sitting right there…. Then again, if his friendship with Wes was so innocent, why did he care whether someone overheard their conversation?

Evan dithered too long deciding, and the call went to voice mail. Probably for the best. "He's probably just wondering how Twist is doing on the trip." Evan felt the need to explain.

"He seems to care about his horse an awful lot, compared to the others."

"Lots of owners call or e-mail, Ricky."

"Sure, but doesn't Mr. Wes own Twist with those other Hollywood people?"

The word "Hollywood" set Evan's nerves on edge.

"I like to only deal with one person in a partnership," Evan explained.

"That makes sense." Ricky nodded. "If it were up to me, I'd pick pretty Julia Compton. The blonde one is smokin' hot too, but I think she's afraid of horses. And she kept squishing up her nose. She certainly didn't like how our barn smelled!"

Evan laughed at Ricky's comments, though he didn't like to encourage his staff to make personal comments about the owners. Some of them didn't use much tact and might accidentally say something in front of the wrong person. Another reason Evan didn't generally like owners hanging around the farm or the barn at the track.

Evan half listened as Ricky told him about a film starring Julia he'd recently seen. Apparently, she was one of a crop of talented female actors starting to get exciting roles that would propel them to the top of the game within a couple of years. He remembered how it had felt once upon a time. The bright future, being recognized on the street or in a shop, being photographed.

Like the photos he'd seen of Wes holding hands with Julia at a romantic dinner. When was the last time he and Gary had such an intimate moment? Evan couldn't remember. Which upset him more: finally realizing he'd fallen out of love with Gary or the idea of Wes Tremayne with Julia Compton? It scared Evan that he wasn't entirely certain.

His phone beeped again. "Text message, Evan. From Mr..... Wes." Ricky put the phone back into the cup holder. Evan pushed away his immediate desire to read the message. Later. He'd wait until he was alone.

They stopped for food in Kettleman City. The In-N-Out Burger there was the best food on I-5, and no one argued. It was a good opportunity to stretch their legs and relax, even though it added time to the trip and they'd arrive in the late afternoon—during the worst of the Bay Area traffic. They'd hit it at one end of the trip or another, and LA's traffic was worse.

Ricky took over the wheel, and Evan stared at his phone, debating whether to listen to Wes's message. Common sense lost, and he listened as soon as they got back on the road and Ricky's full attention was on driving.

"Hi, Evan, Wes here." Wes sounded like he was right next to Evan. "Just checking in on your plans for Twist—" Wes's voice was interrupted by a woman's.

"Evan? We can't wait to see Twister run. We're all heading up there for that!" Evan had no trouble recognizing Vanessa Vandermere's distinctive high-pitched, ultra-feminine whisper. He groaned at the prospect. Another voice boomed in the background—the boorish Lance whatever.

"Bad news?" Ricky asked.

"The worst," Evan replied and erased the message. He wished he could unhear it. No more messages. Nothing personal from Wes. Evan chastised himself for expecting it. He reminded himself he had six other horses to worry about and other owners to work with. It was ridiculous to have let Wes Tremayne take up so much of his energy and expectations.

The rest of the trip was uneventful, and they made decent time until they hit the traffic on Interstate 80. They inched along until Ricky spotted the Golden Gate Fields sign towering over the freeway and clapped in anticipation.

Two and a half hours later, the horses had been bedded down, the equipment unloaded and organized, and they'd all piled into the minivan to head for the motel. Andy, who had volunteered to spend the first night in the barn to make sure the horses were fine, would go back to the track after dinner. Actually, they had all volunteered and rolled dice to see who won.

Evan was pleased at how his staff cared about the horses. Other trainers' employees took shortcuts so they could finish their tasks and leave. Evan's grooms put in extra hours when the horses needed it, even though they weren't paid by the hour.

The hotel was a mile from the track. The grooms doubled up in their rooms while Evan had his own. They had only the minivan, so they would be going to and from the track and meals as a group for the most part. There were a couple of restaurants in walking distance of the motel, but the first night they ate together.

Alone in his room after a refreshing shower, Evan remembered he still had Wes's text message. His thumb hovered over the button for a few seconds before he pushed down to access the message.

I'd like to come up a day or two early for Twist's race—without the others. Let me know when he's running so I can arrange my trip.—W.

Evan quickly pressed the button to close the message, not trusting his eyes. He got a pleasant flutter in his belly at the idea Wes wanted to come up on his own, but it soon turned into a heavy stone. He only imagined there was more to Wes's request than there possibly could be.

Wes would bring Julia, of course. Evan read the message again, expecting his wishful thinking had read all the pronouns wrong the first time around. But at second, third, and fourth reading, it still said "I" and "my." All singular.

Evan's spirits lifted again.

He spent a frustrating ten minutes reminding himself how bad an idea it would be to let himself fall in love with a sexy actor—who had a girlfriend yet continued to send Evan maddeningly mixed signals.

Wes Tremayne embodied nearly everything Evan hated, feared, or avoided, yet Evan couldn't stay away from the guy.

Just how much worse could Evan's life get now?

THE HORSES settled into their new surrounding quickly and by the second morning were back to their usual appetites and training routines. Evan pored over the conditions book, looking for suitable races for each horse based on its fitness level. With the first day of racing a week away, Evan had little time to get his entries in. Here at Golden Gate Fields, entries were made between four and six days before each race.

When he'd found a target race for each runner, he skimmed over the list. Was it chance that Mister Twister's best option was an opening-day race? Evan rechecked his choices, not trusting himself to be completely objective. When he had convinced himself he hadn't selected the race just to get Wes Tremayne up here right away, he e-mailed the list to Nicky.

She called him twenty minutes later. "Looks good to me," she said. "I wouldn't make any changes, unless any of the races doesn't fill. Did you get my list for Del Mar?"

"Yup. Same thing. Your choices look great. Let me know if you want to talk over any of the details."

"Of course I do."

"What in particular?" Evan trusted Nicky implicitly. His only concern was that sometimes she didn't trust herself and insisted on getting his approval on nearly everything. He'd given her free rein with the top string of runners at Del Mar, while he took the less-promising group up north where the competition—and the purses—was a little lighter. The horses in Nicky's care didn't need the same fine-tuning, and she should feel confident about her decisions.

"Did you look at my training plan?"

"Yes. It's fine."

"Just fine?" Doubt echoed from every word.

"I wouldn't do anything differently. You're doing a great job, Nick."

"Really?"

"Yes. Now is there anything that really needs my attention?"

"Well…." This time her tone wasn't doubtful, and that worried him.

"Nick, what is it?"

"We lost another owner. Parker came by yesterday and took his two runners. He wouldn't say why, but he looked a little spooked. He couldn't seem to get out of here fast enough."

"Shit. What the hell is going on? Six in the past month and none of them have given an excuse. Did you mention his outstanding balance?" Evan bit his lip, dreading the answer.

"Yeah. He brought a check, so he's paid up."

"Thank God." Evan let out a breath. "I don't get this. The other horses have done worse running with the new trainers. What do you think is behind this? No one pulls their runners to *lose* races."

"Maybe Wes Tremayne and his friend will buy a few more. I know their month is up soon, but I'm assuming you're gonna keep Twist, right?"

Evan had forgotten he'd given them a one-month test period. Even if he didn't have other reasons to keep Twist—and one of his owners—around, Evan simply couldn't afford to turn away a paying owner.

"I'd like to keep him, but it's up to the owners too. If he can win next week, they shouldn't have any reason to move him."

"Winning didn't stop the others...."

"Thanks for the cheerful reminder, Nick." On that sour note, he hung up.

He took a walk down the shed row, checking on each of his horses. Most had their heads over the partitions, watching activity around them or munching at the hay nets. The gray horse had his rear to the door as usual, while Knotty was lying down, his usual position unless he was eating. He rubbed each velvety muzzle and whispered to each horse. The grooms were cleaning tack or off chatting with their friends who worked for other stables.

Afternoons were quiet around the barns except on race day. Evan went back to the office and pulled his phone out and hit speed dial.

"Hi, Evan!" Wes sounded glad to hear from him. Even two words in his distinctive accent altered Evan's mood for the better. "What's new?"

"We made the trip up here without incident."

"You sound like a news report." Wes's smile came through over the distance. "Why so formal?"

Evan swallowed before replying. He didn't want to sound too chummy, just in case he'd misinterpreted anything. "Is this a good time?"

"Yes. I always have time for you... your reports."

Evan didn't know whether Wes was joking or whether he corrected his personal comment to be less personal.

"I'm looking to enter Twist in a race for next Friday."

"He's ready?" Wes's voice rose in obvious excitement.

"He's ready. I'm going to work him tomorrow, and if he performs as expected, I'll enter him."

"What time tomorrow?"

"Seven fifteen for the workout. Ten thirty for the entry. I'll let you know if anything changes in plenty of time for everyone to make travel plans."

"Sounds good. Thanks for the update."

Wes hung up before Evan got "You're welcome" out. Not quite how he wanted the conversation to go, but it reminded him not to obsess over Wes Tremayne.

CHAPTER 9

THE NEXT morning Evan and his staff arrived at the track by six to clean stalls and exercise the horses. He had arranged for a prospective jockey, Billy George, to work Twist. If they got along well, he'd have Billy ride him the following week. The other horses were doing slower work today with the grooms or hired exercise riders on board.

At six forty-five, the guard at the horsemen's gate phoned Evan's barn.

"Evan, got one of your owners here. I sent him back to your barn, but he might get lost on the way."

One of the owners? "Thanks, Dennis. I'll send someone to the gate, just in case." Evan hung up and scratched the back of his neck. Who lived up here and might show up without notice?

The question had barely flickered through Evan's brain when a familiar shape appeared through the barn door.

Wes Tremayne.

"Hi, Evan. Hope you don't mind the surprise visit."

Evan fought the urge to run up and hug Wes, but that's how much he minded the surprise. He usually hated surprises, but so far he'd loved the ways Wes had surprised him. Ricky's sudden appearance in the corridor made Evan glad he hadn't done any hugging, and the shocked look on the groom's face reminded Evan how extraordinary this visit really was.

"You're just in time to watch Twist. Ricky, you got him tacked up yet?" Evan put his professional face on again and smoothed away his utter delight at Wes's presence.

"Yeah, he's ready." Ricky turned to Wes. "Hi, Mr. Wes. He looks real good today."

Wes pulled his gaze from Evan as if he just remembered he'd come to see his horse. "Thanks, Ricky." Wes stepped toward Twist's stall and rubbed Twist's nose and tugged on an ear playfully.

"Morning!"

Evan turned to see Billy George step into the barn. "Hey, Billy. Come meet Mr. Tremayne, Twist's owner."

"Wes, please." Wes held out a hand to the jockey. "I'm just one of his owners, but—" He stopped talking when Billy glanced at Evan.

Evan knew exactly what Billy was worried about. Some owners gave the jocks their own set of instructions for riding, putting the jockey in a difficult situation. Evan gave Billy a reassuring nod. He'd talk to Wes about that later.

Ricky led Twist out of his stall and tightened his girth again before Evan gave Billy a leg up. Evan walked at Twist's shoulder with Wes trailing behind a few paces as they made their way to the track.

"I've got my eye on Friday's six-furlong maiden for him. Can you work him seven, in about 1:28? He can do more, but I want you to get a feel for how much more. Got it?"

"Yup, 1:28." Billy nodded and adjusted his reins.

They paused at the gap so Evan could give the clocker Twist's official name. Out of the corner of his eye, he saw Wes hovering. Evan smoothed a palm down Twist's neck and stepped away as Billy walked him onto the track. Then he turned to Wes and took a good look at him for the first time.

He looked good in slim-fitting jeans and boots—now dusty—and a navy cable-knit sweater. His dark hair was a little messy, and he appeared tired, except for the way his eyes crinkled up when he smiled. Just seeing him made Evan smile, and he stared a moment too long before he remembered the horse on the track.

"I try to watch from the finish line," Evan said, and Wes walked with him the quarter of the way around the track until they were in front of the grandstand. "He'll jog Twist to warm him up and then start speeding up from the seven-eighths post."

"I remember." Wes grinned at Evan.

He was only a few inches from Evan's side as they watched Billy jog then canter Twist. Too close. Too far, but definitely too close. Evan thought Brits had a different concept of personal space and assumed it was farther not closer than Americans'. But Wes was always just inside Evan's natural comfort zone, and it kept him on edge. Was Wes just completely oblivious, or did he derive some twisted, ironic pleasure from making Evan so completely physically aware of him?

When Twist got to the post, Evan clicked the stopwatch on. He saw Billy effortlessly amp up the pace pole by pole, so smoothly Twist had barely hit his stride before he flew past the finish line. *Yes*—1:29 on the nose.

They waited in silence at the gap while Billy jogged Twist, and Evan was pleased to see the horse had barely broken a sweat. He was breathing hard, but not gasping for air. "How'd he go for you?"

"He's got plenty left in the tank. I could have gone another three furlongs before he tired, I'll bet. He felt good and he wants to run."

"I saw him fighting you the first quarter."

"Just a little. He could have gone in ten seconds less, easily, and he knows it. But he relaxed when he knew I wasn't letting him go yet. Very responsive. He's smart."

Evan nodded. He'd definitely hire Billy for Twist's race, and probably use him for his other entries. They discussed more details of the workout on the walk back to the barn. Outside, Evan held the reins while Billy slid off.

"You booked for Friday's maiden allowance, Billy?"

"Nope. I'd love to ride him."

"Great. I'm entering him this morning. I'll talk to your agent."

"Sounds good." Billy reached out to shake Evan's hand and then Wes's. Then he tucked his crop under one arm and made his way to his next ride.

"Jockeys have agents?"

Evan grinned at yet another of Wes's seemingly unending questions about horse racing. If only he had time to devote to answering them.

"I CAN see I'm in the way right now. I'll let you get back to work." Wes said.

Evan wished Wes would spend the whole day in the barn, but he shouldn't, for so many reasons. He didn't reply or meet Wes's gaze.

"Do you take a break for lunch?" Wes asked.

The question chased away Evan's gloom. "Sure. Around one...."

"Would you spare some time then for a chat? Presumably you have to eat."

"Yes. Of course."

"I'll pick you up at the horsemen's gate around one. Text me if you're running late—or early." Wes waved and headed back to the parking lot, and Evan forced himself not to watch him until he went through the gates and disappeared from sight.

AT TWELVE thirty, Wes sat in his car, enjoying the first rays of sunshine. He was at the entrance to the horsemen's parking lot, facing the San Francisco Bay. The road to the back of the track was right on the water. From here, he could see all the way to the Golden Gate Bridge. Now he understood why they'd named this track Golden Gate Fields, even though it was miles away from the bridge. It must be a gorgeous spot for a sunset.

He glanced at his watch, counting down the minutes to one o'clock, in full schoolgirl mode yet again. Only Evan could do this to him. Interviewers always asked him what it was like to work with beautiful actresses: wasn't it distracting? He couldn't reveal why they never tempted him, but in truth, even working with attractive men wasn't difficult. He could easily separate work from play.

But when it came to Evan Taylor, Wes would gladly drop everything for just the chance of some of Evan's attention. Julia badgered him about following Evan around the track and questioned his spur-of-the-moment decision to drive up here, though she stopped short of trying to talk him out of it. He'd been following his agent's orders to the letter for the last two weeks, and she'd finally eased up on him a little about Evan. She approved of the trip, for her own reasons as well as his.

"Wes, you have two choices. Either you make a move or you step away. You can't keep this pretense up much longer. It's not fair to Evan either. He must be incredibly confused."

"I know." Wes wanted to tell Evan everything, but if he'd misjudged the situation, he'd ruin their friendship. Then he'd be even worse off than just having to keep their interactions casual and friendly.

When he saw Evan's face light up that morning, Wes knew he hadn't been imagining everything. Evan must feel the spark too. But how to approach the subject? Gary's shadow hung over them, not to mention the question of Wes's secret.

A beep from his phone scattered his thoughts. A text from Evan: *I'll be done in about five minutes.*

It would not look cool to go rushing to the gate and wait. Instead, he waited a few minutes and texted back *on my way now*. He had barely hit SEND when he spotted Evan walking through the parking lot. No chance for Wes to hide his recognizable silver Boxster convertible. Evan waved and sped up his pace.

"Hey! Great view, isn't it?" Evan slid into the passenger seat without commenting on Wes's early arrival or slightly untrue text.

Suddenly Wes didn't know what to say. He was great at speaking someone else's dialog but crap at writing his own. "Beautiful," he replied, feeling inadequate. "I hope you know your way around up here. It's my first time."

"First time?"

"I've only been in California for eighteen months, working almost nonstop, till a few weeks ago."

"I forgot. Well, we don't have time to go to San Francisco to eat, but there's plenty of good places in Berkeley."

"Anything with a view of the bay?" Wes liked the water. It would give him something to stare at besides Evan.

"Sure. Let's get back on the freeway heading south and I'll direct you."

"I'm good at taking directions," Wes said with a grin.

Evan chuckled as Wes started the car.

FIFTEEN MINUTES later they were seated at a bayside restaurant with a lovely view. Wes spotted tables outside, but Evan suggested an inside table. "The wind really picks up, and it gets chilly even in the summer. Outside's better in the morning."

"Glad I've got the expert."

The hostess clearly recognized at least one of them, working hard to keep herself from blurting anything as she showed them to a booth. The restaurant was a little dark and old-fashioned. It would probably be nice for a romantic dinner. At lunchtime it was full of people in jeans and light jackets, probably work colleagues from the way they interacted.

Wes watched Evan as he glanced at the menu, taking advantage of the opportunity to stare at him unnoticed. Evan licked his full lower lip as he read, and Wes imagined how his lips would feel, how he would taste. Certainly not here and not now, not until they'd had a discussion, but he played the fantasy over in his mind for the millionth time.

"Would you like anything to drink?" The waitress surprised Wes.

"Iced tea, please?" Evan ordered.

"Same here," Wes said.

She announced the specials. "Do you need more time to decide?"

Evan chose one of the specials, and Wes ordered a crabmeat salad.

"You didn't have to change for lunch," Evan said.

Wes looked down at his clothing. "Oh, I did. I found a hotel and needed a shower."

"Hotel? When did you get here?"

"This morning, pretty early. I didn't think to make a reservation before I left. Stupid, really."

Evan shook his head. The waitress showed up with their tea.

"I guess I surprised you?" Wes asked after she had gone.

"You could say that again."

"I hope it was a good surprise." Wes waited, hoping for the right flicker of response in Evan's face, but the waitress interrupted the moment with their lunch.

Evan nodded and opened his mouth to reply when a fan walked up asking for Wes's autograph. Then another. The rest of the meal turned into a parade, and Wes couldn't begin the conversation he wanted. They finished their meal while discussing Twist's workout and chances in the race the following week.

Wes paid, and neither spoke until they were back in the car.

"Evan, do you need to go back to the track right away?"

"No. I usually have a nap in the afternoon, but...."

"Oh, I'm sorry. Let me take you back to your hotel, then."

"I'm still wide awake." Evan bathed Wes in the warmth of his smile. It would be so easy to suggest another sort of nap altogether.

"Can we have a chat—at my hotel, if you're okay with that. Or yours, if you're not."

"Yours is fine."

Wes needed GPS to find the place again. Thankfully, his key card worked on a side entrance, and he could avoid passing through the lobby. He could do without another parade of fans following him just now and distracting him from what he needed to tell Evan.

He opened the door and ushered Evan inside the spacious room. There were a sofa and two chairs at one end and the bed at the other with a partition in between. It still felt awkward sitting there with Evan, just a few feet away from an enormous bed. Why did they have such huge beds in all the hotel rooms in this country?

All Wes could think about was how much he wanted to share that bed with Evan, even though he knew it was the last thing he should be thinking right now. First, he had to find out if he'd just been imagining everything.

"WANT SOMETHING to drink?" Wes stood at the minibar and opened the door.

"God, no. They charge you about ten times the price for anything."

"Don't worry. I can afford it."

"Yeah, I forgot." Evan felt foolish. He tried not to look at the bed, but it was in his line of vision. He wished he'd chosen a different seat on the couch, but he'd look more foolish if he got up now.

Wes raised an eyebrow. "What would you like?"

If only Evan could tell Wes the truth. Instead, he stared, speechless, at Wes's perfect clothes and hair and his perfect life. And it hit him, like lightning. Wes hadn't mentioned Julia, hadn't brought her up here. He'd come alone, and he'd come directly to the track.

And now he'd invited Evan to his hotel room.

What the hell had Wes Tremayne heard about him? Because as much as Evan was attracted to Wes, he was not about to go into that world again. Not about to humiliate himself to get what he thought he wanted and not about to hop into bed with anyone for the wrong reasons.

Did Wes Tremayne think Evan was just a washed-up Hollywood has-been who'd go for a roll in the hay with some superhot bicurious star? Evan was not that easy lay anymore, and despite how much he enjoyed spending time with Wes, and how fucked up things had become with Gary, Evan had worked hard to regain the self-respect he'd sold out years ago.

"You know, Wes, I really need to get going after all." Evan stood up and headed for the door as quickly as his tattered dignity would allow.

CHAPTER 10

WES STARED at the door after Evan slammed it shut behind him.

What the hell had just happened? He wanted so badly to tell Evan who he was and how he couldn't hide the attraction he felt. And if Evan didn't feel the same way, he still hoped they could be friends. He'd practiced a hundred times, and he knew it wouldn't be perfect. But until he said something, they'd be stuck in this intolerable limbo.

And now Evan had left.

Wes looked around and realized bringing him back here might not have been the best idea, but where else could they find some privacy? Lunch had been a disaster, and there were too many people in and out of the barn. How was he going to talk to Evan?

He grabbed a little bottle of whisky from the minibar and sucked it down in one gulp. Then he grabbed another and one more. He didn't feel any better, but he hadn't expected to. He considered calling Julia and asking for advice. If only those Hollywood gossip columnists could hear him asking his fake girlfriend for advice on how to admit he was falling in love with another man.

He tossed his pride away and rang up Julia.

"Wes? What's wrong?"

"Why do you think something's wrong?"

"Have you been drinking?"

He never could hold his drink. But he could act. "No."

"Liar."

Okay, his acting wasn't top-notch today. "Jules, I could use some advice."

"What happened with Evan?"

"I don't know. I thought he was glad to see me. He looked glad to see me. We had lunch and then came back to my hotel room."

"So lunch went well, I take it. You don't have to give me any personal details."

"No. I didn't have a chance to say anything. Fans…."

"So how'd you get him to your room?"

"It was the only place I could think where we'd have some privacy, but he just ran off. Like Cinderella or something. I didn't even touch him, Jules. I don't know what I did."

"The most obvious explanation is he's just not interested."

"You didn't see the way he looked at me. He couldn't stop smiling when I showed up. And when I told him you weren't coming. No offense."

"None taken." She paused. "Something spooked him. Something about the hotel room?"

"It's a minisuite, but the sofa is still facing the fucking huge bed. Maybe it wasn't that at all."

"He could be feeling guilty about his boyfriend. Even if their relationship isn't very good, he might still have strong feelings about loyalty and cheating."

"But I didn't ask him to cheat. I didn't even get to say anything."

"I'm at a loss. Maybe you should ask Brent. They've been friends for years. He might know."

"How can I ask Brent anything?"

"You could start by being honest with him, I suppose. Good practice for you," Julia said, but there was no humor in her tone.

"Is that your only suggestion?"

"It's a start. You know Brent's not homophobic. He's the perfect person to start with."

"I'll think about it." Wes wouldn't tell her how ridiculous the idea was. "Thanks." He didn't want to burn any bridges with her either.

When he rang off, he found he'd gotten a text in while they'd been talking.

From Evan.

Wes's hopes rose. Had Evan realized there was nothing to be afraid of from Wes?

He opened the text.

I think you should find another trainer for your horse. ASAP.

Wes stared at the message for at least a minute.

He wouldn't give up that easily.

EVAN CALLED Ricky as soon as he left Wes's hotel room.

"I've got a few things to take care of. Can you handle the afternoon chores at the track? I'll meet you guys back at the motel later."

"Sure, boss. You need anything?" Ricky's tone held a hint of concern. Evan hoped he hadn't given him any cause to question his vague excuse. Had anyone seen him leave with Wes? Possibly. But no one could know they'd ended up at Wes's hotel. No one could suspect anything.

Evan started walking in the general direction of the hotel. It was a couple of miles away. He needed to be alone for a while to think through his options.

He was attracted to Wes, but Wes was unavailable. Wes would never be available, so whatever he wanted from Evan was just going to stay Wes's dirty little secret. Evan was past the time in his life where that was acceptable. He was past putting his feelings on hold. And he was past letting anyone else use his body for their own purposes. He'd let himself be put in some degrading situations in the past, trading sex for something he valued—when he hadn't valued himself enough.

It was one reason he knew he was finished with Gary. Evan would not be anyone else's toy ever again. There was nothing he wanted from Gary that was worth the humiliation. Once upon a time, he'd thought he could earn his career or Gary's love with his looks and body, but never again.

He'd rather be poor and alone than sell himself like that again.

He knew what he had to do: cut all ties to Wes. That's how strong the attraction to Wes was. Evan didn't trust himself to say no. Eventually he would give in to Wes's charm, and he'd be happy for a while. Until he woke up one morning and realized nothing was worth sacrificing his self-respect for.

His only tie to Wes was Twist. With the number of horses in his stable so low, he couldn't really afford to lose another, but he would not put one of his staff ahead of himself in this one instance. He'd do anything else to save a job, but he would not risk his own sanity and self-respect.

I think you should find another trainer for your horse. ASAP.

Evan stared at the text message for a long moment before hitting send. He felt better almost immediately. All he had to do was come up with a suitable excuse for Nicky and he'd be home free.

He wandered through the industrial outskirts of Berkeley. Away from the bay and the campus, and the beautiful hills, it was as ugly as anywhere else. Some of the streets didn't have sidewalks, and he didn't see anyone else on foot. A car passed him and stopped. When he caught up, the driver, a woman with an empty child's car seat in back, asked if he was okay or needed a ride. He thanked her and waved her away.

Ten minutes later a man slowed down and offered him a ride, but with an entirely different attitude.

"No thanks. I'm walking."

"I got cash. Fifty bucks change your mind?"

Evan gave him the finger. Only fifty bucks? Had he fallen that far in the looks department?

"Seventy-five?"

"Fuck yourself!" Evan kept moving, and the car sped past him. Guy in a Lexus could afford a lot more than that. Cheap fucking bastard. Evan cursed the man until he ran out of swear words. It made him feel better.

When he saw the sign for Lucky Eight Motel, he felt anything but relieved, and certainly not lucky. The guys would be back from the track pretty soon, if they weren't already here. He had no desire to talk to any of them. He took a twenty-minute detour and was relieved the minivan was not in the parking lot when he finally got back to the motel. He let himself into his room and shut the curtains so no one would know he was back.

He tossed his clothes into a pile and stepped into the shower. He was covered with grime and sweat, along with self-loathing, and he had to wash it away immediately. The ice-cold water was just what he needed. He stood under the stinging spray until he began to shiver, then turned the knob all the way to the left and let the hot water nearly scald him until he could stand it no longer. All the while he thought about Wes's smile and his blue eyes and the smooth seductive tones of his British accent. Connecting every pleasant thing about Wes to physical pain was a crude but effective technique.

He stopped just in time, before he fell into the old abyss he'd struggled to crawl out of years ago. He wouldn't let Wes put him back there.

When Evan dragged his tortured body out of the shower, he wrapped up in threadbare towels and lay on the bed. The cheap, rough sheets chafed his supersensitive skin. Wes's hotel sheets were probably soft and silky, fresh smelling and luxurious, Wes's bed far more comfortable than this ancient mattress, springs broken from the activities of countless bodies before Evan....

Ten more minutes. Then he'd get up and walk to the track. He preferred to spend the night listening to the horses softly snoring than be alone in this room. He closed his eyes.

Pounding on the door nearly made him jump right off the bed.

He ignored it.

"Evan! Are you okay?" The pounding started again. Thunk-thunk. Thunk-thunk. Thunk-thunk. "Evan?"

It was Wes Tremayne. The sound of his voice made Evan's skin ache.

"Evan?" The obvious worry as he said Evan's name felt like a knife though his heart. "Evan?" Wes didn't shout. He wasn't angry or aggressive. He sounded scared. The realization shocked Evan.

"Evan? I know you're there. I saw you go inside. If you don't say something, I'm calling nine-one-one. Just let me know you're all right. Please?"

Evan blinked. Wes thought he'd harmed himself? What made him assume that? When Evan rolled onto his back, his scalded flesh ached as a reminder he *had* harmed himself. Was he crazy? Not again....

"Evan? Ten seconds. Nine. Eight...."

Wes was down to two when Evan finally opened the door.

"Thank God. I was worried sick about you."

Evan wrapped his towel tightly around himself and sat on the edge of the bed. "Why? Are you such a fucking perfect catch you can't put up with someone telling you to get lost? Jesus, I've never met anyone as full of himself as you are. You think I'd hurt myself over you? Why?"

"Because as soon as you left, I felt the urge to do something self-destructive. Something to blot out the big empty hole inside at the thought I somehow upset or offended you. So, here's me being self-destructive. Evan, please don't push me away. I'm crazy about you. And if that makes you run farther or faster, then I'll live with your decision. But I can't not tell you how I feel when I'm with you—and how much worse it is when I'm not with you."

Wes stood there, staring defiantly into Evan's eyes, then once the words were out there, hanging in the air between them, he looked away. Absolutely not what Evan had expected to hear from Wes. He perched on the edge of the bed and stared, mouth open, at Wes.

"What?" Evan asked.

"I know you're involved with Gary. I'm not the kind of person who condones cheating, but you deserve someone who treats you well. Someone who thinks you're the most amazing person he's ever met. And even if you don't have any interest in me, please at least find someone who deserves you more than Gary does."

So many thoughts bounced through Evan's brain, he couldn't organize a coherent response to any of them. All he could take in was that Wes had managed to put into words everything Evan had felt each time they'd been together. He wasn't crazy, and he hadn't imagined the attraction. The possibilities overwhelmed him, and he couldn't breathe with their weight against his chest.

"I'm sorry, Evan. I'll go now, and I'll leave you alone." Wes turned toward the door, head down, shoulders sagging.

"Wait. Don't go."

Wes stopped a foot from the door but didn't turn around.

"I thought I only imagined a connection, a bond growing between us. But I thought Julia…?"

Wes slowly turned. Evan could see how bright and glistening his eyes were. "She's always just been a friend, Evan. It was easier to play it as much more, for my career. But everything with her is as fake as my show. It's just another Hollywood production."

"This isn't just an experiment, or some curiosity? You're gay?"

"I don't have a membership card, but this is me. It's real and it's permanent. It's not some cool new trend I'm following, because God knows my life would be much easier if I weren't gay. But I am. Now you're the second person in this country I've told."

"That's the last thing I expected to hear."

Wes still stood near the door. "What did I say before to upset you so much? I was trying to figure out for the past two weeks how to say something, and I was too afraid. I hoped showing up here might make you realize how I felt. But I'm expecting too much to hope you feel the same way."

"Oh, Wes. I do. As much as I tried not to, not believing there was any way you could possibly return my feelings."

Wes met Evan's gaze. "You do?"

Evan nodded and stood. Wes took a step toward him and Evan closed the gap.

They came together for a quick brush of lips. Wes wrapped his arm around Evan, who flinched slightly at the contact with his sensitive flesh.

"What?" Wes asked, sounding worried.

"Nothing." Evan said. "Everything's perfect."

Evan put his head against Wes's shoulder, enjoying the way his arms felt around his waist. Wes tightened his grip and they stood there, embracing, Evan feeling every breath moving in and out of Wes's chest. The taste of him still sweet on Evan's lips. He wanted another kiss. A real kiss. He wanted to feel Wes's skin against his.

Evan still had the towel wrapped around him and he silently begged Wes to peel it away and take him, touch him, give him permission to undress Wes too. But he didn't make any move. Evan pressed close and leaned up for another kiss.

This one was hot, electrifying, and Evan opened himself up to Wes's mouth and tongue, wondering why it had taken this long for them to find each other. Wes pulled him in tight, deepening the kiss as Evan melted against the hard, solid planes of his chest and the contact soon took Evan's mind off his stinging flesh. He slid a hand under Wes's shirt. He'd seen him shirtless on his television show, and now he traced the familiar contours from memory, fighting the urge to tear the fabric away and give in to his daydreams.

Wes broke the kiss and stepped back half a pace. He licked his lower lip and blinked. "You're driving me crazy in that damn towel."

Evan moved to unwrap it but Wes shook his head. "Not yet. Unless you're done with Gary."

"I'm done. I just haven't told him yet. Not that I think it will come as a shock to him." Evan sat down on the bed again. Wes still held one of his hands, and Evan bent to place a kiss on the palm.

Wes smiled, but his eyes were sad. "I can wait, Evan. I need to wait. I need for you to be completely certain. I'd rather we don't start anything until you can finish with him."

"I'm finished. I'm certain."

"Then it won't take long."

"I don't need to wait, Wes."

"Evan, I would feel better knowing I wasn't the reason you broke up with Gary."

"Of course you're not. Everything you said about him—about our relationship—is true. I've known for a while; it was just easier to ignore the truth and avoid the drama. But I won't put it off any longer."

"Good."

"To be honest, I haven't heard from him for a few weeks. He hasn't answered my e-mails or messages. But I'll e-mail asking him to move out when he gets back. There's nothing ambiguous about that, is there? Then I'm free to be with you." Evan expected Wes to be pleased with the solution.

"By e-mail? That's so…."

"Impersonal?" Gary made Evan feel like an object so many times it seemed fitting, but he wouldn't get into that with Wes. Not now. Now he wanted Wes in his arms, but Wes felt miles away, even though he sat only inches from Evan on the bed. "Cowardly?"

Wes shook his head, but not very convincingly. "Evan, I—"

Evan didn't want to hear it right now. He pulled Wes close and kissed him, hard and deep. Wes curled his arms around Evan's waist and tightened his grip. They lay back on the bed, connected from head to foot. Wes's kisses were hungry and needy, and he pulled Evan in with a hand on the back of his neck.

Evan smoothed a hand down Wes's back and gripped his ass. He felt Wes's cock pressing rock hard against his thigh and knew Wes could feel his erection through the thin towel. He reached for Wes's belt, but Wes stopped him, one strong hand on Evan's wrist, carefully bending it behind Evan's back. The position forced their chests and hips closer, and Evan gave himself up to the new sensations and emotions Wes awoke in him.

He couldn't remember the last time a kiss had been this delicious, this arousing, this perfect.

But it was only a kiss, nothing more. When they separated for air, Wes was panting, chest heaving. He rolled onto his back and Evan lay his head on Wes's chest, listening to his racing heartbeat. Wes stroked Evan's face and ran his fingers through Evan's hair. Evan wrapped an arm around Wes's well-muscled and world-famous chest and snuggled close.

"E-mail's fine with me," Wes whispered into Evan's hair. He gathered Evan close and they fell asleep.

A knock at the door woke Evan. Wes was still wrapped around him. It hadn't been a dream. They were really here, together. The knock sounded again.

"Evan?"

He shifted his weight and Wes let go. He was already awake.

"Hang on, Ricky." Evan pulled the towel around himself and went to the door. He opened it just a crack.

"We're going for dinner. You ready?" Ricky glanced at the slice of Evan visible in between the door and the jamb. "Need a few minutes?"

"I'm more tired than hungry. Go on without me."

"We can bring something back for you?"

"No thanks. I'll wander down the street if I get hungry later."

"You okay?" Ricky cocked his head and frowned.

"I'm fine." Evan forced himself to wake up from the wonderful nap in Wes's arms. "I'm great. Just tired."

"Okay. See you in the morning."

"Yup." Evan shut the door as soon as Ricky turned away. Wes was watching him from the bed. Waiting for Evan in his bed and all he wanted to do was kiss. Damn Wes and his principles. Those principles, and Wes's concern that Evan make a decision for the right reasons, only made him more certain he wanted Wes. He wasn't selfish or domineering like Gary. He wasn't just looking for what he could get out of Evan.

Beautiful outside and inside.

Evan took another step toward the bed.

WES WATCHED Evan's back as he spoke to his groom though the narrowly open door. The towel was wrapped around his hips, emphasizing the curve of his arse through its threadbare texture and hiding nothing. Evan's back was strong, muscled from hoisting hay bales and hauling saddles on and off horses. There were a few uneven pale-red blotches on his back, but the skin slid smoothly over the muscles, and Wes reconsidered his decision to wait until Evan had properly dealt with Gary.

He wanted Evan so much, and those kisses had been torture. His connection with Evan was much more than just physical, and he didn't want to give in to that side of the attraction first. He'd had more casual sex than he cared to admit, but what he really wanted was to make love to a real boyfriend. Wes couldn't until Evan had moved on from Gary.

A quick fuck or suck would devalue their first experience together. Wes had waited this long for someone. He could wait a little longer.

Evan shut the door and turned back toward Wes. He stepped toward the bed and grinned at Wes.

Then he let the towel drop to the floor.

Wes's entire body responded to the sight of Evan, cock half-hard, balls hanging low and loose. He had pink-brown nipples, big nubs in small aureoles. Wes's own nipples tingled at the thought of how Evan's would feel in his mouth. How Evan's mouth would feel anywhere. He shifted as his jeans got too tight again.

"Are you hungry, Wes?" Evan asked, an innocent expression on his beautiful face.

Wes snatched a pillow and lobbed it at Evan's chest. He caught it easily and tossed it away. Wes threw another, harder, and another, but Evan grinned and deflected them, like an unstoppable superhero against a weakening opponent.

Wes chuckled and let naked Evan climb into bed and onto his lap. Evan kissed him, then pulled away to start unbuttoning Wes's shirt. He didn't stop Evan, but he would when Wes felt his self-control slipping. It might be any minute now.

"Does your room have a nice comfortable bed with soft sheets?" Evan whispered.

"I think the barn would be more comfortable than this bed." Wes let Evan kiss his neck and collarbone.

"What about room service?" Evan leaned down to flick the tip of his tongue over Wes's nipple and Wes's cock turned rock hard. Flick. Flick. Flick. Then Evan's hot mouth closed around it, and Wes pushed Evan gently away.

"Maybe we should go out for dinner. Somewhere public?" Wes couldn't trust himself alone with Evan.

Evan sat up and slid out of Wes's lap. He pulled the sheet over his lap. "I'm sorry. I shouldn't have done that."

"Are you trying to test me or something?" Wes asked. He knew he'd give in to Evan's next attack. Gladly.

"No. I'm testing myself, I guess." Evan looked away, sighing and shoulders drooping.

"Well, your test is killing me. But I want to be with you when you're completely free to be… mine." Wes couldn't meet Evan's gaze. "I want it to mean something special. I'm sorry if I sound like a sixteen-year-old girl."

"It's fine. It's nice, Wes. You're the first sixteen-year-old girl I wanted to go to bed with." He reached toward Wes's chest, and Wes leaned back, but Evan scooted closer so he could button Wes's shirt back up. "But I'll respect your virtue until it's the right time."

"How about if I help you write the e-mail?" Wes grinned, trying to lighten up the mood in the room.

"I'd like that, Wes. Thanks." Evan pulled the top sheet out from under Wes and wrapped it around his body. He grabbed some clothes from the dresser and went into the bathroom.

"Okay, now you're the sixteen-year-old girl!" Wes shouted to the bathroom door. He stood up and readjusted himself to be more comfortable. He needed looser pants if he was going to spend much time around Evan. He looked at the bed again before settling into one of the chairs and waiting for Evan to dress.

A few hours ago, he thought he'd fucked things up royally when Evan ran like the proverbial bat out of hell from his hotel room. Wes wondered why he'd left, and hoped Evan would tell him someday soon. Now, they'd made it to the next step. They were both on the same page— or close enough—and the doubts and misunderstanding were behind them. Once Gary was out of the way, they could move forward, together.

The only thing left to deal with was how the hell he could have a relationship with Evan and a Hollywood career. One more thing to put off for another day.

THEY ORDERED Chinese food from a place offering delivery service. Evan went to a liquor store on the next block to get a six-pack of beer. Wes had offered, but Evan didn't want his grooms to spot Wes. When the food arrived, they spread the feast out on the little table under the bare bulb in one corner of Evan's motel room. Wes watched Evan pick up a piece of chicken with his chopsticks and pop it into his mouth. He piled rice onto his plate, plus a scoop from each of the cartons, then reached for a flimsy plastic fork.

Evan looked at the fork, but didn't say anything. He sipped some beer and watched Wes eat.

"What?" Wes asked.

"Not so good with chopsticks?"

"Pathetic. I only use them when I'm watching my weight."

Evan laughed. "Oh, I remember those days."

Wes waited to see if he would open up about his own Hollywood career, but Evan pushed some food into his mouth and chewed it carefully. Wes could wait for that discussion too. There were a million things he wanted to know about Evan, and he could wait to learn them, one at a time. He was looking forward to the process.

"I can teach you."

"Teach me how to watch my weight?" Wes looked down at his body. "Are you saying these jeans make me look fat?"

"God, no. Those jeans make you look like dessert." Evan grinned. "Chopsticks. I can give you some pointers."

"Let me finish eating first."

"Uh-uh. That's the secret to success. You don't learn, you don't eat." Evan took the fork away from Wes and broke it.

"Hey! That's cruel and unusual punishment, which I hear is against your constitution. Shall I call the cops on you?"

"Only if you're still hungry later. Fair enough?"

"Fair enough."

Evan scooted his chair next to Wes's and showed him how to hold the chopsticks. He put his hand on Wes's to get his fingers in the correct position. "Now you just move this finger to make them open and close."

Wes tried and dropped one stick. Evan kept his hand on Wes's this time, so he could get used to the motion. When he let go, Wes dropped the stick again. Evan had infinite patience, letting his own food get cold while he helped Wes.

Wes had the motion down, but he kept messing up anyway. He liked having Evan's hands on his, touching him, guiding him. He liked Evan's serious "training" voice. He must be this kind and patient with the horses, too, Wes thought.

When Wes kept dropping pieces of food, Evan fed him a few morsels. When he succeeded at picking something up, Evan gave him a kiss. Wes liked this game. It would have to substitute for sex, at least for the time being. It seemed a waste, two healthy, horny men playing with chopsticks instead of each other, but that was Wes's choice. He just never expected how much fun or arousing Chinese food could be. It was Evan who turned it into a sexy game.

Eventually, Wes did master the technique enough to feed himself pieces of meat and vegetables.

"We'll work on the finer points like rice and noodles next time," Evan promised with a kiss reward.

"Next time. I like hearing those words," Wes said.

"Me too." Evan closed up the containers. "You want to take the leftovers home?"

"Home?" Wes asked.

"To your hotel." Evan packed them into a bag, then glanced at the clock.

Wes followed his gaze. It was only nine o'clock. Then he remembered that Evan got up by four most mornings. "Right. I should go."

"Yeah." Evan nodded but the look in his eyes begged Wes to stay. "It's late."

"Okay. I'll get going." But Wes didn't get up. He remained in his chair, staring at Evan. If Evan invited him to stay, he would. He wanted to, and he knew Evan wanted him to. The lure of waking up in Evan's arms was powerful.

They stared at each other for a good five minutes in silence.

"Okay. I'm really going now," Wes said.

Evan nodded. He blinked a couple of times, but didn't say anything. Wes wasn't sure he could trust his voice again with the knot growing in his throat. It was just one night. A few hours apart and they would be together again in the morning. But it felt like a century.

Wes finally stood up and collected the bag of Chinese food. He walked to the door, hoping Evan would stop him. He put a hand on the knob, slowly, giving Evan the opportunity to invite him to stay. Then he opened the door.

Evan was a step behind him in half a second flat. He put his arms around Wes from behind and kissed his ear. "Goodnight, Wes."

"Goodnight, Evan." Wes turned and took one last kiss before he left the room. He couldn't look back.

CHAPTER 11

WES SET his alarm for seven, though he was up long before it went off, but Evan had asked him not to show up first thing in the morning. The grooms already knew Wes was becoming passionate about his horse and racing, but there was a line, and if he crossed it, they'd soon cotton on that he'd become passionate about Evan as well.

He rolled into the horsemen's lot a little after eight thirty and showed his owner's credentials to the guy at the security gate, who waved a greeting as he passed. He knew his way to Barn 22 this time around.

One horse was on the hot-walker when he arrived, and another stood at the side of the barn while Ricky bathed him. Wes entered the barn, greeted by the now-comforting smell of horses and hay. He spotted Evan on the phone in the office at the end and fought the urge to head directly there. Instead, he stopped to visit Twist, who nuzzled him and poked his muzzle into Wes's jacket pocket.

"He knows me now," he said to Lonnie, Twist's groom, who was filling hay nets.

"He knows you give him treats," Lonnie said.

"I'd like to think our relationship is stronger than that." Wes laughed and scratched Twist's neck in the spot he'd learned was the horse's favorite. "Right, Twister?" He turned to Lonnie. "How's he after yesterday's work?"

"A little heat on the inside. I'm gonna ice him again."

"Can I check?"

"Sure." Lonnie stopped what he was doing and stood outside the stall while Wes went inside and bent down to smooth his hand along Twist's forelegs.

"Right here?" He felt the tell-tale warmth.

"Yup. He's moving good, though. But best to prevent anything worse." Lonnie nodded as Wes got back to his feet and ducked under the webbing and back into the corridor.

"Thanks for looking after him so well, Lonnie." Wes had learned it was the grooms who were responsible for each horse's day-to-day care, and he wanted to be on Lonnie's good side and not get in his way or appear to question his expertise.

"I like him. He should do well on Friday."

Wes noticed the barn seemed subdued compared to the previous day or his visits to Evan's farm. None of the grooms were chatting to each other or their horses.

"Did someone die? It's like a tomb in here."

Lonnie glanced around and stepped closer to Wes. "We lost another horse."

"Lost? As in died?" Wes spoke softly, though he didn't know if this was some sort of secret.

Lonnie shook his head. "Another owner pulled his colt from Evan. Doug McLean came by and picked up Percy—Positive Negative—first thing this morning. Took him over to his barn."

"*Another* owner?"

"Fourth one this past month. Don't know why. Percy's been improving. He didn't win at Santa Alamita, but he'd clean up here for sure." Wes recalled the horse. He'd run fourth at Santa Alamita. Not impressive.

Wes glanced down the barn. Evan had his back to the door, head down. No wonder he hadn't come out to see Wes.

Lonnie dug into his jacket pocket and handed Wes some peppermint candy.

Wes unwrapped one and held it out for Twist, who slurped it up and crunched happily. Wes fed him two more.

"Good thing you're paying the dentist bills."

Wes turned to see Evan coming toward him. He grinned, then toned it down. Just seeing Evan made Wes's mood soar, even though he knew losing a horse to another trainer was a tough blow.

Evan glanced at the empty stall next to Twist. "You heard about Percy?"

"Yeah. What's going on?"

"No clue. But Nicky had a winner and a second place yesterday at Del Mar. And two happy owners." Wes noticed Evan's smile didn't make it to his eyes.

"Got time for a coffee, Evan?"

"Sure. I need to keep my owners happy." Evan chuckled and nodded to Lonnie as he and Wes left the barn.

"At least you have a good excuse for spending time with me." Wes made a lame attempt to cheer Evan up as they walked into the backside kitchen, a small cafeteria that served food and coffee to the horsemen.

They sat down at a rickety table with their coffees. Half the other tables were occupied, and most of the patrons were speaking Spanish.

"Tell me what happened with the horse this morning."

Evan's mouth drooped, and he glanced around the room before answering. "His owner moved to another trainer. Happens a lot."

"Four times in a month?"

Evan's head snapped up and he stared at Wes.

"Yeah, Lonnie told me."

"Lonnie has a big mouth."

"How many horses?"

"Six."

"That's nearly twenty thousand a month in fees, right?"

Evan shrugged. "But my costs are down too."

"And so is your earning power if the winners are leaving." Wes pushed his coffee away. He was too wound up to want any more stimulus. "Evan, this is bad, and it can't be coincidence. Who's getting the horses? Is someone deliberately targeting and undermining your stable?"

"No. They went to three different trainers. No one person benefits."

"Positive Negative, he's another good prospect?"

"Fantastic. He's still a maiden, but better than the average horse here. I've got—had—my eye on the big purses for him. He's only a two-year-old, but he can clean up here and learn enough to have much more confidence down south. He took fourth in his only race so far; I should run him with less-experienced horses. He's a little like Twist. Just needs a win or two under his belt to move up a few notches in quality."

Wes nodded. Most of what he knew about racing came from Evan, but he trusted Evan's instincts and his rationale. "I have to take care of some things today. Can I take you to dinner?"

Evan smiled—a real smile, all the way to his eyes—for the first time that morning.

Wes pushed his chair back from the table and he was about to get up when Evan put his hand out on top of Wes's and squeezed.

Wes grinned and stood. He wanted spend the whole day tagging along after Evan, but now he had something more important to take care of. He'd taken two steps from the table when Evan broke the silence.

"I e-mailed Gary this morning."

That was the best news Wes heard all day.

EVAN WENT back to the barn to make sure the horses had their meds, vitamins, ice packs where needed and found the place running like clockwork. His grooms were great: reliable and smart. They knew when to consult him and when to handle something on their own. He felt unnecessary most of the time.

He went into the office and checked his list of entries. He had two horses to enter in races this morning. Then he'd get a head start on reports to the owners and take a stroll around the other barns, catching up on track gossip and looking for raw talent.

One way to fill his barn up again was to bring in new horses for his current set of owners, which meant scouting horses for them to buy. Claiming a horse in a race was one option, though he could often get a better price in a private transaction. He'd see which horses were looking good and approach the owners. He hadn't needed to do this for quite a while, but the recent exodus meant he had empty stalls. Wes was right: Evan's income was in freefall, but his payroll hadn't gone down yet. He'd put off firing anyone until he had a chance to bring in some new horses.

After a visit to the racing secretary's office to enter his two runners, Evan spent three hours making the rounds with some of the midlevel local trainers who had been winning lately. They were eager to sell to SoCal owners, who typically paid more for horses than in NorCal. Evan examined countless horses and made notes of pedigrees, workout times, and other pertinent information, and compiled a list of half a dozen prospects to pitch to his owners.

He was on his way back to Barn 22 when his cell phone vibrated in his pocket. "Yeah, Ricky, what's up?"

"You better get back here. You won't believe this."

Evan could live the rest of his life without hearing those words again. "What now?" He tried to keep the rising panic out of his voice.

"No, it's a good surprise. I just don't understand it."

"I'm at the other end of the backside. I'll be there in ten." Evan disconnected and picked up his pace. Now his curiosity was piqued.

He was slightly out of breath when he came into the barn and found his grooms congregating around Percy's empty stall. Only it wasn't empty anymore; Percy was back inside.

"What the hell?" Evan stepped forward and put a hand out to the horse. He peeled back his upper lip to check the tattoo. Not that he expected a switch, but he couldn't understand why the horse had been sent back. Had Bill Ridgeway changed his mind?

"McLean brought him by ten minutes ago," Ricky said. "He's bringing the paperwork later."

Evan shook his head. He went into the office and found Doug McLean's number in the conditions book and called. "What's going on with this horse, Doug?"

"Craziest damn thing I ever saw! Owner wants him back with you. After we just put down fresh bedding. I'm sending you a bill, dickwad." McLean laughed good-naturedly to emphasize no hard feelings. Trainers joked about the cost of bedding—fifteen to seventeen bucks if you did it right.

"Let's have that bet on his next race, then."

"Deal."

"So what is up with Ridgeway? Why'd he change his mind again?"

"Not Ridgeway. Some new guy. Ridgeway sold him this morning, and the new guy sent him back to you. Wes Something…. Australian or English. I can't tell the fuckers apart."

Evan forced out a laugh as the situation became clear. "Me neither. Thanks for playing along, though."

"See ya, Ev." McLean hung up.

Evan went back into the corridor and stared at the horse, slamming his phone against his palm. One loud thwack sent the animal skittering into the far corner of his stall.

Evan punched a speed dial button and waited as it rang. From just outside the barn he heard a cell phone ringing and turned as Wes strolled in.

"Did my new horse show up yet?" Wes was grinning, but Evan really wanted to tear him a new one.

Evan restrained himself and glared at Wes instead, then walked outside. This conversation was not for anyone else's ears.

Wes followed him out again. "You don't look too happy, Evan."

"I'm not!" Evan's voice echoed off the next barn and he lowered it when he continued. "Wes, what were you thinking?"

"I got the horse back."

"By buying him yourself and sending him here?"

Wes shrugged. "What's wrong with that?"

"You can't just do that."

"Didn't you say you're looking for horses for your owners to buy?"

"Yes."

"So, I was looking for a proven winner. You talked me into it this morning, over coffee."

Evan shook his head. "Damn you, Wes!"

"You still haven't explained what I did wrong here."

Evan stared at him. Wes stood in his perfectly fitted jeans with his dark hair whipping in the winds off the bay. Sunshine made him squint slightly, but he just looked so damn gorgeous. And Evan couldn't think of any reason to be mad at him. His solution was perfectly reasonable and logical.

"I just fucking want to… kiss you!" Evan said.

"Wanna go snog in my car?" Wes grinned.

"Yes. But we won't. You've got a convertible."

"Not anymore. I just hired a nondescript crap SUV and I drove through some ugly puddles coming off the motorway. No one will know it's my car unless they see me in it. Plenty of room for making out, or more." He raised an eyebrow.

"I don't even know what to say to you, Wes."

"Show me, don't tell me."

"That's going to have to wait until later."

"Gives you plenty of time to think up something good." Wes strode back toward the barn door. "Now I want to go visit my new horse."

CHAPTER 12

WES PICKED Evan up for dinner at six.

"You weren't kidding about the car," Evan said as he shut the door on the Mazda SUV. "Now you know how the other half lives."

"I didn't even own a car until I moved to LA. I walked or took trains. Don't lecture me about which half I'm in—it's brand new to me."

"That explains it."

Wes stopped near the exit of the parking lot and stared at Evan. "Explains what?"

"Never mind." When he saw the perplexed look on Wes's face, he added, "Maybe you're not used to driving on the right side of the road."

"Are you saying I'm a bad driver?"

"I didn't *say* that." Evan grinned to defuse the situation.

Wes nodded and bit his bottom lip. "Now I see why people always offer to drive." His tone made Evan wish he'd never said anything.

"Wes, I'm sorry. " Evan put a hand on top of Wes's.

Wes turned and blinked before bursting into his usual smile. "Guess I'm a better actor than a driver. But I need practice, right? And you've got your seat belt on, so do you trust me?"

"Of course I do." Evan made a show of clutching at the door when Wes took off again. He really wasn't a bad driver, just inexperienced. "I grew up on a farm, where we learned to drive the day after we learned to walk."

"We learn at seventeen, unless you live in a big city."

"But you didn't learn then?"

"Hey, I said I never owned a car, not that I'd never learned to drive." Wes turned and winked, but he quickly refocused his attention on the road.

Wes seemed to know his way around a little better today, though it may have been the GPS, which he used to find the restaurant, a small Thai place still nearly empty this early.

When they were seated with menus, Wes said, "I would have picked one of the really spectacular restaurants—Chez Panisse or Bay Wolf—but I didn't want too much attention just yet."

Evan didn't respond. He kept his head down, concentrating on the menu. There had been a time when he'd been instantly recognizable and mobbed by fans. He hadn't thought he missed it until Wes's comment. He didn't want that lifestyle again, but that didn't mean he'd hated everything about his brief time in the limelight.

However, something in Wes's tone made Evan wonder what Wes had left unsaid. "But this is just until Gary is gone" or "Get used to it, since we'll always be skulking around." Had it been an offhand remark, or a warning?

When the waitress returned she glanced at him intently for a moment. "Are you Wes Tremayne?" she asked in a cautious voice tinged with excitement.

Wes chuckled and shook his head. "I hear that a lot. Thanks for the compliment," he replied in a perfect American accent.

"Oh, sorry. But you look *so* much like him. Are you ready to order?"

When she left, Evan shook his head. "I can't believe you pulled that off."

"It was worth a shot. It doesn't always work. Obviously never when I'm with Julia." Wes kept to his American accent. It was disconcerting for Evan.

They had wine with dinner, and Evan tried to keep his mood light. Too many things weighed down on him to be very successful at that. If Wes noticed, he pretended not to. Wes was such fun to spend time with: amusing, intelligent, and very attentive, and by the end of the meal, Evan's mood had improved dramatically. Dinner with "American Wes" was almost like dining with another person.

To Evan's surprise, Wes was as kind and gracious to the restaurant staff as he might be as himself, even when he had no reputation to protect. They had just gotten into the car after dinner when Wes turned to Evan.

"Can you wait a couple of minutes? I need to take care of something inside."

Evan nodded, assuming Wes was heading for the men's room. But when he glanced through the window at the front of the restaurant, he spotted Wes at the hostess desk with several of the servers, head bent down, signing something. He came back five minutes later.

"What was that? Forgot to pay?" Evan joked.

"I felt bad about lying. I signed a few autographs for the staff."

Evan liked discovering that Wes really was a kind person even when he didn't have to be. There was an element of common sense too. By revealing his identity after the meal, they were able to have an uninterrupted dinner, and chances were the staff wouldn't remember much about Evan.

He wasn't sure whether he liked that or not.

THEY WERE a couple of blocks away from the restaurant when Wes spoke. "Evan, would you like to stay with me tonight?"

Desire flooded though Evan's body and he fought to rein in his reaction. "I haven't heard back from Gary. Does that matter?" He took a deep breath, dreading a reversal of Wes's invitation.

"A little. But it's a bloody huge bed. We can build our own Hadrian's Wall down the center."

"That's a little extreme."

"You don't know how much I want you in my arms." Wes glanced over at Evan quickly.

The feeling was more than mutual. That was the problem. "Yes. I'd like to stay with you."

Ten minutes later they were in Wes's room again. Evan sat on the couch, in almost exactly the same spot he had the previous afternoon. So much had changed in only twenty-four hours.

"I have wine and beer in the fridge. I got rid of the minibar items. I know how much it offends your frugality." Wes grinned.

"Beer's good. And I'm not frugal." Evan frowned. "Just careful."

"Then let me give you whatever you want." Wes pulled two bottles out of the small refrigerator and handed one to Evan before sitting next to him on the couch. "I want to spoil you rotten."

Evan put the bottle down on the coffee table unopened. "I don't want anything. And you can't buy me." He started to get up as the familiar quavering started in his gut and his knees went weak. He felt like he might get sick again.

"Oh God, somehow I've offended you again." Wes reached out for Evan but stopped short when Evan flinched away. "No. I don't mean that at all. I want to figure out how to make you happy. Treat you to everything I know you deny yourself because you always put someone else ahead of you. And because the one who should notice that—Gary— hasn't done his job very well."

Evan stared at Wes. "I'm perfectly happy. I don't need another person to make me happy."

"Now you see why I'm an actor and not a writer." Wes put on a forced grin, but the color had drained from his face and his shoulders sagged. "I don't think another person can make you happy. At least not so far."

As uncomfortable as this conversation was, Evan's curiosity was piqued. "What does that mean?"

"You're only happy when you're around the horses, or the horsemen. Other than that, you don't like being around people. I'm still part of your horse world."

Evan just stared at Wes. What the hell was he talking about?

"I think someone hurt you very badly in the past, and you just don't trust people anymore. I hope you'll trust me, because the last thing I want is to hurt you. But I understand it's going to take some time, and I'm willing to wait."

"You're awfully patient." Evan hadn't realized how harshly he'd spoken until he saw Wes practically flinch.

"Breaking away from Gary is more than just turning off a switch or sending an e-mail. You'd sooner fuck me than trust me to treat you well. Who made you think your body is less valuable than your feelings?"

Wes met Evan's gaze, and it felt to Evan like he was looking deep inside him. No one had ever said anything like this before, and Evan felt naked and vulnerable. How did Wes know so much? Who told him? Evan realized he was at the end of the couch, back against the armrest. He'd been sliding away from Wes, but now he had no more space to retreat. He closed his eyes to ward off the wave of pain and felt hot tears stinging his eyes. He wiped at his cheeks and tried to calm his pulse rate.

It felt as if the world were pressing down on him, crushing him like a cigarette under the heel of a boot. He blinked away the wetness and realized Wes was still sitting a foot away, worriedly watching.

"Evan, I'm sorry." Wes moved closer, arms outstretched, and Evan tried again to scoot away. Wes put his arms around Evan, holding him loosely, but enough so he could feel Wes's warmth and strength. Evan could hear his slow, steady breaths and felt the tightness in his own chest melting away.

He didn't feel pain or fear, and he hadn't burst into flames. Letting Wes in close hadn't done any damage. Evan inhaled, taking in Wes's scent, a spicy citrus, and he slowly put his arms around Wes. They sat like that for a moment, then Wes pulled Evan in tight and stroked his back in a gentle, comforting motion.

Evan sobbed a few times, waiting for Wes to say or do something frightening, but it never happened. Finally Evan pulled himself together and swallowed hard.

"Wes, you probably want to know—"

Wes shook his head. "You don't have to tell me anything. Not yet."

Evan nodded. He wanted to tell Wes everything. Wanted to trust him, but he wasn't ready yet. Maybe he was like the horses after all. When they are ready, they come to you. If you go after them, they'll run away.

THEY HELD each other for a long time before Wes let go.

"I can take you back to your motel."

"I want to stay."

That surprised Wes. He figured he'd pushed Evan too far tonight. He should have just kept his bloody huge mouth shut. But he saw such pain and doubt in Evan whenever he wasn't talking about horses. Wes just wanted to show him how wonderful he really was, to love him without expecting anything at all back. Someone had fucked him up good, and it made Evan push Wes away.

"It's up to you. I can stay on the sofa. It opens into a bed, or so they tell me."

"Bed's fine. I'd really like for you to just hold me." His voice was soft, unsure.

Wes nodded. "Yes, but you better behave yourself or you're on the sofa."

Evan laughed. The sound was magical. Wes had wondered if he'd hear it again. He'd pulled up something deep and dark and horrible, but it had to come up sooner or later, or Evan would never let anyone love him.

Wes just hoped he wouldn't disappoint him.

They washed up for bed, Evan using one of the hotel's plastic-wrapped toothbrushes. Evan watched as Wes slipped out of his shirt and pants and slid under the covers. Then Wes studiously avoided looking at Evan as he disrobed and got into bed. He'd wait for Evan to slide over or say something. He didn't want to crowd him. Evan was as skittish as one of the horses, and Wes felt huge and frightening, like a tractor, in comparison.

Evan slid into the center of the bed. "Would you hold me?"

Wes flicked the lights off and slid over, wrapping his arms around Evan and spooning up behind him. "Like this?"

"Yeah. Perfect."

"Good night," Wes whispered into Evan's hair. Evan felt stiff in Wes's grasp at first, but eventually he relaxed and snuggled back against Wes's chest.

He'd like to kill Gary or whoever made Evan think so little of himself. Was this what happened when you spent too much time in Hollywood? Did the place eat you up inside so you didn't like or trust yourself anymore? He didn't know any really established actors. All his friends and colleagues were up-and-coming. He wished he had someone he could trust, a mentor, the way he had in London.

He wanted desperately to know what had happened to Evan, but it was the one thing he absolutely could not ask.

IN THE morning, Evan seemed almost like himself again. Wes wouldn't forget what had happened, but he wouldn't bring it up unless Evan did. They both pretended nothing had happened. Wes dropped Evan off at his motel at the ungodly hour of 4:00 a.m. so he would be ready to drive to the track with his crew. Then Wes went back to bed for a while.

He got to the track in time to watch another of Evan's horses work a fast seven furlongs and Percy's gallop. He'd brought a box of donuts for the grooms—something he'd learned—and they ate them gratefully in between their morning chores. Evan took a coffee break with Wes at the track kitchen.

"Wes, don't take this the wrong way."

"That's a promising start to any conversation." Wes tried to grin. Was Evan going to break up with him before they'd even begun a relationship?

"You need to go back to LA."

"What?" That wasn't what Wes expected to hear, but he still didn't like it.

"There's no good reason for you to be here."

Wes flashed him a look that he hoped spoke volumes.

"Owners just don't hang around like this. It's going to be all too obvious to everyone why you're here." Evan gave him a reassuring smile, and the knot between Wes's shoulders relaxed a little. "I want you here, and I want to spend time with you. But until we're official—or whatever you want to call it—then the best thing is for you to go home until your horses run."

Evan searched Wes's face for a reaction. Now Wes got it. This was Evan's way of asking whether they were official, or public, yet. When Wes didn't respond, Evan's mouth turned down.

"Okay. I get it." Evan replied. He fidgeted with his coffee cup and splashed some onto the table. They both grabbed napkins to clean up the mess instead of looking at each other.

"No. It's not that. Not exactly." Wes stopped. He'd begged Evan to trust him, and now Wes was about to lie. "While I do think you need to talk to Gary first, I admit I have to figure out a few things from my end. Can you give me a little time on that matter?"

Evan nodded. He looked less stricken, but still not happy. "That's something we haven't discussed yet. How are you going to handle 'things?'"

"Do you have some advice?"

Evan took in slow breath. "I have some experience…."

"Evan!" Ricky shouted from the kitchen door and pointed to his watch.

"Coming!" Evan called to Ricky. He stood up. "Another of my owners is visiting, and I can't afford to lose him."

Wes opened his mouth, and Evan put out a hand before he got a word out.

"And you can't just buy up everyone's horses, as much as I appreciate that." Evan gave him a genuine smile. "I'll talk to you later." He leaned down and brushed his fingers across Wes's hand as he picked up his cup of coffee and headed for the door.

THREE HOURS later Wes was in his hotel room packing when Evan texted.

I'm tied up the rest of the day. You might as well head home and we'll talk about those issues later.

Wes replied: *See you Friday for the race.* That was neutral enough in case anyone spotted it who shouldn't. He decided it wasn't worth packing or returning the hire car. He kept the hotel room, left some cash as a tip for the maid, and locked the door behind him. They had his credit card, and they'd just keep racking up the bill, even if he wasn't there.

The drive down was uneventful unless horrendous traffic counted as an event. Wes got home well past dinnertime and was surprised to find Julia in his apartment when he walked in. He'd texted her before he left, and she'd been sweet to have some dinner waiting for him. He hadn't stopped to eat along the way and was starving.

"How'd everything go?" she asked as she watched him twirl spaghetti around his fork. She wasn't much of a cook, but she could manage a decent pasta meal.

"Good, I guess."

"Did you figure out how to deal with the problem?"

"Which one?"

"How many are there?" She pulled a bottle of wine out of the refrigerator and poured a glass for each of them.

"There's much more than my career to take into account with Evan. But I figured out part of it." Wes appreciated that she hadn't asked him for any details, just broad strokes.

"Good. Glad to hear. So are you going steady yet?"

"No. Not yet." He ate another mouthful and sipped wine, trying to decide just what to say. "He hasn't been able to talk to Gary—the boyfriend. It's not going to be as easy as he thinks, so I want us to deal with that first."

"Then how will you handle your big problem, with the studio?"

"I'm kind of hoping we get picked up for another season before I have to face that music. What do you think I should do?"

"It depends on what kind of relationship you want, Wes. You can just buy a bunch more horses, and no one will ever have to know there's any more to your relationship than business."

"Because owners always have romantic dinners with their horse trainers and spend the night?"

"You're right. No number of horses could explain that." She laughed into her wineglass. "What does Evan want?"

"He hasn't used the words, but he doesn't want to feel like my dirty little secret." Wes stared at little pieces of tomato at the bottom of his bowl as he pushed them around with his fork. "I asked him to trust me, and I'll lose him if I don't figure this out."

"What's to figure out? You're either open about it or you're single again."

It was so easy for Julia. She'd tried pushing him out of the closet slowly, but now she was ready to plant her foot solidly against his backside. "There's more to it."

"Your career?"

"Of course. Can I afford to be myself yet?"

"Can you afford not to? What's more important?"

Wes shook his head and poured more wine for himself. He drank half of it. "I thought I could wait, but I'll lose Evan if I try to hide him away in my closet. And I risk hurting him if I wait too long to decide."

"I think you have your answer." Julia poured the last of the wine into her glass. Apparently, she was staying, or cabbing it home.

"I guess I do."

Julia raised her glass in a toast, and Wes clinked his, enjoying the cheerful sound.

CHAPTER 13

THE NEXT night Wes and Julia joined Vanessa and Lance for drinks. Lance chose the venue, a popular, but inexpensive spot just off the beach in Santa Monica. The kind of place no one would expect them to go.

Wes stared at the tequila in his glass, needing all of his willpower not to swig the amber liquid. He needed something to steady his nerves after the phone call he'd made to his manager that morning. Wes had been advised to sit tight while Saul arranged the necessary discussions with the network, studio, and producers.

"So, Wes, you hear from Spielberg yet?" Lance asked after downing his own shot of tequila. He waved to the waitress for another.

"Are we going to dinner after this?" Julia asked, picking up Lance's empty glass.

"Yeah, why?" Lance reached for the new shot, but Julia put a hand over it.

"Slow down. This isn't a contest."

Lance looked around. Everyone else still had most of their first drink and were in no hurry.

"What's this about Spielberg?" Vanessa asked. She had glittery things on the tips of each fingernail, and they were making Wes dizzy. She sipped her usual Champagne. She reminded him of Patsy on *Absolutely Fabulous*—a favorite British comedy—who only drank Champagne and chain-smoked. She never ate a single bite of food over the years.

He tried to focus on her face. "Haven't heard anything. I met a fellow who works with him on the Catalina trip." He turned to Lance. "I didn't actually expect to hear back. Perhaps he was just humoring me."

"He spent half the trip talking to you. I figured he just wanted your phone number, but not for a film, you know?" Lance added a wholly unnecessary lecherous wink.

"Lance." Vanessa shook her head. "But that reminds me, how was your trip to see our horse?"

"What does that have to do with the Spielberg guy?" Julia asked.

Wes wished he could go home, or hide under the table. This was not a topic he wanted to discuss, especially the way Vanessa connected Evan to Lance's homophobic remark.

"Well, they're both a little light in the loafers," Lance replied.

Wes reached for Lance's untouched shot and downed it. Then he finished his own drink. Julia stared at him with wide eyes but didn't say anything.

"The horse is fine. He's in good shape for the race on Friday. Evan thinks he should be able to win."

"Right, Evan. I meant to find out what happened to him. I'm sure there was some kind of juicy gossip a while back." Lance turned to Wes again. "So, how is Evan? Did he try to recruit you too? You seem to be a magnet for them. Probably want to know what a big manly man feels like."

"Excuse me, ladies," Wes said and left the table before he ripped Lance's head off. The alcohol made him a little lightheaded. He rarely drank shots and certainly not two in quick succession. He went to the men's room to splash cold water on his face, more to cool his temper than counteract the booze. When he got to the table, Vanessa and Lance were deep in a discussion, but Julia was gone.

"No, I'm not into the pain thing. No biting." Vanessa stirred her drink, fingernails glittering enough to blind Wes.

"I don't mind it. But not like the big mark he had. You noticed it was on his back, right?"

"Yeah…," Vanessa replied.

"So I guess, based on that, he must be the, you know, fuck*ee*."

"Huh?"

Julia came back to the table and leaned in to catch the conversation.

"You know one guy fucks and the other one is the—" Lance said.

"Bottom," Wes said. As soon as the word was out his shoulders stiffened.

"Bottom?" Vanessa asked.

"Yeah, top and bottom. Not fucker and fuckee." Oh, he definitely had to stop drinking. He felt Julia's nails digging into his thigh.

"You seem to know a lot about it," Lance said. "Something you want to tell us?"

"Are you asking me something in particular?" Wes replied, leaning toward him, one eyebrow raised, with the most aggressive expression he could muster at the moment. Under the table he tightened his hands into fists.

"No," Lance said. The little glint of fear in his eyes made Wes smile as he sat back in his chair.

"So what's the plan for the race?" Julia asked, clearly trying to steer the conversation into somewhat safer territory. She still had a viselike grip on Wes's thigh, but he was done talking.

"Let's get a suite at a nice hotel nearby," Vanessa said, ignoring the tension still swirling between Wes and Lance. "Then after the race, we should spend a couple of days in San Francisco. I'll handle the reservations. Let's go up Thursday, then back Monday?" No one said anything for long moment.

"Sounds great, Vee." Julia broke the heavy silence.

"Oh, waiter!" Vanessa fluttered her sparkly fingers, and light glinted off like a disco ball. "A bottle of Champagne. Clicquot, please."

The waiter brought a bottle and glasses in record time—he knew Vanessa was a big tipper.

"Let's drink to Mister Twister's first win." Vanessa held up her glass, followed by Julia.

Lance held his up, and Julia nudged Wes's arm. He was in no mood to celebrate anything with Lance Robbins, but he smiled despite the ten-ton weight on his chest and raised his glass. The girls touched glasses, laughing.

Wes glanced at Lance as he clinked his, wishing it didn't sound like a lock clicking shut.

JULIA FELT unwell and begged off a group dinner, giving Wes a good excuse to get away from Lance. Back in Julia's apartment, Wes leaned back against the soft cushions of her couch and stared up at the ceiling, wishing it would lower and crush him.

"You want to talk, Wes, honey?" Julia sat next to him but he didn't look at her. He could smell herbal tea: peppermint and ginger and a few herbs and spices he couldn't name.

"No."

"Have some tea. You'll relax. Isn't that the British chicken soup, fixes everything?"

"Not herbal tea, Jules."

"This is the stress relief blend."

Wes smiled in spite of his dark mood. Julia was a pain in the ass, but a sweet pain in the ass. He heard her put the mug down on the table, and then she leaned back on the cushions next to him.

"So what's so interesting about my ceiling?"

Wes slid an arm around her waist and pulled her in. She rolled toward him and put her head on his shoulder and her arms around his waist. They lay silently for a few minutes.

"I can't do it, Julia." It sounded like his words echoed through an enormous cavern.

"Do what?"

"I can't deal with all the Lances out there. And he's sort of my friend."

"Wes, he doesn't know he's insulting you. He's just—"

"He doesn't know he's insulting anyone. But he's just like a million others. I'm not strong enough for this."

"Those million others—your fans—already like you. Most of them will keep liking you. You don't have to try and convince a million total strangers they're wrong. It's the personal connection that makes people reconsider their opinions."

"That makes more sense than I'd like to admit."

"And there's Evan." Her voice brightened even more.

Wes sighed. "There will be others, later, when I'm ready."

"Yeah, you're right. He's nothing special. Dime a dozen." Julia lay back against the cushions again, concentrating on the ceiling.

Wes glanced over at her. He looked up and saw Evan's face. Sweet, honest, broken Evan, who felt happier around horses than people. He'd never trust anyone again if Wes bailed. He'd be sadder and lonelier than he was now. Or worse—if he got involved with another Gary, who'd make him doubt himself.

Wes didn't think he could be strong enough for both of them.

CHAPTER 14

EVAN WOKE Wednesday morning to total darkness. Outside, this was usual. In his heart, the darkness had given way to a glimmer of light for the first time in years. In the horse world, days blended together. Awake before dawn and to bed while most people were still up enjoying their lives. For Evan, the joy of working with horses was sufficient to balance the things he missed out on. That had all changed since Wes had come into his life.

Even race days didn't change the schedule much. They only added to his responsibilities—all the other daily chores still had to be done. But Mister Twister was racing on Friday, which meant Wes would be back soon. Thursday night, he'd said.

They'd texted after he left, but last night Wes hadn't replied. Evan had news for him. Big news.

He'd heard from Gary, finally.

Gary was coming home the following week. He hadn't mentioned Evan's e-mail requesting him to move out in his text. Just a simple *Be back next week.* Gary was always to the point, letting Evan know what he needed or wanted, never letting Evan get his opinion in. All that was over. Soon Gary would be gone, and Wes wouldn't merely take his place. Wes would obliterate any memory of Gary, that's how different he was. Where Gary was self-centered, Wes thought of Evan and his feelings.

Wes didn't rush him or pull him out of his comfort zone as if it were a game. Wes had asked for nothing from Evan, though he'd given him so much already: respect, kindness, and a little more generosity than Evan felt comfortable with. Wes had bought Percy just so Evan wouldn't lose another horse from his barn.

And still he'd asked nothing of Evan. Hadn't asked him to explain anything when he'd broken down the other night, or expected sex. Wes had clearly been interested in Evan that way, but the idea of waiting was just another aspect of Wes's charm. Evan knew he'd be a considerate lover when they did give in to their physical attractions. How long had it been since someone had cared how Evan felt in bed?

The thought of making love with Wes got Evan hard again. He glanced at the clock. Fifteen minutes until they'd leave for the track. He had just enough time for a cold shower.

Or a warm one. Evan closed his eyes and recalled the strength of Wes's arms around him and the taste of his kisses as he stroked himself under the spiky spray of the battered showerhead. He needed the release. He felt good, even better when he remembered Wes would be here soon.

Now he was running late. He pulled his clothes on quickly and raced out the door, down the steps, and to the van, hair still wet and dripping onto his shoulders.

IT WAS dinnertime before Wes replied to Evan's texts.

Leaving after breakfast tomorrow. Should get to Berk by dinnertime Thursday.

That was it. No plan to meet. Nothing personal. They hadn't been texting love letters, but the terse message started a little ache in Evan's stomach. Wes was probably tied up with meetings or busy with his friends. He wasn't the inconsiderate type who phoned or texted while he was with others, ignoring them in favor of a piece of glass and metal in his hand.

If Evan wasn't so exhausted from his day, he might have lain awake wondering and worrying. He put his phone on the nightstand and slid under the sheets. He remembered lying here with Wes less than a week ago. He flipped off the light and picked up his phone. He checked the messages, but nothing new. He checked the volume. High enough to wake him if Wes texted late.

When Evan woke up Thursday morning, the phone was still clutched in his hand.

No missed calls or texts.

AT 10:00 a.m. Evan's phone chirped while he was cleaning Lonely Heiress—Lola's—stall and the filly tossed her head, eyes wide.

"Sorry, girl." Evan smoothed a hand down her neck and cooed until she calmed down as he read the text:

Just left LA. Can we meet @ barn @ 6pm?

Evan's mood soared. He hit "reply" then stopped. He didn't want to reply immediately, or Wes would think he was... was what? Of course he was excited to see Wes.

Yes. See you then, Evan texted.

Ding: an almost immediate reply from Wes!

The others want a barn tour.

Evan's spirits plummeted. It hadn't been a personal rendezvous after all. But it was better than waiting another day.

OK.

Eight hours. How would Evan last another eight hours? Because he had plenty of work to do around the barn. He'd given Hector the day off and was covering his duties. Tomorrow Hector would handle Evan's afternoon chores, while he took the horses to and from the track.

JUST BEFORE six, Evan went into the office, put on a fresh shirt, and brushed dirt and straw off his jeans. He ran a cloth across his boots so he looked a little more presentable. He'd asked Ricky to stay to give the tour, since Wes's friends knew he didn't want to deal with them. He'd wait in the office and hope Wes could figure out a good excuse to stop in.

At six fifteen Wes and his friends hadn't yet arrived. Restless, Evan wandered down the barn and into Lola's stall to check her water. Of course it was fine.

He was just moving on to the next stall when they arrived. Wes came in first, followed by Julia, Vanessa, and Lance. Wes wore dark jeans and a turquoise long-sleeved shirt. Even at this distance, Evan could see he wasn't wearing his usual boots. Why not? Wes looked over, and his gaze met Evan's. Then he looked away quickly.

He did not look particularly happy. In fact, he looked like he'd just run over his own puppy. The tiny knot in Evan's gut expanded, and he knew something was terribly wrong. This wasn't just Wes pretending they weren't friends. It felt like Wes had denied Evan's existence.

He moved into the next stall and into the front inner corner, just past the water bucket. He put a hand on the horse's neck for support, for contact with something warm and alive and loving. He tried to breathe around the boulder lodged in his throat and wondered if it might be preferable to suffocate right here, right now.

WES STOOD at one end of the barn as Ricky introduced himself and gave an introduction about how things worked at the track. He spotted Evan farther down the barn, at one of the stalls, but then he was gone.

This was as good a time as any. It would be harder later to explain why he needed a private chat with Evan. Wes strode down the barn, reminding himself it had to be this way. Evan had texted back so quickly today, so attentively. It wasn't fair to drag this out longer.

Wes rehearsed the lines he'd written as he walked slowly toward the stall where he'd seen Evan. "It's just not the right time for me to make a big move like this. I'm not ready, but if we can be discreet about this, then maybe…."

He stopped outside the stall. He heard the horse moving around restlessly inside. He glanced inside but didn't see Evan near the door. He couldn't have gotten out; there was no other exit.

Wes ducked under the webbed barrier and entered the stall. Evan was in the corner, hand on the horse's neck, back against the wall like he'd been hung on a hook.

"Evan?"

No response.

"Evan? I—"

"Please stop saying my name." Pain hung on every word, only it was Wes who felt like he'd been stabbed, punched, kicked.

His eyes got used to the dark and he saw Evan's face more clearly. A sliver of light peeked in from a crack between boards and illuminated part of his face. Wes could hear him breathing, short, shallow breaths. He remembered how Evan's breath felt against his ear and how he sounded when he slept on Wes's chest. And how his arms felt when he held tightly to Wes.

Something big and dark clawed at Wes's heart, and he felt a hole expanding inside him. A hole he hadn't realized was there, but he knew just how to fill it.

"Evan. God, I missed you so much." Wes moved toward Evan and gathered him in his arms, holding him tight to his chest. Evan felt limp and boneless, and Wes backed him against the wall again and tried to get a good look at his face.

Wes leaned down and kissed Evan, needing to feel his lips, taste him.

"What?"

"I missed you. I don't know how I managed to stay away so long." Wes kissed Evan again, and this time Evan kissed back and put his arms loosely around Wes's waist. Wes gripped harder, and Evan melted against him.

How could he have even considered not coming back to Evan? Wes felt whole and strong in his arms, strong enough to deflect the comments of people like Lance. Wes pressed Evan tight against the wall and kissed him hard, deep, drawing in his essence as if he needed Evan to breathe.

Outside the stall, he heard Ricky speaking as Wes's friends filed past. He didn't let go of Evan, kissed him harder, fortifying himself. The horse nickered and moved to put his head over the stall barrier.

"Isn't he pretty," Vanessa said. He could see her stroke the horse's face.

Could she see Wes and Evan from the door? He didn't care.

Evan glanced toward Vanessa, then pulled Wes in for another kiss. Then he pushed Wes back a pace and looked up into his face.

"I wasn't sure—" Evan whispered.

Wes stopped Evan's words with a finger to his lips. "I wasn't either, but I figured things out. Most of them. Tomorrow night, we'll talk tomorrow night about everything."

Evan nodded.

Down the barn Wes heard a horse's steps on the dirt floor. He shifted position to see Ricky leading Twist. Wes pulled Evan out of the stall while everyone's attention was on the horse. He smoothed his shirt and pants. He noticed Evan's eyes were bright and shiny-wet. It had only been a few days, and already Wes had upset him. He hated himself and his selfish fears.

He couldn't keep thinking just about himself if he really wanted to be with Evan. He had to think about both of them. That would take some practice, and perhaps more courage than Wes possessed. Evan was worth it.

Evan blinked in the bright light of the barn corridor, and his gaze held a multitude of questions.

"Tomorrow," Wes mouthed and Evan nodded. This time a smile percolated and finally brightened his expression.

"Twist is looking really great, Evan," Wes said, loudly enough the others could hear.

"Thanks, Wes." Evan came up behind and to the left of the horse and laid a hand on his rump. "He should be in the money tomorrow for sure." He turned to Julia. "How was the drive up?"

"It's the traffic at either end that makes it seem so long, especially in a fast car." She smiled fondly at Evan.

"I could use a drink right about now," Lance boomed, unsettling Twist who tossed his head. "And some dinner."

"Evan, would you like to join us for drinks or dinner?" Vanessa asked. Wes watched Lance's eyebrows rise a good two inches. Vanessa glanced at him, then back at Evan. "We'd like to thank you for doing such a good job with Twist. He looks like a different horse after only a few weeks with you."

Evan looked at his shoes. His discomfort at the compliment was charming. Wes knew it was genuine since Vanessa rarely complimented anyone on anything.

"You haven't seen him run yet... but I'm afraid I should pass tonight. I get up pretty early, so I need to get to bed early. But thank you."

"Okay, ladies. That includes you, Wes. Back to the car. And then to the bar."

"I'm not ready, Lance." Julia turned back to Evan. "May I take some photographs?"

"Sure. Twist likes the attention. You might get better shots outside, though."

"Do you mind?" she asked.

"Ricky, I'll take Twist outside for some photos. Thanks for your help."

Ricky nodded, but before he could walk away, Vanessa stopped him. "Ricky, would you take some photos of all of us with Twist?"

"Yes, ma'am."

Evan led the horse outside and Vanessa arranged everyone around the horse. Ricky took a several shots and handed the camera back to Julia.

"A few more," she said. "Wes and Evan, you two on one side of him, and Vee and Lance, the other."

Wes stood next to Evan and snuck an arm around his waist before Julia snapped the photo. She grinned at him. They took more in different combinations. "We'll get some shots tomorrow before the race, right?"

Evan nodded. Lance was already heading for the parking lot when Evan took Twist back into the barn. Julia and Vanessa were outside waiting for Wes, who had followed Evan inside.

"Julia knows?" Evan asked softly.

Wes nodded. "She's my best friend. She's on our side, always has been."

Evan smiled. "I like her. What about the others?"

Wes groaned. "They don't know, but I'm pretty sure Vanessa would be happy. Lance... well, he can go shag himself. I don't know anyone else who would want to."

Evan chuckled. The sound released the last tension in Wes's back and shoulders. He wasn't sure he'd smoothed things over enough with Evan for the time being, but the laughter made him realize he'd dodged the worst. They'd have time to talk the next day.

"I'll be back before the race. What time is post?"

"Four thirty. We start getting him ready around twelve thirty."

"I'll send them to the turf club for lunch and come back."

"Sounds good." Evan put Twist back in his stall and turned to Wes. "Tomorrow."

"I can't wait." Wes pulled Evan in for a kiss, right in the middle of the barn. He didn't care who saw.

CHAPTER 15

FRIDAY MORNING dragged on for what felt like a week. Wes wasn't hungry and only nibbled on some fruit at breakfast. Lance insisted they order room service in the suite to avoid having to deal with fans.

"Lance, we don't mind meeting fans," Julia said as she buttered a tiny piece of toast. She popped it into her mouth and chewed, eyes closed, experiencing the bliss of genuine butter. Wes wondered how Americans could think margarine was a suitable replacement for the real thing. Normally, he wouldn't care, but since he'd been skipping so many gym sessions lately, he abstained.

"You might not, but it gets to be really annoying for the rest of us." Lance stuffed eggy bread—french toast to the Yanks—dripping with butter and syrup into his mouth along with a piece of sausage. Another thing Wes had never got used to: the way Americans mixed sweet and savory breakfast foods on the same plate. He preferred to keep his eggy bread far from bacon and sausage.

"Speak for yourself," Vanessa said. Today she wore a black-and-white striped dress that was much more restrained than her last race-day ensemble, for which Wes uttered a silent prayer of gratitude. This one had short sleeves and showed relatively little cleavage. Perhaps she had decided not to give Lance—or anyone else—a show. She also nibbled at fruit and yogurt. No wonder she could indulge at dinnertime. Wes had always wondered how she managed to eat seemingly anything she liked and still keep her trim figure.

Breakfasting with friends was quite eye opening.

"Wes, aren't you eating?" Julia asked. "I thought it was only horses that go off their feed."

Wes took some toast and ripped off a small piece but it was all he could manage. He wanted to get to the track, spend time with Evan in the barn. He watched Julia eating. She looked elegant in her dress, gray silk with blue and white flowers.

He'd put on dark gray chinos and a whisper-thin hunter-green jumper. He'd bring a jacket too. He wondered whether Evan would show up in his typical race-day coat and tie. Wes hoped so.

"The clubhouse opens at noon," Wes said. "We can head over and have lunch there."

"What's the hurry?" Lance asked.

"They have a bar," Wes replied.

"Shit, what're we waiting for?" Lance said.

Wes noticed the little smile on Julia's lips. She always knew just what he was up to.

IT WAS closer to one when they left Vanessa's BMW at valet parking and entered the clubhouse. Wes retrieved their tickets from the will call window after autographing a racing program for Betty, the woman who worked the counter. He spent a couple of minutes chatting with her until another person came up to the window.

The place was nearly deserted as they took the elevator to the top floor. Wes handed the tickets to the hostess, and she took them to a reserved table, right above the finish line.

"Best spot in the house," she said. "I thought it was a joke when I saw your name on the reservation. Your waiter will be right here."

"Pretty nice," Lance said, taking in the room. Rows of white-linen-covered tables ran the length of the turf club. Each had its own small television, showing races from other tracks until Golden Gate Fields's races started. At one end of the room was a buffet table and at the other a counter full of self-service betting machines. A complimentary *Racing Form* had been left on their table.

"I'm going to the barn." Wes started to get up before anyone suggested joining him.

"Have a drink first, Wes." Vanessa raised her fingers, the glittering nails a beacon to anyone within a half-mile radius. She ordered a round of vodka cocktails, and he agreed to stay for just one, but he felt like a caged animal between Julia and the glass wall.

"Jules, are you going to the barn too?" Vanessa asked once the drinks had been served.

Julia glanced at Wes before replying. "No, I'll wait till later."

"What's with you two?" Vanessa looked from Wes to Julia and back again. "You're barely speaking to each other, and Wes, you're barely speaking at all."

"Nothing." Julia put on her cheerful face, but Wes couldn't muster the energy today. He looked out onto the track below.

Maintenance crews were restoring the track surface before race time. The turf course, nestled inside the main dirt track, gleamed like bright-green silk. Birds clustered at the infield ponds, and the sun sparkled off the water's surface.

Such a beautiful day and Wes was trapped up here, three stories above the track, in an air-conditioned cocoon of surface elegance.

Lance had his head down, concentrating on the *Racing Form*. Vanessa turned to him then back to Wes, frowning. "Today was supposed to be fun. Why aren't we having fun yet?"

"It'll be fun once the races start." Wes squeezed her hand, then raised his glass in a toast. "To fun!" He held his glass out until the others clinked theirs. Lance's was already empty.

Vanessa smiled and Wes sipped his drink. The vodka was blended with grapefruit juice and something else, and it felt acidic and bitter in his stomach. Why was he so nervous? He had no doubts about Twist's chances of winning today. He missed Evan, and the guilt over nearly pushing him aside hadn't completely subsided yet. How could Wes make it up to Evan? Certainly not while he was stuck up here, quite literally chilling.

"Looks like our horse has a great chance today." Lance finally came out from behind the paper. "He's definitely got the speed on the other horses." He read off race and workout times of the competition and rattled off some statistics. Wes's mood brightened. He actually understood what Lance was saying, now that he'd learned so much about racing.

Julia and Vanessa listened, but the jargon went over their heads.

"Okay, let's just bet already. I'm convinced." Vanessa glanced toward the betting machines. "Jules? Come with?"

"Sure." The two women got up. "Wes, you want me to place a bet for you?"

"No. I'll do it myself."

"Okay." Julia followed Vanessa.

"Vee's right, dude. You've been ignoring that sweet little—"

"I'm not ignoring her." Wes didn't want to discuss Julia with Lance, not today.

"Come on. Nothing but silence from your room last night. That's what I call ignoring."

Wes shook his head. "You think we'd do anything with you next door?" They should have put Vanessa in the next room and Lance in the room on the opposite side of the suite. Major mistake.

"You seem awfully eager to get away from her and run off to the stables. I'll bet you met some cute little thing up here last week." Lance stared at Wes, but not with his usual nudge-nudge expression.

"I didn't."

"I hope not. If I hear you're cheating on sweet Jules, I'll punch your lights out. Fuck you and your pretty TV-star face." Lance spoke low, under his breath. The pent-up emotion and violence took Wes by surprise. "She deserves much better than that. You should let someone else treat her right."

"So now you're after Julia?" Wes couldn't stop himself in time and the words forced their way out. "Tired of Vanessa's rejection? You've got even less chance with Julia. But go ahead and try if you're the better man." Wes leaned across the table into Lance's space.

Lance held up his hands, palms out. "Hey, I didn't say that. Just wanna make sure you're not phonin' it in with her and giving it to someone else on the side."

"I'm going down to the barn. Not off to see some other woman." Wes stood. He glanced around, wondering whether they'd raised their voices. A few people looked up from other tables, but their expressions told him they recognized him and not because of the little tiff with Lance.

"Okay, okay, I believe you. Nothing down there but some horses and our pretty little trainer. Watch he doesn't try to pull you into the hay!"

Wes let Lance's insults bounce off his back. He balled his fists up as he strode away. If he turned around, he would surely use one on Lance. He went down the stairs to the ground level and walked around the track toward the backside. He'd call Julia from the barn.

His throat tightened even as he exited the building into the air. Lance's accusations weren't completely off-base. Wes had been seeing someone else and ignoring Julia. She wasn't his girlfriend, but she was a friend, and he hadn't been playing his role in their charade, which made her look a fool. He owed her an apology. Just a few more days, a week at most, and they could both move on. He could come clean, and she would find a real boyfriend who treated her like a queen. She deserved that at the very least.

But not Lance. When had he become so solicitous of her? Had Wes failed to notice if this was reciprocal? Perhaps Julia did like Lance; there could be some redeeming quality Wes hadn't yet noticed. His attention had been elsewhere for the past month, and anything could have happened under his nose.

When he got to the security gate, he waved at Dennis who returned the greeting. "Good luck today, Mr. Tremayne."

"Wes. Just Wes." He nodded and headed for Evan's barn.

Inside he spotted Evan in front of the last stall, wearing faded jeans and a pale-blue button-down shirt with the sleeves rolled up. His hair was mussed and dark strands clung to his temples as he stopped at each stall, pouring grain into the feed buckets hanging at the door.

"Need any help?" Wes asked.

Evan spun around, nearly dropping the can of grain in his hands. "I didn't expect you yet." He dumped the grain in the next bucket and scooped more from a large tub at the end of the shed row. "I-uh, look like…." He rubbed damp hair off his face with the back of his hand and pressed his lips together for a moment. They plumped back to normal when he relaxed.

"You look good enough to eat," Wes said softly.

Evan glanced around, scratching the back of his neck. Such an adorable expression of embarrassment and pleasure on his face. "I'm sure I don't smell that good right now."

"Come closer." Wes cocked his head and waited. When Evan didn't move, Wes ducked under the webbing of the closest stall and moved to the back, taking care not to get in the way of the horse's rump and hind legs.

Evan glanced around again and followed Wes inside. Wes took hold of Evan's shirt with a finger hooked over the top button and pulled him close. He let out a sigh as Evan melted against him, sliding his arms around Wes's waist. They merged in a deep, slow kiss. When they broke apart, Wes gazed down into Evan's eyes, searching them for an answer to a question Wes hadn't yet asked. The answer was clearly yes.

He slipped a paper into Evan's back pocket, letting his fingers explore the curve of Evan's arse on the way down and back up again. Evan pressed his hips against Wes, and Wes sucked in a breath, calming himself. He was on the verge of arousal. The look in Evan's eyes and his body pressed close pushed Wes right to the edge, but he forced himself back. Now was not the right time.

"Later, Evan. The note has the plan."

"Plan? Secret notes? I feel like I fell into a James Bond film." Evan ran a finger down Wes's chest. "I never thought about being a Bond girl, but suddenly the possibility appears very attractive. Unless I'm just one of many."

Wes frowned.

"Oh, I'm sorry. I shouldn't have said that. I'm not usually the possessive type." Evan blurted the words then turned his attention to the horse, contently munching hay and ignoring them….

"I don't mind the possessive part. But the Bond thing? It's not happening."

"I read it somewhere. Is there any truth to it?"

"I thought you'd given up the Hollywood gossip rags and your connections." Wes traced a finger along Evan's face.

Evan gave a tiny shrug. "I have, but I was a little curious about you. If someday they ask about Bond, you'd be a fool to turn it down."

Wes had no intention of turning down a role like that. It would be a dream come true. How ironic if he had to come to the States and be on a television show here just to get a chance to head home and play Bond. Crazy world.

"You think the world is ready for a gay Bond?"

"Not in our lifetime." Evan looked up and planted a soft kiss on Wes's mouth.

Wes had been only half joking when he asked. Gay Bond? No. Gay actor playing Bond? Probably just as unlikely. "You're probably right."

"I need to finish up feeding, and then I've got to get Twist ready."

"Evan? The vet's here!" Ricky's voice boomed down the shed row.

"Coming!" Evan disentangled himself from Wes. He smoothed his clothes and hair and ducked out of the stall. Wes waited a moment and followed, hoping the attention would be on Evan and no one would notice he'd come out of the same stall—it wasn't even his horse.

Evan introduced him to the vet as Twist's owner. He watched as Evan took Twist outside and walked then trotted him between the barns. The vet ran a hand along each leg and had Wes show her Twist's hooves. She made notes on a clipboard.

"He's fine. Good luck today."

"Thanks."

She patted Twist's neck and got back in her SUV and drove off.

"She's the state vet. Has to check every runner to make sure they're sound. If not, she won't let them run."

Wes led Twist back to his stall while Evan finished feeding.

By that time the grooms had returned, presumably from lunch. So much for having the barn to themselves.

Wes made small talk while Evan painted Twist's hooves with a protective coating, then wrapped ice on his forelegs. One and a half hours to the race, Wes noted as he glanced yet again at his watch. Outside, the temperature soared, and he was grateful to be in the shade, though the barn was far from cool. Evan even set up a portable fan in front of Twist's stall for ventilation and to keep him calm.

Evan had just finished strapping on the ice packs when Julia, Vanessa, and Lance arrived. Ever practical, Julia had brought a comfortable pair of flat shoes to wear into the barn. Vanessa tottered on high heels and kept tripping on the uneven dirt floor of the barn.... She must have had an awful time navigating the rutted road between the track and the barn. Perhaps Lance had been chivalrous and carried her.

"How's Mister Twister doing?" Julia asked Evan as he stood up and brushed straw from his jeans.

Wes tried not to notice how well the denim emphasized his assets. Lance cast an appraising gaze over Evan, taking in his sweaty, disheveled appearance.

"He's great. Let's try and stay on the other side of the aisle so we don't crowd him. He's not used to this many visitors in the barn, are you?" Evan scratched under Twist's chin, and the horse raised his nose to give him better access.

"What's wrong with his legs?" Vanessa pointed at the ice packs with wide eyes.

"Just icing them down to take care of any residual inflammation. I'll take these off just before we head to the track."

"Who's our jockey?" Julia asked.

"Billy George. He's one of the top riders in Northern Cal. He worked Twist last week and galloped him the other day. They get along very well."

"He looks good on paper," Lance said, as if the real horse didn't meet his expectations.

"Yes, he does. He's the favorite for a reason." Evan replied.

Wes held his breath, not trusting Lance, but Evan and Lance had a discussion of speeds and the competition that even Wes couldn't follow. As he spoke, Lance glanced at Wes, then at Julia, who stood a few feet away. They hadn't touched or held hands at all that day. Wes watched Evan talk about horses, hands gesturing, eyes bright, clearly enjoying the subject. Wes couldn't touch Julia around Evan. He simply wouldn't do that to either of them.

Just a few more days of this.

"Wes, show me your new horse?" Vanessa asked, and Wes reluctantly left Lance with Evan. Julia was there to mediate if Lance's usual personality resurfaced.

In front of Percy's stall, he introduced him to Vanessa.

"Wes, you sound just like Evan, talking to horses like they're people." She gave a little laugh and reached out to stroke the horse's muzzle. "He's beautiful. Bigger than Twist. Is he going to run soon?"

"Thursday, I think, if the race goes. Evan said if there weren't enough entries it would be cancelled or pushed back a few days."

"Are you coming back up to watch?"

"Probably. I have some meetings next week, so it'll depend on my schedule."

"Oh, a new part? Or a film?"

"I can't say anything about this project yet. Soon, though."

"Good." Vanessa moved down the shed row, away from Percy. Wes glanced back and saw Lance was still chatting with Evan, but the second time he looked, Evan was nowhere in sight. A weight descended again. What had Lance said? Adrenaline pumped through his veins, and he felt his shoulders tensing. He fought the urge to find Evan.

When Vanessa had tired of looking at the rest of the horses in Evan's half of the barn, they headed back. Evan had reappeared. He'd changed, and Wes had to fight off other urges this time. No suit today; instead, Evan wore a pair of slim, dark jeans, topped with a mint-green shirt, and a jacket and tie. Wes would have swept him into his arms if he'd had more courage. Instead, he devoured Evan with his gaze, noting he'd smoothed his hair and put on a nicer pair of boots. Definitely good enough to eat.

Ricky took Twist's ice packs off, and a loudspeaker made an unintelligible announcement.

"That's our call to go to the test barn."

"What's that?" Julia asked.

"An official will check each horse's identity and select two for prerace drug testing."

"Testing for what?" Vanessa asked.

"A variety of drugs. Pain meds, performance enhancers, that sort of thing."

Lance's skeptical expression returned. "Of course he's clean, right?"

"Absolutely. If he has anything in his system, he didn't get it from me." Evan didn't appear insulted by Lance's accusatory tone. "You can come to the barn with me and then walk to the saddling paddock, or you can meet me there. It's probably pretty boring to stick around." Evan glanced toward Wes. "But you're welcome to."

"I think I need a head start back to the track," Vanessa said pointing one high-heeled foot out in front of her. "Should we wait at the paddock?"

"Yes," Evan replied. "Owners can stay in the paddock while he's being saddled."

"Mind if I tag along?" Wes asked.

"It's really just a lot of walking in circles and waiting." Evan took Twist out of the stall.

"If it's too boring, I'll head for the track."

"Fair enough." Evan took Twist outside, and they all walked together to the test barn, which was on the way back to the track. Julia and Lance went with Vanessa.

"Evan, you're not being tested today," a track official said when they got to the test barn. Another official stopped at each stall, comparing the horses to a set of photographs to make sure no one had brought in a ringer.

"Don't they look at the tattoos?" Wes asked. He knew each Thoroughbred had a unique number tattooed on the inside of its upper lip for identification purposes.

"Nope. They do the first race at a track, but Twist's run up here before, so his photo is on file. They only check the number if the horse doesn't look like its picture."

"How hard is it to fool the official on the ID?" Wes asked.

"It's probably not as hard as it should be. But I've only ever seen it happen once in California."

They moved to the receiving barn and walked around in a circle. It was just as boring as Evan had warned, but Wes didn't want to be anywhere else right now. Excitement was building for him, for the upcoming race and because he was with Evan, away from the all-seeing eyes of his friends.

FINALLY, THEY got the call to head to the track. The grooms or trainers led the horses out in post-position order, and they filed through the gap and onto the surface of the track. Wes glanced ahead at the grandstand, now filling with people. They were about a quarter of the way around, and the walk to the saddling paddock took just over five minutes.

Walking here on the track, next to his horse, Wes's pulse raced again. Butterflies swarmed in his stomach and his throat went dry. Of course, Evan's presence might have contributed to his emotional response, but even without him, this would be one of the most thrilling moments of Wes's life. The realization surprised him. Even winning a Tony award hadn't been that much more exciting. And he'd been on top of the world that night.

But being here on the track had nearly beaten out the single most amazing night of his life. They hadn't even gotten to the saddling area. He'd be a total wreck by the time the horse got into the starting gate, much less started running.

Calm yourself, Wes. Pace yourself. So much excitement planned for today.

They met Julia and Vanessa in the saddling paddock, and Wes stepped back to wait in the center of the ring, out of Evan and Ricky's way.

"Where's Lance?" Wes hoped he wasn't at the bar.

"Placing some more bets," Julia replied. She'd put her fancy shoes back on and pulled a small camera out of her bag.

"Now he really looks like a racehorse." Vanessa grabbed Wes's arm in excitement as Lonnie led Twist around the ring with the tiny racing saddle and his numbered saddlecloth.

Julia was snapping photos of everyone and everything like a mother at her kid's first play. To Wes, the buildup reminded him of waiting for the curtain to rise, hearing the audience fidgeting in their seats from the same anticipation. He glanced at Evan, who looked calm, as if he'd done this a million times.

The jockeys filed in, and Evan leaned close to Billy's ear to give him instructions.

"Can I get your picture, Billy?" Julia asked, then took a group photo with their jockey. Evan took one with Julia in the shot, then he gave Billy a leg up onto Twist and steered him to the well-worn path inside the paddock. It was much smaller than the one at Santa Alamita, and they would walk the circumference with the other runners until they headed for the track.

"Post is in about ten minutes," Evan said. "Let's go upstairs to watch." He led them up one flight to a good vantage point, closer to the track than the turf club or their reserved box in the grandstand. Vanessa called Lance to let him know where they were.

The announcer's voice echoed through the grandstand.

"Oh, he's English," Vanessa said. "Isn't that odd?"

"Am I odd as well?" Wes asked.

"No, of course not.... Oh, I see." Vanessa shrugged, a frown erasing her excitement. "Sorry."

Wes gave her a grin, and her face brightened.

They took turns with Evan's binoculars, watching Twist's warm-up around the track before the horses were led into the starting gate right in front of the stands. For a one-mile race, the starting and finish lines were the same spot.

"How do they get the gate out of the way?" Julia asked.

Evan pointed to the two tractors. "One is a backup in case the main tractor doesn't work. Then they'll pull it out of the way and take it off the track there." He indicated a spot to their left past the grandstand. Wes had wondered himself and was glad Julia had asked.

"I am so excited." Julia was bouncing on her feet and grabbing at Wes's arm. Vanessa had her program balled up from her own excitement.

Evan had one hand on the railing in front of them. Wes stood next to him and slid his hand next to Evan's so their fingers touched. He saw Evan smile without turning toward Wes.

Finally, all the horses were in the gate. Wes gripped the rail so hard his knuckles were white. Julia's grip tightened on his arm hard enough to stop circulation.

The two horse broke ahead of the pack. Twist was somewhere in the middle, and it took a moment for Wes to spot him. Evan's bright purple silks made the job easier, but the horses were bunched close. They were already around the first turn before he could make out that Twist was in third and on the outside of two other horses, not a good position.

"Come on, Twist! Come on, Twist!" Vanessa and Julia chanted.

"Come on, Twist," Evan said calmly. "Billy, hold him back...."

Twist was second along the rail on the backstretch. Wes wished he had binoculars because he couldn't make out what was happening, and the announcer's voice sounded like noise despite the familiar accent. Twist was nearly even with the leader, number six, going into the third turn, but Wes couldn't see anything. It was farthest from their position. Coming into the last turn, Twist had fallen to third, on the outside again, and he had trouble keeping up with the second-place horse.

Then, as if Billy had stepped on the gas, Twist hurtled forward, legs digging into the track, propelling himself faster and faster, passing the second horse and two lengths back from the lead.

Everyone around Wes shouted, and he blocked the noise out. "Come on, Twister! Twist!" His heart pounded, adrenaline pumping as Twist caught up to the leader as they stormed across the finish line.

"There's a photo finish for first," the announcer's voice boomed.

Evan pulled his binocs down and turned to them, cocking his head. "I think he got it, but I'm not sure. They were on the same stride, so it's hard to tell. Billy looked like he made it."

Wes stared at the results board, willing the "official" sign to pop up, but when the board lit up, it wasn't what any of them expected.

"An inquiry?" Vanessa asked. "What happened?"

"I didn't see anything," Evan said. "But it might have happened on a turn when we can't see much from the stands. I'm heading down to the track. Wait for me next to the paddock."

They filed back downstairs, but Lance excused himself when they hit the ground level.

Wes went onto the track and talked with Billy, who had just slid down from Twist. The horse was gulping in air and had sweat streaks along his shoulder and flanks. Lonnie unsaddled him and handed the tack to Billy, who had to weigh in after the race with the other jocks. Then his valet took the saddle while he answered questions about the race.

"This is taking longer than the race," Julia said.

Evan came to join them while waiting for the result of the inquiry. "Billy said they bumped another horse around the turn because the inside horse went wide. It's why they lost ground on the third turn." He pointed toward the curve. "But that jock is claiming Billy hindered him."

"Which horse?"

"The six horse." Number Six, the one in the lead until Twist caught up with him at the wire.

"He's just a sore loser!" Vanessa said.

"I think it means Twist beat him," Evan said.

"We have the official results for the fourth race." The announcer's voice drowned out whatever else Evan said. "The winner is number three, Mister Twister, owned by Wesley Tremayne—" Cheers from the audience—some shouting Wes's name—drowned out most of the announcement. "The inquiry does not affect the results."

"Oh my God!" Julia and Vanessa shrieked.

Wes turned to Evan and pulled him into a hug, and his lips brushed Evan's cheek as Julia moved to hug him and she collided with Evan. Wes caught himself before it was too late and stepped back. Had anyone else seen that? Vanessa stared at him and Julia's eyes were wide, worried. She hesitated only a fraction of a second before grabbing both of them into another hug, and Vanessa joined in.

"Time for our Winner's Circle photo," Evan said, completely unfazed, compared to Wes. Now his heart pounded again but not from excitement. Had anyone in the crowd noticed that interrupted kiss?

"Where's Lance?" Julia asked.

Wes looked around and saw Lance staring at him, mouth wide enough to comfortably fit a six-horse trailer. Wes donned his usual role, grinning as if nothing had happened, and waved Lance toward the track. "Hurry up, Lance!"

Lance broke into a jog and met them at the Winner's Circle, producing a couple of bottles of Champagne for the photo. "Sorry, no glasses!"

Wes held Twist's reins in the photo, with Evan on one side of him and Julia on the other. Vanessa and Lance stood on the other side of Evan as the photographer snapped a series of shots.

Lance gave Wes a sidelong glance before shifting his gaze to Evan standing next to Wes, but he didn't say a word.

CHAPTER 16

"EVAN, YOU must come join us." Vanessa took his hand and squeezed it. "We won thanks to you." They had crowded around the Winner's Circle so long the track personnel moved them out so they wouldn't interfere with the next race.

"Well, Twist did all the work," Evan said. "I need to get him back to the barn. But thank you for the invitation."

Wes watched from a couple of feet away, noting that Evan wouldn't make eye contact with Vanessa.

"Please, Evan." Julia came up to add more pressure.

Wes grinned and joined in. "You can't miss this. It's quite a bash Jules and Vanessa have planned."

"I have a lot of work left here."

"How long will that take? We can wait. It's still early," Vanessa said. Wes was surprised; he expected her to tell Evan to ignore his duties. She'd surprised him several times during the trip, and he found himself liking her more than he'd expected. He began to understand what Julia saw in her, and Julia didn't suffer fools.

"Another couple of hours. I need to cool, bathe, and ice Twist and check on the other runner today."

"Evan, you should go. I'll finish up with Twist." Lonnie hooked Twist's lead into his halter. "And I'll call if there's any problem when the ice packs come off."

"Can we send something round to the barn for the grooms?" Julia asked Evan. "How about some Champagne, or order in some dinner from a nice place?"

Vanessa offered to bring more bubbly from the track bar while Julia, Wes, and Evan walked back to the barn with Twist and Lonnie. Lance made himself scarce and said he'd meet them at the valet parking when they were done fucking around. Wes suspected he just went back to the bar, but he was relieved Lance was gone. Maybe he hadn't seen as much as Wes thought he had.

While Evan oversaw Twist's cooldown and bath, Vanessa poured bubbly for the grooms, and Julia ordered dinner from the best place that would deliver, a local Italian restaurant.

Wes tried not to get in anyone's way, but he willed the clock to move more quickly. He couldn't stop meeting Evan's gaze and grinning like an idiot. Only Evan knew it wasn't just about the big win.

An hour later they met Lance at the car.

"I should really go back to my motel and change." Evan hesitated when they were getting into the car.

"Why? You look great." Vanessa gave Evan's tie a tug.

Lance screwed up his face in an all-too-real grimace. "Why are you wasting your time on him?" he said, not particularly quietly, but his eyes were on Wes.

"Lance, you're such a killjoy. I'd rather spend time with Evan than you if you're gonna be in that mood."

Julia burst into very unladylike laughter, and Wes joined in

"If you'll be more comfortable, we can drop you off to change."

"I'm not changing." Vanessa twirled in her dress, and the beads danced around her with a delightful sound. "I love dressing up."

"This is California. There is no reason to wear a tie except maybe at your funeral." Lance shook his head and got behind the wheel. Wes's stomach took another nosedive.

"Are you okay to drive?" Julia asked and pulled him out. "Vee, I'll drive if you like."

"Thanks, Jules."

Lance took shotgun while Vanessa and Wes sat in the back with Evan, who looked even more uncomfortable than usual. But Vanessa's cheerfulness and kind demeanor had a positive effect. Wes wished Evan could relax more around his friends. Maybe once they told everyone, he'd feel more comfortable.

Up in the suite, several bottles of Champagne were already chilling in ice buckets, and an array of cold appetizers awaited them. Vanessa called room service to arrange for the rest of the food while Wes started popping corks.

Vanessa made the first toast to Evan, and each of them made successive toasts to the day, the horse, and to the winnings—the last was Lance's.

Wes and Julia stood by the buffet table while Vanessa chatted with Evan on the couch.

"I don't know whether to cut Lance's booze off or give him more so he passes out. I'm worried something bad is going to happen between him and Evan—or him and you." Julia smiled as she spoke so no one else would guess what they were discussing.

"I vote for drugging his drink." Wes watched Lance help himself to food from a platter a few feet away.

"So, Lance-a-lot, how do you like owning a winner?" Julia asked with more patience than Wes had for him.

"It's great. I love it."

"Really?" Wes replied in what he thought was a perfectly polite tone, But Julia gave him a warning glare. "I didn't think you were enjoying this trip at all."

"It's certainly got its downside. But I'm hoping things will pick up when we get to San Francisco." Lance raised his eyebrows and glanced over at Vanessa.

"You came up here for Vanessa?" Wes asked.

"I bought the fucking *horse* for Vanessa. I just didn't realize she was so into the actual horse racing part of owning a racehorse."

"Hard to fathom, isn't it?" Wes said, watching Julia's face.

"What am I doing wrong with that chick?" Lance asked. He was watching Vanessa—still talking a mile a minute to poor Evan—with a lovesick expression that surprised even Wes.

"Maybe thinking of her as a chick is a bad place to start," Wes replied. Julia twisted her mouth into a smirk, and he could see she was having trouble not responding.

"You gotta give me some pointers, dude." Lance's tone had turned sardonic. Wes hoped he wouldn't openly say what he'd implied. "How do I get someone as hot as Jules here to give me the time of day?"

"You know, Julia's Vanessa's best friend. I'm sure she could advise you." Wes grinned, pretending there wasn't more to Lance's words. He spotted a "rescue me" look on Evan's face and grabbed a bottle from one of the ice buckets and left Julia to deal with Lance.

"You look parched, Vee. How about a refill?" Wes poured Champagne into Vanessa's glass. He wanted Lance to think he'd gone to talk to her and not Evan, but he spared a quick wink at Evan, giving him a chance to escape. With a grateful nod, Evan made a beeline for the bathroom.

"Thanks, Wes. You are a perfect gentleman."

"Thank you for noticing." Wes sat on the couch in Evan's spot, still warm from Evan's body. The heat reminded him of their plans, and he hoped everything would go smoothly.

"So, Wes, I'm loving owning Twist, you know. I want to buy a few more horses. I was talking to Evan about my options."

"What did he think of your plan?"

"He doesn't really talk much, you know? But he says a lot with a few words."

The description summed Evan up pretty well. "Which means?"

"He's going to look out for some horses for me to claim."

Wes wasn't sure how to react. Part of him wanted to keep Evan to himself, to be the only one of his friends who had any ties to him. But Evan needed more horses in his stable. Vanessa could afford to buy enough horses to replace the ones whose owners pulled them out.

"That's great. If you're sure you want to."

"I do. I was going to give him a check. Told him to just buy what looked good, but he won't buy without my explicit approval."

"He's pretty honest."

"A little too honest. I almost got the impression he didn't want to deal with me." Her voice rose and Wes was surprise to hear the hurt in her tone.

"He's also not the best salesman when it comes to these things."

"You two get along *so* well. Would you put in a good word for me?" She batted her eyelashes at Wes, bouncing back to her usual ebullient self.

He grinned. "Yeah, sure."

"Thanks." She pinched Wes's cheek. "You're a sweetheart."

"I know."

Vanessa went to get some food and stood talking to Julia and Lance. Evan came out of the bathroom and headed for the buffet as well. He didn't even look at Wes, sitting alone on the couch. Wes got up and headed for the others.

With Vanessa's attention, Lance was fairly good company. He didn't aim any more digs at Evan or Wes. Perhaps Julia had admonished him. Wes couldn't wait to find out what she'd said.

EVAN GLANCED around the room. He'd been at the party for less than two hours, and he was mentally exhausted. He was also physically worn out. He'd been up since four that morning, and it was closing in on eight. Not particularly late, but it had been a trying and emotional day.

Vanessa and Julia introduced him to several people and formed a barrier between him and the insensitive, odious Lance. Every time the guy opened his mouth, Evan could see Wes cringe. Clearly his acting skills deteriorated when he was personally involved. How had Wes ever become friends with him?

Evan was chatting with Julia and Theresa, one of Vanessa's San Francisco friends, when he spotted Wes across the room. Wes was on the phone, one finger stuck in his ear. The music and voices were just loud enough to make conversation difficult. Wes caught Julia's attention and pointed to his phone and left.

"His agent," she told Evan and Theresa. "Hopefully, it's something good. They don't usually call on a Friday night."

Theresa was a writer of some sort and she went into a detailed diatribe on agents. Evan did his best to follow the conversation. Finally, he gave up. Wes still hadn't returned.

"Julia, I'm beat. I'm going back to my motel. Early morning," he said to Theresa.

"It's barely cocktail time on a usual night." Theresa put a hand on Evan's arm and squeezed. "Don't go just yet." She didn't take her hand off his arm. Boy was she barking up the wrong tree. Julia had an amused smirk she couldn't quite contain.

"Sorry. Maybe next time." He leaned in toward Julia and found himself giving her a hug and air kiss.

Get me away from these Hollywood people! Their bad influence was already rubbing off on him.

He nearly ran for the door, not even stopping to say good-bye to Vanessa. He knew she'd call him. Her kind always followed up when they were interested and wouldn't take no for an answer. He walked down the hall and past the elevator, all the way to the other end. He opened the door to the stairway and went down four flights. On the sixth floor, he went back into the hotel corridor and stopped in front of 602. He straightened his tie and knocked.

The door swung open, and Wes tugged him in and wrapped his arms around Evan's waist before the door was completely shut.

Evan leaned up for a kiss and pulled Wes close.

The kiss lasted a very long time. Evan was hot—overheated—and longed to take the damned tie off again.

"So what did your agent say?" Evan asked when he finally let go of Wes.

"He said I should lock the door and not let you out until tomorrow."

Evan grinned. "I like him already."

"The feeling's probably not mutual." Wes pressed his mouth to Evan's again and parted his lips. Evan let Wes push him up against the closed door, and he heard the bolt slide in, making the door vibrate against his back.

He let out a sigh as he took in Wes's taste and scent and felt heat radiating from Wes. Evan reached up and slid his hands beneath Wes's shirt, tracing fingertips against the smooth, firm flesh. Wes's weight pinned him, but he didn't want to be anywhere else.

Wes stepped back half a pace and took Evan's hand, dancing him away from the door and toward the couch.

"Why do you get to lead?" Evan asked.

"It's my room."

"Fair enough." Evan hadn't slow danced in a million years and never with another man. Wes actually knew what he was doing and skillfully maneuvered them around the room. All Evan had to do was keep from tripping on anything, and it felt like they were in a movie.

Cut.

Life wasn't like a movie, at least not for him. The momentary loss of concentration made Evan miss a step, and they both stumbled. But Wes's arm around Evan's waist tightened so he didn't fall, and Wes barely missed a beat. He leaned down to kiss Evan, but that wasn't as successful.

"No wonder no one kisses while they're waltzing." Wes said, stopping, slightly breathy.

"We were waltzing?"

"In my mind we were waltzing. In reality, I don't think anyone would put a name to that step."

Evan laughed. How could Wes always put him at ease, no matter what? Almost. He still hadn't forgotten that sickening moment the day before when he was certain the sky really was falling. But Wes had swooped in and played the part of hero yet again. Would everything with Wes be a rollercoaster of emotion?

They were at the foot of the king-size bed. Wes let go of Evan for a moment and glanced at it. The spread had been peeled back, and a pile of foil-wrapped chocolates sat on each pillow.

"Would you like to stay, Evan?" Wes's voice had a surprising waver, as if he wasn't sure how Evan would respond. They'd planned this. Was he giving Evan a way out—or himself?

"I want to stay. This is so much better than the celebration upstairs."

"Evan, I want this to be a celebration too. I want to celebrate you."

"Us. This should be a celebration of us."

"To us." Wes gave Evan a kiss, passionate, but not hungry or deep. It was exactly how Evan felt. He wanted to be with Wes tonight, on their way to starting their relationship more officially.

"So what did your agent say? About us?" Evan asked as he started on Wes's shirt buttons.

Wes pulled one of Evan's hands away for a kiss then let it go again. "You really want to know?"

"Of course."

Wes peeled Evan's jacket off and was loosening his tie. "You want to stop this and have that conversation?"

"No way." Evan yanked the front of Wes's shirt—not caring about the last two buttons his fingers just couldn't manage to work. Wes laughed and pulled Evan's shirt over his head.

They worked at each other's belts as they kissed until they wore nothing but underwear, Wes in silky blue boxers that almost exactly matched his eyes, Evan in dark gray boxer briefs that announced his arousal. Wes glanced down at him with a beautiful emotion shining in his eyes. Even in the low light of the room, it warmed and brightened Evan.

Wes stepped forward and hooked his thumbs into Evan's waistband. The warmth of his fingers, the gentle caress against his hips, made Evan suck in a breath. Wes slid his hands inside, palms against Evan's ass, and pushed the shorts down until they shimmied down Evan's legs on their own.

From Wes's smile, he liked what he saw. He stepped forward and wrapped a hand around Evan's cock—loosely, but enough to engage every nerve ending. Evan's balls ached, and he felt his cock throb with each beat of his heart. His nipples tingled, and all he wanted was for Wes to never take his hands off.

Wes leaned down for a kiss, still holding Evan's cock. He didn't tug or squeeze, exerting just the right amount of pressure to flip every switch in Evan's body. Evan pulled away from the kiss and lay down on the bed, on his side, facing Wes.

"Your turn." Evan made a motion with his finger in the direction of Wes's erection, tenting his boxers out sufficiently for Evan to estimate what lay beneath. He shuddered with delicious anticipation.

Wes let out a soft chuckle and turned his back to Evan, slid the shorts down to reveal his ass—A+ in Evan's opinion—then slid them back up and turned around. The little tease eased some of the tension between them. So much had led up to this, Evan felt worse than on any opening night.

Wes slid his boxers down unselfconsciously and let Evan look at him. His cock had an upward curve and he was cut, which Evan hadn't expected. Evan was no good at guessing cock sizes, but he liked what he saw. And he would like how it felt, and that was what really mattered.

Evan held his hand out, and Wes climbed onto the bed and lay next to him. They kissed again, and their cocks rubbed together. Wes rolled Evan onto his back and leaned down to lick at a nipple. He took it fully into his mouth and probed it with his tongue and sucked, and the pleasure overwhelmed Evan.

"I've been thinking about doing that all day. More than all day." Wes licked at the other. "Pretty pink. Like sweets."

Evan let out a choking sound, and Wes let go. "Did I hurt you?"

"No. Just I'm locked and loaded here. I don't want to lose it too soon. You're killing me here."

"Rather the opposite of my intentions." Wes slid back toward Evan's head and brushed hair off his forehead—a gentle, intimate gesture. "What would you like me to do for you?"

For you. Not *to* you. Or "lie there till I'm done." Evan didn't even know how to respond.

"Let's simplify. Top or bottom? Or would you like a blow job?"

The word sounded so dirty with Wes. Because for Evan, this wasn't about sex, not just about sex. It was much more. "Bottom."

"I go both ways."

Evan nodded. "Do you have…?"

"Yeah." He nodded toward the nightstand, then reached over to pull a box of condoms and a tube of lube from the drawer. Evan took the lube from him. "What can I do?" Wes asked.

"Watch?" Evan let out a laugh because he didn't know what else to do. At least if he lubed himself, there would be plenty. A shiver went through him at the memory of that last morning with Gary. He swallowed, willing himself to forget it, or he'd never relax enough for Wes. Then a cold, sick feeling washed over him. That was the day he'd met Wes. Out on the porch. He recalled how their gazes met and the look in Wes's eyes. Only it wasn't pity. It was something unexpectedly positive. "Hang in there." Something words couldn't quite express.

And Wes had never once mentioned that day, that moment. But he knew Gary hadn't been good to Evan. Or good for him. How did Wes see below the surface?

Evan slicked his fingers and spread his legs to apply lube. Wes watched as if he'd never seen this before. He reached for the tube and squeezed a lot of lube into his hand. Was he planning on getting more than a few fingers or his cock in there? Evan's hole squeezed shut of its own accord. He was not into fisting—and definitely not ready to even consider it on a first time. Was Wes really kinky under his vanilla exterior?

"Let me help." Wes waited for Evan to nod approval, then applied some lube. He didn't do a very smooth job, and Evan laughed again. Could it be macho star Wes Tremayne really didn't know what to do with a man in bed? They hadn't discussed past experiences yet. Evan wouldn't mind showing him how things worked. It would be better than dealing with any bad habits. The thought made him smile; Wes already came out far ahead of Gary.

Wes pushed a few fingers inside and took an inordinate amount of pleasure in the task, to the point of embarrassing Evan. He wasn't really used to that much activity in there. But it felt good, and there was more than enough lube. "I think we're good to go."

"Now you help me?" Wes balanced on his knees and pushed his cock—still hard as a rock and now pointing straight out—in Evan's direction. Evan squeezed and tugged, though it wasn't necessary. But it was fun, and Wes obviously enjoyed the attention. Evan reached down to play with his balls. Wes ripped open the condom and started rolling it down.

"Back or front?" Evan asked.

"What?"

"You want me—"

"On your back, facing me. Of course."

Of course.

Evan lay back and Wes lay on top of him. He wanted to kiss first and play with Evan's cock until he was really hard again. Then he shifted position and lined up and pressed himself to Evan's entrance.

WES PAUSED before pushing inside. He glanced down into Evan's face. His eyes were closed. Wes sat back on his heels.

Evan opened his eyes. "What's wrong?"

"Nothing." Wes looked down at Evan, from his face down his body. He felt he was missing something he'd never get back if they started out here. He pulled the condom off. "We'll get back to that later."

Evan raised himself to his elbows, eyes wide, wary. Wes could see hurt and fear mingled with surprise. He lay down on top of Evan and kissed him. He didn't want to talk right now. He wanted to get to know Evan in every single way first. They could make love later, but there would never be another first time for them to be together, and suddenly even making love was no longer the main event tonight.

Most of Wes's experiences had been with sex partners, not boyfriends or lovers. It had always been about getting off. For the first time, Wes's priority was to make Evan feel great. He wanted nothing more than to please Evan. That would make Wes feel good too. He kissed Evan and held him tight, knowing Evan felt he'd somehow failed Wes if Wes didn't want to fuck him.

As they continued to kiss, Evan relaxed again, and Wes moved lower, kissing his throat and shoulders before visiting Evan's nipples again. He loved the way Evan arched against his mouth, letting out whispery gasps and moans.... When Evan tangled his fingers in Wes's hair, he knew he was finally giving in and letting himself enjoy this.

Lower, to Evan's navel. Wes flicked his tongue inside and then traced the trail of almost invisible hair as it led below Evan's waist. Wes lifted his head and looked at Evan's cock. It was perfectly shaped with just a slight curve. The head was smooth and plump, and all Wes wanted was to taste it, to taste Evan.

He leaned down again and licked along the underside, causing Evan to make some delightful noises. Wes glanced up to see Evan watching him. He went back to his task, exploring every inch of Evan with hands and mouth and eyes before he finally took Evan completely into his mouth. Wes glanced up again. Evan was leaning on his elbows, head thrown back.

Wes smiled around Evan's cock. He'd never taken this much time before, but he'd never cared to get to know much about a sex partner before. He learned what Evan liked most and how each part of him tasted. He played with his balls and slid a couple of fingers inside. Evan was slick and ready, and Wes's fingers encountered no resistance. He couldn't coordinate his fingers and his mouth no matter how hard he tried. When he stroked Evan inside, he felt him tremble and come with little warning beyond Evan tugging at his hair.

He sucked through Evan's orgasm, still stroking inside, until he'd swallowed everything Evan had to offer. Then Evan let out the sweetest sigh and tugged Wes off him. He slid up Evan's body and pulled him close while he listened to Evan catch his breath. At least now Wes knew Evan did enjoy being penetrated. He wouldn't have to wonder whether Evan wanted to bottom, or felt he had to.

Evan clung to him, making Wes feel like the luckiest man in the world. He didn't even mind that Evan fell asleep, face pressed against Wes's neck.

IT WAS still dark when Wes woke. It certainly wasn't the alarm going off or daylight that woke him. He felt warm hands and wet lips around his cock and smiled. What better way to be awoken. He didn't even care what time it was. Evan glanced up, his smile visible even in the dim room.

"Come here?" Wes wanted to hold Evan, kiss him a while, but Evan shook his head and kept working on Wes's cock. Wes played with his hair instead, feeling the silky strands of Evan's sun-streaked hair between his fingers. Evan's tongue worked magic as his fingers drew fiery trails along Wes's ultrasensitive skin. He didn't even try to fight back the pleasure as it slowly rolled through him until he was totally overwhelmed.

"Oh, ah, now," he warned Evan, but he didn't pull off, and Wes felt Evan's throat tightening as he swallowed. He lay back, unable and not particularly wanting to move as he let himself enjoy Evan's gift. Finally, he found words. "Evan, thank you."

Evan slid up and nestled himself against Wes's chest and side and let Wes pull him in for a kiss.

"Is it morning?"

"Close enough. I woke up and realized you let me sleep last night, leaving my work unfinished."

Wes took Evan's chin so he could look into his eyes. "Evan, you never need to feel as though you have to reciprocate. If it's 'work' then—"

"No, it's not what I meant. Besides, 'work' doesn't have to mean something is unpleasant. I love my job." Evan grinned, and Wes didn't know if he meant his work with horses, or in giving Wes a blowjob.

"Can I offer you anything this morning?" Wes grinned and slid a hand down Evan's chest, but Evan took his wrist before he got past his navel.

"Later. First...."

"First?" Wes kissed him again, but Evan broke the kiss quickly.

"Can we talk first?"

"Of course."

"What did your manager say?"

Wes nodded. Evan deserved to know. "I talked to him when I was in LA, and he's setting up a meeting with the studio and network for next week. He wants to give them a heads up."

"Are you going to make an announcement?"

"Do you want me to?"

Evan stared at Wes. "Would that matter?"

"Yes. Evan, this is for us. At least that's how I look at it. Am I wrong?" Wes felt a twinge of worry. Had he moved too fast with Evan? Should he wait until Gary had moved out and Evan was completely free?

"No. I want us to be together, not hiding from the studio or your fans or the press. That would quickly ruin anything between us."

Wes agreed.

"But no, you don't have to tell the world or bring me into it, if that's what you're asking. I'm happy to remain in the background. But I'm worried you think I'm forcing you into this."

"Julia's been after me for months to stop hiding. I just never had any reason until I met you. Now I know what I'd be missing. I never met anyone worth the risk before."

"But there is a risk," Evan said, voice barely louder than a whisper.

Wes kissed the top of his head and tightened his grip around Evan.

There definitely was still a risk.

CHAPTER 17

EVAN TOOK Wes's rental car back to the motel to change for the track. Wes's friends were heading to San Francisco after lunch to spend a couple of nights there before returning to LA. Wes would go along for the afternoon, but come back to the Berkeley hotel in time to have dinner with Evan. He wondered what Wes would tell his friends.

As he knelt down to check Twist's legs, a mass formed in the pit of his stomach. The horse was fine, just a tiny bit of heat in one fetlock—the lower joint on the forelegs. He'd worry only if another round of ice didn't eliminate it. Twist's condition didn't overly concern him, nor did Wes making excuses to his friends, or even what the network would say.

Evan still hadn't told Wes he'd heard from Gary.

"Coming home next week" was the whole message.

It was too neutral, too impersonal. Part of Evan was glad he could get Gary out, but another part felt offended Gary hadn't addressed Evan's request to move out. Didn't he care? Didn't he want Evan to change his mind?

It had taken Evan a long time to admit their relationship had deteriorated so badly the word no longer applied. Far longer than it had taken Gary to grow tired of him, or bored, or simply apathetic. He suspected the only surprise to Gary was that Evan had said anything at all....

Nothing to fight for. Nothing to salvage.

Now nothing to stand in the way between Evan and Wes.

Or was there? As Evan cleaned out Lola's stall, his body was on autopilot, but his mind raced. Wes hadn't given details of what his manager had said or planned. But now, in the light of day, not in Wes's warm embrace, the enormity of Wes's decision loomed over Evan. He didn't want to put Wes's career in jeopardy. One day—possibly quite soon—Wes would move on. Would he consider the time with Evan to be worth it?

Evan had so easily fallen for Wes in the first few times they'd met, despite his abhorrence of nearly everything he believed Wes stood for and strived for. Evan had seen the real man under the Hollywood façade he realized he'd only imagined. Wes wasn't a walking persona; he was a kind, caring, honest man with principles and an amazing ability to give people what they really needed, not what they wanted. He'd made Evan feel better about himself in an hour of discussion over lunch than Gary had in the last several years.

It would be even easier to fall in love with Wes, and Evan suspected he was at least halfway there.

But what did Wes see in him? Would Wes really risk his career—one he'd dreamed of and worked toward more than half his life—for Evan? He said he would, but Evan didn't want Wes to resent him if things didn't work out.

He pulled his phone out of his pocket and dialed.

Wes's phone went to voice mail. Of course, he was out with his friends.

"Wes, it's Evan. I was thinking maybe you shouldn't...." He didn't know what to say. Evan hung up without finishing the message. He balanced his pitchfork against the wall of the stall and closed his eyes, remembering the night and morning with Wes. They still hadn't made love "officially." But Evan felt more connection and emotion from Wes than he'd gotten for a long time. It would just get better and better.

Evan didn't want to give that up, but he knew it was the right thing—for Wes.

AN HOUR later, Evan was in Twist's stall, unwrapping the ice packs from his legs and examining him for any residual heat or injury.

"Let's take you for a little walk," he told the horse and snapped the lead to his halter. They had just stepped out of the stall when Evan heard an unexpected voice.

"Where are you going with my horse?"

Evan swung around to see Wes striding toward him in Evan's favorite pair of jeans and his boots. Wes came up and hugged Evan, right in the middle of the barn. Then Wes kissed him, and Evan didn't trust his knees to hold him up. Luckily, Wes still had a good grip around his waist.

"How's Twist this morning?" Wes asked as if this appearance was nothing special.

"A little heat. I'm just going to walk him around a little and see how he's moving."

"Let me."

Evan nodded. Wes led the horse outside. He'd apparently learned a lot in a short time. As Evan watched, Wes walked Twist between the barns, up and back, then did another pass at a jog, just as he'd seen Evan or the grooms do. When Wes brought Twist back, Evan slid his hands down Twist's legs again, then straightened up.

Wes repeated the movements. "A little warm on the inside near foreleg?"

Evan nodded. "The ice didn't eliminate it, but he's moving just fine."

"So, is there a treatment? Some meds?"

"No. Just another day off and some easy walking to stretch his muscles. I don't think a shot is the answer to every ache or pain. Like I said before, human athletes are sore after a hard workout or race. The difference is the horses can't treat themselves. I have to do what's best for them, and it's not drugs."

"Okay, I get it."

Evan hadn't realized he'd raised his voice, but the topic was one that infuriated him. He was in the minority, and he didn't care who disagreed with him. "Sorry about that."

"I'm glad you do. I knew you were a good choice to train him. I trust you to take good care of him and do what's best for him."

"Thanks. You want to walk him around for about ten or fifteen minutes?"

"Yeah." Wes clucked to Twist and they went off.

Evan relaxed. His care was one of the reasons his horses won, even if they raced less frequently. He paid attention to what they needed and didn't use meds to get them ready to race on his schedule.

The thought reminded him of something Gary had said before he left, about running Jet on his birthday. Gary was coming home next week. Evan watched Wes, now two barns away. He wouldn't mention Gary just yet. It might not even matter. Evan would wait until the end of the weekend to decide what to do about Wes. He should let Wes go, and Evan was being selfish not saying so now, but he wanted just another day or two of Wes's warmth and companionship.

Wes and Twist made their way back toward Evan, Wes grinning at the horse and occasionally catching Evan's eye. He looked so peaceful, happy, as if he really enjoyed being at the track with his horse. And the looks he gave Evan went straight to his heart every time, skewered him into helplessness.

How long before Wes got bored with horses, and Evan?

CHAPTER 18

WES SENSED something with Evan when he arrived at the track Saturday morning. The cryptic half message worried him. Evan's tone was shaky, and Wes had to know what was wrong. Evan hadn't seemed particularly thrilled with his arrival.

Wes couldn't wait to pull him into his arms, so he did, not caring who saw. Soon it wouldn't matter. Despite his qualms, now he was completely on board for being totally open and public. Evan made him feel like he'd been awarded an Olivier—Britain's Tony Award. No, *better*. And Wes knew because he'd won both. With those accomplishments behind him, he could give up the chance for another, because Evan made him feel so much more special.

As he walked Twist around the backside, he watched Evan's face. Something roiled beneath the surface, something he wasn't sharing with Wes. Something new. This wasn't the old pain Evan had buried deep and Wes had almost unearthed. The new problem was something *Wes* had caused. He would have to wait for Evan to tell him.

"He's moving well, Evan? What do you think?"

Evan slid a hand to the warm spot again. "No change. Can you manage another ten?"

"Okay." Wes turned to Twist. "C'mon, mate, let's take another spin." He smoothed a hand down the horse's sleek shoulder, and they did another circuit.

Some people waved or nodded at him. He wasn't sure if it was because they'd seen him here with the horses or from his show. No one asked for an autograph, so he suspected they weren't fans. He liked having a group who were beginning to accept him for himself and not his connections. What would they think when they found out he was seeing Evan?

For the first time, Wes was looking forward to finding out. He couldn't wait for the meeting with the studio the following week.

He brought Twist back after another ten minutes of walking.

"Still the same. Let's put him back away for now."

"What about the heat?"

"It stayed the same. I'd worry if it was worse after walking. If he's not back to normal tomorrow, I'll call the vet." Evan put Twist into his stall and checked his food and water. "When are you meeting your friends?"

"I'm not." Wes waited to see Evan's reaction.

"What?"

That wasn't the reaction Wes had hoped for. He wanted a "Really?" or a flicker of joy. Evan looked like he'd been shanked. "I told them I was tired, and I wanted to watch Percy work tomorrow. I didn't want to keep running around. Plus, I don't want to drive back to LA with them—with Lance."

Evan nodded and moved to the next stall. Wes peered at the water. It was full. "Evan, the grooms just fed and watered all the horses. What's wrong?"

"Nothing." Evan rubbed the horse's neck over and over, like a robot.

"Want to grab a bite? I'll bet you haven't had lunch. Everyone else had their break, and the horses are fed. Now it's your turn."

The loudspeaker crackled and belted out an announcement for the horses in the first race of the day.

"Lunch." Evan mouthed the word like it was in a foreign language.

Ricky was sweeping straw from the walkway into a pile near the door. He stopped and said, "I've got things under control here, boss. You don't even need to come back to feed dinner. I'll have Sticks take care of it."

"I need to check on Twist."

"You'll get a full report." Ricky shooed Evan away. "It's Saturday. Have a real night off for a change."

Wes had the feeling Ricky was encouraging Evan to have some fun with Wes. Whether he suspected just what kind of fun it might be was another issue.

"Okay, you've talked me into it." A smile finally brightened Evan's face.

"I've got the hire car." Wes moved toward the barn door. He stood at the entrance as Evan grabbed his bag from the office. They didn't speak until they were at the car. Wes clicked the locks open and settled into the driver's seat.

When Evan sat down, Wes put his hand over Evan's. "You okay? I'm kind of worried about you."

"No, I'm fine. Just trying to sort out some things going on back home."

"If you want to talk—"

"I don't."

Wes had never heard Evan use such a dismissive tone before. If he didn't want to discuss the issue, Wes wouldn't push him. Was it something about the night before? He pulled his hand off Evan's and held onto the gear knob instead.

"Are you sorry we spent the night together, Evan?" If the world could see him now. Wes Tremayne, newly minted television star, wondering if he had been good enough in bed. They would laugh. But the doubts had the opposite effect on Wes.

Evan spun his head toward Wes, and his features softened. "No. God, no." Evan reached for Wes's hand. "No. It was wonderful. You're wonderful." He squeezed tightly.

Wes's mobile started buzzing.

EVAN STARED at Wes and pulled his hand off the gearshift, bringing it to his chest. Confident, strong Wes hadn't looked so self-assured. He blinked a few times, and he sat back against his seat with a nauseated look on his face. Evan had wanted to push him away, and now he saw how much Wes really cared for him.

And it made Evan feel even more miserable. He didn't want Wes to doubt himself because he was one of the most amazing, honest, and genuine people Evan had met, not just in Hollywood—where he stood head and shoulders above everyone Evan had ever encountered—but anywhere. Wes had always focused on Evan, not himself, and he'd already risked so much.

Evan felt ungrateful and unworthy. He'd always dreamed of someone like Wes, and now the only way to be with him might destroy him. But pushing Wes away would hurt him too. Evan wasn't worth Wes giving up his career now, when he'd just had his first taste of Hollywood success and had such a bright future ahead.

The cell phone had been a welcome interruption. Wes's gaze met Evan's while he listened to someone on the end, someone practically shouting though Evan couldn't make out any of the words.

"Yeah, it's fantastic news," Wes said brightly into the phone, though his eyes were hollow. "Ring you when I know when I'll be back." Wes's face was drawn as he hung up. "Got some good news," he began.

Evan's gut twisted. This mess between them had dampened Wes's news. "Really?"

"*Zero Gravity's* been renewed for two more seasons and I'm in line for a raise. My agent's working on it now. This could fix everything, Evan. Saul's got some bargaining room when he negotiates my new contract."

"That's incredible news." Evan tried to sound cheerful. "Really, it is." Wes was headed for the top now, and rocking the boat had become more risky not less, but Wes just didn't get it yet. Evan was more determined not to hold him back, and he wished he could be celebrating with Wes instead of breaking up with him.

Wes just nodded, unconvinced.

"We should celebrate. Let's go somewhere now, Wes. San Francisco, wine country, the beach? Have you been across the Golden Gate Bridge?" Evan couldn't bear to upset Wes anymore, not today. Not tomorrow…. He'd save the truth for Monday, in enough time for Wes to call off the meetings with his manager and the network if necessary. The two-year pick up might just make the point moot. But whatever happened, this weekend would be one last special time for them.

"No. I've never been up here before, but I'd love to celebrate with you."

"You came back here instead of seeing the city in style with your friends?" Evan still couldn't fathom Wes's priorities.

"San Francisco isn't going anywhere. But I missed *you*." Wes's lips trembled again, and the only remedy was for Evan to kiss them. He leaned forward and pressed his mouth to Wes's, sliding one hand behind his neck and pulling him close. Wes was tense, shoulders rigid, but as Evan kissed him, he began to relax and wrapped his arms around Evan.

They held each other for a while, neither speaking, but Evan knew Wes's mood had shifted. "Where should we go?"

"Why don't you show me around?"

Evan nodded. "I'd love to. Under one condition."

Wes raised an eyebrow.

"You have to let me drive."

Wes got out, opened Evan's door for him, and slid into the passenger seat, finally smiling. Not the one he wore on his show, making millions of young women adore him, but a special, private smile Evan had come to crave.

THEY DROVE over the Bay Bridge and into San Francisco. Evan parked the car near the water, and they got lunch from a busy stall at the Ferry Plaza Farmer's Market and ate huge pork sandwiches within view of the Bay Bridge and Treasure Island. They spent a pleasant twenty minutes sampling fruit and other offerings at stalls, and Wes surprised Evan with a bright sunflower from one of the florists.

Stuffed and tired of the crowds, they got back in the car, and Evan drove through the city and over the Golden Gate Bridge. With the usual weekend traffic, he could spare a few glances at Wes enjoying the incredible view of the bay on one side, Pacific Ocean on the other.

"This is Sausalito," Evan told him on the other side of the bridge. The fog was advancing in waves and obscured their vision occasionally. "A ferry runs between here and San Francisco."

"I'd love to take the ferry."

"How about saving that for another day? There's somewhere else I'd like to show you." Guilt stabbed through Evan's chest at the lie. There wouldn't be another day, but he thought Wes would enjoy today's destination more. He swung through enough of the town to give Wes a taste of Sausalito, then drove to the Golden Gate National Recreation Area, winding high into the hills and coming out on his favorite panoramic view of San Francisco. He parked and they walked to the edge of the hills high above the city and the bridge.

"This is incredible." Wes put his arm around Evan. Wind whipped through their hair and they were underdressed for the location. But with Wes holding him, Evan felt warmth radiating through his whole body. Perhaps a bit too much. "We're so high above the bridge, and you can see all the San Francisco landmarks."

"And the fog."

"Yes, the fog. We have a bit of that back in London, you know."

"Ours is much more picturesque."

"Absolutely."

When Wes had his fill of the view, they drove back over the bridge and down to the Palace of Fine Arts in the Marina District. They walked past the small lake and watched swans elegantly gliding on a surface as still as glass. Several wedding parties posed for photographs while children ran or threw bread to the swans.

"This was part of the World's Fair, I think." Evan led Wes along a broken path down to a series of Greek-style domed buildings with high open arches. They encountered another wedding party.

"Let's take pictures too." Wes pulled his phone from his pocket and they moved through the structures, some in ruins held up with wire netting to keep them from crumbling. They ignored the signs warning them not to climb on the structures and took shots of each other and a "couple selfie." Evan held his breath when Wes asked another tourist to snap a photo of them, arms around each other's waists. The girl seemed to recognize Wes but didn't say anything or ask for an autograph.

For a while Evan felt as if they were a real couple, enjoying an afternoon at one of the most romantic settings in San Francisco. Could every day be like this? They sat near the edge of the lake to catch their breath after racing around the grounds. Wes was like a kid at Disneyland, boundless energy and curiosity about every aspect of the place.

"This place is gorgeous. I could live here." Wes lay back and stared at the sky. He held Evan's hand close to his body.

"Here at the lake, or in San Francisco?"

"Both. It might get a bit chilly living right here, though. None of those domes really has doors or windows. And the lack of privacy."

Butterflies took flight in Evan's stomach as Wes gushed about the place. And a little extra kick at his pronunciation of privacy: "priv-uh-cee" rather than the American "pry-va-cee." Despite Evan's acting experience and practice with accents, he couldn't get enough of listening to Wes speak.

Wes pulled Evan down so he lay on his side next to Wes. Then Wes tugged him closer, but Evan resisted.

"No, Wes. Not yet. We've already been too public today."

Wes's smile drained away. "You're right. I just want to kiss you so much, right here and right now."

"I know," Evan said, hoping Wes would get the *Star Wars* reference.

Wes burst into laughter and Evan joined in. God it felt so good to hear Wes laugh, to be able to laugh with him. Evan drew in oxygen because he felt as if all the air had gone out of the world when Wes stopped smiling. "Later. I'll collect double on that."

"Fair enough. Let's talk about dinner, then how about a jazz place?" Evan didn't know what kind of music Wes liked. How wonderful it would be to have forever to discover every little thing about him. He pushed the thought out of his head.

"I'm not hungry yet. How about a drink? Take me to Castro Street." Wes sat up and reached for Evan's hand.

"No. That's just not a good idea. You'll be looking over your shoulder the whole time."

"No, Evan, I won't."

"One of us has to use common sense. It won't be much longer, and we can come back here. I'll be at Golden Gate Fields the rest of this month and then again in the fall. You'll come up to watch your horses run, won't you?"

"Of course." Wes looked into Evan's eyes with an expression that conveyed much more than a kiss.

It took all of Evan's willpower to resist. "Now dinner? Chinatown, North Beach for Italian food, or the Mission for Latin American. What do you like?"

"Anything is fine. You choose."

"You have to pick one." What did Wes like to eat? So far they'd eaten at places near the track without much thought to the food.

"I love Italian food. Pasta. Homemade ravioli or gnocchi. Know a good place for that?"

"I do. But first, there's a great bar on the top of Mark Hopkins. It's the perfect place to watch the sunset. Or we could go out to the beach and watch from a local place that's not so fancy."

"Let's go to the posh bar."

They had drinks at the Top of the Mark, an elegant spot on the top floor of one of the most expensive hotels in the city. Then to North Beach for dinner. They strolled along Columbus Avenue, past Italian bakeries showcasing mouth-watering arrays of pastries in the window.

"Maybe we should skip dinner and go directly to dessert." Wes stared at some chocolate-dipped cookies and let out a little moan.

"Let's get something for later." They went inside where there were even more items to choose from. They couldn't agree on what to get so they got one each of several different delights: chocolate-dipped biscotti, pignoli, amaretti, and a huge slice of tiramisu....

Wes held on to the bag, and Evan saw him sneaking a cookie. "Hey, you'll ruin your dinner." Evan took custody of the bag.

"You have one too." Wes took the bag back and they each fished out a cookie.

The amaretto had the perfect crunchy outside and light inside. Evan immediately wanted another. This time Wes folded the bag shut and kept it out of Evan's reach.

They went down a side street and around the corner to a nearly deserted narrow street, a stark contrast to busy Columbus Avenue, swarming with tourists.

Dinner was wonderful. They shared lobster ravioli, gnocchi with fresh tomato sauce, and roast chicken. Because this place was full of locals, no one asked Wes for an autograph, though several recognized him and waved or said hello politely. Many celebrities lived in San Francisco and valued their privacy when they went out, and residents were used to seeing them.

"This was such a great choice," Wes said, finishing the last of his wine. "I never would have found it. I'd have ended up eating on Columbus with the world and his wife."

Wes had enjoyed every place Evan had taken him, snapping photos, asking questions, and making jokes. But never once had he asked whether Evan had come here with Gary or someone else. Evan liked how Wes didn't dwell on the past or make Evan's history a major topic of discussion.

"The jazz place is on the next street. It used to be a secret, but maybe it's gotten too popular. I haven't been for years."

They got there early enough to get a table, but the place was small and got crowded as the evening went on. They ordered drinks and held hands under the tiny table as they enjoyed the music.

During the second set, Evan couldn't help yawning. Wes bent close to his ear. "You must be exhausted. We should go."

As much as he hated for their perfect day to end, Evan nodded, and they headed for the car. "I'm sorry. I'm just not used to staying up so late."

"It's fine. I know you didn't get a full night's sleep last night." Wes quirked one corner of his mouth.

"Yes, Cinderella's about to turn into a pumpkin."

"Either you're very tired or your parents played a spectacular joke on you."

"Probably both." Evan laughed as they strolled through Washington Park Square—a green refuge in the heavily built-up city.

Wes stopped. "I'm the one who feels like Cinderella today, visiting a magical new world."

Wes looked up at the night sky, too foggy to see any stars. Birds and insects chirped from the trees lining the park. Evan could see he didn't want to leave just yet, didn't want to break the magical spell. Evan's throat tightened.

"No, not Cinderella," Wes suddenly said. "Like Audrey Hepburn. The princess in *Roman Holiday*, being shown a new side to everything. You've taken me on such a tour today I'm dizzy. It's been the best day I can remember."

Evan just nodded because he didn't trust his voice. Wes was exactly like the princess, usually the center of attention and unable to experience the city as herself. Wes wasn't exactly invisible, but today he'd put away his celebrity and been himself. Evan took Wes's hand and pressed a kiss to it, then hand in hand they walked to the car.

CHAPTER 19

WES DROVE back across the bay. It was nearly midnight, and Evan could barely keep his eyes open. He'd slept only a few hours in the past twenty-four, and he wouldn't have it any other way.

Today had been wonderful. Better than he'd imagined, and he felt his resolve wavering. Did he have the strength to leave Wes behind? If he didn't, and Hollywood spit Wes out like a rotten apple, how long before Wes blamed him and everything would be ruined? This way, they'd fast-forward to the pain, without the irreversible damage to Wes's career.

They were in the hotel parking lot when Evan woke up, Wes's hand on his knee shaking him.

"You can sleep in the car, but I wanted to give you the choice." Wes squeezed Evan's knee. "You're welcome upstairs with me."

"I'm awake." Evan rubbed his face to kick-start his senses. They rode the elevator in silence, the air heavy with unspoken thoughts. As soon as they got inside Wes's room, they crashed together, Wes's back against the door. Evan had never needed to kiss anyone as much as he needed Wes at that moment.

Wes reciprocated. As their tongues tangled and they fought for breath, Wes's hands slid beneath Evan's shirt and pressed against his back, burning through the skin. Then Wes smoothed them toward Evan's chest, higher, until he could rub his thumbs across Evan's nipples.

Evan groaned. If he hadn't already been rock hard, that would have done it. He thrust his hips against Wes, feeling his hipbones and cock rigid against him. He tried to unbutton Wes's shirt, but with his tongue, hands, and hips hitting all of Evan's hot spots, he lost control of his fingers. The last stubborn button remained between him and Wes, and he gave up and ripped it away.

He felt laughter bubble up through Wes's body. "You really don't… like my… shirts." He breathed out the words against Evan's lips.

They removed each other's clothes without further incident, and Evan backed toward the bed, forcing Wes along with him.

Then Wes stopped. He pulled his mouth off Evan's and looked down, brushing hair from Evan's face. Why had he stopped? Evan was so ready right now.

"Evan, I want you to come back to LA with me for a couple of days. Be there for the meetings. There's no racing till Thursday, so…." He emphasized his request with a soft kiss, then continued. "I want to be with you so much, but…." Wes's chest heaved against Evan's as he took two deep breaths. "I don't want to make love with you in this hotel—any hotel. Come home with me, stay with me, in my bed."

Evan nearly bellowed. It had to be here, now. There would be no next week and no meetings, and Evan wouldn't be welcome in Wes's apartment or his bed. He opened his mouth, but Wes kissed his rebuff away. A firm "no" morphed into a "maybe" by the time it left Evan's lips.

"How about a shower?" Wes said, throwing Evan off his bearings. The way he firmly cupped Evan's arse meant this would be more than a shower.

They kissed until the water was warm enough and never let go as they moved inside the large glass-walled shower. Steam floated from their bodies and hovered above them, thickening the air, as warm and comforting as the fog over the Golden Gate Bridge had been cool and bracing.

Wes sudsed up a handful of body wash and applied it to every inch of Evan's body, down to the soles of his feet. He took his time, massaging each hand and arm and leg, with plenty of attention to the parts in the middle. His fingers were firm but gentle as he soaped Evan's balls and the cleft of his ass and slid his cock up and down again, sending more shockwaves through Evan's entire body. After a good rinse, Wes slid to his knees and took Evan's cock into his mouth.

"Not yet. Not too much," Evan whispered. When he got too close, he pushed Wes's head away. "Not quite yet."

Evan traded places, pushed Wes against the glass wall, and starting his explorations with Wes's cock. He traced its unique curve and tasted every part of it, leaving Wes shuddering but not letting him come. "Not yet," Evan said again. "Soon."

Still reversing Wes's actions, Evan soaped Wes, visiting each mound and valley of his muscular torso and legs, memorizing his curves and shallows the way he'd already memorized his taste. He kissed Wes, then pinned his arms above his head, pressing him against the glass, and turned down the shower spray. It was warm enough in the shower without it.

He slid along Wes's soap-slick torso, his cock gliding along Wes's thigh and up against his cock. They were both hard again, and Evan repeated the motion, up and down against Wes's body, just the right amount of friction as their cocks rubbed together. Wes sucked in his breath. With their height difference, Wes's peaked nipples drew lines a few inches above Evan's, and he pressed himself hard against Wes.

He was so close it wouldn't take much to reach climax, but Evan kept thrusting against Wes until he heard a little catch in his breath and Wes's eyes closed.

"Very soon. Very, very soon." Now Wes was meeting Evan's thrusts and moaning on each stroke. He let out a soft gasp and sprayed hot jets up Evan's abs and chest. Evan let Wes ride the wave for a few moments before taking his release.

When he let Wes's wrists go, Wes pulled him close, their come mingling on each other's chests. Evan slid down far enough to taste. Now his exhaustion caught up with him, and his knees buckled slightly. Wes caught him and held him up, then rinsed them clean and wrapped Evan in a soft, thick towel before half carrying him to bed.

They lay together, hair still wet, bodies warm and damp.

"That was the best shower I've ever had. Thank you, Evan." Wes kissed Evan's temple and snuggled close.

A RINGING cell phone woke Wes up. He was spooned up behind Evan, who had reached for his phone on the nightstand. Wes sat up enough to see the clock. Two seventeen. Who would be calling now?

"What is it?" Wes whispered, worried but not wanting to disturb Evan.

"Sorry," Evan mouthed and carried the phone into the bathroom.

Wes watched him, admiring the view of his arse as he walked away. What was he doing? There was an emergency and here he was perving on Evan. It must be something with one of the horses. He got up and went into the bathroom. Evan was perched on the edge of the bathtub.

"Call me back when the police leave, unless they want to talk to me. It's going to be fine, Nick. Take the keys and stay in my house if you're not up to driving home."

Wes couldn't hear Nicky's side of the conversation. He sat next to Evan and slid an arm around his waist for moral support.

"As long as no one's hurt. ... Check in the morning. ... Don't worry, just call, no matter the time."

Evan spent another few minutes and Wes waited. Evan let out a long sigh when he disconnected.

"What happened? Has someone been injured?"

"Not as far as Nicky can tell. She's been worried about that filly, Jet, so she decided to sleep in the barn. There's a stall with cots in case someone needs to stay with a horse overnight."

Wes nodded, not wanting to interrupt with the thousand questions racing through his brain.

"The dogs' barking woke Nicky, and she went outside to investigate. Apparently, someone had driven up to my house. She saw headlights, but by the time she started up the hill, the car drove away. Then she discovered the filly out of her stall, running down the driveway. In the dark she could seriously hurt herself. The filly's okay now, but she might have been injured, and we'll find out tomorrow. Anyway, Nicky called the police. They were pulling in when she hung up."

"Were they trying to steal her?"

"Only if they planned to ride her away. They didn't have a horse van."

Wes nearly smacked his head for overlooking that detail. "What were they doing?"

"I'm not convinced they were there for any mischief. The noise and dogs probably just spooked the filly, and she was able to get out of her stall. Frightened horses have a lot of strength."

"What can I do?"

"Nothing. I'm sorry for waking you up."

"I don't mind. I'm more worried about Nicky and the horses— and you."

Evan put on his stoic smile. Wes could recognize it now. "I'm fine. Let's try to get whatever sleep we can before I have to go to the track."

"Can you take the morning off?"

"I took half of yesterday off. I need to pull my weight, not throw it around."

The phrase amused Wes. "Okay, I understand."

They climbed back in bed and held each other tight to regain the warmth they'd lost standing on the cold bathroom tile.

"What time are you leaving for LA?"

"I thought we could leave after the horses' lunch, when you normally take a break."

"Wes, I can't go with you."

"Why not?" Wes felt a chill at his core. Like a ghost had settled inside him, scratching at his insides with icy fingers. "We can fly. Then you won't—"

Evan shook his head. "It's not—"

"I'll pay for the tickets."

"It's not the money, but thank you for the offer. Let's talk about this later. In the daylight."

Evan rolled away, but he scooted back against Wes's chest. It wasn't enough to push the icy ghost away. Evan wouldn't say what the issue was, only what it wasn't. Wes bit his tongue, quite literally, to stop from asking. He had to back off and give Evan space. He'd been pursuing Evan, following him up here and leaving his friends to come back to Evan. Wes had never been in love before, and he wasn't sure what it felt like. But rumor had it that it made you crazy. He had the crazy part down.

He lay quietly, remembering all the lovely places Evan had shown him yesterday. For all their fun, Evan had been slowing things down, at least in public. Inside—in bed—Wes was the one who wanted to take things slow, make everything special. He pressed closer to Evan and inhaled. Even though they'd used the same body wash, Evan still had his own special scent. It filled Wes's lungs, and he felt the ghost melting away.

NICKY CALLED back a little after four. When Evan went into the bathroom to speak with her, Wes didn't follow. He lay on Evan's side of the bed, absorbing his warmth from the mattress and blanket.

Evan came back and sat on the bed, stroking Wes's hair. "Don't get up just yet."

Wes stared up at Evan. The call hadn't put him at ease. His mouth was a tight line, and tension frayed the corner of his eyes. Wes put a hand on Evan's thigh. For more support, he told himself.

"Wes, I will go back with you today. Fly, drive, I don't care. Just want to be there before dark."

Wes sat up. "Why?"

"Nicky's a wreck. She insists on sleeping in the barn. The filly's stall door wasn't broken. The latch was opened. It's a horse-proof latch. We put it on because she got out of her stall before. Now it looks like something *is* going on."

The hair on the back of Wes's neck stood up. Horror movies and Stephen King novels didn't scare him. But this was real life. Something *was* going on.

"Let's fly. I'll get the tickets. I'll call a cab to take you to your hotel in time to go with the guys. Then I'll pick you up. I'll let you know what time."

"Okay. Thanks." Evan leaned down for a kiss that put Wes's worries at ease. Especially when he added, "I wish we had some extra time for a proper good morning."

"I'll let you tuck me in tonight…."

Evan gave a cryptic smile and turned to hunt for his clothes, scattered between the door and the bed.

Wes grinned as he watch Evan dress, this time not at all ashamed to be staring at his gorgeous boyfriend, a man who changed his plans only for horses. Wes chose not to take it personally that Evan had accepted his invitation only after Nicky's upsetting calls. Wes could wait to be with Evan, and he loved that Evan cared so much for his animals and his staff.

THEY FLEW out of Oakland, more convenient than SFO. Wes donned one of Evan's Golden Gate Fields caps, hoping to preserve a shred of anonymity. The crowds and lines in airports and the sheer number of people who recognized him were one reason he liked to drive. But time was of the essence today.

With three-days' growth of stubble, he'd lost the more instantly recognizable clean-shaven look fans were used to. The flight had been nearly full, and they couldn't get seats together. Even business class was booked up. At least it was only forty minutes in the air.

It was three thirty when they touched down and headed for the taxi stand. They cabbed to Wes's apartment. No delays, no huge traffic jams. Evan crossed his fingers, hoping his luck held out the rest of the day. The taxi deposited them on the sidewalk in front of Wes's building on a palm-tree lined street near the hills. Exclusive but affordable for up-and-coming stars who had outgrown a roommate but weren't ready for their own homes.

Wes shuffled his feet on the pavement. "Do you want a drink or something? Or should I take you home now?"

Evan glanced at his watch. He had plenty of time. That wasn't the issue. But Wes looked so forlorn and somehow so young suddenly. He still hadn't regained his usual confident demeanor.

"Water or something cold would be great."

"This wasn't quite how I wanted you to see my place." Wes fumbled with his keys at the street-level door. He opened it and picked up Evan's suitcase, then waved him in and closed the door behind them.

Evan remembered his own bachelor days and almost expected pizza boxes strewn all over the kitchen, tipped-over beer bottles dripping on the furniture and floors. But Wes didn't eat pizza.

Wes opened the door for Evan and followed him into the living room. The place was immaculate. Nothing seemed out of place. No bad smells, no stains on the floor or couch. Evan glanced around. "What were you worried about?"

"Oh, not worried. But if I'd had time to plan, I'd have bought you flowers or strewn rose petals around or something special."

Evan stared at Wes to see if he were joking, but the expression on his face jolted Evan's entire set of assumptions. He was Wile E. Coyote, and the Roadrunner had just dropped an anvil on his head. Rose petals? Flowers? Wes was completely serious.

Had Evan ever looked at anyone with the love radiating from Wes's smile? Evan had been waiting his entire life for someone to gaze at him with such open affection. He looked back on the past two days. Wes had told him in every way except words he was falling in love with Evan. But with his blinkers on, Evan had seen only his side of the equation.

The stunning realization didn't make him mock or belittle Wes's emotions. Instead, it set Evan's free. Free to receive what Wes wanted so badly to give him. Free to take Wes's kindness, concern, generosity, honesty, optimism, and sheer zest for life. Wes wouldn't have taken the chance with his career if he hadn't found Evan worthy of the potential costs and sacrifices.

That expression, everything Wes had said and done, washed away every doubt in Evan's mind. The doubts planted by Gary and the cruel and manipulative men he'd let use him and make him feel worthless without their attention and praise. With his mind clear, Evan's heart took control.

Wes was two feet away, reaching to hand Evan a glass of water. "Do you have time for a tour?"

Evan took the glass and put it down on the nearest surface, then pulled Wes close and let his heart and body pay back everything Wes had already given him. They fell to the couch, embracing, kissing, hands traveling under shirts, seeking skin.

"Can we start with the bedroom?" Evan said, hating to let go of Wes's mouth to get those six words out.

Wes nodded and stood. "Until now there's never been much to see in there."

"Show me everything."

THEY LAY facing each other, naked and needy. Evan couldn't remember getting out of his clothes. He had one hand wrapped around Wes's cock, thumb sliding across the slit and listening to the little sounds Wes made as he got more aroused.

"My bag."

"Forget your bag," Evan said.

"The condoms."

"Hurry up and get your bag."

Evan slicked and prepped himself quickly. They could take time and play later. Now he'd accepted there would be a later. That today wasn't the last time he'd be with Wes. He was ready to accept Wes and support him through what may come.

Wes knelt between Evan's knees and rolled the condom on. He was panting, and his nipples were hard swollen buds. Evan still had the taste of them in his mouth. He grabbed and pulled Wes toward him as if the world would stop turning if Wes didn't make love to him this exact second.

Evan put his legs up to give Wes better access and forced himself to relax. Wes caught his gaze then pressed the tip of his cock to Evan and, still looking into his eyes, pushed in slow and deep. Evan watched the smile bloom across Wes's face, living in the same moment, the same joy, and the same feeling that together they were so much better.

As Wes started to move, Evan let out a gasp at how well they fit together. No pain, just a perfect pressure filling him up. Wes slid in and out slowly, stopping to kiss Evan between strokes. Heat and pressure continued to build at Evan's core, and Wes was a little too tender and gentle. Evan thrust his hips to meet Wes's, and he soon got the message.

Slow and tender went out the window when Wes pushed in harder, rougher, forcing little groans and gasps from Evan. And Wes's hands were everywhere, gripping Evan's cock or pinching a nipple, holding his hips. Just as he was about to let himself go over the edge, Wes slowed.

"Care to try something else? What position do you like?"

"From behind?"

Wes slid out slowly and let Evan move onto hands and knees. A long time ago, he'd loved this position, and being with Wes blocked more recent memories of Gary until Evan was already in place, ass up, legs wide. It was too late to shift. As Wes hovered behind him, Evan felt a dark weight pressing on him, and he fought for breath as Wes slid in. He went deep and made small, slow thrusts, never moving more than a few inches. Evan arched his back, craning his neck back. Wes put a hand on his head and curled his fingers in Evan's hair without pulling. He traced along Evan's throat and neck while he pumped, and his hand came to rest on Evan's shoulder.

The pain was gone, but the memory flared up. He felt Wes tracing the skin. Had the scar healed yet? Evan wouldn't look. Wes leaned down, and Evan's gut clenched as his lips brushed the spot, but Wes only planted a soft kiss there.

"Let's change again."

Evan nodded and let Wes lay him down on his side and enter him from behind. Evan felt Wes behind him and relaxed, letting the first waves of pleasure ripple through his body. The buildup had been slow and steady, but he would come hard and fast and soon. He squeezed Wes's fingers as they gripped Evan's cock, and Wes shifted them again, back to the first position.

"Are you close?" Evan puffed the words out.

"Yes, but I want you to go first."

"Not together?"

"I want to watch you."

Now Evan felt self-conscious. He put a hand up over Wes's eyes, and Wes peeled the hand away. Wes closed his eyes and played with Evan's cock just the way he liked it.

"Did you come yet?" Wes asked, a grin spreading across his face, eyes still closed.

"Yes. Twice."

"Try for a third?" Wes opened one eye and Evan couldn't help laughing.

He closed his mouth, embarrassed.

"I love to hear you laugh."

"I'm not laughing at you—or this."

"I know. Now show me some fireworks." Wes tightened his grip and Evan was so very, very close. He gulped air and felt the ripples become a tidal wave. He came and came. Something in the way Wes kept brushing his cock against his gland prolonged the pleasure until Evan thought he'd explode in quite a different way.

Only then did Wes speed his strokes again and take his own pleasure. His soft groans sent delicious aftershocks up and down Evan's body. Wes rolled them onto their sides carefully, still inside Evan. Then he traced his finger through the glistening puddle on Evan's chest, now dripping slowly toward the bed.

"Now that was worth waiting for," Evan said.

"I agree. But I still can't wait to do it again."

"I'm not sure I could survive another round anytime soon."

"No. Not too soon. I should get you home." Wes started to pull out, and Evan stopped him.

"Wes, can you stay at the farm tonight?" Evan had no idea where the thought originated, but he loved the idea. His mouth spoke of its own accord when he was with Wes.

"For you or for Nicky?"

"A little of both."

"Sure. I'll call my manager from the farm to find out what time the meeting is. But first maybe a shower. Quick. No funny business."

"Scout's honor." Evan held up his hand in what he thought was the Boy Scout salute. "No funny business. Now, I could use that water."

"Let me get it for you." Wes rolled away slowly and stood, then padded into the living room.

"FUCK, WHAT the fuck are you doing here?" Wes got the shock of his life when he saw Julia sitting on the couch. She looked pretty shocked too, which probably had something to do with the fact he was naked. "I thought you were staying in SF till Monday."

"Your manager called mine for a meeting first thing tomorrow. I guess he's going to break the news to me that you're gay."

"I guess that will be our official breakup. I'm glad Saul is doing that for me. Why the hell didn't he include me in that meeting?"

Julia shrugged and stood up. "It's too bad. Now that I see what I've been missing." She dropped her gaze to his cock, but it was too late to be self-conscious. "Lucky Evan." She winked.

"But why are you *here*?"

"I left my car here when Vanessa picked us up, and I thought I'd use the bathroom."

"And you just stayed?"

"I'm sorry. I didn't realize you had company."

"The trail of clothes on the floor didn't clue you in?"

"Well, now that I look, I see two of everything. But I didn't look very closely." She held her hands up and shook her head. "Evan?" She mouthed.

Wes nodded.

"I guess your celebration lasted more than last night? Loved that pic you sent me. I'm thrilled about the renewal. And about Evan."

"Ta on both. Now get out of here." He heard the shower go on in his bathroom. "He's kind of shy, and if he knows you know he's here, well, you know."

"Okay. I'm going. You don't need to walk me to the door."

"Bye, Jules."

"Bye, sweetie." She blew kisses to him and fluttered her fingers, then left.

CHAPTER 20

AFTER THEY had showered and dressed, Wes packed up some more clean clothes. They were at the door when he started patting all his pockets.

"What did I do with my phone?"

They looked around the living room. "Here it is." Evan bent to retrieve it from under the coffee table and handed it to Wes.

"Thanks. I guess it fell out when I wasn't paying much attention." He gave Evan a look that made him want to drag Wes back into the bedroom. Later.

In the elevator to the garage, Evan steeled up his courage again. "There's just one condition on staying at my place."

"What's that?" Wes asked as they approached his car.

"You have to let me drive."

Wes grinned. "Very funny." Then the smile drained away. "You're serious? I'm not that bad."

"We'll practice on deserted country roads."

"Fuck you!" But Wes was smiling, so Evan didn't take it personally. He was relieved Wes could joke after the insult to his driving. Evan was shaky enough with whatever was happening at the farm, and he didn't need more agitation.

When they got to Evan's farm, they parked near the house and left the suitcases there before heading down the hill to the barn.

"I'm so glad you're back," Nicky said. Her boyfriend, Mark, hovered behind her. Evan was glad she wasn't alone, even during the day. Nicky glanced at Wes, and he gave her a nod but didn't say anything. Evan would tell her later if she hadn't figured it out on her own. It wasn't the most important issue today.

"Let's take a look at Jet." Evan went to her stall, and the others followed. The screw securing the metal latch on her stall wasn't loose. He ran his fingers over it, but the only conclusion was someone had opened it. Then he checked the filly for injuries, but she was fine, only a little spookier than usual.

"What do you think?" Nicky asked.

"We can hire a guard for the barn at night."

"Evan, that's so expensive." She glanced at Wes and Mark, then pulled Evan away for a private discussion. "Can we afford it?" She kept her voice to a whisper.

"Can we afford not to? What if someone or one of the horses is hurt? A guard might just scare them away. Let's do it for a week, and if nothing happens, we'll drop it."

Nicky nodded, but she was still pale and exhausted looking. "How much will it cost?"

"Don't worry about that." Evan would worry about that too. "We won some over the weekend with Twist, and you were in the money at Del Mar."

"Come on, our share of the purses is peanuts."

Evan made a snap decision. "I'll be getting a couple of new horses soon. It'll even out."

"Who?"

"Vanessa Vandermere wants to buy a couple. I'll be looking around while I'm down here this week."

"That's great." Her shoulders relaxed a little. "It was starting to feel like a ghost town around here."

"I'll sort out the guard. You go home and get some rest. I'll stay here until someone shows up."

"I can't leave you alone, Evan."

"Wes is here."

Nicky glanced over at Wes again. He was chatting with Mark, not paying Evan or Nicky any attention. "Wes is... oh. I see."

"That's not public information yet, okay?"

Nicky nodded, lips pressed together. She gave a disapproving look. "Gary?"

"That's over. I ended it. Before."

She gave Wes another sidelong look. "Well, congratulations, you lucky bastard."

"We'll see."

NICKY AND Mark left, and Evan and Wes went into the barn office.

"I know some bodyguard agencies. Let me get the numbers." Wes reached for his phone. "Okay, I had it before." He retraced his steps around the barn and came back with the phone. "Here you go." He read the numbers off, and Evan called the first one.

"He'll get here by seven and stay until six in the morning." Less than an hour to wait. Evan let out a sigh. The cost was more than he'd expected. He better find a horse for Vanessa soon.

"Great. Then I'm going to need some dinner."

"You did exert some energy this afternoon." Evan flashed Wes his approval of the experience. "There's not much in the house since I didn't expect to be back. So, pasta or delivery?"

"I don't care. As long as I have company."

Evan wasn't particularly hungry. Nicky's worries had rubbed off on him, and he'd lost his appetite.

THE GUARD arrived on time. Peter Martinez was an off-duty LA County deputy and occasional stuntman. He was as big and beefy as the occupations implied, but he was solid and fit. And he had a gun. Evan wasn't sure he liked that, but Peter should deter anyone who showed up unless they were also armed.

If he recognized Wes or Evan, he didn't let on. Evan appreciated the professionalism.

Evan showed him the filly and gave him a tour of the grounds with Wes tagging along silently. His presence felt as comforting as the guard's.

"I'll walk the barns, the perimeter of the barn and residence area, and keep an eye on the drive. If anything happens I'll notify you and the sheriff's office. Just to be safe, I recommend not wandering around during the night. If you want to come to the barn, call me to escort you down here."

"Okay. Thanks." Evan wasn't sure what to do now.

"You don't have to stick around."

"There's fresh coffee in the office and a bathroom in there."

"Got it." Peter gave him a little salute, and then Wes and Evan walked up the hill to the house.

THEY HAD a relatively satisfying dinner of homemade lasagna Evan found in the freezer and some frozen veggies.

"It's half-homemade," he said as they sat down to eat. They decided against beer or wine in case they needed to deal with any intruders later.

Wes wanted to be on Evan's schedule, so they went to bed by nine thirty. Evan phoned Peter, but so far, no sign of an intruder.

As they started down the hall to the bedroom, Evan stopped. Being with Wes, having him here, seemed so natural already, but in fact, it was their first time as an official couple in the home Evan had shared with Gary for nearly five years. He couldn't pretend Gary wasn't still very present, beyond his mere belongings.

"Can you wait a few minutes?" Evan asked. Wes went back to the living room while Evan changed the sheets. He'd already changed them a few times since Gary left, and he planned to buy new ones for Wes, but it was the best he could do on short notice. He glanced in the nightstand at lube and other things he and Gary had used. He wanted to throw all of his stuff away and anything that had been "theirs." It would take too long. Tomorrow. He tossed a few things into the trash and invited Wes in.

Wes seemed to understand Evan's worries.

"Should I just stay on the couch tonight?"

"No. I want you with me. I just wish…."

"I understand. If it's too soon or I pushed you, let me know."

Evan put his fingers on Wes's lips, then silenced him more effectively with a kiss. They slowly undressed each other and got under the sheets.

"Just cuddling is fine," Wes said against a spot behind Evan's ear that drove him wild.

They kissed for a while, until it was clear cuddling wouldn't be enough, then made slow, comforting love. They made love again after Evan's alarm went off at four. It would be torture to leave Wes in bed every morning. The thought warmed Evan after the months and years of eagerly getting out of bed with Gary. He really didn't need to be at the barn that early. He hired grooms and a foreman to oversee those tasks. Now he had a good reason to shift his work hours.

"Let me turn the coffee machine on, and I'll be right back." Evan slipped into his underwear.

"Why bother putting those on?"

"So you can take them off again."

"I like how you think." Wes let out a satisfied sigh.

Evan passed through the living room on the way to the kitchen and stopped dead in his tracks. His heart thumped as if were about to explode.

Gary was sitting on the couch.

"What are you doing here?"

"I live here."

"W-wh-why didn't you tell me you were coming? I didn't even hear you." Why hadn't Peter called Evan when Gary showed up?

"Yeah, you were occupied. In the literal sense."

Evan felt like ice water had just been poured down his back. "I told you it's over."

"Oh, I got that message loud and clear. Very loud."

Evan wouldn't let Gary manipulate him into guilt. It should be the other way around after his treatment of Evan.

"So the mighty, manly Wes Tremayne is on our team? I wouldn't have guessed it. He's a great actor."

"Wh-what do you want?" Evan felt years of weight pressing him down, crushing his heart, and soul, his new happiness. He hadn't stuttered in years, since junior high, but Gary rattled him so much he couldn't think straight. Gary could make things ugly by his very presence. Why had it taken so long to realize how toxic he had become? Wes was such a contrast, a new breeze blowing the ugly stench out of Evan's life.

"Just to pick up some of my gear. I'll be out of your hair in an hour, then we can arrange a time for me to come back for the rest."

"Th-that's it?" Evan realized his hands were shaking at his side.

"Yeah. Just one other thing." Gary held the pause so long Evan lived a whole lifetime waiting for the rest. "I still want you to run Jet. Soon."

Jet? He came to talk about the filly? "When she's ready. But I'm thinking of selling her, Gary."

"She's half-mine. I'm not selling my half."

"Why do you want her?"

"She's an investment, you could say." Gary stood up and seemed to tower over Evan. Was he that much taller? Wes had more than a few inches on Evan but never *loomed*. Evan breathed a small sigh when Gary went into the office and shut the door.

Evan dashed to the bedroom as quickly as his shaky legs could carry him.

Wes sat up in bed and opened his arms, letting Evan melt against his warmth and strength.

"God, you're trembling." Wes tightened his arms and kissed Evan's hair until he stopped shaking. "I should have gone out there with you."

Evan shook his head. "It's better you didn't. It could have been so much worse. It still might be. Brace yourself."

"I can handle him. I've got mad fighting skills." Wes flexed a bicep. He did outweigh Gary and had the muscle to pound him to dust. Evan knew he was too nice to actually carry out his subtle threat.

They took quick showers and dressed, foregoing coffee in the kitchen. There would be some in the barn.

Peter was at the barn entrance with Nicky when Evan and Wes arrived.

"No disturbance or intruders at all." Peter's radio squawked from his belt and he lowered the volume.

Evan begged to differ, but technically Gary wasn't an intruder. "You should have called when Gary arrived."

"I stopped him, and he said he lived here. Showed me his DL, and he wasn't lurking or going into the barn."

"You couldn't have known he doesn't live here anymore."

"Tonight, you give the agency a list of everyone who is supposed to be here, then we'll keep everyone else out, or call you."

"Sure." Evan held out his hand to shake Peter's as he prepared to go off-duty.

"Seven again tonight?"

"Will it be you again?"

"Not tonight. I'm on day shift today. I'll alternate with two other guys. I'll brief them before they arrive with what you've told me, but you might want to give them a tour of the place their first time."

"Got it. Thanks."

Peter left and Evan went into the office with Nicky.

WES FIGURED they had plenty to discuss and stayed out of their way. There was activity around the barn as the grooms mucked stalls and tacked up horses for workouts. The daily schedule didn't change around here, no matter what drama happened in Evan's life. He went outside to watch the sun come up.

He hadn't heard from his manager yet, but he might have missed a call while he'd been occupied with Evan. He'd left the phone at the house.

Gary's car was still parked in front, but Wes didn't let that stop him.... Evan had come back to bed shivering, and it wasn't the temperature. The meeting with Gary had terrified him. He wished he'd stood up for Evan before, despite Evan's desire to fight his own battles. There was some heavy baggage between them. If Evan confided in him, Wes would know how to help obliterate it for good.

He let himself into the house and saw video gear arranged near the door. Next to it were some of the framed prints that had been hanging around the house. He heard Gary rustling around in the office. Would he take something that belonged to Evan?

Gary came down the hall toward Wes. He looked fairly harmless. Short, neatly trimmed salt-and-pepper hair and dark wire-rimmed glasses gave him the appearance of a university lecturer, sans the leather patches on the elbows.

Wes found his phone on the living room table and slipped it into his front jeans pocket. Now, in daylight, he noticed the huge print of Evan with the intimate, loving look on his face had been taken down. He spotted a large print stuck between the couch and the wall, back facing out. Evan must have taken it down sometime after Wes's last visit here. He hadn't done it last night; they'd been together every moment but the few minutes Evan had spoken to Gary. Whether it was the memories it evoked or Evan not wanting Wes to see it, the little touch pleased Wes.

Then Gary entered the living room. Wes's presence startled him and Wes stood tall as Gary gave him a silent once-over. There was nothing Gary could say or do to hurt him, but he'd had a devastating, demoralizing effect on Evan after just a few minutes.

"Good luck with Evan."

For a moment, Wes thought Gary's words were sincere. Until he continued.

"He seemed fine when I started with him too. But his issues run deep. Very deep. One day he'll hear a name or see a face in a crowd and... he'll be afraid of his own shadow for a while. And whatever you do, don't mention Larry Fenton or Hummingbird Lane. Probably best not to even mention hummingbirds. Or any birds. Don't even order chicken in a restaurant." Gary smiled and his voice was even, steady, but the words sent chills through Wes. How could Gary find such glee in Evan's fears?

What happened to Evan on Hummingbird Lane? The name Larry Fenton sounded familiar, but Wes couldn't place it.

Gary moved past Wes and reached for the print behind the couch. He pulled it up and reversed it; it was the remarkable print of Evan. He looked so damn beautiful—and content—in the portrait. How sad to see what his relationship with Gary had become.

Wes worried Gary might damage the print, but what happened next shocked him even more.

Gary put it under his arm and walked out the front door.

Despite his unsettling words and menacing remarks, could he still care enough for Evan to keep the print as a memory of their good times? Or was there something else behind his actions?

As long as Gary stayed away, Wes wouldn't give him any more thought. He watched from the porch as Gary stowed it in the back of his car and turned back to the house. They passed each other on the front porch, but Gary didn't meet Wes's gaze. Wes continued toward the barn, flipping through his phone to see whether Saul had called or texted.

Nothing.

WES WALKED into the barn office just in time. Nicky had her arms crossed over her chest and was kicking the leg of his desk.

"I don't think you can afford to be so damn picky, Evan. Money is money." She punctuated the last sentence with three more jabs that rattled the coffee mugs.

"Okay, I can come back." Wes did a quick one-eighty.

"No, Wes. Please stay," Evan shouted at his back.

"Yes, Wes, stay." She gave Wes a smile. "Maybe he'll listen to you."

"Nope. I'm leaving." Wes waved her away as if she had the plague. "I wanted to let you know Gary just drove off."

Nicky glanced from Wes to Evan. "Maybe I should be the one leaving."

"Not necessary. Wes is going to be spending more time here and Gary won't. Nothing for anyone to be embarrassed about. It's a change for the better." Evan leaned back in his chair, enjoying a moment of relative peace in what had already been a trying day. Thankfully, both Wes and Nicky were here to ease some of his strain.

Nicky left anyway with an excuse about mending a saddle, and he didn't stop her.

Wes leaned on the edge of the desk. His face was drawn and pale.

"What's wrong?" Evan asked and put his hand on Wes's thigh.

"Gary's a bloody bastard."

"What did he do?"

Wes rubbed Evan's hand. "Nothing." Clearly he was lying. Evan would find out sooner or later.

"What was Nicky talking about before, if you don't mind my asking?"

"No. She thinks we should take on a new owner and I don't want to."

"I thought you're looking for new owners."

"Yes, but not this guy. Something about him isn't right."

Wes waited.

"He has some good horses. One was in the Derby last year. So why is he coming to me and not one of the elite trainers? Bob Baffert, Todd Pletcher, Lukas. Those guys are in his league."

"Maybe they turned him down too."

"Right. Why? They want winners as much as the rest of us. If he's coming down this many rungs on the ladder, there's a reason."

"Maybe you should just be flattered by the request." The corners of Wes's eyes crinkled as he smiled.

"I'd rather do business with Vanessa. I'm going to call her today."

"That's a great idea. I'll leave you alone. I need to make a few calls too." Wes slid off the desk and came around to kiss Evan.

"It's only eight, Wes. Most people aren't up yet."

Wes looked at his watch. "I hadn't realized. We've been up for hours."

"Welcome to my world. Sometimes I start dialing before I remember. The only people working at this time are horsemen. And people like Starikov."

"Starikov?" Wes stopped in the doorway.

"The persistent owner. Hey, that's a good name for him. Starikov the Persistent."

"If he were a medieval warrior."

"I need to watch some workouts on the track. Want to come? I'll let you ride my pony." Evan flashed a grin.

"God, I hope that's a euphemism for something."

"In this case, it's not. But later we should put the other thing on the agenda."

THAT EVENING they sat in Evan's kitchen sipping beers with dinner. Wes had gone to the grocery store for Evan, who had cooked dinner.

Evan shook his head. "I still can't get over Vanessa."

"She trusts you. That's a good thing. She gives off the impression of being a stereotypical blonde, but she's sharp. She learned something from her father and grandfather. She might end up running the family businesses before she's thirty-five."

"She wired fifty K to my account. 'Or should I send a hundred?' she asked me. Does she have that much money?"

Wes nodded. "She has more money than God. *He* comes to her for a loan."

"She's interested in buying my share of Jet. I'll keep working on Gary to sell his half. He must need the money, too. His backers don't pay for his personal expenses once the film's shot; the funding drops dramatically once he moves into the editing phase."

"Are you having any second thoughts about him, or me?"

"Of course not." Evan gripped Wes's hand. "I probably could have given him more warning to find a new place, but I didn't want him back here. Especially if you weren't here."

"Are you afraid of him?" Wes held Evan's gaze and Evan turned away. He wasn't ready to have this discussion just yet.

"Not physically."

Wes nodded. He didn't press the issue, and he could interpret that answer however he chose.

"Back to Vanessa," Evan said, steering the conversation away from the reef called Gary. "I'm going to Del Mar to see a few horses with her tomorrow. Do you want to join us?"

"I do, but I've got a meeting with the network tomorrow. Finally."

Something moved in Evan's gut. Not butterflies. This time it was crows, pecking at his insides with pointy beaks and razor-sharp claws. He put a hand to his abdomen, but they wouldn't stop eating at him. "Is that good or bad?"

"I think it's good. Saul didn't say. I know they saw Julia today, working on her story. Something along the lines of 'we're dear friends but we were never more than that.' We've both said point-blank we are not dating."

"But you've been photographed together. Touching. Kissing. How can you explain that without looking like it was a huge lie?" Evan wished he hadn't been so blunt. He waited for Wes to fight back, be hurt, or worse, hostile.

Instead he just nodded. "You're right. We never kissed on the mouth, just cheeks. But it did look like we were a couple. It was good publicity for both of us, though it was never intended that way. We just let it happen." His tone wasn't defensive. "Do you have a better suggestion? You've probably had some experience with this."

Nothing particularly relevant, or that Evan wanted to discuss, so he didn't reply. The crows were back. Now he realized they weren't for Wes; they were Evan's past trying to claw its way out of him, one way or another, even if it killed him in the process.

"If you think of something, please let me know. Otherwise we'll brainstorm tomorrow."

CHAPTER 21

WES WAS in a great mood when he walked into the conference room at the studio. Only his manager was there.

Wes glanced around the table that seated ten. "Am I early?"

"No. Right on time." Saul didn't stop blinking. Wes's smile disappeared, and a huge black cloud floated right into his sunshine.

"You sound like I'm scheduled for execution."

Saul did an odd movement of his head, a nod mixed with a shake. A bad sign. "Funny you should say that."

"Please tell me you're not being ironic."

"The studio and network are not happy. In fact, they're shitting themselves. They need more time to process this issue."

"This 'issue' is my life."

"Yes. And they're going to kill you."

"Huh?"

"They're going to kill your character. By the third ep of next season. Then you're free to love whoever you want. Until then, tone it down with Julia and don't do anything gay. Their words."

"You're fucking kidding me."

"Hey, I didn't tell you the best part."

"There's a best part? Please, tell me."

"You'll have some choice in how you're gonna die." Saul had a grin on his face like he'd had the only ticket to a record Powerball jackpot.

Wes just stared. He was numb. He didn't feel anything, not yet.

"Look, kid, that's huge. In this town actors don't get a say about anything."

"That's it? No discussion, no negotiation? They just picked this series up for two seasons and the best you could do is get me three episodes? What the hell do I pay you for?" Wes slammed the table. The sound sent Saul six inches out of his chair, but Wes barely noticed the impact.

"What are you talking about? They wanted to write you off with some unexpected off-screen accident and have your funeral in the first ep. Like Charlie Sheen. I got you three more eps and the chance for a memorable death—on screen. That's not nothing."

Fuck. The studio wanted to Charlie Sheen him? Being gay was on par with Charlie Sheen's substance issues and public meltdown?

Wes stood up so fast he knocked the chair over. "You're fired." Wes stabbed at the air between them.

"Oh, and did I mention I got you an extra 25 percent over last season's salary?" Saul looked awfully proud of himself.

"You're still fired. Twenty-five percent more than last time," Wes roared as he strode out of the room. The next stop would be his solicitor's office.

Saul chuckled and shouted after him, "I'll call you next week for the meeting about your death. They're already rewriting the beginning of the season."

EVAN WAS on the top of the world when he got home that night. Wes's car was parked in front, but there were no lights on in the house even though it was dusk. Evan unlocked the door and headed toward the flickering light coming from the living room.

Maybe Vanessa had called and told him their good news, and he was going to do something sweet and romantic with candles. That sounded like Wes.

But there were no candles. Wes sat on the couch, the only light coming from the television. He had his elbows on his knees, hands holding his chin. The sound was muted.

"Wes?" No answer. Wes didn't even look up. "Wes?"

Evan sat down next to him. He glanced at the screen. It was an old Bond film, one with Sean Connery looking young and debonair and irresistible.

"I have really great news, Wes." Evan wanted to share, but something was wrong.

"Me too. You go first." His voice was low and listless.

"Can we pause that?" Evan asked. When Wes didn't reply, Evan reached for the remote and stopped the DVD. Wes continued staring at the screen, seemingly oblivious to the fact the picture had ceased to move. "Wes? You okay?"

"Right." Wes turned to Evan, eyes again showing signs of life. "What's your news?"

"Vanessa bought two horses and my share of Jet today. The new horses are arriving here tomorrow. So the financial situation has improved drastically."

Wes smiled. It was his stage smile; Evan knew the difference. "That's great. I'm happy."

"What's your news?" Evan had been so excited about his own day, Wes's condition hadn't fully sunk in. But now he saw the dark circles under his eyes, the pale skin and dark smudge on one cheek. His clothes were wrinkled. Maybe he'd just fallen asleep on the couch. Evan's schedule had caught up with him.

"My news." Wes nodded.

Evan rubbed a thumb over the smudge. "Tell me this is chocolate."

Wes rubbed at his cheek. "Yeah. I had some chocolate for lunch."

For lunch? "Wes?"

"I'm dying."

"What?" Evan's heart thundered and his head spun. "What? Are you ill?"

"Well, I'm not dying, exactly. I'm going to be killed." He turned to Evan and quirked one corner of his mouth. "My *Zero Gravity* character, Lt. Wallace. Not me. Not literally. But I'm still pretty fucked." He pronounced it "leftenant."

"Did you know that was coming? How long is your contract?"

"One year to start, with the usual options on series renewal. But Saul couldn't get them to extend, and this is the best they would offer. I'm too big a risk, and they saw this as an opportunity to eliminate risk." He waved his hand in the air.

"But they just picked up the show for two seasons. Multi-season renewal is rare, and you're a huge reason for its success. They can't just do that."

"Yup. Even if the contract was longer, I'm violating some morals clause. They tell me it's okay to be gay. But it's immoral to have a boyfriend in public."

"That has to be illegal. After the Supreme Court decisions last summer—"

"I called my solicitor—whatever you call them. He's looking into it."

"Good." Evan put an arm around Wes. "Have you been alone here like this all day? Why didn't you call me?"

"I knew you were busy. Julia wanted to come over to cheer me up, but I didn't want to see her."

"Tell me the whole thing from the beginning."

Wes recounted the meetings with his manager and the lawyer.

Evan's mood grew darker and darker. This was all his fault. He should have walked away and stayed away. He'd ruined everything for Wes because of his selfish desire to have someone love him. If he loved Wes—and Evan thought he was pretty close—he wouldn't let this happen.

"Is this final, Wes?"

"It sounds pretty final. Unless my solicitor figures out an angle, but by then I'll be dead."

"I can't let this happen, Wes. I can't stay with you. This was a bad idea, the two of us."

Wes grabbed Evan's shoulders and looked him right in the eye. "No. We're great. You're great. This will not break us up. But I love that you're willing to make a sacrifice for my career. Thank you."

This wasn't quite the end. Evan wasn't ready to give up. "What's next? What's going to happen?"

"They asked me not to go public with our relationship in any way until the big death episode has aired. But it's months from now. I don't want to hide until then."

Evan found a sliver of light. "Maybe we don't have to wait that long. Just until they shoot that ep. What are they going to do? They won't have time to write and reshoot three episodes and still make the schedule."

Wes nodded. "Right! Who gives a toss about breach of contract, right? And I can start looking for a new job now. And a new manager. I fired Saul."

"There are plenty of gay actors with good roles."

"They all came out after they were established. I'm not Zach Quinto or Jim Parsons or Matt Bomer—"

"You're all three rolled into one."

"At least I'm lucky in love." He leaned forward to kiss Evan. "Even so, I may end up playing the quirky gay neighbor-slash-lead female's best friend until I get gray. Then I can play the quirky gay dad."

"I'm sure it won't be that bad."

"I could always go back to Broadway. Who *isn't* gay there?" Wes laughed. This time it was a real laugh, and Evan was swept up too for a few moments. But his job, his land, was here. He couldn't pick up and move to New York. They'd sort this out, but if New York or London was Wes's only chance for good roles, Evan would let Wes go for good. Maybe he *should* let him go now.

"Wes, I am so sorry about this. What can I do? What if we aren't seen in public? I can handle keeping private. It's better than the alternative."

"No, Evan, it's not. If we let them force us to hide then we're really lying. I want to go places with you like I did with Julia. I won't let the studio keep me from living my life—with you."

"I'm willing to stay secret for a little while. Until you can find another way, either with this show or another one. I can wait. We can still be together. No one will question our friendship since I'm training your horses…."

"You're too special to hide. I want you to know that. No matter what anyone said or did to you before, you're the most amazing, incredible, every superlative in the book, person I've ever met. Except maybe my mum."

Evan felt tears welling up, and the mention of Wes's mom chased them away. He let himself laugh away the pain because it was exactly what he needed to hear. But tonight was about comforting Wes. He pulled Wes in tight and listened to him exhale against Evan's ear.

Then a shudder went through Wes, one short, sharp tremor before Wes wiped at his cheek and was still for a while as Evan cradled him. He knew how Wes felt; he'd been in a similar place before—a choice between two bad options—only Evan had been alone. He hadn't given up his dreams for love; he'd given them up to save himself. Yet somehow, now, he'd found love in the least likely place.

"Evan?" Wes's voice was shaky.

"Yeah, hon?"

"I kind of wanted to be James Bond." Wes nodded stoically, which made Evan's heart ache all the more.

CHAPTER 22

WEDNESDAY WOULD have been a black hole for Wes if it hadn't been for Evan. He included Wes in his tasks and gave him some work to do around the barn. Then Vanessa's new horses arrived. Wes got one of the stalls ready, under Nicky's eagle eye. He was grateful for the manual labor to tire him out. He might actually get some sleep that night.

Then again, Evan was driving back up north early Thursday—this time with Jet and another horse ready to run. Wes didn't want to waste their last night together sleeping. He needed to stay in LA for meetings with his lawyer and additional negotiations with the studio and network. Wes's team racked their brains for alternatives—everything but pretending Evan didn't exist and wasn't Wes's partner/boyfriend/whatever the phrase of the day was.

Peter was on duty that night, but since the guards had been hired, nothing untoward had happened. Evan and Wes went to bed early Wednesday night. There would be time to make love and say good-bye to each other and still give Evan enough sleep to drive safely on Thursday. They fell asleep in each other's arms.

EARLY THURSDAY morning, Wes's cell phone woke them before Evan's alarm clock. It wasn't even four. The caller ID showed a number he didn't know, so he let it go to voice mail. Five minutes later the phone chirped again.

"I guess we better just get up. Who's calling?" Evan asked, rubbing sleep out of his eye. "God, I want coffee."

The phone rang again and Wes silenced it. Someone might have gotten his number and tweeted it, or some business accidentally printed his number on their flyers. He was halfway to the kitchen when a commotion outside got his attention. "Evan? What's going on at the barn?"

"Dunno. Can you take a look while I call Peter?"

"Yeah." Wes went back to the bedroom for his boxers. It might just be Nicky or one of the grooms having trouble with the van.

He had his hand on the door when Evan came up behind him, phone to his ear. "What? Can't you get rid of them?" Wes opened the door and twenty reporters were outside, carrying cameras and microphones, and he saw flashes popping. He stood there until Evan pulled him inside and shut the door.

"What the fuck?" Wes said. "What's going on out there?"

"Wes, tell us about Evan!" someone shouted from the other side of the door. Then the doorbell started. "How did Julia Compton take the news?

Wes peeked through the front window. Evan came up next to him. "I guess this makes me Julia Roberts."

Wes stared at him until he connected the dots. He was living *Notting Hill*. This might be the closest he got to a film role. And playing the Hugh Grant role in real life wasn't what he had in mind.

Evan left Wes on the couch and went to get dressed. Wes pulled at his hair, then held his head in his hands, wondering who had talked. Someone had told the press.

"I'm going outside, Wes. You should get dressed too."

Wes nodded, still not quite believing what was happening. When he came back, Evan was on the couch. He thrust a newspaper at Wes, one of the local tabloids.

The headline read: Wes's New Hobby. Underneath: "The real reason Wes Tremayne goes racing." There was a photo of Evan and Wes with Twist, then next to it, one of the photos Wes had taken of them in San Francisco. He dropped the paper.

"How the hell did they get that photo?" Wes asked.

Evan was flipping through another paper and folded it open to a big spread of other photos from their special day, including a selfie of them kissing. "And those too!"

Evan pressed his lips together. "They came from your phone."

"Papa-fucking-razzi!"

"How could they get photos from your phone, Wes?"

"They hack into phones all the time in the UK. They record calls and sell them to papers, radio stations. For years it was condoned by the papers, encouraged even."

"How?"

"I don't know."

A few reporters still shouted from the front of the house, but they'd stopped knocking. Wes just realized. "How did you get them to stop?"

"I told them you'd make a statement later if they behaved. I also told them they were disturbing the horses. Some of them actually apologized."

"Great."

"Here's your chance to say what you want, not what the studio wants." Evan looked up at Wes. "It's a good thing, actually. Just take some time to collect your thoughts. Call your lawyer and get his advice, too. If you want, I'll help you write it or whatever."

Wes sat down on the couch and stared at the papers spread on the table. "It really couldn't get any worse, could it?"

Evan shook his head. "Coffee." He went into the kitchen and brought back two steaming mugs.

Wes took one and sipped. "I'm gonna need a bigger mug."

DESPITE THE early hour, Wes phoned his lawyer, Bob Kellerman, who was already awake, thanks to the many Wes-related calls he'd already received from the studio, production company, and the network.

"Bad news, Wes. The studio terminated your contract completely and rescinded the extension for three episodes to resolve your character's storyline on-screen."

"How can they do that?"

"They claim you're in breach of the morals clause. They're enforcing it because you didn't handle this to their satisfaction while negotiations were underway... bad faith, yada yada yada."

"I don't know what that means."

"Don't worry. That's what you pay me for. But basically it's curtains." He chuckled. "I made a theater joke!"

"I'm laughing inside," Wes replied, not bothering to hide his sarcasm. "Now what?"

"They're sending out a press release about you. I'll e-mail you a copy."

"You have a copy? Can't you stop it?"

"No. Nothing's false so there's no libel here. They sent it to me for approval."

"Why didn't you tell me?"

"I've been trying to call you for an hour."

"Right, I turned the phone off."

They discussed Wes's statement to the press, and Wes agreed to e-mail it for approval before he spoke to anyone.

Evan helped Wes write, and while Kellerman was checking it, Wes showered and dressed. Or half dressed. He couldn't decide which shirt to wear.

"Evan, which is better. This one?" He held out a blue-and-white striped button-down. "Or this?" From behind his back he produced a rainbow tie-dyed T-shirt.

"You were in my drawers?"

"Well, yeah, and I also looked for clothes in your dresser."

Evan threw a pillow at him. "I have one with a unicorn *and* a rainbow."

"You should wear that." Wes couldn't believe he was able to joke about this.

He was about to put on the striped shirt when Evan took that away too. "Vertical stripes look awful on TV. Go with a solid color."

"Thanks, Heidi Klum."

"Now that's even better than Julia Roberts."

Wes took a few breaths and stepped outside with his statement. He wasn't prepared for the number of reporters—there must have been dozens. He took a few more breaths to steady himself.

Before he could open his mouth, they shouted questions at him: Why had he lied? How long had he been seeing Evan? What about Julia? He held up a hand, and most of the reporters quieted down.

"I know you have a lot of questions. Give me a few minutes and I should answer most of them."

A few reporters shouted again, but most just waited.

"First off, I want to thank Julia Compton. She's been a very dear friend since we met doing *Les Mis* on Broadway. She wanted me to stop hiding long ago, but she always supported my decision on that. I do love her—like a sister."

There was a mix of applause and hostile comments. He ignored the angry looks and focused his gaze on a few individuals who nodded or smiled.

"Julia and I played roles, for lack of a better word. I didn't expect to meet someone who would change my mind about that decision. And then I met Evan."

He took in a few breaths, hoping to slow his racing heart. Now most of the reporters were nodding; a few shouted words of encouragement. He let himself relax a little, smile a little.

"When I realized how I felt about Evan and told him, he wasn't interested. That's not accurate. He wouldn't go out with me because he didn't want to harm my career. I was scared about the possibility, too. But after a few days apart, I decided he was more important. Luckily, he went along with me. I've been working with the studio to find the best way for them to accommodate my reality, and they decided to write me off the show, kill me off."

The reporters booed. Wes hadn't expected that support.

"But the photographs preempted their schedule. I'm actually glad I can stop pretending now."

The applause and cheers grew in intensity. Wes started to speak and they quieted again. "When I told Evan the network's decision, he wanted to break up or keep our relationship a secret. He still didn't want to hurt my career. I can't possibly give up a man who keeps putting me first. I won't let him do that, but knowing he would reinforces my knowledge that he's worth giving this up. I might not get another role on a television program or the stage, and I'm okay with that. I'm glad I came here, or I wouldn't have met Evan. I'm thankful to my fans for supporting me and making my show popular.

"I love acting. I started as a child, and enough people thought I was good at it to get some great roles and a Tony award here in the States. But there's one role I won't play. I won't pretend to be someone I'm not. Not anymore. I'm sorry for misleading my fans and I'm sorry I'm not exactly the man you thought I was. I didn't much like him anyway."

The reporters laughed and cheered.

"I hope soon we won't have to hide to keep our jobs or friends, and I don't just mean celebrities. I mean everyone, from the postman to the CEO of a big company. And I hope you all—gay or straight—find your own Evan."

Wes looked around, locking gazes with several of the reporters as he spoke. He hadn't been sure about getting so personal, but he had nothing to lose at this point. And the response here was supportive and many applauded when he finished. The average American probably didn't give a flying fuck about who he dated. But average Americans didn't run television networks. Risk-averse bean counters controlled everything from storylines to wardrobe. The writers, actors, and production staff only thought they had a say in the process.

At least he'd said his piece, expressed his opinion, and he could move on knowing he hadn't buckled under their pressure.

Reporters shouted questions, but Wes's brain was overloaded and exhausted. His hand felt like lead when he gave a small wave and went back inside.

This is not the end; it's the beginning of something new. He had options. And best of all, he had Evan.

CHAPTER 23

EVAN WAITED a few feet from the door when Wes shut it behind him, and was in Wes's arms in seconds. They embraced and Wes was grateful for Evan's support—literally. His knees shook and buckled, and he realized he had been holding his breath.

"Come sit down." Evan led him to the couch. "I have coffee, beer, vodka, or hot chocolate. Which would make you feel better right now?"

"Mix them up. Perhaps one of them will work." Wes leaned back against the couch and closed his eyes.

Evan cocooned him in his arms and they sat together. Outside, Wes heard voices and radios squawking. The sheriff's office had sent a couple of cars just in case. Hopefully, they were encouraging the reporters to leave.

A sound from the back window caught his attention. Someone had a camera pressed to the window. Evan leaped up and shouted something uncharacteristically vulgar, then shut all the shades and blinds.

"I'll let the sheriff's department know about this. Wait here." Evan was at the door before Wes summoned the strength to protest. He came back a few minutes later.

"One of the deputies got him. He's cuffed in the back of a cruiser." Evan's smile was big enough for both of them. "If they ask, we're pressing charges. Okay?"

Wes nodded. He liked when Evan said "we." It warmed him up a little, filled some of the black emptiness swallowing him from the inside out.

Evan came over and rubbed Wes's shoulder. "You need tea. I'll make some."

Tea sounded perfect. At home it was the answer to everything. He hadn't had a proper cuppa for ages. "Hey, none of that herbal shite, either!"

Evan hovered in the doorway. "The 'h' is silent."

"No, it's not."

"Chamomile?" Evan cocked his head.

Wes threw a pillow at him and lay back on the couch. Evan clattered in the kitchen and came back with a tray and a proper teapot. Wes hadn't seen one—except for his or at a restaurant—since he'd left London.

"Darjeeling work for you? If not, make your own." Evan poured tea for both of them. It was good and hot and strong enough to stand up to some milk and three sugars. Usually, Wes only had one, but now he didn't need to listen to his personal trainer anymore, he threw caution to the wind.

After three sips he turned to Evan. "Have you got any biscuits?"

"If you mean cookies, yes. If you mean the—"

"Yes, I mean cookies."

He ate four. After his second cup of tea, he felt almost human again.

"Evan, I'm sorry this whole thing has bollocksed-up your plans today."

Evan had been eating a biscuit, and he coughed out crumbs. "You're apologizing because you've inconvenienced me? I'm fine in comparison."

"You should be on the road now. You'd be halfway to Berkeley."

"I can handle the delay." He finished the biscuit and turned to Wes. "But I'd like for you to come up with me. Unless you have some meetings or...."

Wes didn't want to take another bloody Hollywood meeting. The word made him sick, but Evan's offer balanced that black hole inside. "I'd like to go with you. I have to get out of here for a while and collect my thoughts. We should think about what's next."

"How about just thinking about 'now' for a while?"

Wes had never stopped looking forward, planning his steps, his path, his future. But that version of his life stopped today. He didn't know what he'd be doing tomorrow or next week or next year. It was a new feeling, and it unsettled him, as if he stood at the edge of a cliff with no clue how to get down the mountain.

He put his teacup down. "Evan, who do you think did this? And why?"

"Does it matter? You can't undo it. But you can make yourself miserable wondering."

"Do you think it was Gary?"

"Why? I don't think he wants me back."

"To split us up, fuck with me. I left my phone here the other day, when he was alone in the house."

"Wes, you leave your phone everywhere. The barn, your car, the floor. If that's your rationale, anyone could have gotten your photos. Even Peter the guard. And you don't use a password."

"I can never remember when I'm in a hurry." Wes pressed his lips together. A dozen people could have had access, including Nicky, the grooms, Vanessa, Julia, Gary. *But who...?*

"Where's your phone right now?"

Wes patted his pockets. "I don't know."

Evan pulled it out of his shirt pocket and handed it over. "Forget the pictures. It's over and done. When do you want to make our escape?"

THEY LEFT shortly after lunch. Nicky and the grooms were glad to see them leave so the barn could get back to their usual routine. They drove Evan's SUV and towed the two-horse trailer with Jet and one of Vanessa's new horses. Nicky would keep the other there until it was ready to race.

This time Evan and Wes checked into the hotel together. A few other guests recognized Wes in the lobby and gave him the same friendly greetings as before the Big News went public. In his mind, it deserved capital letters. His life was now BBN and ABN. Before the Big News and After.

Today he wasn't checking in as Wes Tremayne, television star. He was here as a horse owner. The only real change was getting flirty looks from men instead of women. He was here with his boyfriend, for God's sake. What were they thinking?

Upstairs, Evan plopped onto the bed and lay face up. "Oh, it feels so good to just relax."

"You didn't have to drive the whole way yourself."

"Yeah. I did." Evan tugged Wes's wrist until he lay down too, and Evan rolled up next to him.

"That joke is getting old."

"Sorry." Evan kissed Wes.

"Not good enough."

Evan kissed him again. And again.

"A little lower. Like here." Wes put Evan's hand on his cock.

"So much for subtle." Evan started unbuttoning Wes's shirt, then leaned down to lick a nipple. He raised his head.

"Don't stop yet."

"What did that guy whisper to you by the elevator?"

Wes raised his head. "Nothing." Evan's stare hardened. "Okay, he gave me his room number if we were up for a three-way."

"Which room?" Evan started sucking Wes's nipple.

"I don't remember."

Evan stopped sucking and fixed his gaze on Wes.

"Four one three. You're interested?" Wes stared at Evan, who started working at his belt and fly.

"We'll see how you feel after I tire you out." Evan slid his hand into Wes's pants and took firm hold of his cock.

Little ripples of pleasure radiated through him. "I like it when you get possessive."

"I'll remember you said that." Evan tugged Wes's jeans and shorts part way down his hips and took most of Wes into his mouth.

Wes didn't like this new version of Evan. He loved it.

CHAPTER 24

OVER THE next two days, the new horses settled in at Golden Gate Fields while Wes settled into his new reality.

Evan's grooms had made a point to congratulate him and Evan. They had come to like Wes because he took genuine interest in the horses and treated Evan's staff nicely. Ricky took Evan into the tiny office at the end of his barn for a private discussion while Wes kicked dirt from the floor into a pile and then smoothed it out again. He visited Twist and Percy and fed them peppermints. Most of the work had been done, and he was at a loose end.

Ricky nodded when he came out and went into Jet's stall to saddle her for a half-and-half workout. One lap of jogging and one of galloping, if she worked well at the jog. Evan waved Wes into the office and shut the door.

"Ricky wanted us to know it wasn't any of the grooms who spoke to the press."

Wes nodded and waited.

"They suspected our relationship, but they're loyal, and I can't see them risking their jobs. They dote on their charges, and they'd hate getting fired and not seeing their horses."

"Okay. I'll take your word for it."

"I still don't think it matters, but I know you want to find out. At least you can rule my guys out and relax while you're here. Now let's go to the track and watch Jet. Vanessa's other new horse, Ancient Romeo, will be jogging after. I have races for both of them in the next week."

WES CONTINUED to get calls and e-mails from people he hadn't spoken to in months and years, all supportive, commiserating with his termination from the show, and wishing him and Evan all the best. His publicity agent forwarded hundreds of e-mails and a bag of mail. He sat on the bed and opened a few letters at a time. Ninety-five percent were positive. He'd disappointed some of his fans, and he accepted full responsibility.

Vanessa called. Brent called. Even Lance called with a "no hard feelings, are we good?" apology. Of his close friends and family, Julia was the only one he hadn't spoken to. She hadn't even returned his several calls and texts. Given how she came out in the whole debacle, he wasn't surprised.

"Just give her some time," Evan said. He had another pile of Wes's letters at the table by the window. They took turns reading each other the best lines.

The internet buzzed with discussions of how the network had dropped him. Popular opinion was in his favor, and viewers were boycotting the network's other shows. He received hundreds of requests for interviews. Even Ellen DeGeneres called personally to invite him onto her show.

He refused all of the invitations. He simply didn't want to talk about it. People were on his side, but it didn't change anything. No one had offered him a new job or even an audition. Public opinion counted for squat.

Positive Negative ran on Saturday and took second place in his race. The purse was modest, and Wes's share was just under $10,000, after 10 percent to Evan and another ten for the jock. Wes wasn't hurting for money, but until he got work, he should cut back on living expenses. He wouldn't dream of selling the horses.

SATURDAY NIGHT they went into San Francisco to celebrate. They had dinner and drinks at a few bars in the Castro. They were bombarded the whole evening with cheers, handshakes, high fives, and more than a few additional invitations to three-and-more ways. Strangers bought them drinks, and no matter how much they tried to return the favor, they couldn't have paid for anything if they'd wanted.

Finally, they found a small late-night club with live music. They could kiss, hold hands, anything they wanted. The freedom felt amazing. In between sets, they revisited a topic Wes had brushed off every time Evan mentioned it.

"I've got plenty of room at the ranch for you. There's a spare bedroom so you can have your own space. I don't want to blow it by moving too far too fast." Evan put his hand on Wes's.

"Would you be offended if I say no?" Wes searched Evan's eyes for his reaction.

"Of course not." But Evan's gaze was downcast, and he worked at an imaginary spot on the pristine tablecloth.

"Give me a little time to decide. In case another role comes along, I'd need a place in the city. It's too far to travel in for early calls."

"We're here for another two weeks. Is that enough time?"

EVAN TOOK Sunday morning off. Ricky could handle everything on his own. He'd done fine while Evan had been in LA most of the previous week. When Wes came out of the bathroom after his shower, he found Evan on the bed staring at his phone.

"Did you teach it a new trick?" Wes asked. He sat next to Evan and shook his head so droplets from his wet hair splattered Evan.

"God, you're worse than a dog."

Wes tackled Evan and lay on top of him, getting Evan's clothes wet and Wes's cock hard.

"Sorry, Wes, but not now."

Wes sat up. It was the first time either of them had rebuffed an advance. It had to happen sooner or later, but after their wonderful night before, it sent tremors through Wes's gut.

"What's up?"

"I have to call Gary. Tell him when Jet's going to run. He's been after to me run her. And I need to tell him I sold my share to Vanessa."

"Just text him. Or e-mail if it's too much to text."

Evan leaned over toward Wes and planted a sloppy kiss on his mouth. "Perfect solution."

"Sometimes technology really is the answer." Wes unwrapped his towel so Evan could see his cock, thick and jutting out from his body. "A natural feat of engineering."

Evan leaned in close to examine it. "Wow. It does that all by itself, with no one touching it." He hovered a few inches away.

"It does much more interesting things when someone touches it. Go on, see what I'm talking about."

Evan shook his head. "Nah. I've got one of my own."

Wes pushed Evan down and went for his belt. "You should let it out. We can introduce them and let them play together."

"Like dogs at the park?" Evan's cheeks dimpled, and he pressed his lips tight, trying to hold back laughter.

"That wasn't what I was thinking. Let me show you."

By the time he undressed Evan, he was as hard as Wes. He got on his knees and leaned forward, pushing his ass up. Wes took one firm globe in each hand and kneaded gently, then spread them wide, revealing Evan's pink, puckered hole. He planted a kiss on one cheek and a very gentle bite. He'd been careful not to apply much pressure. He'd found other pale curved scars, presumably from Gary's teeth.

He added more soft kisses then went lower to lick Evan's balls. He sucked one into his mouth and felt shudders coursing through Evan's body. He kissed the other cheek and was about to grab lube when he did something he'd always wondered about.

He pressed his lips against Evan's pucker, making him go weak in the knees. Wes liked that reaction. Evan had just showered, and he exuded a light soapy fragrance, so Wes got more adventurous. He licked at the hole. Evan made an absolutely amazing noise, so Wes flicked his tongue across, then drew circles. Everything made Evan groan or gyrate. In for a penny, in for a pound. Wes pushed the tip of his tongue in, just a fraction of an inch.

The reaction from Evan encouraged him to push in farther. Evan gasped and sucked in a breath and let out a long low moan. Wes kept going. Evan's hole was slick with saliva now and loose enough for Wes to get deeper. He licked, he sucked, he tongue-fucked Evan. When he reached for Evan's cock it was rock hard and dripping. Wes moaned into Evan.

"Oh God, Wes." The rest of his words melted into another low groan.

For variety, Wes stuck two fingers in, pushing deep. He was caught off guard when Evan clenched down and came. Wes kept playing until Evan's tremors subsided.

"Jesus, Wes." Evan pushed a condom toward Wes. "Hurry, fuck me right now."

Wes wouldn't dream of disappointing Evan, so he rolled the condom on quickly. He was so hard and ready. He hadn't realized how hot eating Evan's arse would be—for both of them.

"Lube?" Wes reached out.

"Probably slick enough." Evan usually liked lots of lube, but Wes would give it a try.

He slid in slowly, but Evan was loose and spit-slick. The lubricated condom was just enough, but Wes still took his time and waited for Evan to respond.

"Yeah, good. Deep and hard, please."

Wes laughed at the incongruity of Evan's polite request to fuck him and obliged. Evan was vocal and demanding, and Wes wouldn't last long. The extra friction rubbed him the right way, and he pounded into Evan so hard Evan lost his balance but kept asking for more. Wes came hard, exhausted, and lay across Evan's back for a few minutes.

"Uhhh, Wes, that was incredible."

"Not bad, was it?" Wes caressed Evan's back and sides. Sometimes he was very ticklish, particularly after sex, but not today. In the bright daylight he noticed another pale ghost of a scar, about three inches long on Evan's hip. "How'd you get this?"

He felt Evan's entire body tense, like a board. "Don't ask me." Evan's voice was hard and sounded like he was deep underwater.

"I'm sorry." Wes played with Evan's hair instead, but the moment was gone. Evan rolled Wes off him and stared in the opposite direction.

Evan didn't reply. Wes thought he heard him whispering, but clearly not anything he wanted Wes to overhear. Evan didn't take a breath for so long, Wes thought he was trying to asphyxiate himself.

Finally, Evan sucked in some air and his muscles loosened. He rolled back toward Wes. "Sorry. I—"

"Tell me when you're ready. I won't ask again." But Wes desperately wanted to know because Evan had scared the crap out of him just now, and he didn't know how much of that he could bear. It wasn't Evan's cold shoulder, but the evident pain Evan fought off on his own. Wes needed to help him. How long before Evan trusted him?

Evan snuggled up to Wes as if nothing had happened. Had Wes been in bed with a stranger for those strange, painful moments? Now his warm, wonderful, loving Evan was back. They kissed long and slow.

Then Evan's cell phone rang. Wes had to get used to Evan always checking caller ID. An emergency with the horses took priority over snuggling and lovemaking.

"Vanessa?" Evan's voice was postcoitally gravelly.

"Oh, Evan, I am so sorry if I disturbed you." Wes was close enough to hear her voice, tinny this far from the speaker, but full of overwhelming emotion.

"Are you okay?" Evan sat up, and Wes couldn't hear her reply.

"What? When did this happen? ... Did you get the number? ... Slow down ... Repeat exactly what he said. ... Call the police and report this. Tell them to call me if necessary. ... I understand if you want to.... Talk to the police first. ... Bye."

Evan looked pale and drawn. Any remnant of their incredible sex had been washed away by a fresh disaster, apparently.

"Vanessa got a threatening phone call, warning her to take her horses to another trainer, or she'd be sorry. 'In ways you can't even imagine.'"

"Aw, fuck. Who was it?"

"No caller ID. She's going to have the police trace it. Or FBI. I don't know. Maybe Homeland Security can access the records."

"Homeland Security? Don't they deal with terrorists?" What the hell was going on? How would terrorists be connected with Evan and Vanessa?

"All she recognized was his accent. Russian."

CHAPTER 25

WITHIN AN hour both LAPD and the FBI called Evan. Wes ordered room-service breakfast so they could deal with the phone calls in private. Apparently, if your last name was Vandermere, government bureaucracy sped up, even on a Sunday morning.

It would take a few days to get court orders to trace the call. Vanessa refused to take her horses elsewhere and offered to pay for round-the-clock guards on the farm, the Golden Gate barn, and any runners at Del Mar. Evan didn't even try to argue. He wanted the security as much as she did and appreciated her covering the expense.

"Evan, I'm not going to let this scare me away. Whoever is trying to hurt you won't do it through me." She sounded more confident than either Wes or Evan felt. "This is the second personal attack this week on people I care about. I won't cave."

When Evan had hung up, he turned to Wes. "Until she said that, I didn't even connect this to the photo thing. Could it be the same person?"

"I don't think the Russians are trying to ruin my career. But you've been losing owners for two months. Did any of the others get a threat?"

"No one told me if they did. The guy warned Vanessa not to tell the cops because it wouldn't do any good. A threat like that would make anyone else keep their mouth shut. I'll have to let the FBI know about the others. One of the owners is in Oregon, so the FBI has automatic jurisdiction."

"Sorry, I'm not up on those details."

"Interstate—any crime occurring in two or more states is automatically a federal case, not a state or local case, though the LAPD might still be part of the investigation."

Wes's head was spinning with American legal minutiae. "Sure."

THE INVESTIGATION into the threats revealed the other owners who took their horses from Evan had received similar calls with threats to their families and their horses. They'd followed instructions and told no one. But the calls were untraceable and there were no leads.

"Are we just supposed to wait until someone else gets a threat, or something worse happens?" Evan paced back and forth along the shed row in Barn 22 at Golden Gate Fields.

"What did the police say?" Wes didn't have an answer for Evan. He was so exhausted dealing with his own recent career setback, he wasn't much help with this one.

"Keep the guards on until they get a lead."

"Vanessa's coming up to watch Jet run on Wednesday. We can discuss this in person then." Evan sounded confident, but he hadn't been sleeping. He had dark circles under his eyes, and his clothes were looser. He had no appetite, and Wes couldn't get him to eat.

VANESSA ARRIVED late Tuesday, after Wes and Evan had gone to bed, but they met for breakfast at her hotel before heading to the track.

"Evan, I am not letting this affect me. I'd buy two more horses if you could find some good prospects."

"There's a yearling auction next week. It's a longer-term investment, but we'd have complete control of the training and conditioning. It's not a sure thing, though. We'd be working with a blank canvas, so to speak, with no idea of how the horse will mature."

"Let's go, and if you see anything you like, we'll decide then."

Wes noticed Evan's color came back when he was talking about horses. He really was more comfortable dealing with them than people, and law enforcement. Would Wes's life be any more satisfying if he gave up the idea of acting and devoted his life to horses, the way Evan had?

Over the past two months, he'd come to love being around the horses, getting to know their personalities and seeing the progress in their training. It had its appeal, and Wes could be happy living with Evan at the ranch and getting up before sunrise and going to bed early, sharing days and nights with Evan. But if he didn't make one last attempt, even if he crashed and burned, he'd never know whether he'd given up too early.

Evan had given up, though Wes still didn't know the story. He hoped Evan would tell him, given Wes's predicament, but if anything, Evan was clammed up even more tightly after the threat to Vanessa.

"Let's head to the track," Evan said and reached for the check.

"I'm buying," Vanessa said and hit Evan on the head with the paper.

Jet was alert and eager when they arrived. Her groom had rubbed her so her coat gleamed under the dim barn lighting. He'd even braided her mane. "Why'd he only do the top part?" Vanessa asked. "Is he going to finish?"

"The jockeys always pull the braids out on the lower part, so they can get a grip."

"Oh really?" She watched Evan and the groom do the prerace prep, icing her legs and painting her hooves with a special protective coating.

Vanessa rubbed Jet's muzzle and kissed her cheek. She pulled mints from her pocket and fed Jet a few. Wes had never seen her so affectionate with a horse, then recalled she'd noticed Jet on their very first visit to Evan's ranch.

She snapped photos and Wes remembered Julia had been camera-crazy when Twist ran. Was that only a week ago? Not even seven whole days. In the meantime Wes's entire world had been tipped upside down and shaken, like an ominous snow globe.

"Is Gary coming too?" Wes asked out of Vanessa's hearing.

"He hasn't told me if he is. Are you okay if he shows up?"

"Yes. He doesn't worry me." But he did. Not because Wes suspected him of sending the photos to the tabloids—of all the suspects, Gary had the most experience with cameras and digital cards—but his implied warnings about Evan's mental state worried Wes. He didn't want to be reminded Evan had some dark secret that could send him over the edge with an unknown trigger.

As Evan walked Jet toward the test barn, there was no sign of Gary.

"We'll wait for you at the paddock," Wes said.

"Okay. Jet's been chosen for prerace testing. She'll probably do better if it's just me and Andy taking her to the paddock."

Twenty minutes later, when the horses arrived to be saddled in the paddock, Jet looked alert and ready. She was a little hot, dark patches of sweat visible on her flanks. Andy sponged her to cool her down.

"I'm so excited!" Vanessa snapped photos of everything that moved. She'd worn a dress the same color as Evan's purple silks, and she glowed like a dark, exotic jewel under the bright sun. She wasn't wearing the usual glittery nail art, after Evan had told her it distracted the horses.

In the paddock stall, Jet stamped her feet and skittered away when Andy tried to saddle her. She tossed her head and swatted her tail.

"It's only her second start," Evan said. "She's just not used to the routine. I brought her to the ring the other day so she would feel more comfortable here, but she's more animated than I'd like to see before a race."

When the jock, Billy George arrived, Evan gave instructions. "She's a little excited. Watch the warm up so you loosen her up just enough. Then keep her one or two back until the last turn. She's got late speed, unless you take her too fast in the first four furlongs."

"Got it." Billy tugged at the brim of his helmet and Evan tossed him easily into the saddle. One more turn around the ring and they headed onto the track.

By now Wes knew Evan's favorite vantage point, and they waited for him there while he stayed at the edge of the track for a few minutes.

"She's not settling down the way she should. If she gives any trouble at the gate, I told Billy not to run her. I don't want her hurt or to have a bad experience or she may dislike running."

Vanessa looked worried, and she nibbled at a fingernail for the first time since Wes had met her. Evan's fingernails were too short to chew, or he probably would have too.

Jet didn't give any trouble at the gate, and the announcer called out "Racing!"

She broke with the pack and surged to the front.

"Keep her back, Billy," Evan muttered.

Wes had his own binoculars now and saw Jet was back in third place by the first turn. At the second turn, heading into the homestretch she was second on the outside but went wide and was back in third as they straightened out. Evan and Vanessa were shouting at Jet, at Billy, at the front-runner, and Wes joined in as Billy made his move, bringing her up into second and then half a length from the lead with a furlong to go. The crowd jumped to its feet, and Wes lost sight for a split second, and she was only yards from the finish line, directly in front of their position, then the shining bay filly went down.

CHAPTER 26

A COLLECTIVE wail echoed from the stands. Evan was gone before Wes had a moment to process what had happened, and he saw him sprint across the track toward the prostrate horse and drop to his knees near her head.

Sirens blared from the ambulance and veterinary van. Billy George, her jockey, was sitting a few feet from the horse, and medical personnel attended him. At least he was conscious and talking.

"Should we go?" Vanessa asked, hands gripping Wes's arm. He barely felt her nails digging into him. His senses were entirely focused on Jet and Evan.

The horse thrashed and tried to lift her head but couldn't stand.

"I can't tell if she's broken a leg...." Wes looked through the binoculars to no avail. What he could see was the anguish on Evan's face as he moved to hold the filly's head in his lap.

They were surrounded by veterinary personnel and track staff who unrolled a green barrier around the drama so the bystanders couldn't see what was going on.

"Wes, that can't be good." Vanessa was crying. "She's my horse, I should go."

Wes led her to the track level, holding her up, and she supporting him in turn. They were stopped at the gap near the finish line.

"She's my horse, please let us by."

"Sorry, ma'am, I can't let you. I'll check on her, but you don't want to see. It could be very upsetting."

"She's already upset," Wes said, then turned to Vanessa. "He's probably right. Let's stay here for now."

She clung to Wes, and he put his arms around her. If not for the devastating circumstances, it would have been a relief to focus on someone else's problems.

JET HADN'T even hit the ground before Evan was heading for the track, pushing spectators out of the way and shouting her name and Billy's. He thought he might be sick before he reached her, and he forced himself to take a few breaths.

As he moved across the track, he saw Jet's eyes: wide, the whites visible, blood dripping from her nostrils as she thrashed her legs around. They all looked fine; if she hadn't broken anything, there was an excellent chance she would recover. He'd do whatever was necessary, any surgery, rehabilitation, anything. He couldn't lose her.

"Jet, baby." He held her head in his lap and stroked her face and neck, and she calmed slightly. Her chest and belly heaved and her entire body shook and shuddered. Blood sprayed over Evan with each labored exhalation. Everything blurred, and hot tears streamed down his face. "Jet, I'm sorry. Jet."

He remembered buying her from her breeder's farm less than two years earlier. She'd been a gawky yearling, but the fastest in the pasture. He'd worked with her every day. She'd been a gift for Gary, and so many memories of her were connected to him. He loved this filly, and he'd naively believed selling his share in her would sever his ties to Gary too. That she'd be just another horse in his barn, the sale a business decision when he desperately needed the cash infusion.

Only now did he understand what a mistake he'd made. He couldn't blame her for Gary's actions, and he couldn't break the connection to her as easily as his connection to Gary.

He kept Jet calm while the vet checked her legs and a vet tech checked her pulse and breathing. Behind him the staff erected the barrier, and down the track, he knew the race had finished. The announcer gave the results, avoiding any mention of Jet.

"She hasn't broken anything, Evan," Dr. Elizabeth Lucas, the track vet, said. She put a hand on his shoulder. "She's shaky and dehydrated. We'll give her fluids. I'm running a blood test too. But if you gave her anything, please tell me now so I know how to treat her. If we wait too long, she could die."

"I didn't give her anything. You know me, Liz. I don't even do Lasix unless they have a history…." He stared at Jet. She had been unsettled since they hit the track, but she'd calmed enough for Billy and the starter to keep her in the race. "They already tested her today."

"You know what kind of shit happens around here. Someone else could have slipped her something."

They gave her water and she gulped it up, coughing because she had difficulty swallowing on her side. But she was still too weak to stand.

Liz came back from her truck. "Evan, she's got a huge dose of Lasix and about three other substances in her. I'll administer something to counteract, but the doses—"

Jet started shuddering again, and within moments was convulsing and thrashing her legs. Liz injected something into her neck and someone else tried to pull Evan away, out of reach of her wildly flailing legs.

"No. No!" He only held onto her more tightly. One of her flying hooves caught him in the thigh and the sound startled him more than any pain. After what seemed like an hour, the convulsions subsided.

He stroked her face, hoping the worst was over.

It was. She was completely motionless, not kicking and not breathing.

Jet was dead.

CHAPTER 27

EVAN DEMANDED to ride in the van with her to the hospital barn, and eventually the vet tech gave in. He watched them haul her lifeless body into the van with a winch and sat down on the floor, cradling her head for the short drive around the track.

"I want a necropsy," he told Liz when they'd put the filly in the exam room. "Can you arrange for one with an expert?"

"Was she insured?"

"What does that matter? I'm not thinking about collecting insurance money right now."

"Calm down, Evan. They'll require a necropsy before they settle, if she's valued over the threshold."

"Yeah, she's insured." *Was*, he reminded himself.

A track official came in to talk to Evan, along with a rep from the California Horse Racing Board. He knew both men, though he'd never had to deal with them on an inquiry.

"Evan, let's sit down here." Raul Betta, the GGF official took him into a small office with a door. The CHRB man remained silent. "There's got to be an investigation into this. I know you're upset. We all are. We don't like to lose horses."

"Especially not on the track," the CHRB rep added.

Evan tried not to punch the guy. Betta cared about the track's reputation and publicity more than the animals. And the CHRB was ineffectual at enforcing its rules. Doping happened constantly and Evan, who never doped his horses, was caught in one of the few inquiries.

"I didn't give her anything. She tested clean prerace."

"Liz is running another test, and it will be confirmed by a state vet and an independent lab if necessary. Until we find out what happened, there will be a hearing. You're suspended from all tracks until we have a definitive explanation or your hearing date. I'm sorry; it's CHRB policy."

Evan stared at the two men, then down, only now realizing he had blood on his pants and shirt. He looked from one to the other, and he wasn't sure if he saw empathy or pity in their eyes. At least it wasn't apathy. Maybe they were human after all.

He stood and walked out without saying a word.

Liz nodded silently as he walked out of the hospital barn and into the sunshine.

Vanessa waited outside the door, Wes beside her, arm around her shoulders. Vanessa pressed a plain white handkerchief to her red-rimmed eyes. It was probably Wes's.

He wanted nothing more at this moment than to feel Wes's arms around him, supporting and surrounding him, holding him up because he couldn't keep it together much longer. But his own comfort would have to wait. He owed Vanessa an explanation before he could think of taking any personal comfort.

"Evan?" She blinked silent tears away. He'd expected dramatic, but dignified sobbing from her, but this was genuine pain.

Wes stepped forward, arms out but Evan stopped him with a glance and took Vanessa's hands in his.

"She collapsed, possibly from dehydration, heat exhaustion, they're not sure. She didn't break a leg."

"But she's—" She shook her head, knowing the answer without asking the question.

"She died on the track. It was very quick." He wouldn't let her know how awful those last moments were. "They're going do to a postmortem—a necropsy—and some tests. Do you want to see her?"

She nodded, and Evan put an arm around her waist and led her back inside the hospital.

WHEN EVAN came out of the hospital barn, the sight of him nearly brought tears to Wes's eyes. Evan had blood splattered on him and track dirt on his clothes. He looked like he'd been run over by a steamroller from his expression and slumped shoulders. Wes wanted to hold him, but Evan's eyes told him not to.

The rebuff hurt, but Wes understood, and he followed Evan and Vanessa inside, there for whichever of them needed him, but as an outsider to their distress.

Wes wished he hadn't seen Jet's body lying on a metal table. It hadn't been like a cold, impersonal forensic television show. This was a flesh-and-blood filly, who hours ago had munched carrots out of Wes's hand and searched his pockets for more hidden treats.

He'd rubbed her, filled her water bucket and hay bag, and formed a bond with her during the time he'd spent with Evan in the barns. He turned away and fought nausea.

"I want to go back to my hotel now. Is that okay, or do I need to do anything?" Vanessa asked when they were outside again.

The sun was shining, but Wes felt ice moving through his veins. Everything floated past in slow motion, and time came to a stop.

"You should go. I'll be back in an hour or so if you want to talk."

"Okay." She turned and walked away.

Wes waited to see what Evan needed, but he just held out his hand, and they walked back to Barn 22. While Evan spoke to the grooms, Wes waited in the little office. Evan came in and shut the door, then he fell into Wes's arms and cried. Wes wrapped his arms tight and tried to absorb Evan's pain. They stood together for ten minutes, maybe more, then Evan pulled away, wiped his face, and stepped out of his ruined clothes. He put on a pair of jeans and a thin sweatshirt.

"Let's get out of here." He dumped the clothes in a trash bag and stuffed it into a can at the end of the shed row as they left the barn.

Evan let Wes drive back to the hotel. Now Wes knew things were really bad.

When they passed a seedy liquor store a couple of blocks from the track, Evan tugged at Wes's sleeve. "Hey, stop there."

"What? Why?"

"Get one of those really big bottles of something. Vodka or gin."

Wes kept driving. "Unh-uh. You don't need that."

"Think tea is going to fix this?" Evan's tone was sharp, and it cut through Wes.

"Of course not. Maybe a bath and a nap."

"A little bottle of vodka?"

"No. It's the middle of the afternoon. If you still want something later, I'll get it."

Evan slumped against his door and didn't speak even when they were in their room again.

Wes started a bath and poured a glass of water. "Drink that. You'll get dehydrated and feel worse." Evan drank without argument. He undressed and got in the tub. Wes sat on the edge and wiped Evan's face with a damp flannel to remove the blood and tears.

Evan took his hand and held it against his cheek. "Wes, I was supposed to be cheering you up this week. How'm I doing?"

"You're doing a brilliant job. My problems have faded into insignificance now."

Evan let out a huge sigh. Wes's heart weighed him down like it was made of lead. He'd wanted distraction from his career implosion, but certainly not like this. He'd give anything to turn back the clock and have another go at today from the time the alarm went off.

"I'm cold." Evan raised his head. "Really cold."

Wes reached for the hot water tap.

"Come in here with me, Wes?"

He slipped out of his clothes and got in the tub with Evan, nestling him against his chest. They held each other until the water cooled.

Wrapped in hotel robes, they lay together on the bed.

"I got a suspension. There will be a hearing in a few weeks, after they finish the tests."

Now they both had lost their jobs. What a pair.

"Nicky and Ricky will have to run everything. I'm not allowed at the track. They'll let Nicky run the horses since she has her own trainer's license."

The punishment served to drag Evan further into despair.

Wes's cell phone rang.

"It's Vanessa. She wants to come up and talk to you. You up for a visitor?"

Evan nodded. He didn't bother to get out of bed, but Vanessa didn't seem to mind. She sat in a chair Wes pulled up for her.

"Evan, this is my fault. I'm sure of it."

"How can you say that? Unless you doped her. But I didn't think winning was so important to you."

"Of course not. But that guy who called. He told me something bad would happen if I didn't take my horses away. This is bad. Really bad."

"That's ridiculous, Vanessa." Evan sat up and reached for her hand. "Please don't blame yourself."

Evan's phone went off and Wes answered. The state vet wanted to speak with Evan, who listened for several minutes without speaking, but his wide-eyed expression indicated more bad news. After he hung up, he turned to Wes and Vanessa.

"They won't do the necropsy until tomorrow, and the results will take weeks, but they did some preliminary blood tests." He paused. "Something odd is going on. The prerace test blood was not from Jet."

"What?" Wes and Vanessa said at once.

"They checked all the samples against hers, and none of the blood was hers. But I saw the tech come into her stall and take blood. I saw him."

An idea bloomed in one corner of Wes's brain. "Did you see him draw blood, or just stick a needle in her neck? I don't know the procedure, but is it possible he injected her with something?"

Evan stared at Wes. "I didn't watch very closely. But it's possible. I didn't know this guy, thought he was new. I told the officials. I remember distinctly because he had…." Evan touched his ear. "He was missing part of his ear. He had a buzz cut, and it was very obvious."

"Or he didn't belong there…." Vanessa added. "Okay, half an ear? Now I'm getting chills and goose bumps. I don't like this at all. I don't want to take any more chances, Evan. Maybe I *should* take my horses. Not because I don't trust you, but because I think someone is after you and your stable. I don't want you or anyone else—or another horse—to get hurt."

"That's crazy. It sounds like something from a movie or television." Evan shook his head.

Wes stood up. "Is anyone hungry? We could use a break. How about room service?" No one was interested, but Wes ordered food anyway. Evan and Vanessa would eat once it was here.

He ordered bacon cheeseburgers and garlic fries, mac and cheese, and other comfort food none of them would normally eat. For fifteen minutes they picked at the food, trying to talk about any other subject besides horses and Hollywood. Vanessa used to have plenty of inane topics of conversation, but today she couldn't even summon the interest to talk about shopping.

Wes pushed the room-service cart into the hall and sat on the couch. "I have an idea to find out what's going on. It might be dangerous, though. We should definitely involve the police."

Evan and Vanessa listened as he explained. When he was finished, Vanessa all but rolled her eyes.

"Come on, Wes. You've been watching too much *Masterpiece Mystery*."

Evan gave Wes an apologetic glance. "I have to agree. I'm sorry. It would make a good script though. Very exciting."

Now he wished he hadn't said anything. "Fuck you both." But as soon as the words were out, Wes wanted to take them back and maybe sew his mouth shut. "God, I am so sorry. Really, really sorry."

"It's okay. We're all under too much pressure right now," Evan said. "But you might have a future as a writer, as a fallback."

Now that really made Wes's day. The last thing he wanted was to be a damned writer.

"I think I'll stop by the liquor store after all, Evan. Seeing as how this day can't get any worse."

Vanessa's phone went off, playing some hip-hop song Wes was glad not to recognize. She answered almost immediately. "Hey, I didn't expect to hear from you again today. ... What? ... Yeah, he's here. Hang on."

She held the phone to Wes. "It's Julia."

He had worried when she hadn't called after the tabloid disaster, but his worry had fermented into a kind of grief, the loss of her presence in his life at the time he needed a friend the most. "Hi," he said, with absolutely no emotion. He'd used it up.

"Wes, I've been trying to call you, and I keep getting your voice mail. I need to talk to you. It's very important."

"This isn't a good time. Vanessa and Ev—"

"I talked to Vanessa already. I know what happened today, and I'm so sorry. But this is just as important."

He got up and took the phone to the far side of the room. "What is it? Are you okay?" His concern rekindled. He wasn't so hurt he wouldn't help a friend, even though she'd hadn't been there when he needed her.

"No, Wes. I'm not. I'm sick to death over what happened with the tabloids. I just couldn't call until now."

"I'm sorry you got blindsided by those stories before we had a chance to fine-tune our excuses...."

"That's not the problem."

"Julia, my ESP isn't working today. What *are* you talking about?"

"Wes, I'm the one who sent your photos to the papers."

He sat down on the bed so hard the headboard thunked against the wall, and he thought the box spring might have broken.

Even two big bottles of the worst gin wouldn't be enough to wash away the horrors of this day.

CHAPTER 28

WES SAT on the couch with Evan, Vanessa in the chair opposite.

"She did what?" The revelation upset Vanessa more than Evan, based on the way she balled up her hands into white-knuckled fists.

"Did you know Julia was involved?" Wes asked. Vanessa shook her head violently.

"Why on earth…?" Evan's shoulders slumped even more.

Wes should have waited until Evan recovered from Jet's death, but he was devastated by Julia's revelation.

"Her manager wanted to paint me as a lying, cheating gay bastard with her as my victim, and she wouldn't have it. Then she showed the photo I sent her to her manager, to prove to him how happy we are together. She confronted him after the photos came out, and he said it was in her best interests and not to make a fuss about it. That this had been the only way to avoid the Evil Wes story. She accused him of having my phone hacked, and he didn't deny it. She's looking for a new manager."

"And you really need to start using a password." Evan glared at Wes.

"Lesson learned."

"I won't mention that adage about the barn door."

"Wow." Vanessa didn't have more to say. "Poor Jules. She's probably been too embarrassed to tell anyone. I'm going to give her a call." She stood. "Let's talk in the morning."

"Good night." Everyone hugged and she left.

Wes put the Do Not Disturb sign on the door and turned to Evan, who was on the couch, knees tucked up under him.

"Don't say it, Wes. Don't even think it."

Evan had read his mind. "Yeah, the hotel might burn down, or there would be a Class 11 earthquake or something."

Evan laughed. "The earthquake scale only goes to ten, and 'classes' are for hurricanes."

"Sorry, I'm not a Weather Channel junkie. We don't have many of either back home…. Cut me some slack, dude." Wes used his worst American accent on the last line, hoping Evan might laugh again. If Evan could laugh, maybe Wes would again someday.

"Come here, dude." Evan overemphasized the last word, then put his arms around Wes. "Let's talk about Julia."

"We already did."

"Now that we're alone, tell me how you really feel."

"I can't really be mad at her for making a mistake, can I?"

"I'd be furious, in your shoes."

"Really? You would?" Wes thought about that. He'd felt guilty for being angry, and he'd held his tongue with her and when telling Evan and Vanessa. "I am upset."

"Why?"

"Do you seriously have to ask?"

"Yes, you will feel better once you get it out, and you'll know what to do next."

"Yeah, I'm mad. I'm bloody furious I lost my job over this."

"They were going to kill you, Wes. The photos only preempted the original plan."

Wes stared at Evan. He was right. He'd already been shown the door; Julia's unintentional error didn't make it much worse. "Well, we were going to propose another solution. It wasn't certain."

Wes got up and paced around the couch. He was breathing hard, and he wanted to kick down a door. He'd never been so angry before.

"I thought it was Gary, Evan. I was furious he'd looked in my phone and then pulled this stunt to punish both of us." Evan nodded, without commenting, so Wes kept talking. "That would have been bad, but it's worse coming from Julia. Even if she didn't give the photos to anyone, she told her manager about us, without asking me—or you. This isn't just about me. She invaded your privacy too. And if that wasn't bad enough, she waited nearly a week to even admit her role." A small black mesh wastebasket stood by the desk. Wes went over and kicked so hard it hit the opposite wall.

"Ow, fucking, fucking, fuck!" He sat in the chair and inspected his toes. "That would have been much more satisfying if I were wearing shoes." His big toe was scraped and hurt like fuck, but it wasn't bleeding. It only felt like a dozen piranhas were gnawing on it.

"What are you going to do about her?"

"I haven't decided. We have some things to talk about, but I'm not ready for that quite yet."

"There's still time for gin," Evan said.

"No gin. Let's just go to bed."

"Sounds good."

THEY WASHED up and slid into bed. Wes was grateful for Evan's comforting heat. He was so lucky to have a man who, in the midst of his own worst day, still found room in his heart to console Wes. He pulled Evan close, wanting to take his grief away. If they were close enough, maybe Wes would absorb some of it and allow Evan some peace.

A few hot tears puddled on Wes's shoulder, and he pulled Evan in more tightly, anticipating heart-wrenching sobs, expecting Evan to let the pain take over. But Evan was still and silent. After he fell asleep, Wes remained awake, listening to Evan's breathing and the sounds of cars driving past. The traffic never stopped around here. Twenty-four hours a day. Out at Evan's ranch, the nights were filled only with the sound of insects. Until the tabloids camped out.

One Christmas holiday when he was twelve, his family had gone to Spain for two weeks. They'd stayed in a hotel right on the beach. It didn't have air conditioning, so they kept the windows open at night. The sound of the surf was so loud, he couldn't sleep. He was used to city traffic—cars, buses, lorries—but the ocean crashing on the beach kept him awake at night. If only that were the worst of his concerns.

Sometime before first light, Evan woke Wes. He pressed a kiss to Wes's lips and then his body against Wes's. "Hold me, Wes."

He wanted more than being held, and they made love in the last shreds of night, with daylight creeping in around the edges. They started slow and gentle, but ended hard, rough, and messy.

Afterward, Evan rolled to face Wes, watching him across the pillows supporting their heads.

"Wes, I want to tell you something."

Wes put out a hand to stroke Evan's cheek. "Hey, it's okay. I told you it didn't matter to me."

"I need to tell you. It's the right time. I'd like to do it now."

"Okay." Wes's curiosity had grown over the weeks, but now he wondered if some things were best kept secret. What if this changed his opinion of Evan? Gary's taunt echoed through his brain. Wes needed to know, but he didn't particularly want to anymore.

"It's not a pretty story. It's very ugly. But I'm scared right now, and you need to know why."

"Scared of what?"

"Let me start at the beginning." Evan took in a breath. He was still lying face-to-face with Wes, and a few tears slid onto the pillow. Evan swallowed. "You haven't asked why I left Hollywood, and I appreciate that. Your unconditional affection was one of the reasons I was so drawn to you. You didn't let my secret put a barrier between us. Gary used to find ways to force me to do or say something…." He stopped. "This isn't about Gary. I'm sorry."

"Go on. I'm listening. I'm here."

"When I first came out here I landed a few little parts. Not enough to pay bills, but enough to meet people, get my face noticed. Like other actors—men and women—sometimes there are shortcuts to money. More money than waiting tables or temp work. 'Modeling sessions' or videos. Serving at private parties or very private parties."

Wes nodded. He didn't need or want more details. He hadn't realized how lucky he'd been until he came to LA and found out what other actors had done for parts or money.

"I wouldn't do videos, but I did a few photo sessions. I worked at a few parties—but nothing I wouldn't do with someone I hooked up with at a club, so it didn't seem so wrong. And I did a few escort type things. Shortly after, I got a part on a soap and that led to my first series, and then two years later some film roles. I never connected that success to any of the people I'd met when I was a party boy."

That last line sent shivers through Wes. He hated hearing what Evan had to do—or felt he had to do—but he wouldn't judge. Everyone has a different path, and Evan had tried to make it in the most competitive entertainment market in the world.

"Do you hate me for that, Wes?"

"No. Not at all." Wes kissed Evan's hand and waited for him to go on.

"The day before a big audition—for a film—one of those clients from years before called me. He was a producer, not a headline exec producer, but he brought in plenty of funding. He said he arranged the audition for me. If I wanted the part, I should go to his house for just two hours. That was a great part—supporting role, but really fantastic. But I said no. I would get the role on my own merits. Someone else got it. He was nominated for an Oscar for that role. I won't say which film or which actor. And I don't know if he visited this producer to get it.

"Two months later, the same sequence of events. Within six months I could only get auditions for third-rate horror or direct to DVD. Then he called again. 'Come over for a few hours, and I'll tell you about a role we're casting soon.' I'm not proud to say I went. Two days later I got an audition and small part in a very good film."

Wes flashed back to the Catalina boat trip and how Saul had told him to suck cock for the guy who worked with Spielberg. Maybe it hadn't been a joke. No wonder he never heard back.

"You don't have to tell me more. I get it. I don't judge you."

"There's more. This went on for a couple of years. Sometimes he wanted me before a part. Once he threatened to get me killed off on the series he'd gotten me. He convinced me those very first successes I had were because of him. I couldn't get away from him.

"Then a really great film role came up. Starring role, big budget, sure to make me a megastar. I wanted that so bad. I figured once I got a role like that, I'd get to work with other producers and escape from this horrible man. But this time he wanted me for a whole weekend.

"I wished I didn't feel the need to go. I wish I'd been more confident in my skills. But over the years, he'd drummed into me that I wasn't talented, I was just lucky to have met him to pave my way. I thought I was a fraud, worthless, no matter how many roles I got or how much I got paid. And of course, I was terrified he would tell the world what I'd done to get the parts."

By now Wes had tears in his eyes. Listening to Evan doubt his talent and self-worth was more painful than he could bear right now.

"What did he do to you?" Wes couldn't hold back the question.

"He liked playing games, but they'd been mild. A riding crop, handcuffs, nothing too rough. But this weekend he wanted a lot more. I don't want to dwell on the details, but he didn't have any limits, and he was a true sadist. You asked about the scar on my hip?" Evan didn't need to explain more. "He threatened to mess up my face. I didn't believe he'd do it, or I wouldn't get any roles except maybe Phantom of the Opera. He wasn't bluffing." Evan traced his fingertip across the scar on his jaw line.

"Half the things he did were psychological." He paused and Wes reached out for his hand. "I wasn't strong at the time, and I had a… breakdown after I got home. He pushed me to such ugly places, and made me believe ugly things about myself. I tried to kill myself."

He said it so matter-of-factly that Wes took in all the pain Evan must have experienced. "Oh God, Evan." Wes wanted to find this man and hurt him. He balled his hands into fists.

"I'm okay, Wes. It took me a while. Now you see why I left Hollywood, my career. I thought so little of myself, and I hated myself for letting it happen. Maybe I just connected with the wrong person—the actual devil—or I didn't have the right constitution to hold up to the meat grinder in Hollywood. But I got out and followed my other dream, working with horses. They don't judge you, and they usually make you feel better about yourself."

He gripped Wes's hand tight.

"You're the other bright thing in my life now. Gary was just a scaled-down version of that man, and I let him manipulate me because he kept me in the mindset no one else would want me. The first time I met you, you touched a spark in me, and I could see Gary was wrong. Not that I think you fell for me the day we met, but you saw *me*, not the cardboard version Gary had me believing was reality."

"Whether we ended up together or not, I hoped you'd get away from him."

"Wes, you made me realize I could choose to move toward you. I wasn't just running from Gary. I made a conscious decision."

"I wish I could wash away all those terrible memories."

"You will. You have already. And replaced them with more realistic ones. I ran away from you at first because I couldn't deal with any connection to Hollywood. It terrifies me still sometimes. And I was scared for you. Now that coming out has lost you your series, I'm still very afraid you'll get chewed up and spit out too."

"Thank you for worrying about me. I don't know what I'll do next, but spending my life raising horses doesn't sound like the worst idea."

"I love those understated British compliments."

"Evan, I love you."

Wes could taste Evan's tears when they kissed.

"I was worried that telling you would have the opposite effect. I thought you've already seen me at my worst after Jet dying. If I scared you away, one more loss at this point wouldn't hurt so much."

"It's going to take more than that to scare me away."

"Good, because I fell in love with you, too, no matter how much I fought against it. That day we spent in San Francisco; it was going to be our last day together. I didn't want you to ruin your career over me. But instead of breaking up, I knew that day that I loved you."

"Care to show me how much?"

"Try and stop me."

CHAPTER 29

THEY DROVE back to LA later that day, taking the scenic route along the coast instead of a quick run down Interstate 5. They snapped photos at ocean vistas, then stopped around lunchtime in Monterey where they strolled along the water before deciding where to eat.

"The aquarium here is fantastic," Evan said. "Do you want to check it out?"

His tone wasn't particularly enthusiastic, and Wes knew they wouldn't enjoy it today. Better to keep that for another time when the place wouldn't be associated with bad memories. "Let's come back to see it. We'll be getting home awfully late as it is."

"Right." Evan tightened his arm around Wes's waist. "You're right. It would take half a day to see it properly."

Wes let Evan justify the decision to make himself feel better.

After a lunch of fresh seafood, they got back on the road, winding past incredible views of Carmel and Big Sur. Wes realized how little he'd seen of California's natural beauty. How wonderful it would be to visit here with Evan another time.

Along the way, Evan pointed out landmarks or related historical tidbits about places and sights they passed. Wes collected a list of places to visit: Hearst Castle, Santa Barbara, Monterey Bay Aquarium.

It was nearly dark when they arrived at the ranch. Even at this relatively late hour for horsemen, Nicky and the rest of Evan's staff were waiting to greet him. Wes took their things from the SUV up to the house and waited for Evan. He wouldn't intrude on their discussion.

Wes tossed their clothes in the washing machine and busied himself around the house. After an hour he went out onto the porch and noticed the only car parked down at the barn was the night guard's. Where was Evan?

Worried, Wes hurried down the hill, but the barn was empty of people. The office door was locked, and one stall door was open. Wes knew exactly where Evan had gone. He went out the barn's side door and followed the sound of thundering hooves to the track. Even in the moonlight, Wes could make out Evan hurtling around the oval on his favorite mare, Sable.

His face was against her neck, her streaming mane hiding Evan's expression, but Wes knew both man and horse needed and wanted this late-night run. Wes stayed back from the rail, not wanting to intrude on them. It was a perfect bond of horse and rider, much different from the way the jockeys rode their mounts in a race. Evan belonged on a horse, that was obvious, and the mare comforted him in a way Wes never could.

With each lap the pace slowed. Wes could hear Evan talking to the mare, and she made the little snorting sound with each stride that Evan told him meant the horse was relaxed and enjoying the run. She was breathing hard when Evan slowed her to a jog and did a cooldown lap. Then they made their way through the gap.

"Wes!"

"Have a nice ride?"

"We did."

Wes kept at Evan's knee as they moved back to the barn. "How are you?"

"Better. I'm better." Evan pushed his fingers through Wes's hair. "Thank you."

"Should I wait for you at home?" Wes asked when Evan slid down from the mare's back at the barn door.

"At home. Sounds perfect." He pulled Wes toward him for a kiss. "Perfect."

As Wes climbed up the hill, he realized it was the first time he'd used the word "home" rather than "house." Until now it had been Evan's house. So much had changed in a week, and now it was home, even if Wes hadn't wanted to move in yet.

It was just a matter of time.

He remembered to put the clothes in the dryer, and then washed up before climbing into bed. Evan came in later and tasted like toothpaste when he kissed Wes. He still smelled faintly of horse soap and leather.

AFTER MORNING workouts, Nicky flew up to oversee the horses at Golden Gate. Evan would focus on the horses here, including Vanessa's other new horse, Deadly Verdict. Del Mar racing was finished, and those horses came back from the track.

Evan was glad to have more horses to look after here. He needed to take his mind off Jet with more work, more decisions to make. He was in the barn office after workouts when the landline rang.

"Mr. Taylor, this is Bill Emerson, Western Equine Insurance."

"Hi, Mr. Emerson. We don't need any insurance; everything's covered. Thank you."

"No, Mr. Taylor, I'm from the Claims Department here at WE."

"I don't have any policies with you."

"You are an owner of record for Shapely Shadow. We had a claim filed yesterday…." He left the sentence unfinished as if gently reminding Evan.

"Our insurer is American Equine. There must be some mistake."

"The claim was filed by a Mr. Gary Laurent, listed as the animal's primary owner."

Had Gary put his own insurance on the horse? Why?

"What can I do for you, then, Mr. Emerson?"

"Even though the policy is only $15,000—" Evan nearly choked at the figure, far less than Jet's value. "—due to the circumstances of the death, we are going to require additional paperwork beyond the death certificate." He rattled off a list, including blood tests and necropsy results.

"I can supply those when I receive them. Who purchased this policy?"

"Mr. Laurent. He is listed as sole beneficiary."

What the hell? "Let me get back to you regarding the documents."

Emerson gave Evan his contact information before disconnecting.

Evan still had his hand on the phone, rolling the information around his brain. He had to find out why Gary had insured Jet for much less than she had been worth. He didn't particularly want to talk to Gary. He'd chickened out and left a message on Gary's phone about Jet…. Evan could use Wes's advice on how to handle the call.

He went back to paperwork, and an hour later another claims representative called, from a different insurance company, requesting documents regarding Jet.

Two policies, totaling Jet's approximate value. Very strange.

It only got stranger. Three more insurance companies called over the next two hours, all for relatively modest policy amounts, but totaling far more than the filly had been worth.

Evan's pulse raced, and a buzzing started in his head, soon approximating the roar of a jumbo jet taking off. He wrote down the rep's contact information and hung up.

Evan needed air. Fresh air. He pushed out his chair, but when he stood, his knees buckled. He was going to be sick. Just in time, he made it to the trash can and heaved up the morning's coffee and toast. He was shivering and had to sit down for a while to calm his nerves.

Evan sipped water to settle his stomach. This didn't make any sense. Gary wasn't the sort of person to even think about insurance, much less buy multiple policies. He'd only really paid attention to Jet for the first few months after Evan had bought her. Lately, Gary's only mention had been asking Evan to run her and refusing to sell his share.

Gary's words came back in a sickening flash. "It's kind of like an investment."

Well, he'd hit the jackpot this week to the tune of nearly $100,000 in insurance money, far more than Vanessa would have paid for his share of Jet.

It was time to call his lawyer.

WES CLEARED their lunch dishes and served bowls of fresh fruit salad, even though Evan had barely touched his soup.

"Starving yourself isn't going to help. You need energy to deal with everything."

"You sound like my mother."

"I hope that's a good thing."

Evan reached for Wes's hand and squeezed. "It's not a bad thing. I'm glad you're here looking after me." He emphasized the statement with a few kisses on Wes's hand.

"Did you talk to Julia?"

"Not yet. I had a missed call from her this morning."

"Have you talked to anyone?"

"No. They all say the same thing. I appreciate the support, but I don't want to keep talking about it." He pushed cubes of melon and mango around on his plate.

"I'll call Gary if you call Julia." Not that Evan wanted to make that call, but he had to know what was going on.

"That seems fair." Wes speared a chunk of watermelon and stared at it as if it had the answers to all of his questions. He put it back down on his plate.

Evan went into the living room and retrieved Wes's phone.

"Oh, you meant now?"

"Or when you're done torturing that fruit."

Wes looked at his plate, then pushed it away. "Okay. I'll ring her." He took then phone. "What should I say?"

"Wes, I'm not a scriptwriter." Evan was glad to hear Wes laugh. At least someone could. "You'll figure it out."

Wes called and held the phone so Evan could hear it ringing.

"Wes! I'm so glad to hear from you." She sounded more excited than relieved.

Wes put the phone to his face. "I saw you called me." He glanced at Evan, apparently seeking approval for the line. "What? No, I haven't been watching TV or online. Say that again? … He did? … I'll call him. … Yes, now. Talk to you later."

"You're smiling. What was that about?"

"She says there's been a lot of talk online about how the network handled my situation. Apparently, there are some unofficial rumors they are reconsidering their decision."

"Hey, that's great." Evan hoped it was more than just rumors. "You should talk to Saul."

"I've been ignoring his calls." Wes shrugged. "I guess I shouldn't. Of course I'll never get another job if I don't talk to my manager."

"I thought you fired him."

"I did, but he seems to have ignored me."

"What are you waiting for? Call him!" Now Evan felt the prickle of excitement.

"I'm going to use the office."

Evan nodded. He got up and cleaned up the kitchen. There was half a pot of soup on the stove. Wes had cooked, saying his break was a good opportunity to improve his cooking skills. Unfortunately, he was a better driver than cook. Evan didn't have the culinary talent to repair what Wes had prepared, but he put the leftovers in the refrigerator. He wouldn't insult Wes by throwing them out.

The conversation with Saul was shorter than Evan would have liked. Wes came back into the kitchen sans the smile he'd worn when he left. "Those unofficial rumors are still unofficial."

"What does that mean?"

"The network wants to talk, but that's all they'll say. I told Saul I don't want to talk to them."

"Are you crazy? Wouldn't you like your job back?"

"I don't know. I loved the role and the show. I don't like the network's policies."

"That's fair enough. See what they come back with. You can always change your mind."

"Your turn. Gary."

"Okay, but I need to be more comfortable for this." They sat on the couch, and Evan dialed.

"Evan, I got your message." Gary sounded subdued, somber. "I'm sorry about Jet. I know how much you loved that filly. It must have been awful."

"It was awful. It's still awful. It's going to haunt me for a long time."

"Shit, Ev, I really didn't expect…."

"Expect what? That I'd be upset? I'm more than upset." Evan stopped himself. This wasn't why he called. "I got several calls from insurance companies today."

"Already?"

"What do you mean already? Why didn't you tell me you had these policies on Jet? I don't understand why there are so many small policies."

"It's complicated. I need a favor from you."

"What the hell is going on here?"

"Ev, I'm in some trouble, and you might be too."

"Gary, you better explain."

"The insurance money is part of a debt. They made me take out the policies, and I couldn't tell you. But it's only because—"

"You lost me. Who are 'they'? And what does Jet have to do with anything?"

"I borrowed money to finance part of my film, Evan. And not from a bank. I didn't realize until it was too late what I'd gotten into. I thought he was just a rich guy who owned racehorses. I mentioned you're always looking for horses to train. But then you wouldn't take his horses, and he said he'd only give me the money if we had a fallback plan."

"Gary, just spell it out."

"Starikov. He's Russian mob."

Evan had read news stories of their brutal methods—on people and on animals. Recalling the details made his stomach churn. Now Evan was terrified. Puzzle pieces clicked into place, but the picture wasn't complete.

"Evan, you have to take his horses. He's got some scam he's running, but he needs a small, relatively unknown stable. It won't come back on you. I don't understand the whole thing, but you won't get in any trouble."

"No trouble? You're saying this guy killed my horse for insurance money—plus my license is suspended, and we might be party to insurance fraud. And they want more money? No, Gary. I will not bail you out of this mess you got into. I'm going to call the authorities."

"No! No. Please, Ev. I really need your help." He sounded desperate. "Look, just take his horses for a month. That's all he needs to make back the rest of what I owe."

"You have to be fucking insane. No. Find someone else. I won't risk losing my license or going to jail. If you help the cops, you may not get into trouble."

"Ev, I know things are over and you moved on, but if you ever cared about me, please help me. They will hurt me, Evan. And they may hurt you too."

"Are you threatening me?"

"No. I'm just passing on their message."

"I'm going to call the police. Now."

"Don't do that."

Evan hung up. He blinked a few times. He couldn't believe what he'd just heard. But he was numb. In shock. Something was disconnected in his brain or his body. He felt an invisible wall closing in on him, squeezing him until he'd pop.

He was going to be sick at the horror Gary had exposed him and the horses to. He flung open the office door and ran for the bathroom.

"Evan, what's wrong?" Wes followed him into the bathroom.

When he'd emptied his stomach again, he wiped his mouth and turned to see Wes in the doorway, eyes wide. "That wasn't just my lousy soup, was it?" He knelt next to Evan. "Tell me."

EVAN SIPPED weak tea with lots of sugar to battle the mix of fear and rage in his gut.

"Do you believe it, Evan?"

"It all adds up. I can't understand how Gary got tied up with those guys, but now everything makes sense. They thought scaring my owners away would make me take Starikov's horses. Then Vanessa didn't listen to their threat, and they killed Jet—I'm still not sure how—for Gary's insurance, not because Vanessa owned part of her. They were sending a message to me that they would make me do what they wanted."

"We need to call the authorities, Evan. Maybe we *are* in danger. Those guys are monsters."

"Really? Are you trying to make me feel better?"

"You will once the cops get involved. Or FBI. I don't know who handles what in the States."

"Okay. But they're going to think I'm nuts."

"Not after the threat against Vanessa. Aren't they already investigating that?"

"You're right. I'll call the lead agent on it. I have his number somewhere." Evan dug through his messenger bag and found Baxter's business card.

They wrote a list of the events, dates, and times that they could remember, organizing the details before Evan called. But Agent Baxter wasn't in. He made a statement to another agent and was told Baxter would call him within twenty-four hours.

"Do you feel any better?" Wes asked. He'd made more tea while Evan was on the phone.

"A little. I still feel like throwing up."

"Now that's probably the soup."

Evan let out a weak laugh. "God, Wes. I can't believe they killed a horse to scare me. A beautiful, innocent, helpless horse." Knowing Gary was involved only made the situation more painful. Well Evan wasn't going to let another horse get hurt. And despite his new loathing of Gary, Evan hoped he would protect himself by cooperating with the authorities.

Wes held him close and helped ease the pain and rage.

He woke up in bed, and it was almost dark. Wes sat in a chair reading a book. "Hey." He squeezed Evan's leg through the blanket.

"Did you hear from Baxter?"

"Not yet. Are you hungry?"

"A little."

"We're low on everything, including headache pills and that pink stomach stuff. You'll probably need more of both. How about if I run up to the shops and bring back some real food someone else prepared?"

"I'll go with you."

"Peter's on guard duty tonight, and he'll be here soon, probably before I even get back. Or I can wait till he arrives."

"No, I'm just being paranoid. You're right. Get some chocolate too. And biscuits?"

"You mean the breakfast kind?"

"No. The kind you like with tea. The things I used to call cookies."

Wes leaned over and kissed Evan. "I really do love you."

WHEN WES came back an hour later, he spotted Peter's car by the front gate. It was dark, and the moon was bright. Lights were on in the barn as he drove past on the way up to the house. There weren't any lights on there. Evan must have fallen asleep again or he would have put them on. Wes pulled the bags out of the back of the SUV and headed for the porch.

A noise from the barn caught his attention, and he turned to look. A high-pitched whinny. He was used to those now. Something on the ground caught his eye as he was turning back to the house. A dark splotch on the path.

Dark red. Blood?

He heard another noise from the barn.

He dropped the groceries and ran down the hill.

CHAPTER 30

HE RACED along the trail of blood, hoping and not hoping it would lead to Evan. He fought the urge to shout because he didn't want to warn the bad guys he was here. Even though he couldn't see anyone, there were always bad guys. Maybe they hadn't heard him drive in.

The trail ended at the body of one of the guard dogs two-thirds of the way to the barn. A dark German shepherd with a hole the size of tennis ball in her chest. She must have been shot and dragged herself down here. Wes's instinct made him slow down and reach for the dog, but it wouldn't do her any good now. He left the body and picked up his pace.

He had to find Evan. Now.

Then he spotted Peter standing at the barn entrance. His back was to Wes, but he was wearing his uniform. Wes had just overreacted. As he got closer, he noticed something strange about his ear. Half of it was missing. Not like Peter, who had two regular ears. But it was like the guy Evan saw in the test barn the day Jet died.

Oh shit.

He needed to call the cops. He reached into his pocket. No phone. He patted his entire body. He'd left the fucking phone in the SUV.

A weapon. He needed a weapon. What could he find outside the barn? He didn't have all day. If they'd shot the dog, what would they do to Evan? And where was Peter?

He found pitchforks and shovels behind the barn. They would have to do. He went back to the door, but the one-eared fake guard was gone. Wes went inside, looking around, shovel ready in defense.

The guard had one of the horses, and they were standing outside an open stall. Jet's stall. Wes moved carefully along the opposite wall, keeping out of the man's sight. Ten feet away. Eight. Six. Four. In the light, he saw the flash of a knife, pressed against the horse's neck. He raised the shovel and moved behind the man, bringing it down as hard as he could on the guy's head.

The metallic thunk echoed through the barn, and the horse ran off in terror. The guard lay crumpled in the doorway of the stall, and it was only then Wes realized the guard hadn't been alone. His partner was inside the stall. Wes dropped the shovel and grabbed his pitchfork.

Evan was inside, tied to a chair. The accomplice looked up at Wes.

"Join the party." His Russian accent was thick and tattoos covered both forearms, visible because his sleeves were rolled up. He didn't move.

To his horror Wes saw a knife at Evan's throat.

"Evan!"

Wes's heart stopped, or maybe it exploded, because his chest felt like it had been ripped open. Evan was gagged and shirtless, and there were lines of blood along his chest and torso where the man had sliced him.

The man moved the knife so the point pressed against Evan's crotch.

"Stay there or your friend won't be much good to you if he lives."

Wes stopped. He stared at Evan, who gazed back at him, eyes sunken and glassy but still full of sadness. Not pain; it looked like regret that Wes had seen this or gotten involved or might get hurt.

"A little birdie told me how much Evan likes to get tied up, and he likes knives. He's having a good time. You like this too, Wesley?"

Wes stared. Evan's story came back in sickening clarity. Had Gary told these men the thing that would frighten Evan the most? He'd kill Gary after he killed the guy grinning over Evan's bruised and bleeding body.

Evan said something unintelligible through the gag.

"Yes, Evan, I know you agreed to help us. This is just a thank-you party."

The bastard already got what he wanted, and this was just for his sadistic pleasure? Wes put aside his fear and hesitation and moved into the stall, knocking the man down and pushing the pitchfork against his chest. As the man fell, he slashed out with the blade, and Wes felt something scrape against his face. He ignored it and tried to push the pitchfork through the thug, but it was much harder than it looked in horror flicks.

He was bellowing and ineffectually stabbing at the man when someone grabbed him from behind. He swung around and clocked the guy—a cop—in the head. Then he dropped the pitchfork. Several sheriff's office deputies swarmed the stall. One walked him out, and he broke away and ran back toward Evan.

Everything happened in slow motion, with no sound. Just flashes of color. The blue uniforms. Red blood. Evan's pale white skin streaked with more bright red dripping lines.

CHAPTER 31

WES WOKE up in a white room. All he could see was white. He felt someone touching his hair.

Evan.

He raised his head. He'd fallen asleep face-down on the edge of Evan's hospital bed.

"I thought you'd be here when I woke up. I just didn't think you'd be sleeping on my lap."

"I'm sorry, Evan. I—"

"The nurse told me you'd been here all night and all day."

Wes stared at Evan. He looked and sounded pretty good after what had happened. The wounds weren't as bad as they looked, but he'd been hit on the head pretty hard and had been in and out of consciousness since he'd been brought in.

But Wes was thrilled he sounded okay. He smiled and wished he hadn't as pain ripped across his face. He reached up and remembered the bandages.

"Wes, your face."

"Just a little scratch. I'm fine."

"Half your face is bandaged. That's not a scratch. Oh God, your face." More pain filled Evan's eyes. "I'm sorry. It's my fault."

"No, it's not. And it's not bad. A really good plastic surgeon patched me up. If it doesn't heal properly, I hear I'm a shoo-in for a *Scarface* remake."

"How can you laugh at that?"

"I'm tired of crying. Please promise me you'll never leave your house again. I can't bear the worry."

"What happened? Who called the cops?"

Wes felt his face heating up. "I would have but... I need to tie the phone to my wrist or something. But they came when Peter didn't check in."

"Check in?"

"Apparently he had a routine of calling the sheriff's dispatch every hour if all was clear. They knew if he didn't call to send a unit. And our address flagged the system since the LAPD and FBI were on an investigation connected to you. They sent extra units."

"Thank God for technology."

"The FBI agent you spoke to yesterday relayed your statement to Baxter, and they fast-tracked additional wiretaps, and they traced the call that sent the thugs. If Vanessa hadn't got the investigation started, this wouldn't have gotten wrapped up so quickly."

"My head is spinning. You'll have to tell me again later when I can think clearly."

"Gary's in jail."

Evan stopped smiling. "I don't know if I'm happy about that or not. I wish he hadn't got caught up in this…. Jet would still be alive."

"He took your advice and turned himself in. He wanted to tell the FBI what he knew. If he has enough information to make a difference, he may go into witness protection."

"At least he'll be out of my life for good." Evan gave a sad half smile. "I wish it didn't end like this."

A nurse popped her head in. "You have some very insistent visitors, if you're up for them." When Evan nodded she opened the door to let Vanessa, Julia, Brent, and Lance in. "Ten minutes. And I mean it!"

They gave Evan careful hugs, except for Lance who nodded from near the door, apparently not sure he was welcome.

Julia stood next to Wes. "Check out today's *Variety*." She pushed the paper into his hand and pointed to a front-page story.

"'Spielberg announces new project.' So?"

She shook her head and snatched the paper back. "Steven Spielberg has a new project on the drawing board. If you think you've seen everything there is about Shakespeare, you're in for a surprise. Still early in development, he would only go so far as to say he's taking a very alternative approach to the familiar classics by presenting them from a different viewpoint, introducing us to characters who have been on the sidelines until now. 'We haven't begun casting but I'd love to bring in a pool of talent like Michael Fassbender, Wes Tremayne, Benedict Cumberbatch, among others. In fact, the project got its start after a chat with Tremayne.'" Julia squealed. "Wes, Spielberg mentioned you in the same sentence as Michael Fassbender!"

Wes was more shocked that Spielberg had mentioned him at all. "Is it the first of April or something?" Wes grabbed the paper. He didn't believe a word of it. But there it was in black and white, Spielberg talking about him.

"Since when do you have informal chats with Spielberg?" Brent asked.

"I'd like to know too," Evan said. "Where was I?"

"I have to thank Lance for that." Wes looked for Lance, who was near the wall. Wes went over to him and was about to hug him, then held out his hand to shake. He knew Lance still wasn't comfortable around him. Lance grinned and they shook hands, then Lance pulled him in for a hug.

The nurse came in—thanks to Julia's squeals—and shooed them all out, even Wes.

"I'll be waiting outside. Oh, your parents are at home."

"My parents?"

"I called them and they flew in and came directly to the hospital but they were so exhausted, I sent them home to rest, till you woke up. They'll come back next visiting hours. Your mom's cooking something lovely for whenever they let you out of here."

Evan shook his head. "Just don't even offer to help her, please?"

Wes laughed. Now he was sure Evan would be okay.

CHAPTER 32

EVAN STAYED one more day in the hospital, then came home to a completely clean house and more food than even an army could eat.

The first night was a cozy welcome-home dinner with Wes, Evan, and his parents. During the meal Wes kept getting calls, but no one minded that he took them. He was on cloud nine that Evan was safe and more or less healthy.

"That was Saul. The head of the network called him, begging—his word, not Saul's—me to come back to my role, with the original storyline they planned for this season. Even offered to double my salary."

"I'm sure your costars would be thrilled with that." Evan shook his head.

"Now it's the writers who want to kill me."

Everyone laughed.

"And?" Evan asked.

"Told Saul to tell him to get stuffed. Oh, sorry." Wes apologized to Evan's mother.

"I think he should get stuffed too," she replied. "Whatever that means. I hope it's nasty."

More laughter bubbled around the table.

"What will you do instead?" Evan asked. He glanced at the scripts piled in the corner of the living room. There was another pile in the office.

"That HBO miniseries looks really good. A couple of films scripts look promising. There are a few TV pilots. Do I want to take a chance like that, or stick with a new role on an existing show?"

"What does Saul say?"

"Not to rush into anything. I should take a look at everything and let him start talking to producers for the projects I like."

"That sounds like good advice."

BY THE following Friday, Evan was well enough to be bored from inactivity. Most of the cuts hadn't been serious, just painful, and the doctor okayed a trip back up to Golden Gate if he promised not to muck stalls or exert himself.

"Gee, that takes a lot of the fun out," Wes said when he heard the doc's report.

"I'll let you do the hard work. I'm sure that will be fine." Evan kissed Wes.

"Are you going to check with the doc?"

"Of course not. I'll know if I'm overdoing it."

They flew up late Saturday, hoping to avoid crowds in the airport, but Wes attracted more attention than before. He signed autographs on ticket folders, baseball caps, and even on one guy's bare shoulder, earning a mild glare from Evan. Few of the details of the attacks at the barn had been reported, but people treated Wes like a hero, and he wished he could crawl into Evan's backpack and hide from the attention and praise.

"You're a hero to me," Evan said when they were in their seats. They held hands the whole flight. Wes still didn't think Evan should be traveling, and Evan realized Wes's overprotective streak was far preferable to Gary's treatment.

Nicky and the rest of Evan's staff gave him a warm welcome back, and other trainers, jockeys, and assorted friends and acquaintances stopped by. He even had several new owners interested in placing horses with him.

On Wednesday, Mister Twister was entered in another race, and Julia, Vanessa, and Lance flew up.

Evan's stomach churned as Billy warmed Twist up before the race and headed for the starting gate. He hadn't forgotten the last race he'd watched, the day Jet died. But Wes stood by and offered silent support. If it were up to Wes, he'd be holding Evan's hand twenty-four hours a day.

"Wes, you can just let go, already. I won't break or get lost," Evan finally said as they watched the horses enter the starting gate.

"Sorry." Wes took his hand back and picked up his binoculars. Evan knew he'd spoken sharply, and as much as he loved Wes's concern, he wasn't an invalid, either physically or emotionally.

"Me too," Evan whispered and squeezed Wes's hand briefly.

"Racing!" the announcer shouted and everyone focused attention on the horses.

Twist broke well and held the lead until the first turn. He lagged in second or third until the last turn and the horses thundered toward the finish line. Twist surged forward and didn't stop accelerating until he was four lengths ahead, winning away to a deafening roar. When Evan looked around, he realized most of the noise came from Wes and Vanessa.

They hugged him, hard at first then backing off. "Did I squeeze too hard?" Vanessa asked. Julia was still subdued around Evan and Wes, though they had both forgiven her repeatedly.

This time they drank Champagne toasts in the Winner's Circle while what seemed like millions of cameras flashed in their direction from the stands, as well as the official photographer.

Evan hoped the camera didn't capture his tears of joy and relief. A couple of weeks ago, he'd thought he'd never want to stand on a track again, and then with his suspension, he'd thought he'd never be allowed to. Then when the Russians dragged him out of the house, he wasn't sure he'd live to see Wes's face again, much less a track.

But today, he was here, with the man who returned his love, and a winner, safe and sound and so many good things in the future for both of them. Wes kissed him and more cameras flashed.

Could life be any better than this?

CHAPTER 33

EVAN WALKED Twist back toward the barn only as far as the gap, then Ricky took the horse from him.

"I'll cool him, bathe, and ice him. Don't worry."

"I'm not worried. I just feel obsolete," Evan said. The barns had functioned just fine without him. He needed to be useful.

"Just a little more rest," Wes said. "But I still need you. You're not obsolete to me."

"Thanks." But the compliment didn't allay Evan's worries that he wasn't really needed except for a few executive decisions.

"Come here, I want to show you something." Wes tugged Evan's hand and they walked through the horsemen's parking lot out to the two-lane road leading from the highway to the grandstand. Wes led him across the road and up to the edge of the bay, the gray water slapping softly against the boulders.

They stopped at a flat place and Wes pointed across the bay.

"I wondered why they called this track Golden Gate, when it's nowhere near the bridge. But I see it's the perfect name for the place."

Evan stared across the bay at the familiar, soaring orange-red towers of the Golden Gate Bridge, now partially obscured by the late-afternoon fog. The sun shone through, lighting up the bridge so the color glowed brilliantly.

"It's a beautiful view," Evan said. He loved this spot, and today the view was more magnificent than ever.

"I feel like the bridge," Wes said, holding Evan's hand. "Out there at the head of the bay, one side pounded by the ocean and the other side, the bay. And some days are so foggy I can't tell what's going on around me."

"That's very poetic—"

Wes put a finger on Evan's lips. "But no matter how dark or foggy or how rough the wind and waves, there's always some sunshine breaking through." He turned to Evan and looked into his eyes. "That's you. Sunshine on a cold, foggy day, making me know there is still light and warmth and love there, all the time."

Evan couldn't see for the tears welling in his eyes, and a lump the size of Alcatraz formed in his throat. How had he gotten so lucky, that Wes was still here with him? Their relationship had turned Wes's world upside down and cost him a job he loved, and nearly a career.

Wes hadn't walked away when things got tough; he'd loved even harder.

The love shining in Wes's eyes overwhelmed Evan, and he pulled Wes into an embrace. There were no words adequate to describe his feeling, this moment, the bond that strengthened every day.

They held each other for a while, the wind sweeping across the wide expanse of water and whipping their hair and chilling Evan. He loosened his grip enough to kiss Wes.

"I do remember you telling me something about your being a marvel of engineering. That's true in more ways than one." Evan held his breath, hoping the joke hadn't ruined the beautiful moment.

Wes's laughter melted the knot in Evan's throat, and he joined in.

"That wasn't exactly what I was talking about," Wes said, looking away. "But my drawbridge is in perfect working condition."

When they'd stopped laughing, Wes took Evan's hand again. "Thank you for sticking by when things got rough for me."

Evan felt like the luckiest man alive. Almost, but not quite. Only one thing would be better than the way he felt at this moment. He pictured a velvet pouch in the bottom of a drawer back home, containing the family engagement ring he'd asked his mother to leave when his parents flew home. One day in the future, when his and Wes's lives smoothed out and they'd weathered these storms, he would have the stone reset and offer it to Wes.

Wes kissed Evan's hand and wrapped his arms around him from behind while they watched the sun lower behind the beautiful bridge.

This would be the perfect spot.

AUTHOR'S NOTE

LIKE A lot of girls, I fell in love with horses at an early age. I read every horse story, saw every horse movie, and asked for every model horse over the years. I was lucky enough to be able to take riding lessons and go to horse camp every summer. Though I never convinced my parents to buy me my own horse, I continued to ride until heading off for college.

I also found a love of horse racing along the way. Growing up in Miami, where there were several tracks, I was allowed to go on occasion. Even after I outgrew (literally) my dream of being a jockey, I kept visiting tracks, betting—and winning more often than not. And I never miss a running of the Kentucky Derby, even if it's only on television.

For years I've wanted to incorporate my love of horses and racing into a story, and this is the result. The research was as much fun as writing. I contacted several trainers at Golden Gate Fields—my local track here in Northern California, and one very accommodating trainer, Donna Hjort, welcomed me into her barn, let me tag along after her, and answered a thousand and one questions. This book would never have been written without her hours of help and her unlimited patience.

It was a thrill and a privilege to be allowed on the backside, access to barns, horses, jockeys, trainers, and to hang out on the rail and in the saddling paddocks. It's truly a world unto itself with a very close-knit community.

The story of Jet's last race came from personal experience. I saw a lovely young filly go down in the homestretch and never walk away. I felt a sense of loss, even though I had no connection to the horse, and it brought home the risks of horseracing to me in a way nothing else could have done. I've tried to present a very real picture of the horseracing industry today, and explore a few of the issues and challenges the sport faces, including the dangers of drugging race horses.

In addition to Donna's assistance, I would like to thank Kate Pavelle, Sarah Madison, AJ Llewellyn, Con Riley, Lissa Mitchell, and Suzie Bass for their help with this story, Britishisms, and an inside look at an actor's life in Hollywood. I owe them a debt of gratitude for making this book so much better. Thanks also go to Andi Byassee, my editor, and Reese Dante, my wonderful cover artist.

EM LYNLEY has worked finance, the wine industry, and high-tech, though she'd rather be writing hot man-on-man romance. She spent ten years as an economist and financial analyst, including a year as a White House Staff Economist, but only because all the intern positions were filled. Tired of boring herself and others with dry business reports and articles, her creative muse is back and naughtier than ever. She has lived and worked in London, Tokyo, and Washington, DC, but the San Francisco Bay Area is home for now.

Visit her website at http://www.emlynley.com
her blog at http://emlynley.livejournal.com
her Twitter page at http://twitter.com/emlynley
and her Facebook at http://www.facebook.com/emlynley.

A Novella in the *Delectable* Series

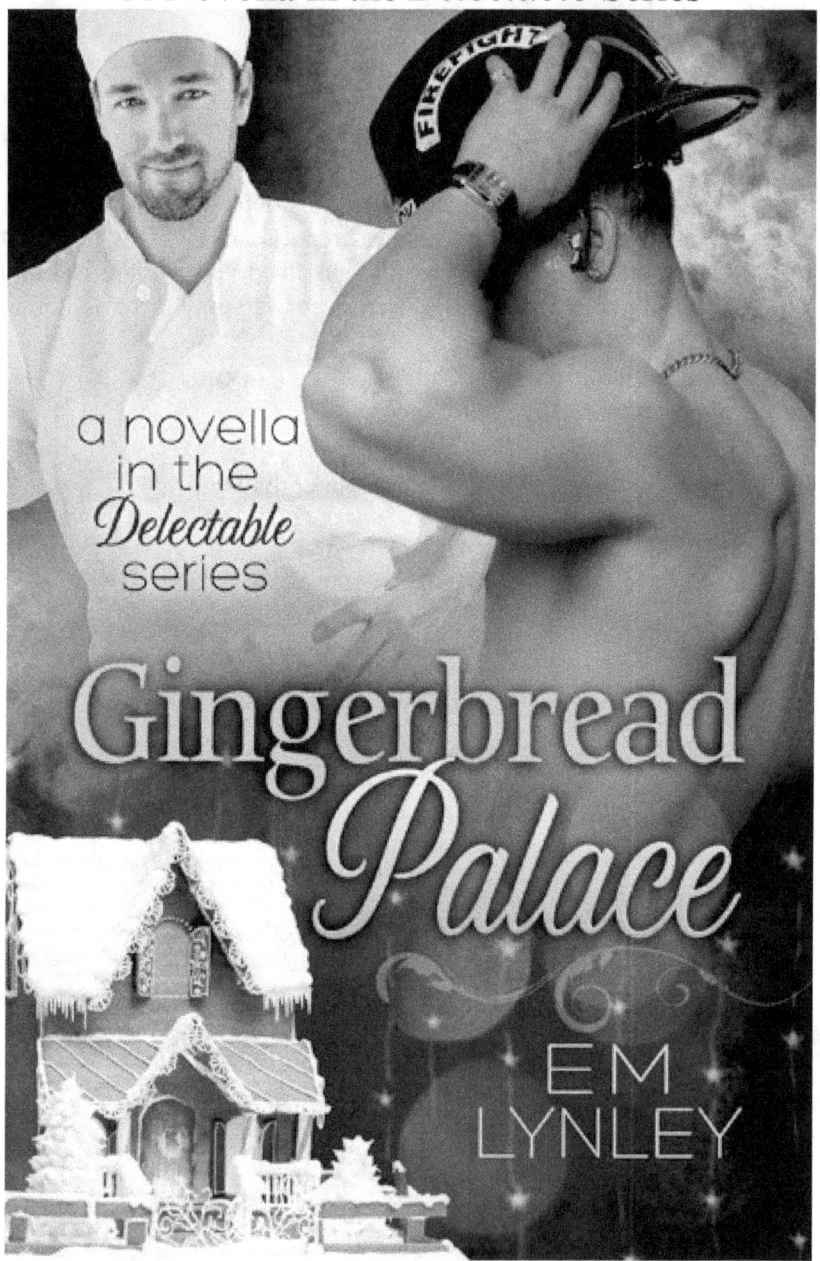

a novella
in the
Delectable
series

Gingerbread
Palace

E M
LYNLEY

http://www.dreamspinnerpress.com

A Novella in the *Delectable* Series

Brand New Flavor

a *Delectable*
novella

EM LYNLEY

http://www.dreamspinnerpress.com

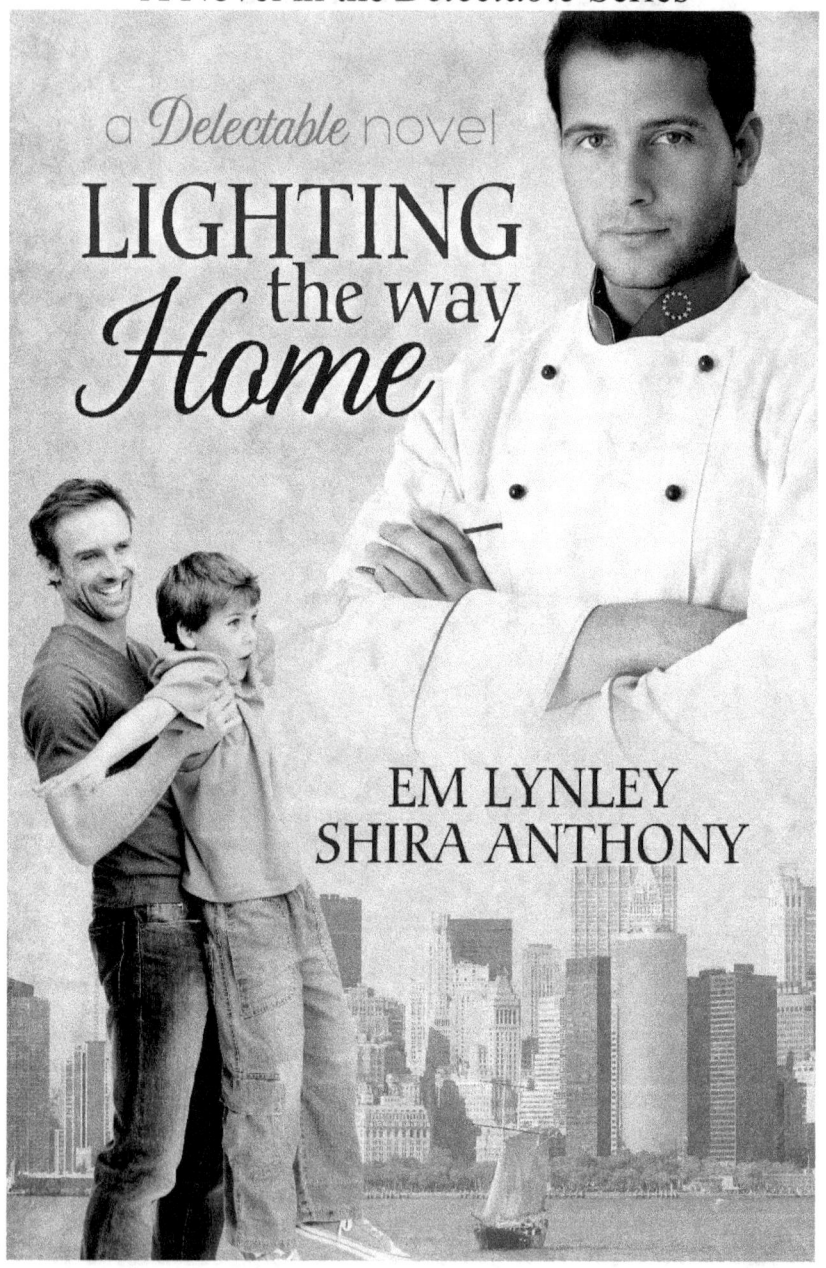

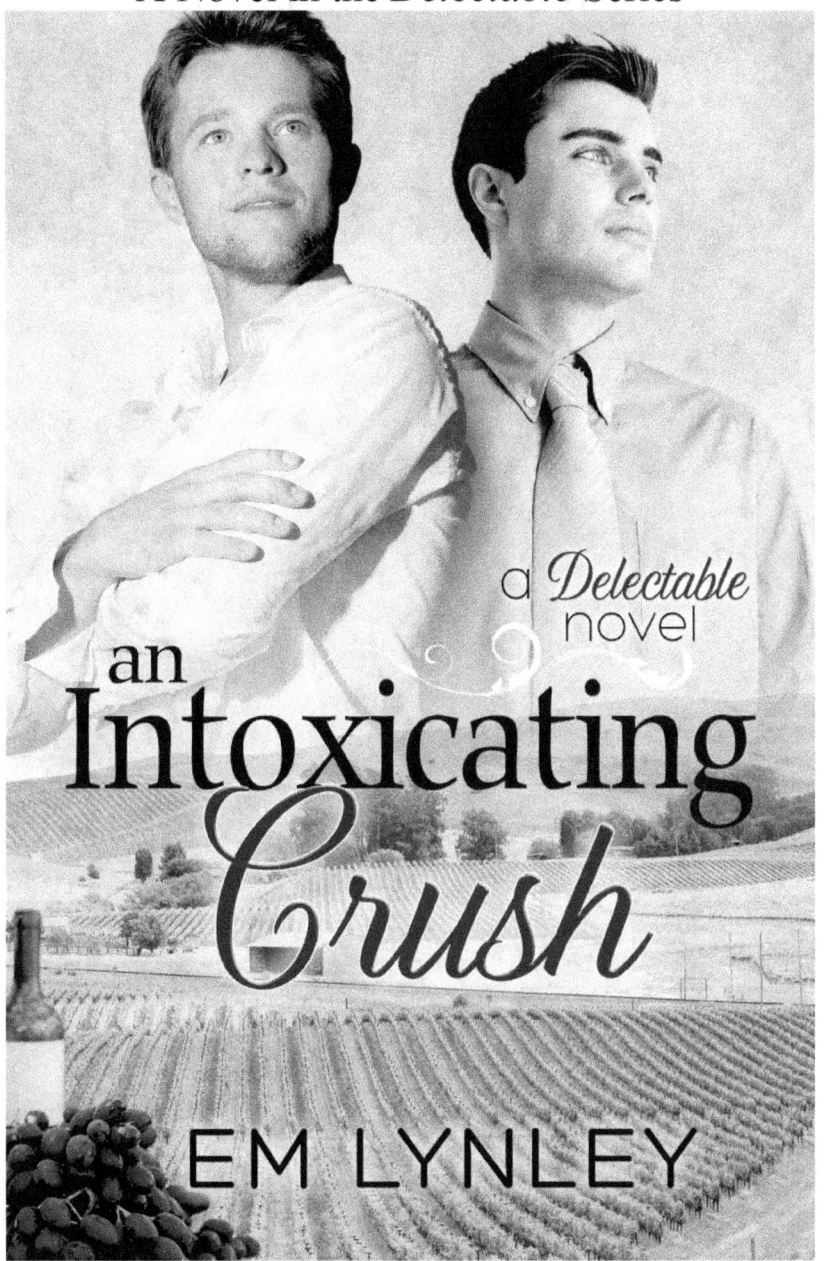

A Novel in the *Delectable* Series

a Delectable
novel

an
Intoxicating
Crush

EM LYNLEY

http://www.dreamspinnerpress.com

Precious Gems from EM LYNLEY

EM LYNLEY

ITALIAN
ICE

A
PRECIOUS
GEM
STORY

http://www.dreamspinnerpress.com

Precious Gems from EM LYNLEY

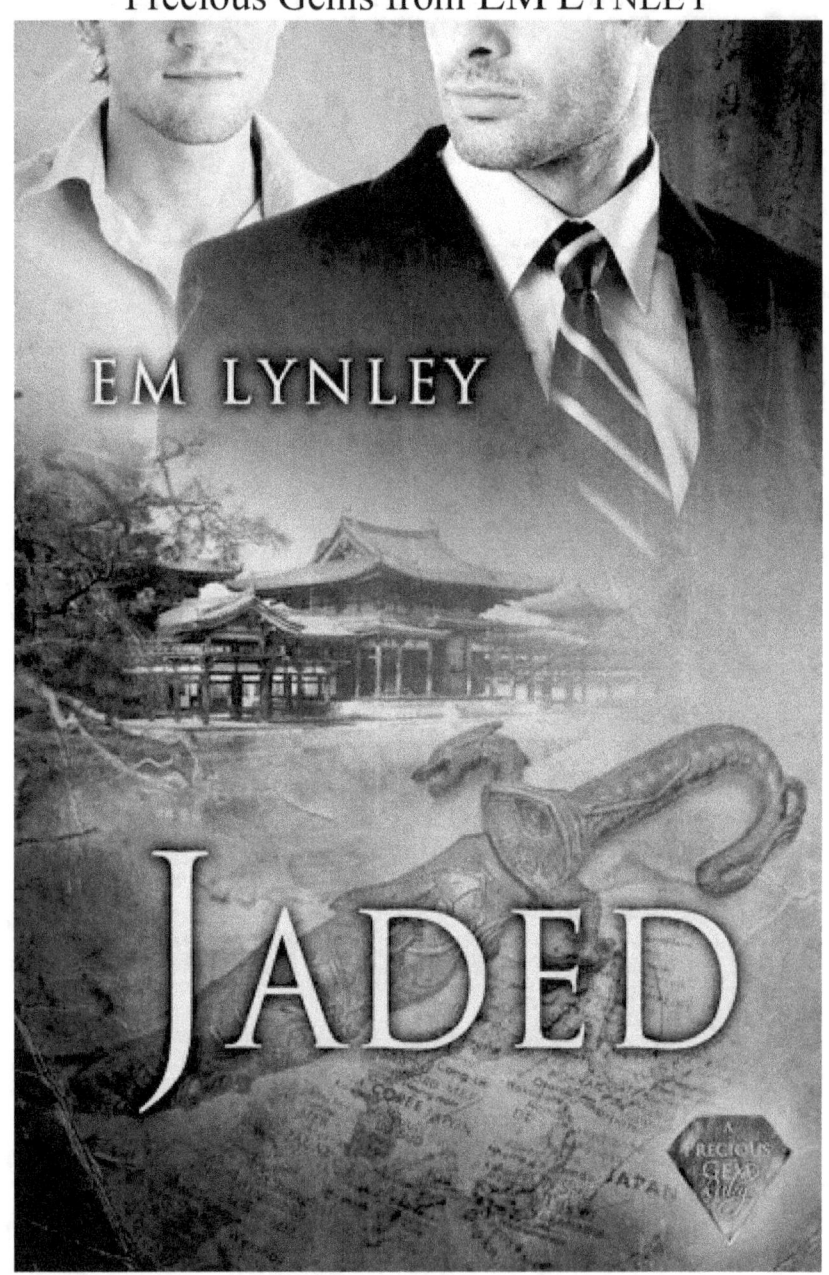

EM LYNLEY

JADED

http://www.dreamspinnerpress.com

Also from EM LYNLEY

DISGUISES
EM LYNLEY

http://www.dreamspinnerpress.com

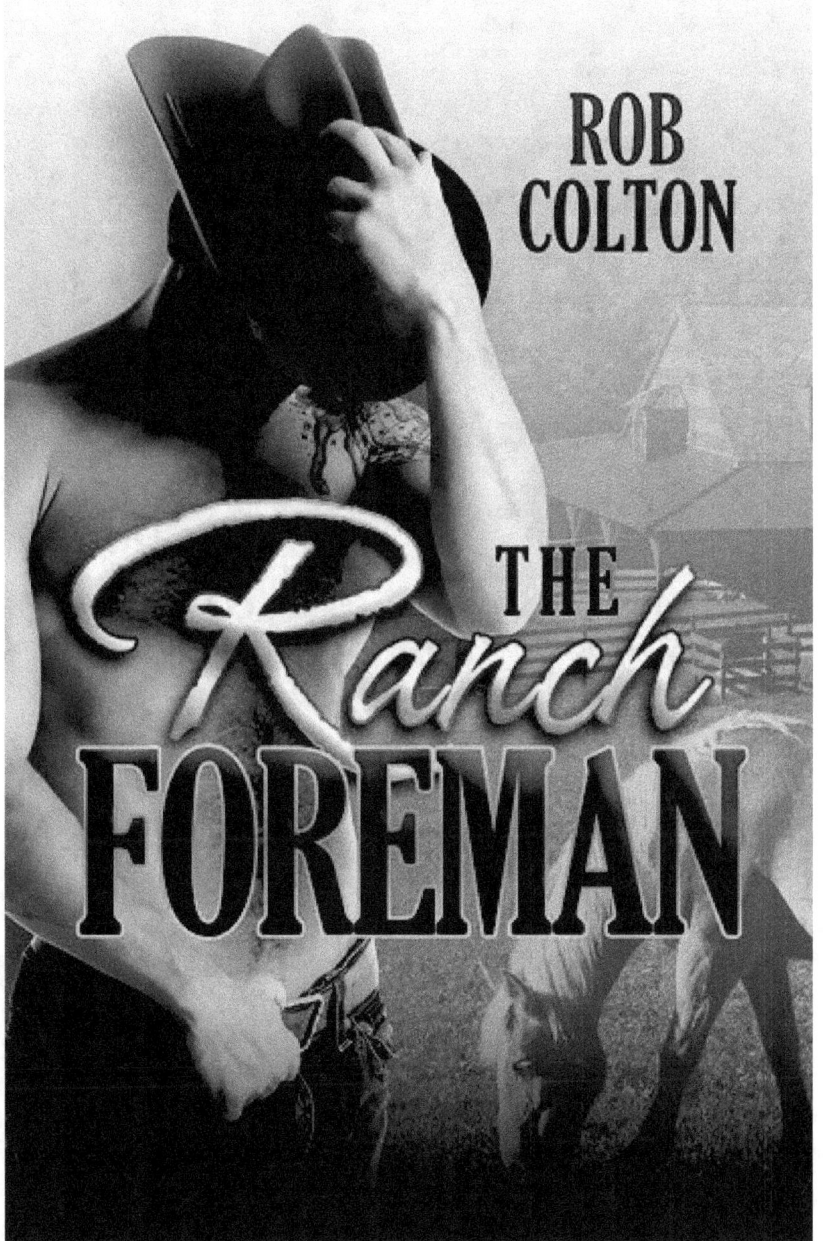

ROB
COLTON

THE
Ranch
FOREMAN